THE PROMISE OF FOREVER

HOLLY RIDGE

MORGAN ELIZABETH

To the girls with mommy issues.

PLAYLIST

Landslide - Fleetwood Mac
So High School - Taylor Swift
Old Recliners -ROLE MODEL
Vienna - Billy Joel
Ruin the Friendship - Taylor Swift
You're My Best Friend - Queen
I Will Wait - Mumford & Sons
Beast of Burden - The Rolling Stones
Elizabeth Taylor - Taylor Swift
Stubborn Love - The Lumineers
Mine - Taylor Swift
Your Song - Elton John
We Are Gonna Be Friends - The White Stripes
Forever - Noah Kahan

https://open.spotify.com/playlist/5QnSi1GVGocGwanxgoL4YJ?
si=1BmU2DGMRq2EkNaZYs1C5w&pi=1qJATgAvRoa3q

AUTHOR'S NOTE

Dear Reader,

I always say my stories are personal, a bit of me in each of my characters, because at the end of the day, I've only ever been inside my own head. That being said, I have to admit that has never been truer with this story.

When I was little, I loved the song "Landslide." In 2002, The Chicks covered it, and the song was inescapable. But because I was raised by my dad, and thus all of the rock albums that came out between 1975 and 1985 (also why the playlist has a lot of it, despite my typical playlists mainly being Taylor Swift and the occasional 2000s pop punk, though I would argue I can totally picture Emma and Jesse having an air guitar battle while jamming out to "Highway to Hell") I've always loved the original most of all. I never really understood why that song always spoke to me so much or why, if I listen to it at the wrong time, it makes me uncontrollably sob, but it clicked when I wrote this book.

While editing this book, I randomly got the urge to listen to Fleetwood Mac, and the 1997 Live at Warner Brothers version of the song came on. Before the song really starts, Stevie Nicks says, "This is for you, Daddy," and when I say I *immediately* started crying, I mean *immediately*.

If you want a song that perfectly encapsulates Hallie in this story —her fears, her limitations, her endless love—listen to "Landslide." I've always thought it was twelve-year-old Morgan's song, but now I'm sharing it with Hallie.

The Promise of Forever is my most personal story to date. I see so much of myself in both Hallie and Emma; my own childhood is incredibly similar to theirs in different ways. While writing it, I joked that while *All My Love* was my seasonal depression book, this is my therapeutic book.

Though, don't worry: this is not a sad book, not the way AML is.

Unless you have mommy issues. Then maybe a little. My bad.

That being said, I said this book is for the girls with mommy issues, and it is. But it's also for the single dads of the girls with mommy issues, who knew they couldn't heal that hurt or bridge that gap but did the best they could with the hand they were dealt, regardless. The ones who were okay with being the villain and the bad guy if it meant their daughters could make it out in one piece.

As always, there are a few things for you to note before jumping in: this book contains mature language and adult situations. It also heavily features narcissistic parents, as well as the emotional turmoil that creates both immediately and in the long term. There is a lot of mention of mothers in many senses, but heavily in mothers not being in the picture by choice. Remember, reading is meant to be our happy place! Put your mental health first, always.

I hope you love this story as much as I loved writing it. Love you all to the moon and to Saturn,

Morgan

ONE

JESSE

The brand-new cellphone in a glittery pink case buzzes on the countertop, and I glare at it like the enemy it is.

A cellphone for an eleven-year-old girl. Who the fuck gets that as a gift?

An irresponsible, absent parent trying to make up for not actually being in their child's life—that's who, I remind myself, because that's exactly what Emma's mom is. *Mommy!* with a bunch of emojis behind the name flashes along with a new message.

> I can't wait to see you next Saturday!

I groan as I read it, knowing the chances of that actually happening are near zero and already seeing the meltdown that will result.

Running a hand over my face, I decide that will be a concern for next week. Future me might hate me for it, but current me knows the fact that it's nearly seven thirty and my daughter is still not out of bed is more concerning. Last year, I let Emma sleep in during winter break, and the first day back was an absolute nightmare, so I won't be making that mistake again.

Padding down the hall, I poke my head into my daughter's doorway and sigh with defeat. The lavender blankets she begged for last spring, when she decided the pink ones with princess crowns were for babies, are pulled up over her head, blocking out the light I flipped on ten minutes ago on my fourth entry into her room.

"Get *up*, Emma," I say for the sixth time. "Aunt Wren will be here soon."

I never thought I'd miss the days when a tinier version of my daughter would rise with the sun and wake me by jumping on my bed and demanding breakfast, but this phase makes me yearn for the early mornings and long nights. Now, I find myself constantly battling an almighty stubbornness, intertwined with the attitude my parents have been warning me was impending. Call me delusional, but I couldn't imagine my sweet little girl ever being anything but sugar and sunshine.

I have since been proven wrong.

I'm convinced something happened the moment she walked into the halls of the Holly Ridge Middle School, turning my sweet baby girl into a preteen tyrant with more attitude than one small person should be able to hold in their body.

"It's not even a school day," Emma grumbles, rolling over and tugging the blankets up higher. Tipping my head back to the ceiling, I take in a deep breath and force my voice to sound neutral instead of revealing the brewing irritation that's crawling in my veins.

Don't let her know she's getting to you. Don't let her sense your weakness, I remind myself before speaking aloud. "We're sticking to our routine, so when you go back, you're not out of the rhythm." That was my theory, at least, but it's not going well. Obviously.

"Daaaaaad," she whines.

"Get up, or I'm throwing you in a cold tub. Again."

Three weeks ago, Emma refused to get up for school, and eventually, knowing she would miss the bus if she didn't get going soon, I started a cold tub, then grabbed her from her bed, blankets and all, and dropped her into it. The water that splashed everywhere was a bitch to clean up, and the shrieks were nearly ear-splitting, but the giggles that were intertwined with them and the fact that she actually got up and out the door on time made it worth it.

Thankfully, it doesn't seem like I'll have to face the cleanup again, my threat seeming to work when her head pops out of the blankets, a burning glare hitting me.

"You're the worst," she grumbles, but pushes the blankets down and slowly rolls out of bed.

"Yeah, well, I'm the worst dad ever who happened to steal some cinnamon rolls from Grandma's yesterday, so get up, get dressed, and head to the table before I eat them all." Another glare shoots in my direction, this one less barbed now that my threat of freezing water is replaced with pillowy soft cinnamon rolls.

"Fine," she says, rolling out of bed and stumbling sleepily to her door before she closes it in my face. I could argue with her about the attitude and rudeness, but she's out of bed, and I have learned I need to choose my battles.

This will not be mine.

Less than ten minutes later, Emma is dressed and sitting at the kitchen island, picking at the center of a reheated cinnamon roll, when there's a knock on my front door. It's probably my sister, Wren, coming to watch Emma while I start on the decoration takedown at my family's Christmas tree farm, where I live and whose maintenance I manage, but there's no reason she'd be knocking. Not only is the door unlocked, but she also has a key and could walk in at any time.

"Who's that?" Emma says around a mouthful of cinnamon roll, and I cringe at her.

"Jeez, Em, chew, swallow, then talk," I say, moving toward the door. I don't see the exaggerated eye roll she gives me, but considering it's her newest trademark move, I'm sure it's aimed my way.

"Who is that, Father?" she asks in a sugary sweet tone.

Glancing over my shoulder, I give her a glare I know will have no impact on her.

Emma, the unexpected gift that arrived when I was twenty-two, is what my mom calls the ultimate payback, given that from ages eight to twenty I was a headache—and then some. When I found out I was going to be a father to a girl, I thought maybe she'd be like Wren, sweet and cajoling, a daddy's girl at her finest.

Instead, most days it feels like Emma got my sister's best friend, Hallie's, personality—full of fire, snark, and enough attitude to take down a bear.

"Drop the attitude, Emma," I scold, another common refrain these days.

I turn back to the door to let Wren in. But when it creaks open, letting in a gust of cold air, I wonder if I summoned the woman in front of me.

Long strawberry-blond hair is draped over one shoulder, an over-sized brown bag slung over the other, and a puffy coat with a furry-lined hood hides what I know is a perfect figure. Instead of my sister, her best friend, Hallie Young, stands before me, a smirk on her full pink lips. Her cheeks are pink, probably from the cold, but maybe because of the pink blushes she loves to wear, and mischief is written all over her face.

Somehow, I know I'm not going to like whatever it is she's here to say.

"You're not Wren," I say, the first idiotic thing that comes to mind spilling from my lips and making her smile go wider.

"You really are the smart King, aren't you?"

My jaw tightens as she reaches up to pat my cheek, then turns her body, brushing along mine as she steps into the mudroom.

"What are you doing here?"

"Well, hello to you, too, Jesse. So good to see you," she says.

I stand in the doorway for a moment, staring outside to see if maybe my sister is coming behind her, but it's just Hallie's shitty green car parked right beside my white truck. Instead of standing there like a moron and letting all the heat out, I close the door and turn to where Hallie is removing her coat and sliding it onto one of the hooks, as if she plans to stay for some time, setting her bag on the bench and toeing off her brown clog slipper shoes.

Hallie is here.

In my house.

Without Wren, my brother, or my parents.

Just Hallie in my house, smiling at me like the last year of us avoiding one another didn't happen at all.

"What are you doing here, Hallie? Is everything okay with Wren?" She turns to me with that mischievous look, and somehow, I know I'm not going to like what she says next.

"Oh, Wren is great. She's on a plane headed to Paris right now, so I'm really not sure if she could be any better, you know?" Her smile goes wider somehow with her words, entertained by whatever game she's playing before turning and walking away from me.

I stare at her retreating back, blinking as I try to decode her words.

"Paris?" I ask, needing just a few long strides to catch up to her short ones, following her as she moves through my house as if she belongs here.

"Yeah, Adam took her to Paris as her Christmas gift. That's why I'm here bright and early. I'm taking over babysitting duties for Wren," she calls over her shoulder before turning into the kitchen and out of sight.

"Hey, Hallie!" my daughter says, her lips wide and excited.

I ignore the happy look on her face, instead turning to Hallie with irritation brewing in my veins. "What do you mean you're taking over for Wren?"

Hallie sets her bag on the counter, then turns to me. "Well, she can't quite babysit from Paris, so I'm taking over."

"Aunt Wren is in *Paris*?" Emma asks with stars in her eyes.

Hallie nods enthusiastically. "Don't worry, I'm sure she's going to bring you back the best gifts. Probably even better gifts, since Adam will probably be paying for them. She has a bigger budget."

She winks at my daughter, who grins deviously, and I don't bother to remind either of them that she doesn't need anything, not after she was just spoiled rotten yesterday. Instead, I choose to focus on the important topic at hand.

"I'm sorry, can you rewind?"

Hallie rolls her eyes at me, and the urge to argue with her moves through me, but if I want to figure out what the hell is going on, I can't give in to that. Hallie has always been able to irritate me, to get under my skin better than anyone I've ever met, and I can't fall into that trap right now.

"Adam called me..." She purses her mouth as if trying to remember something, the freckles dotted over her pert nose scrunching up before she shrugs one shoulder. "I don't know, some-time last week, and said he wanted to take Wren to Paris for a Christmas gift, since, you know, she's always wanted to go. But he knew if he just planned the trip and expected her to drop everything and go, she never would."

While I don't necessarily know about my sister's travel dreams, I do know that her boyfriend's last-minute surprise trip without a plan in place would have gone poorly. My younger sister helps everyone and anyone, and the idea of falling short on that would send her into a tailspin. Her new songwriter boyfriend has done a good job in the last few months of helping her restructure her priorities so she doesn't burn herself out, which I'm happy about, even if it's seeming to make my own life a bit more difficult.

"Okay...?" I say, slightly confused as to what that has to do with anything.

Hallie moves to the oven where the rewarmed cinnamon rolls are.

"Are these your moms?" she asks, pointing a light green-tipped nail at the baked goods. I nod, then watch with reluctant fascination as she plucks one out of the pan without asking, puts it on a plate, and licks the brown sugar and cinnamon goo off her fingers. "So I found out about all the million and seven things she promised to do and either redistributed them or took them on myself, including hanging with my best girl this week."

"Yes!" Emma says excitedly, clearly looking forward to time with Hallie, who she thinks is possibly the coolest person on earth.

I am considerably less impressed.

"And no one thought to tell me that the plans had changed and my child would be being watched by someone other than my sister?"

Hallie looks at me like I'm being dramatic as she grabs her plate and sits next to Emma, slowly peeling the first layer of the sweet bread roll off, then gesturing to me with it.

"After the bullshit you and Madd have been putting her through? No. I wasn't going to give you any room to argue and make her feel guilty. Your mom agreed. And don't put this on Wren. She didn't even know they were going until last night, so it's not like *she* was lying to you." She's right, of course: my younger brother Madden and I have been giving her more than her fair share of responsibilities as of late, but I can't seem to focus on that. Not when Hallie slides the pastry between her lips, something I've caught myself doing more times than I should admit over the past few years.

Hallie Young is temptation in the most basic, primal sense, and over the past four years or so, I've begun to think it's a brand of temptation calibrated to torture me specifically.

"My mom knew? And she didn't tell me?"

Hallie gives me an exaggerated eye roll as she chews. "Jeeze, Jess, it's not like I'm a stranger. I've babysat her more times than either of us can count."

With Wren, I want to remind her, but Emma pipes in before I can speak.

"Yeah, Dad, chill."

I snap my head to my daughter, who is giving me her most signature sassy look that now I'm noticing looks a bit like Hallie's.

"I'm not sure how I feel about you and Emma spending large chunks of time together. You're a bad influence."

"Sorry, I'm not a precious second-grade teacher you can take advantage of," Hallie counters with a raised brow.

"I don't—" I start to say, but with Hallie's look, my words sputter out. The truth is, I *have* taken advantage of my baby sister's kindness for some time now, even though I didn't mean to. I sigh, a mix of bone-deep exhaustion and resignation in the sound.

Running a hand through my hair, I glance around my small house, which is currently a disaster. When I found out Emma was coming into the world, I dropped everything to become the parent she needed, and my parents, always the parents *I* needed, began building the small house on the family property for Emma, me, and Emma's mom to live in before she decided full-time parenting wasn't for her.

They also built one for Madden, though it sits relatively empty. He lived there for just over a year after graduating from college before deciding he did not want to live that close to all of us and moved to the center of town. Usually, I keep the small space relatively tidy, but since yesterday was Christmas and I didn't expect anyone other than my sister over, it currently looks like a tornado tore it apart, and I haven't had time to clean it up. Even more, with the tight schedule I have over the next week, I won't have time for it.

"I have shit to do today," I tell Hallie.

Normally, right after the holidays, I start organizing the decorations and taking them down, so setting up next year is easy. Although my family's Christmas tree farm isn't too busy in the winter, I have a lot to get done before the snow hits again, making it near impossible to take things down until it melts.

"That's why I'm here," Hallie says, and then I watch with intrigue as her face goes soft just a bit, an unspoken apology in her tone. "I promise, I'm here to help. I can handle one preteen girl for a week. I was one, after all."

Her face is sincere, and despite my reservations, I know she's right.

"Yeah, Dad, we'll be fine! God, I'm not a *baby*," Emma says with sass in the words.

Hallie snaps her head toward my daughter and raises an eyebrow. "Emma, check it," she says under her breath, and to my utter shock, my daughter nods.

"Sorry, I just meant it's no big deal for him to leave me with you."

Hallie nods, and I watch the exchange in disbelief. Emma's growing attitude has been an ongoing issue, and I've found combating it to be like walking a tightrope: pushing too hard or being too frank with her about it can make it worse, but not pushing enough, and she thinks it's a game. Somehow, it seems Hallie found that balance on the first try.

"I know, but we still need to be respectful. It's normal that your dad would be worried about who will watch you. You don't need to give him a hard time for wanting to make sure you're safe."

You could push me over with a feather when Emma nods instead of giving that same attitude to me.

"You're right." Then she turns her face to me. "Sorry, Dad."

I blink a few times, trying to see if this is some kind of dream, but nod all the same, not wanting to ruin the exchange.

"You're done?" Hallie asks, tipping her chin toward Emma's empty plate, and my daughter nods. "Good. Get ready for the day. Get dressed, brush your hair, brush your teeth, whatever you would do on a normal school day."

Again, I'm in utter shock as my daughter stands without an argument, puts her plate in the sink, and heads for her room. I'm still watching her retreating back when Hallie's soft voice knocks me out of it.

"Hey. I know this was a surprise, but I hope you know you can trust me to take care of Emma, no matter what happened between us. I may make the occasional questionable decision, but I'd never let anything happen to her."

With her words, her lips tip up with a soft, rueful smile, and my eyes dip there.

For a brief moment, a flash of memory hits me, sending me backward ten months.

The bitter cold of February in Vermont and the contrasting warmth of her soft hand on my cheek. Her body pressed to mine, my arm wrapped around her waist after having caught her when she slipped.

Her soft, full lips moving against mine.

Fuck.

I shake my head to knock the memory away, not needing that, especially not now. Her brow furrows in confusion, interpreting my head shake as a dismissal, but I can't focus on that.

All I can think is that I need to get out of here and away from her presence.

Now.

"Okay, well, I guess you've got this covered. Are you sure you're good with her? I'll probably be out until about five, once it starts getting dark."

Hallie nods. "No problem at all. I have nowhere to be today, so if you're later, it'll be fine."

I stare for another moment before the phone in my pocket buzzes, probably a text from my dad asking when I'll be at the main house to get started, and I make my decision.

"Fine," I say, then turn in the direction of where my daughter walked off to. "Be good, Emma!"

She shouts something indecipherable from her room, but I have to get out of here, so without another word, I head for the door and away from Hallie Young.

TWO

Hallie

The house rattles as Jesse slams the door behind him, and finally, I let the facade drop, if only for a moment. I allow the easy friendliness I'd put on my face to make him feel slightly more confident to slip away, and I take in a deep breath. The air doesn't get to where I need it the most, to the bottom of my lungs, which feel like they haven't felt fresh air in a decade, anxiety tightening my chest to stop it.

It's been sitting there ever since Adam asked me to help take over Wren's responsibilities while he took her on a trip, and I realized one of those would be watching Emma. I *knew* Jesse wouldn't be happy to see me today, but I think in some delusional part of my mind, I had convinced myself it would be fine. At some point during my drive over here, I'd told myself he would welcome me in happily, and we could go on with our lives.

Maybe we could go back to the way things were before that trip.

Clearly, the delusion was *very* strong this morning. Thank goodness I can always count on reality to knock me down a peg or four.

"Hallie! Come here! I want to show you something!" Emma's voice calls from down the hall, knocking me from my thoughts.

With the reminder that Emma deserves the most fun week ever, and I'm here to make that happen, I take in another deep breath that doesn't make me feel any better, brush my sour thoughts aside, put on a happy, animated look, and make my way to her room.

Two hours later, my phone rings, and the name *Madd Dawg*, accompanied by the world's worst photo of Madden King, lights up the screen. Madden added the name when he was going through a phase where he was trying to convince everyone to call him that (thankfully, the phase only lasted a few weeks, but I've never had the heart to change it), but the photo is all me, and something he complains about regularly. His eyes are bugged out, his lips curled back in the most alarming, horror movie-worthy grimace, and his chin is deep into his neck, looking more like a meme than my friend and pseudo-boss.

"Is that Uncle Madden?" Emma asks with wide, horrified eyes when she catches sight of my screen, and I nod, letting out a laugh.

"Yeah, he's a big goofball. I'm gonna take this, are you good in here?"

"Yeah, I'm going to keep organizing my clothes," she says, and I try not to look too self-satisfied, though I'm loving that my plan is falling into place, before walking through her room and into the now-clean living room.

What Emma wanted to show me earlier this morning was all the new clothes she'd gotten the day before as gifts. As she was flipping through them, I told her we could totally do a fashion show in the living room, if only it were clean. I added a bit of dramatic disappointment to the words, which had the exact reaction I had hoped for, and put a fire under her ass to get the living room cleaned up.

If there's one thing I've learned from my best friend, it's that you can convince kids to do just about anything you need them to, so long as you give them the proper motivation. Together, we cleaned up piles of her things strewn around the house, making sure they were all put away and not just thrown into a closet, and then put on music for her fashion show. Once she showed me her new clothes, I told her we should put them away and sort out any clothes that don't fit, which is where we're at now. I don't know if I'll be able to convince her to completely clean her room before Jesse gets home, but it's a start.

Once I'm out of earshot of Emma, I hit accept and put the phone to my ear. "Hey, Madd—"

"What the fuck did you do to my brother?" he asks before I can finish my greeting, and my entire body seizes up.

Does he know? All this time, I assumed neither of the King siblings knew, since neither of them is good at keeping secrets or being casual. I figured if they had even a *hint* of it, I would never hear the end of it, and the silence was a good sign, but maybe...

Okay, Hallie. Play it cool. Play dumb. Easy as that, I tell myself, desperate to keep myself from going into a full-blown panic.

"Me?" I ask, my pulse beating like a drum. I sit down on the arm of the couch, worried my legs will give out. Maybe everything I worried about was *real*. Maybe—

"Yeah, you," Madden says with a laugh. "He came into my parents' place on a fucking rampage, bitching about Wren not telling him she was going to Paris."

Relief washes through me as understanding creeps in.

He's talking about Jesse's bad mood. Not great, but I can handle that.

"Well, in her defense, *Wren* didn't know she was going to Paris," I say, standing once more and moving toward the kitchen to grab a glass of water. I balance the phone between my ear and shoulder as I open the cabinet to grab a glass, then fill it from the fridge dispenser.

"Yeah, yeah, I got that. Mom came in when he started getting loud and put him right in his place."

I take a sip of the water and can't help but chuckle at the idea of Mrs. King, who is barely five-four and in her late fifties, marching in and giving her eldest son, who towers over her at six-two, a piece of her mind. I can picture it perfectly, and even more, I can picture the way Mr. King would have gone from defensive for his wife to impressed by his wife's attitude in the blink of an eye.

I've seen similar exchanges more times than I can count since Mrs. King pseudo-adopted me in middle school.

"So is he mad that Wren went away and didn't tell him? Or that I'm the one watching Emma this week?" I ask, morbid curiosity winning out. There's a beat of uncharacteristic silence that comes over the line, and I set my glass down, the nervousness I thought I'd set aside coming back with a vengeance and making my stomach flip.

"I don't know. You never really know with Jess, but he mostly seems pissed you're the one watching her."

"Hmm," I say noncommittally, my finger moving along the rim of the glass. That's not good. My mind moved over the look he gave me when I stood at the door, then the way his irritation grew as I explained what the new plan for the week was.

But mostly, it goes to the way how, for a split second, his face went soft after I talked to him when Emma left, and the way I desperately want to know what was going through his mind in that moment, right before the wall slid back down and he stormed out of the house.

"You've got nothing to add to that?" He's fishing, trying to understand something he doesn't quite have all the intel for, but I stick to the threads of a story I have.

"I mean, he clearly looked pissed that I was the one who showed up, but other than that, who knows why Jesse is the way he is," I say, echoing his sentiment, something I've long discovered to be the best way to deal with Madden.

Silence fills the line again, and I feel the urge to fill it but manage to keep quiet for long enough.

"What happened with you two?"

"Hmm?" I ask, walking down the hall and peeking into Emma's room. Her music is blasting, Willa Stone pouring from the speakers, and watch as she puts a dress on a hanger and places it in her closet.

"I don't know. He never used to be like this with you."

He's right. After high school, I spent a lot of time at their house, even when Wren was at college. During that time, Madden and I grew close, and he became somewhat of a second brother to me. Jesse kept to himself after Emma was born, but when her mom left, he started spending less time staying secluded in his small home on the King property and more time at the main house, where his parents lived and I often was. Over the years, we became friends, picking on Madden together and laughing over the way Mr. and Mrs. King bicker. He even used to take me out on the UTV when I needed to take pictures of the farm for the Three Kings Tree Farm website and social media channels, which I manage.

But then Vermont happened.

The memory of it comes fierce, pulled from the depths of my mind where it's buried deep. The dark night sky with the shining stars and fresh snow on the ground over ice that I slipped on. The warmth of his body when he caught me.

The four words that I whispered that changed everything.

I shake my head to rid myself of the memory before speaking again.

"No idea. Who knows why Jesse does anything he does? Anyway, I don't want you to worry about me getting things done this week while I watch Emma. I have a bunch of content scheduled, and I'm going to make sure the emails are all answered when I get home at night and again in the morning. I also brought my laptop, so if there's an emergency, I'm around." I pin the two together as casually as I can, desperate to change the topic but also wanting to reassure him.

I started working for the Kings right out of high school, desperate to find a few jobs to support myself since I wasn't going to college. My older brother had graduated four years before and was already out of the house, and I knew my dad was waiting for me to be settled on my own before he could move down to Florida, where his two other brothers lived. He already gave up so much to raise Colt and me after our mom left, staying in the town he never wanted to be in so we could finish out school here, that I wanted to get out of his hair as quickly as I could. I offered to run their social media for free to help me build up a portfolio, and not only did they hire me, but they also refused to let me do it for free, becoming my first and longest-standing client.

Six months later, with the constant glowing referrals from Mrs. King to everyone in town, I had more than enough clients to move out on my own. The second I moved out and into a shitty apartment across town, my dad sold our childhood home and moved to Florida, just like I knew he would.

Madden manages the business and wholesale side of the Three Kings Christmas Tree farm, Jesse manages the maintenance and labor, and Mr. King covers everything in the middle. Because of this, I mostly report to Madden for my work with the Kings.

"Uh, I'm really not worried about it, Hal," Madden says, confusion in his words. "You know that. I just called to fill you in and see if —" I step into Emma's room, and the music is louder once I'm inside, working in my favor. I don't need or want Maddena singing any more questions right now.

"Okay, well, let me know if you need anything, and I'll do it! Emma needs me right now," I lie. Emma's face turns toward me, confusion written there.

"Okay, well, bye—" he starts, but I hang up before he can finish.

"I don't need you for anything," Emma says, looking at me skeptically.

"I know," I say with a smile. "But your Uncle Madden is a yapper, and I would much rather have girl time. How are we doing over here?"

That's enough to distract her, and she launches into an explanation of the shelves she's moved onto organizing. Then she gives me a task of my own, a distraction for which my lingering guilt and I mind are grateful for, as I throw myself into it.

THREE

"Dad is going to be so shocked," Emma says hours later with a giggle as she looks around her room.

While we were cleaning, we found the vision board Wren and I helped her make at the beginning of the year, of all the things she wanted to do during the year. It's something Wren and I started with Mrs. King when we were kids, and we've continued it into adulthood. Once a year, Wren, Nat, and I get together to eat, drink, and cut up magazines, setting goals and aspirations for the year ahead. Somewhere in my room, I have years and years' worth of vision boards, a lifetime of dreams and desires and aspirations.

Last January, Emma heard Wren and me planning our vision board night and begged us to do one with her, too. Later that week, we met at Wren's place after school, armed with magazines, stickers, poster boards, and glue, and had a girls' night with the youngest King.

When we unearthed Emma's board, she noted that some things—like getting into the town soccer championship or graduating from fifth grade—had already been accomplished. Others, like learning to do her makeup or redecorating her room, weren't. Loving a plan, and with barely a week of the year left, I decided we should try to knock out as many of them as possible while she was on break.

Since we were already halfway through cleaning her room, we finished that task, reorganized and moved her furniture around, and then ordered her some new decorations for her room on my phone. She promised to pay me back with the Christmas money her dad has, and I agreed, knowing full well I wouldn't accept it.

Afterward, we put together a simple dinner of grilled cheese and tomato soup, which we kept warm in the kitchen. Jesse might not be happy I'm here, but I've been around long enough to know that the week after Christmas is always tiring for the guys as they take down the decorations and put them away for next year. He shouldn't have to come home and worry about dinner, too.

But now that he's here, that panic and nervous energy are brewing in my stomach once more, cresting as the door creaks open. Emma turns to me with wide, excited eyes, the complete opposite of how I feel in this moment.

"Emma?" he calls, confusion clear in the word.

"In here!" The telltale sound of boots on hardwood floors gets louder before his presence fills the doorway. "Tada!" Emma shouts with a flourish, her arms moving as if she's a game show model showing off the grand prize.

His eyes scan the room, and I force myself not to scan *him*, his worn baseball hat on backward, a worn Three Kings hoodie hanging off his shoulders perfectly, and a pair of old jeans that I know from experience if he turned around would fit his ass *perfectly—*

Jesus, Hallie, there's a child in the room.

And it's your best friend's brother.

And it can and could never happen.

"What do you think?" Emma asks, and I snap myself out of my internal debate.

"Your room is clean," Jesse says, shock written all over his face, the mustache he started growing three or four years ago quirking a bit with his joy-filled awe.

"And the living room!"

"I saw." Then his head turns to look at me, and I get the full force of the handsomeness that is Jesse King. "You cleaned her room?"

I shake my head. "Emma did it."

His eyes widen then, somehow that being even more of a shock. "You convinced her to clean her room?"

I smile then, a genuine one. "It was her idea."

It's not a lie, even though I very heavily guided her in the direction I wanted her to go. From the mix of shock and relief written across his face, I know it was a good choice.

"I cleaned the living room so I could have a fashion show, and then I cleaned *my* room because I remembered on my vision board, I wanted to redecorate my room this year. Remember when I told you all the things I wanted to do this year?" Emma asks, and I fight back a laugh as she barely even waits for her dad to nod. "Well, Hallie and I found the list, so we're doing a last-minute race to get them all done. I don't think we'll get them *all* done, since, like, you probably won't let me get a cat." She pauses just long enough to see if Jesse will proclaim his love for cats and the idea of his daughter getting a pet, but when he stays silent, she continues. "But the others, we're totally doing. Come on, I'll show you dinner. Hallie and I made it." She tips her head toward the kitchen, then moves around us and out the door, leaving Jesse and me in her small room.

"I, uh..." I take in a deep breath. "I hope this was okay. I figured getting her room clean was worth a little redecorating." I gesture toward the project we worked on today.

"Considering I was concerned things were living in here, yes. A little bribery is definitely worth a clean room."

A moment passes, his eyes on mine, his mouth opening then closing as if he wants to say something, but he doesn't. Then again, he doesn't have to. Despite himself, Jesse has always had an incredibly expressive face, and right now, reluctant gratitude lies there.

I give him a soft look before nodding and taking a step out of her room. "Anyway. Dinner is in the oven. Emma knows the deal, and you'll need to help her get the sandwiches out of the oven." I move down the hall toward the front door, and he follows me. "Did eight this morning work? Or should I try earlier or later tomorrow? Just let me know." I try to keep my tone as light as possible.

"Eight works."

I nod, but don't turn around. "Cool. Okay. Bye, Emma! See you tomorrow!" I call out toward the kitchen.

"Bye, Hallie, thanks for hanging out with me!"

I reach the mudroom and grab my jacket, sliding it on almost frantically before putting on my shoes.

"I'll walk you out," Jesse says, and I fight back a groan. Madden almost always walks me to my car on the days when I work from the small office on the farm, so I know arguing it is a lost cause. Mrs. King raised those boys with manners, and even though they're both grown, when they're on the King property, they still fear the wrath of Mrs. King.

Still, I try.

"There's no need," I say with a shake of my head anyway, but he ignores me.

I let out a quiet sigh of defeat as I dig through my bag to find my keys before stepping into the biting December cold. Quietly, we walk to my car, his boots crunching on the gravel, the only sound between us. I think I'm home free, my hand on the door handle, but before I can pull it, his voice breaks the silence.

"Was Emma okay with you?"

When I look over at him, his face is unreadable, so I answer the best I can, giving him a small, forced smile.

"Yeah. She was great. We messed around with some of her Christmas gifts, cleaned her room, made some plans for the week, and then she wanted to learn to make something for dinner. It's nothing special, but she did almost all of it herself, so she's really excited."

He nods, hesitating as if he wants to say more, but he shakes his head and stops himself.

I pull the door of my car open fully, his hand reaching out to grab the top and hold it open for me, and I snap. Maybe it's the anxiety of the day and knowing that more of the same is coming tomorrow, or perhaps it's the way he suddenly looks so tired. Either way, I speak without thinking.

"Are you okay?" I ask, and he looks as surprised as I feel that the words left my mouth.

"What?" I shift, leaning against the side of my car to face him fully, and crossing my arms on my chest. Might as well get this over with now, so I can get on with the week knowing where I stand. Where *we* stand.

"Are you okay? With this? Me being here, helping out, and watching Emma?" A moment passes, and I bite back the inherent need to continue to ramble and explain and fill in the silence. Eventually, a reluctant Jesse speaks.

"Yeah. We're good. You're good with her."

I stare at him, so many unspoken words hanging in the freezing cold between us, tangible in the clouds our breathing creates.

"I just...I know you were annoyed this morning about my watching Emma, and I know I'm not as good with kids as Wren, but I promise everything was okay today. I made sure we followed your rules, or at least the ones—" He shakes his head, and I stop my rambling.

"No, no. It's not that. Wren deserves to have some time to herself. I'm just having a rough go of it with her lately and wasn't sure if she was being a brat with you."

I nod, understanding, but I still can't let it go. I can't sleep tonight knowing I'm coming here tomorrow without a firm answer. "But this." I gestured between us. "Us. We're good?" A long beat passes, and his eyes bore into me in a way that Jesse King has always been good at. I hold my breath, waiting before finally, he nods.

"Yeah. We're good, Hal."

Hal. A nickname I once hated, considering it a boy's name, then begrudgingly accepted because it was *Jesse* saying it, then missed when he stopped.

A name I hadn't heard in almost a year, and definitely not in that soft, sweet tone. We stand there quietly, both of us looking at the other, lost in our own thoughts for a moment before I break the silence once more.

"Okay, well, good. Then, I guess I'll see you tomorrow," I say, my voice soft as I force my body to move. His hand stays on the top of my door as he watches me slide into my car and turn the key in the ignition. Then he nods at me, a small thing that holds all those unspeakable words that still linger.

I hope he never says them.

"Later, Hal," he says, then slams my door.

I put the car in drive, turning out of the gravel drive in front of his house and down the road toward town. As I drive down the familiar road, I let myself take in the first deep breath since he came home.

One day down, eight to go.

FOUR

Hallie

When I show up at Jesse's house the next morning, he looks slightly less perturbed to see me, but definitely doesn't chat with me any more than the previous one. That being said, I don't think he had much of a chance, considering this morning, Emma seems much less tired and starts chatting with me the moment I walk in. With a few grunts and a *let me know if you need anything,* he's out the door, and I can breathe.

After she finishes her bowl of cereal, Emma cleans up breakfast, and I take her to my car to show her the few small things I got last night on my way home to help decorate her room. It's not much—a small rug, a poster, two frames, and a makeup organizer—but she squeals and jumps and gives me the biggest hug before running to start putting things in their place.

Afterward, we decided to have lunch with Mrs. King, a double-duty task since we were also there to pick up a few things for today's cooking lesson and activity. While cleaning yesterday probably wasn't the most fun, I think I made up for it with Emma by agreeing to play restaurant for her dad today. This required us to borrow some china, decorations, and linens from her grandmother. We spent the afternoon making dinner and decorating the kitchen and dining room to be *Emma's Restaurant*.

Learn to cook was also on her vision board for the year, which at first confused me because she bakes all the time with Wren and her grandmother, but she clarified that she meant cooking meals, and then confided in me that she really wants to be able to help more with her dad.

I'm not nearly as good a baker as Wren, but I *can* cook, something I taught myself mostly out of necessity. Colt and I were latchkey kids entrusted with frozen meals and fast food. When I was about four-teen, I got tired of eating pasta and jarred sauce or grilled cheese (Colton's specialty since he was the one watching me most of the time) and started watching the Food Network and following cooking blogs. I started small, but by the time I was sixteen, I was making dinner for my small family every night, and I still love the ritual of cooking, even if these days it's just for me.

When she asked me to teach her how to make dinner for her dad, she was a young girl who, while she has a support system to teach and guide her, doesn't have a mom here for the day-to-day, a mirror of who I once was. As it always happens when I spend time with Emma, I felt that deep kinship of a girl raised by a single dad.

Emma's excitement can't be contained as she spends every minute between four forty-five and five fifteen staring out the window for her dad. She actually *shrieks* when she sees him coming up the drive.

Looking around the kitchen and the chaos we created one last time, my heart is in my stomach. Maybe this was a bad idea. He's already frustrated that I'm here, and even though we did a bit of cleaning yesterday, which may have bought me some goodwill, we also made a bit of a mess with this little scheme of ours. But I don't have any extra time to overthink it as the doorknob turns and the door pushes open. Emma greets him, and an excited look spreads across her face.

"Hey, Dad!" she says as he walks through the door.

I step to the side to get a better view of them from my spot in the living room without interrupting their moment. Jesse steps in with a cautious look on his face and hangs his jacket on the hook in the mudroom, then takes off his worn Three Kings Tree Farm hat and flips it around in an incredibly smooth move. My heart flutters in the way it always does, my childhood crush flaring up momentarily before I stuff it back into the box where it belongs.

He looks down at his daughter, who is nearly jumping up and down, a small smile spreading across his lips, and for a moment, the stress and exhaustion that seem to haunt him constantly fade away.

"Hey?" he asks, confusion and entertainment in the single word.

"We made a restaurant!" She's nearly jumping in place now, smiling from ear to ear, and it's contagious. I can't help but let a smirk of my own grace my lips.

"You did?"

"Yeah! Hallie helped me cook it. Meatloaf, mashed potatoes, gravy, corn." She ticks the items off on her fingers, realizes she forgot something, and quickly adds it. "And a salad! We even made the dressing!" While she wasn't super excited about the basic dinner at first, Emma had a blast mashing the potatoes and shaping the meatloaf, and she's already asking about what we can do tomorrow. I have a night of Pinterest scrolling and a trip to the grocery store on my to-do list once I get out of here, but the unencumbered joy on her face makes it completely worth it.

"You cooked?" Jesse asks. "You did something nice for me? On *purpose*?" It's a joke, but there's something in the words as well, a hint of a disbelieving tone. It's as if he can't believe his eleven-year-old daughter, who clearly thinks the world of him, would willingly make him a meal. In response, Emma rolls her eyes, not nearly as shocked as I am.

"Yes, Dad. God, you're so dramatic." She waves off her father and heads toward the kitchen, where everything is keeping warm, and Jesse watches her walk off in shock.

I roll my lips between my teeth, trying to fight back a laugh, but a slight sound comes out, and Jesse's eyes snap to me across the room like he forgot I was here. I give him a small wave, and that smile still graces his face when he tips his chin in my direction before he follows her.

Emma and I had to take three trips to and from Mrs. King's house to grab linens, candle holders, candles, and, of course, the dishes to make the place look *extra fancy*—Emma's words, not mine. The menu Madden printed and delivered to us sits on the plates, along with placeholders Emma decorated, and it brings me so much joy to see her so excited about it.

"We got the fancy dishes from Grandma, and Uncle Madd made us menus. There are rolls in the oven, though they aren't from scratch, just the kind that explode out of a can, which was really fun to do. Hallie screamed." I give her a faux stern look, and she shrugs, the sass that is ever-present shining bright. "Do you like it?"

Jesse looks around, then shakes his head as if snapping himself back into this reality before nodding and smiling at Emma. He puts an arm around her shoulders and tugs her into his side in a move so sweet and intimate, I immediately feel like I'm intruding.

"You did great, kid. It's better than a fancy meal out, for sure."

She looks up at her dad with pride and bliss on her face, and when it settles uncomfortably in my chest, I mark that as my time to leave.

"Okay, well, I'll let you two get to it," I say. "Emma, remember what I told you about afterward." I give her a stern look, since my number one rule with doing this was that I didn't want her dad to come home to more work just because we were being fun and whimsical. "Tomorrow morning we'll bring everything back to your grandma's, so just leave it in a pile, okay?"

"Yup! And I'll make sure everything gets cleaned up and that Dad doesn't have to do it all."

I nod, a hint of relief moving through me, knowing I did my best. I don't know if she'll actually stick to her word, but it's the thought that counts, right?

"Okay, good. Remember, I'll be here bright and early tomorrow, Em, so if you don't stick to our plan, I'll be so disappointed." She gives me a dramatic roll of her eyes, one I've seen a handful of times today, and each time, I have to bite back a grin. Her antics are much more entertaining than they are annoying, but I don't want *her* to know that.

Without another word, I wave to Emma as I move to the front door. Jesse, still in his boots, moves as well, tipping his chin toward the door.

"I'll walk you to your car."

I don't bother to argue today, knowing it's no use. When we enter the mudroom, he watches me grab my bag, slide my shoes on, shrug into my jacket, then open the door and step outside. We're almost to my car, the keys in my hand, when I speak, rambling uncomfortably as is my way.

"I know the dinner thing looks like a mess, but anything she doesn't handle with the cleanup, just leave, and I'll take care of it tomorrow. She actually did make most of the dinner herself, and I think it's pretty good, but try not to make a big deal if it's not. There's a pizza in the freezer just in case," I say. He looks at me for a moment, then shakes his head as I stop at my car, turning toward him.

"What's with the sudden need to cook?"

"Hmm?"

"She's never wanted to cook dinner. What's with the sudden interest? Is it just something you're doing or..." His words trail off, and I shake my head before explaining.

"It's all Emma. Learn to cook was on the list we found, so I'm teaching her a few easy meals."

Her interest in cooking isn't just about her need to cross something off her list, though, something I learned this afternoon when we were standing side by side, peeling potatoes.

"Did your mom teach you how to cook?" she asked.

I let out a loud laugh and shook my head.

"No, no, my mom didn't. I uh..." I hesitated, unsure of how to tell

her that she and I have a lot more in common than she might realize. But then I realized that, when I was her age, I would have loved to know someone—anyone—who had been in a situation like mine. My best friend was Wren, whose family was basically picture-perfect, and none of my friends were being raised by a single parent. If she's in the same boat, it has to feel isolating, especially living so close to her grandparents and knowing her dad was raised under much different conditions. So instead of avoiding the topic, I faced it head-on and prayed it was the right choice. "My mom wasn't around when I was a kid. I saw her occasionally, but not all the time. I taught myself to cook because my dad worked a lot, and I wanted to help out by making dinners a couple times a week."

"So you were like me?"

It panged in my chest, but I forced my voice to sound happy and positive. "Yup."

Her face went contemplative with my new addition before she nodded. "That's why I want to learn to cook too. To help out my dad."

My chest is still warm with the memory of it, and I decide Jesse should know that too.

"She wants to be able to help out. She might give you a hard time, but that's because she's eleven and has a lot going on. She knows you work a lot and work hard, and she wants to do something to alleviate that," I add, shaking myself out of the memory.

With my words, something crosses his face that I can't quite understand or pin down, but he looks uncomfortable as he sits with it, so I continue rambling. "Then I told her about how Wren and I used to play restaurant and make a big thing out of it, and she was super into it." When he doesn't speak, I start to panic, rambling on even *more.* I was never blessed with the ability to shut up, unfortunately. "I probably should have asked, but I didn't want to bother you while you were working, and your mom said it was a good idea, so I kind of ran with it."

He's still giving me a look I can't decode, and it amplifies my anxiety.

I did the wrong thing.

Fuck.

I genuinely did just want to do something fun with Emma, but maybe I should have pulled a Wren and brought a ton of educational crafts or whatever.

"Okay, so the way you're looking at me, I'm really starting to think I totally fucked this up, so if I did, I'm sorry. I didn't—"

"No, no. It's okay. It looks like she had a great time with you. I just...you're really good with her. You seem to get her."

Instead of giving him the revelation I had this afternoon, I let a snarky grin spread across my face. "Don't look so happy about that," I say with a laugh, the tension that was in my chest melting just a bit.

"I'm really fucking trying."

Something about the way he says it, or maybe the way he's looking at me, has my breath stop in my lungs, my pulse pounding, and my lips parting. The once forgotten crush has been dusted off and placed back on the shelf, it seems, and for a split second, I think I see a similar look on Jesse's face. He opens his mouth to say something, and I hold my breath as his eyes drop to my lips, but before he can, the front door opens, and both of our heads turn that way to see Emma standing in the doorway.

"Dad! The rolls are done—can you help me get them out of the oven?"

I clear my throat and step back toward my car, increasing the space between us, though I'm worried a *mile* wouldn't be enough space. "I told her she can't do anything with the oven without adult supervision."

He gives me a relieved look, and I can't quite tell if it's because of the distance or my answer. "Good call. Well, I guess that's my cue."

"It is. See you tomorrow, Jess."

"Later, Hallie.

I slide into my car, smiling up at my best friend's oldest brother with new eyes, seeing the boyish crinkles that are turning into fine lines. His tan from a summer of working long days on the farm has faded, and his thick mustache over his lip needs a trim. His hair is getting a bit too long as well, with locks of it curling around his ears and at his neck beneath his hat. His neck has always been hot to me, corded and thick and disappearing beneath the collar of a flannel that I know hides strong, broad shoulders.

I'm probably being much too obvious with my perusal, but really, a woman can only be so strong for so long, and I can't seem to feel weird about it, not when he's looking me over as well. For a moment, I wonder what he's seeing, but when his look turns to a scowl, I don't have to guess anymore.

"Those shoes are shit for the winter, Hallie," he says, eyes locked on my warm, suede, and fur-lined slip-ons.

"They're winter boots," I say, my lips spreading into a teasing grin. This isn't the first time we've had this argument, after all.

"No, they're not. They're glorified house slippers, and you're going to break your neck in them."

I give a dramatic eye roll. "Whatever. See you tomorrow, Jess," I say, closing my door and turning the key in my ignition before waving and driving off. But as I do, Jesse King stays in my rearview mirror until I'm out of sight.

FIVE

On Sunday, I roll out of my bed bright and early, then get ready as quietly as possible, knowing my brother, who owns a bar and thus typically has late nights, is still asleep and will be for some time. I rent one half of the duplex from him, but the walls are paper-thin, and we've had more than one argument about our contrasting schedules.

Once I'm ready, I gather all of my things together and head toward the front door. When I slip my foot into my boots, I smile, knowing that it's going to annoy Jesse. The drive over is short and familiar, something I could probably do in my sleep, and before I know it, I'm at Jesse's front door.

"Hallie! How was your morning? I love your jacket! What's in your bag?" Emma asks, opening the door before I even get the chance, words spilling out fast.

"You'll find out in due time, my girl," I say with a laugh. Stepping inside, I look over Emma's head and see Jesse.

"Morning," he grunts out, and I bite back a snort of laughter, shaking my head and stepping inside.

"Don't seem too excited to see me now, Jesse, or I might start getting ideas." For the slightest moment, there's a twinkle on his face that's so reminiscent of how he used to joke with me, and it causes an ache in my chest.

"Don't worry, I'm not." He leans in the doorway of the kitchen, a mug that says *#1 Dad*, one I know Wren helped Emma make for Father's Day years ago. His hair is a tousled mess, a small smile is on his lips, and that fucking mustache is a tease I remind myself to ignore. Unfortunately, Jesse King has *always* done it for me, regardless of whether or not we've been on speaking terms.

I was fourteen the first time I realized he was the hottest boy known to mankind. He'd come home from college for Thanksgiving, something he hadn't done since he left in August for school, despite being barely an hour away. His hair was messier than his usual short-cropped look, which his mom forced him into during high school; his posture was more relaxed, and a new, effortless cool surrounded him.

At nineteen, he ignored me, waving hello when he walked in on Wren and me helping Mrs. King bake pies for the big dinner, but never acknowledged me any more than that. I barely said a word to him the whole week he was home, despite my being at the King's house nearly every day, too tongue-tied and dazed to attempt it.

My childish crush started then, writing *Mrs. Jesse King* in the margins of my diaries, cutting out pictures from magazines of models with the same thick, floppy hair and hazel eyes to add to my vision boards as my ideal match, and each visit home, he got more and more handsome, and my crush grew deeper.

Three years later, my girly dreams were crushed by reality when, during a sleepover, Wren whispered the real reason he was home out of the blue and why Mrs. King was crying: Jesse had gotten some girl at school pregnant, and he was going to be a dad. He finished school over the next year before moving Emma and Emma's mom into the house that the Kings had cleaned up for him. By then, my crushes had become more appropriate: boys my own age or pop idols I'd never actually meet, and in the years since, I've buried the mere *thought* of Jesse King beneath metaphorical *tons* of reality.

But my *god*, when he's standing there all sleepy and casual and none of the everyday stress of the farm and life as a whole weighing on him this early, it's hard not to see the boy I once daydreamed could be my everything.

Plus, now he has a mustache. A fucking *mustache*. It's basically my own personal catnip. If Nat were here instead of a literal child and it wasn't *Jesse*, I'd probably whisper some joke about riding it.

"This is your doing?" he asks, knocking me out of my thoughts and gesturing to his kid with his mug. I furrow my brow, not understanding in the least, my mind still stuck on much more inappropriate places.

Get it together, Hallie. You're being weird, I silently chide myself before speaking aloud. "I'm sorry?"

"I normally have to drag her out of bed." His smile goes wide as he rinses his mug in the kitchen sink and puts it into the dishwasher. Once it's closed, he leans on the counter and crosses his arms across his chest, those muscled arms honed not from a gym, but from hours working on his family's tree farm, flexing beneath the dark green Henley he's wearing over jeans. "She's not what you'd call a morning person."

"One time, Dad threw me in a bathtub filled with ice water," Emma adds happily, sitting at the island again and spooning more cereal into her mouth.

Jesse turns to her with an exasperated look. "Okay, it wasn't ice water, Em. It was just cold. And I didn't *throw* you into it. I simply placed you."

"Well, it *felt* like ice."

I bite back a laugh and shake my head at their back-and-forth. Jesse said he's been having problems with her lately, with the two of them clashing over her sass and his inherent stoic sarcasm. I can see it, but I don't know if he realizes how much she adores her father beneath her age-appropriate attitude.

It's bittersweet to see, as it always has been, Wren engage with her parents, knowing I will never have the same close relationship with my parents. From the age of ten on, I was raised mainly by a single dad who never imagined himself as the primary parent but did the best he could with the hand he was dealt. It's not to say I never felt loved or appreciated or supported, just that I don't have...this.

I'm glad Emma has Jesse, considering the stories Wren has told me through angry whispers when she gets on a tangent about how shitty Kim, Emma's mom, is.

I'm pulled from my dreary musings when Jesse's phone rings, my attention darting to him as he checks it and groans.

"Shit, that's Dad."

"Everything good?"

"Mom's having us meet her in the office for a *formal meeting.*" He sighs, clearly exasperated by the entire ordeal. "She's trying to get him to install a pick-your-own flower field, and he's trying to see if I can talk her out of it."

I roll my lips into my mouth, knowing that the way Mr. King loves his wife, by spring, he and Jesse will be out in the field of her choosing, tilling the ground and planting the most beautiful flower garden you've ever seen.

From the resignation on his face, Jesse knows that as well.

"Well, feel free to head out whenever. I've got it from here. Right, Em?" Emma nods eagerly, and I turn back to Jesse. "Anything I should know?"

He shakes his head, and I'm pleased to see the same hesitation that's been on his face the past two mornings isn't there as he speaks, eyes on me.

"Nope. You girls have fun. Be good." Then he turns to his daughter. "Dinner at Grandma and Grandpa's tonight, so no fine dining restaurant today, okay?"

A wide grin spreads on her face, and she nods before he pulls her in for a big hug and heads for the door.

From what I know, Jesse doesn't usually work on weekends, and Sundays in particular are reserved to spend time with his daughter. Still, since the holidays are the busiest season at the farm and there's a ton of decorations to take down before the next big snowstorm, he works nonstop in the days following Christmas to get things done.

Once the door slams behind him, this time seeming to be more functional than intentional, which is another improvement, I turn to Emma. "Okay, girlfriend, what do you want to do today?" I ask, even though I already have a plan in mind.

"Another thing from my board?" she asks with hope written on her face.

Although I agreed to watch her, finding that vision board was kind of a saving grace, since I had no real idea what to do this week. Now we've crossed off decorating her room and started learning to cook. Some of the items are entirely unfeasible for complete in one week, like watching Willa Stone perform live or learning to play the guitar, though I did file that one away to bring up to Wren, since I know child music prodigy Adam could probably teach her. But there are still a few things we can do, like make s'mores, learn to do her makeup, or get her hair professionally done.

Watching Emma's excitement to get as much accomplished as she could before the end of the year has admittedly lit a fire under my own ass, and when I got home that first night, I found the vision board I had made around the same time she made hers at the beginning of this year. I couldn't help but feel a bit surprised when I realized just how many items on my yearly vision board I *hadn't* accomplished.

While I did accomplish most of the items related to my career on the board, like finally creating social media channels and a website for my business and getting two new clients, that's all I accomplished.

I wanted to move out of the duplex I rent from my brother and get a pet.

I wanted to travel, to find more time to be silly, childish, and creative, and to visit places on the travel bucket list Wren and I made as kids.

I wanted to get more into photography.

I wanted a relationship—a goal I quickly crossed out the second the catastrophe that was Vermont happened—but it's more than just that.

It was an alarming reminder that, lately, I've felt stagnant. My best friend finding her voice and standing up for herself while simultaneously finding the love of her life was a bit of a reality check for me, but finding that list nailed just how complacent I've become, leaving so many things unchecked.

But I can't fix any of that right now. That can be a next year thing—thoughts and concerns, and goals to address when I make next year's board. What I *can* do is make sure the girl in front of me gets the excitement of crossing things off her yearly list and has the best winter break possible.

Knocking myself out for my dull thoughts, I give Emma an excited look. In my bag are makeup, hair tools, and more nail products than two people could use, but I packed this morning on a mission.

"We have a family dinner at your grandparents' today—how about we cross off learning to do your makeup and get all dolled up?"

Her eyes light up with my suggestion, and I grin.

SIX

JESSE

After I get Dad to concede that we will build Mom a pick-your-own flower garden this spring, I head out onto the property to continue cleaning up. After two days of working harder than I have in some time, definitely *not* in an effort to distract myself, I can finally see the light at the end of the tunnel in terms of the decorations being taken down, and it couldn't come soon enough, with a big storm forecasted for Tuesday. By three o'clock, I'm tired and cold and can't stop thinking about my nice warm house, where my girl is probably having yet another perfect day with Hallie.

Hallie, who, when she walked in this morning, looked at me in a way I hadn't seen in a long time. Like she was interested in me, like she liked what she saw.

A hundred of those glances and my clear misinterpretation of what they actually meant is how this mess started, though, so maybe I'm not the best judge of that.

Either way, with frozen fingers and little motivation to spend more time outside, I pack things up and make sure to feed the goats, chickens, and other small animals in the petting zoo area before heading home. When I walk in, a loud, carefree laugh fills the space, followed by a lighter, younger one, and suddenly, the cold is gone. Warmth floods my system at the sound of my daughter laughing and chatting, and Hallie occasionally adds her own indecipherable murmurs. Quietly, as I take off my boots, jacket, and gloves, I listen to their murmured conversation and head toward the noise.

They're sitting on the floor around the coffee table, makeup palettes scattered about. On a plate are a few cookies and some crumbs, and Emma is sitting with her hands splayed out on the table, chatting with Hallie. Or, more likely, chatting *at* Hallie, who is adding a coat of clear polish to her own nails as Emma rattles on, telling her the gossip from her school, with a few names I recognize as friends or middle school-level enemies popping up. Her hair is down and in loose curls, not like the ones she naturally has, but more refined, the kind that I've seen Wren do a dozen times with a curling iron, and it throws me back as I realize Emma is also wearing makeup.

"How's it going, girls?" I say, and Hallie jumps, clearly caught off guard, turning to me with wide eyes. Emma turns as well, smiling wide at me.

"Good! We're painting our nails," my daughter says, wiggling her pinkies, her nails pink with little white polka dots.

Emma had been begging for makeup and girly stuff, since apparently the girls in her class are already wearing those kinds of things, and I've been at a loss for what to do. I hadn't gotten around to asking Wren about her thoughts on it, but I have to say, I was both grateful and panicked when Emma opened the giant gift Hallie got her on Christmas morning at my parents, revealing makeup and hair stuff of all kinds. She looked at me immediately, and her face went soft as if feeling my panic across the room.

Don't worry, Jess. It's all very age-appropriate. No full faces or lash extensions, I promise, my sister had told me. I wasn't sure what either of those things was, but the knot in my stomach did release just a bit.

"Hallie's been teaching me to make up." There's an excited tone in her words, and when I step closer, I see what she means. There's a thin glide of blush over her cheeks, her lashes are a darker brown color, and there's something shimmery swiped over her eyelids. Her lips are glossy and pink, and even though it cuts deep to see it on my daughter, who just last week couldn't have been older than five, I'm grateful to see that Wren was right: it's nothing crazy, but something that, based on the grin on her face, makes Emma feel good. I know her friends wear makeup, and I've seen some of their work and worried that Emma would try to use a heavy hand, but this feels like the perfect compromise.

"Looks good," I say, pushing past the sudden annoying lump in my throat.

"Doesn't she look gorgeous?" Hallie asks.

"And Hallie! I did Hallie's makeup."

"You both look beautiful, but you both always look beautiful."

Emma rolls her eyes, but I don't miss the blush that pinkens Hallie's cheeks and down her neck. For the first time in a long time, I find myself wondering just how far it goes, her fair skin always showing her emotions so quickly. She looks away, fingers gently tapping on the tips of my daughter's before nodding.

"You're all dry. You want to wear that for dinner at your grandparents?"

"I'm gonna change. This face deserves a good outfit."

Hallie looks at my daughter, something soft and easy, before nodding. "So true. I'll neaten this up, and you go change, okay? I'll set it aside, and you can clean it up after dinner, if that's cool with your dad. But when you get back, it's your responsibility to put it all away. If I find out you didn't, then we're not doing another makeup lesson tomorrow."

With Hallie's words and firm look, I brace for Emma's attitude. Her nose scrunches just a hair in irritation, but then, to my astonishment, my daughter, who hates cleaning up almost as much as she hates ultimatums, nods, then grabs a few of the things out on the table, stacking them in her arms and walking toward her room without even being asked. I watch in awe as Emma stands and moves toward her room without a single argument.

"How do you do that?" I ask in awe once she's out of earshot and eyesight.

"Do what?" Hallie asks, looking at me quickly before wiping a makeup brush on a paper towel, leaving a trail of faint pink in its wake. I watch the way her hands move back and forth, deepening the color until the brush is cleaned.

"Get her to talk to you? Get her to drop her attitude? Agree to clean up? Not freak out about going to my parents' for dinner?"

She looks at me, confused. "We've been talking about going to dinner all day, so it wasn't a surprise. I asked her to clean up and made a deal that seemed fair to her. Easy as that."

"When I ask her to do anything, I get the attitude. When I ask her to clean up, I get a fit. Same for Mom and Dad, even Madden and Wren. But she just...did it."

Hallie's face clears when she looks at mine, then nods as if she understands and gives me a knowing look. She neatly arranges the remaining items into a pile as she explains.

"Well, unlike all of you, I treat her like she's a person instead of a little kid," she says bluntly.

"She is a little kid," I counter.

She lets out a small, reluctant sigh meshed with a laugh. "Not for long. Soon, she's going to be a woman, and right now, she's in a very awkward stage. She wants you to treat her like someone whose opinions matter, not like someone who needs to be told what to do."

I open my mouth to argue, to tell her that Emma does, in fact, need to be told what to do. If I don't, she might not bathe regularly or clean her room, or, actually, remember to do her homework, but then I look at Hallie's face.

And then I remember who Hallie is.

A woman who was once a girl being raised by a clueless single dad. She's a woman whose mom up and left her when she was barely ten, a woman who clung to my family in an effort to find a place to belong.

A woman whose childhood probably looked a whole lot like Emma's. When I don't speak, lost in my thoughts, Hallie stands, pushing her hair behind her shoulders and giving me the same stern look she gave my daughter.

"Go. Take a shower, get dressed—do whatever you've gotta do. I've got things handled with Emma, and then we can head over to your parents."

I look down at my outfit, a thick flannel and a pair of jeans, with a couple of smears of dirt along the knees, and I wouldn't be surprised if there were some pine needles stuck to my shirt.

"Are you coming to dinner?" I ask, though I know the answer.

"It's a family dinner."

Sunday is family dinner no matter what, and if you're nearby, unless you're deathly ill, my mother expects you to come. It's the one time a week I see Hallie, though she always does her best to avoid me on those nights.

Because, regardless of blood, Hallie Young is family, something I'd be wise to remember if I want to make it out of this week with my head on straight.

BREAK

"How did I get stuck carrying all of this?" I ask, shifting the box in my arms filled with dishes and a tablecloth into my mom's house. Since the girls hadn't been outside, they decided they wanted to walk to the main house on the Three Kings Christmas Tree Farm property, which is my parents' house and my childhood home. It's barely a quarter mile, so I had no argument, until Hallie walked out the door holding a cardboard box filled to the brim.

"I think you offered," Hallie says, and when I turn to her, there's a slight smirk on her lips like she's trying not to laugh. It brings a feeling so akin to nostalgia that it warms me up, despite the biting cold.

"Oh, yeah, definitely. Insisted, even," Emma adds, and I sigh, shaking my head.

"Because Hallie could barely see over it," I say, and the girls look to one another, sharing an exaggerated eye roll before breaking out in laughter.

"Look who the cat dragged in." My dad stands on the porch of my childhood home, door opened wide with a grin on his face. Emma runs up ahead and barrels into him with a hug. "Oof!" he groans as she slams into him. The sound is Oscar-worthy since, despite nearing his sixties, the man would definitely need much more than a small-for-her-age eleven-year-old to take him down. "Oh, my! Who is this grown-up hugging me?"

Emma pulls back, and even though I can't see it, I know she's giving him an irritated glare.

"Grandpa, it's just some makeup. God, you're so dramatic."

I look to Hallie, who is rolling her lips between her teeth, fighting a laugh. I let out a silent one, shaking my head before tipping my chin for her to go ahead.

"And my Hallie girl, gorgeous as ever." He reaches for Hallie next, pulling her in for a hug and kissing her hair. My parents may not have *actually* adopted Hallie when she was a kid, but they might as well have. My parents treat her no differently than they do Wren or even my brother and me. Knowing she doesn't have that from her family but gets it here always brings me some small form of joy.

When she pulls back and steps into the house, I hear her greeting my mom, and my dad tips his chin to me. "Jess. Looks like you're the bellhop today."

I shake my head. "You should've seen her trying to bring it over. Hallie could barely see over it. She was going to trip and bust her ass, along with every single piece of china in this box."

My dad just nods, ushering me into the chaos that is Sunday dinner at my parents' place.

Moving down the hall, I catch Hallie greeting my brother, his arm wrapped around her shoulder, and her leaning into him, chin tipped up to smile at him as he looks down at her, and I remember the truth.

No matter how well she fits in here or gets along with my daughter, it's because she's meant to be Madden's.

SEVEN

Hallie

"I sit next to Hallie!" Emma yells when Mrs. King announces that dinner is ready, and we all start moving toward the dining room.

"I'm sure your grandma has the table how she wants it, Em," I say, but Mrs. King hip bumps Emma and winks.

"Already got you two girls next to one another. Madden, you're next to your brother tonight."

Madden groans because when Wren is home, it's usually Wren, me, and Madden, with Jesse and Emma on the other side of the long table, but since Wren isn't here, it seems Mrs. King and Emma have new plans.

For the past year, I've dreaded sitting across from Jesse, but things seem to be a bit easier between us since I've started helping out at his house, so for the first family dinner I can remember, I don't feel that nervous energy of having to sit across from him.

We've shared casual updates about our lives, with everyone telling Mr. and Mrs. King about the best and worst parts of their weeks, a tradition they began long before I started joining these dinners, when Mr. King speaks. "Jess, make sure you put the plow on your truck sometime before the storm comes on Tuesday."

I groan out a sigh. "A storm is coming?"

Mr. King looks at me with a hint of confusion, and I have to assume it's a storm that he, and probably the rest of the town, has been tracking for a bit. Unfortunately, I am more of a *fly by the seat of my pants and see what the weather is when I wake up* kind of girl.

Mr. King, who would probably be prepared if an apocalypse hit, can never quite understand when I say I don't foresee things like massive storms coming, but looking ahead in the forecast only makes you think about the bad. I'd rather every day just be a fun surprise.

"A big one," he says. "Nor'easter. Could get eighteen, twenty inches."

I scrunch my nose with irritation. Typically, a snow day wouldn't be that big of a deal: I'd stay home, watch shitty movies, make soup, and dilly-dally until the streets are plowed. But this week, I'm helping Jesse with Emma, and when a storm hits, Jesse has a lot on his plate since he picks up odd jobs plowing around town and has to ensure everything is okay here on the farm. Mrs. King could probably take over, but I know she'll be busy making sure Mr. King is safe out on the property, and the last thing I want is for Wren to come back from her trip and find out I added to the stress instead of easing it.

"Do you mind if I spend the night in Wren's old room on Wednesday night?" I ask Mrs. King, knowing it's what Wren would do if she were watching Emma this week, wanting to stay close but knowing getting home would be too risky. "That way, I don't have to worry about getting home after watching Emma if the snow is crazy."

"Of course not," she says with a smile and a shake of her head. "I'll make sure it's all good for you."

"No need, really. I just need a bed to sleep in." She rolls her eyes at my dismissal, which is expected.

"You also could just stay home," Jesse says. "Emma could have a sleepover with Mom."

"Dad, no!" Emma whines. "We have to keep working on our makeup and cooking lessons!"

Jesse turns to his daughter, frustration evident on his face. He mentioned he's been butting heads with her a lot, which, from spending a few days with her, I can understand—especially since he and Emma are complete opposites in personality. To try and prevent the coming argument, I drape my arm around her shoulders and pull her in close. When she looks at me, irritation fades into disappointment, softening something in my chest.

Wren has told me there's a history of her mom making promises she never keeps, so I tread that line carefully.

"No need to pout, Em. Even if, for some reason, it doesn't work, I can come one day this week. I promise to make it up to you, but there's no need to give anyone else a hard time, especially your dad, who is trying to make sure I stay safe." Jesse looks at me from across the table, and relief and appreciation are written clear across his face. I give him a wink, feeling like we're on a secret team right now, working together to keep Emma happy. He gives me a slight nod before looking down at his plate again.

"Okay," Emma grumbles, then picks up her roll and takes a much larger-than-polite bite, but I don't mention it.

"You should just move into my old place," Madden says, waving a fork in my direction. "You keep bitching about living next to Colt, and the house is just sitting there."

"I don't bitch," I say, glaring at Madden.

He gives me wide, disbelieving eyes. "Sure you don't."

"I don't!" I repeat, balling up a napkin and throwing it at him. It hits him in the nose and falls into his lap, making Emma giggle. "I occasionally *complain*, the same way Wren would if she were stuck living in a house with paper-thin walls right next to you."

"It's not like you're bringing home anyone where the thin walls would actually matter," he mumbles, a smirk playing on the edges of his lips like he knows that's going to annoy me. This is our way: teasing and taunting and irritating until one of us cracks and we start laughing so loud and hard, neither of us can breathe.

"I'm sorry that I'm not constantly out looking for some—" I start, but Mrs. King cuts off our bickering in a smooth, practiced move she's used a hundred times.

"That's actually a good idea, Madden. Hallie, you're here nearly every day anyway, so it would probably save you gas money," she says. "You absolutely should move in there."

I stare at her with wide eyes and shake my head. "No, no. I really couldn't. That's...that's not necessary."

"I disagree. It makes perfect sense to me," Mr. King adds, and the panic in my chest builds.

"I appreciate the offer, but I don't want to impose," I say, knowing I've imposed on the Kings more times over my life than I'd like to admit.

Mr. King shakes his head. "No, no, it wouldn't be an imposition at all. That building is just sitting there! Hell, I'd actually feel better having *someone* there. It would make me feel less silly about building it."

"And I'd feel better about having you close! I love having all of my kids close by," Mrs. King says with a broad, genuine grin that strikes me in my chest.

There were a few buildings on the King property other than the farm, office, storage barn, and a small retail shop at the base of the farm: the main house where we are now, the one that was built for Jesse and Emma, and a second, smaller home intended for Madden that now lies vacant. From what I understand, they were also going to build a small house for Wren, but they learned she would be inheriting her grandmother's home and figured Wren would enjoy that more. Mr. and Mrs. King love having all of their kids close, and since they have the means and the land, they have done what they can to ensure that.

Never in a million years did I think *I* would be included in that.

"I don't—"

"Madden just said you're not loving living with Colt, and Wren told me you were looking for a new place, right?"

I mentally shake my fist at my best friend, who listened to my whine about living in the split home with my brother, who is incredibly nosy and has no concept of personal space—something that says a lot when coming from me. Two weeks ago, I was telling her that the sheer number of times he's come over without knocking and almost walked in on me having a date with my vibrator is honestly getting obscene, and she was laughing so hard, tears were coming down her cheeks.

"I mean..." I hesitate, unsure of what to say. "Yes, but—"

"So it's settled. You'll move in," Mrs. King states with a grin.

I open my mouth, looking around the table for a single person to vouch that this is crazy, but find none.

"I really don't think this is necessary," I say with a laugh. If it were any other family, I could laugh it off and move on, but this is the King family, and I know if any of them get an idea in their head, they'll be going for it within twenty-four hours.

"It makes total sense, Hallie. I mean, you're here more than Madden even is," Mr. King says, sending a glare to his son.

"I never asked you to build me that house," Madden grumbles.

"Plus, you could help more with me!" Emma adds.

I turn to give her a soft smile, latching on to the one piece of leverage I might have.

It's not that I wouldn't love to live closer to where I work or to the Kings, since I love them all completely. It's that I've learned my lesson over and over not to ask too much of anyone because when I do, they get tired of me. The second I become too much work for someone, they begin distancing themselves from me, and losing the Kings would absolutely destroy me.

"I love hanging with you, but I also don't know if your dad—" I start, looking to Jesse for help, but he also surprises me.

"It would be a help, honestly," he says with a shrug of his shoulders, and for a moment, a look of shock crosses his face, like even he isn't sure why he said it. Still, he doesn't backtrack. "I like to make sure there's someone there to get her off the bus, but it's not fair to always rely on my mom, so a lot of the time I have her walk over to Wren's after school, who has to drive her up here."

I bite my lip, knowing this is true and desperately wanting to encourage Wren to keep setting boundaries and putting herself first.

"I mean, I could easily get her off the bus, whether or not I'm living here. Most of the time I'm working in the office with Madden —" I start, which is true. Although I work for myself, I like working from the office at Three Kings so I don't sit alone all day.

"You work from home some days, though, especially in the winter," Madden adds, and when I turn to him, he has a smile on his face like he knows I've already long lost this battle and he's *happy* about it. "It would be an extra drive when there might be ice or snow on the ground. And the place is nice, Hal. Not too big, probably as big as the duplex. It's perfect for you. The kitchen is huge and faces the woods."

I scrunch my nose because he knows me too well. I like living in town, but I *love* the woods, especially the woods out here on the farm. Being able to wake up and look out my window at them every day would be a dream.

"I don't—" I start again, though even I can hear the fight is gone from my voice.

"Jess, do you think Hallie could move in tomorrow?"

My eyes bug out. *Tomorrow?!* Before I can argue, though, Jesse is answering.

"Yeah, it should be good now, but I'll double-check everything later. I can show you tonight before you leave, if you'd like," Jesse answers, looking across the table at me. I glare at him, a traitor, especially considering that just two days ago, he could barely even stomach the sight of me. Now he's encouraging his family to move me in next door, basically.

"It's settled. If you like the place, you can move in tomorrow," Mrs. King says with an excited clap of her nails that are painted a pretty light green color with red tips for the holidays, a giddy grin on her face.

"I appreciate it, really, but I'm paying Colt rent for my half of the duplex—I can't in good conscience—"

"And you can keep paying him until he finds someone to live there," she replies with a shrug.

I narrow my eyes, already seeing where she's going with this. "Mrs. King, I can't afford double rent," I start, and she shakes her head, confirming my fears.

"You'll only be paying rent to Colt. And I told you, call me Mom. My god, you've basically been my kid for years. This Mr. and Mrs. King thing has to die eventually."

Warmth fills me at the common argument, but I push it back, trying to stay focused, knowing her goal is to distract me. "I can't live in Madden's place and not pay—"

"If you try and tell me you want to pay rent, I'm going to be offended, Harriet Young."

Mrs. King breaking out the full name makes me smirk a bit, but I force myself to stay focused. That fight isn't one I'm going to win right now, but maybe I can table it.

"Okay. I'll move in, but I'm not dropping the conversation about rent."

"Yay! After dessert, Pete will give you the keys, and Jess will take you over to your new home. How exciting!" She claps her hands excitedly. "Now. Everyone, help me clean up. I've got an apple crostata waiting for everyone if things get cleared quickly!"

As I've witnessed happen a dozen times before, everyone at the table stands, moving efficiently to clean up the table, each person having their own task. I gather the plates and scrape them, which is usually my and Wren's job, and it's not until I'm laughing with Emma as she steals a scoop of whipped cream off my plate that I realize she never agreed to talk to me about rent later.

EIGHT

JESSE

I'm lurking in the hallway like a creep as Hallie, Madden, and Emma play Uno. Simultaneously, I'm attempting to decode what the fuck I just did, not just *agreeing* but *encouraging* Hallie to move into Madden's old place. She looked to me for help, for someone on her side to say the idea was bonkers, but in the moment, I couldn't seem to think of why it *wasn't* a good idea.

And now, watching the unwavering smile on Emma's face and realizing I haven't had any actual arguments with her in a few days, I can't find it in me to say having Hallie closer and spending more time with my daughter would be bad. It's mostly just for my own sanity, but I've been putting Emma above my own surface-level wants and needs since Kim left.

"Seems Emma and Hallie get along pretty well. It will be good to have her around here more," Dad says, scaring me as he steps beside me in the hall. I nod, unable to argue that. "She always did fit in around here. Even when she was a kid, she always seemed to love being out this way. She gets the magic of the farm, like you and I do."

I shrug, not sure of how to feel about that, about Hallie loving this place the way Dad and I do.

Madden doesn't. He needs people and entertainment, and business at all times of the day. It's why, when he came back from college, he only lasted here for a year. He needs the hustle and bustle of downtown, even if it is a sleepy small town like Holly Ridge. Mom and Wren are the same way, but Dad and I...we aren't. If it were up to us, we'd never leave this place.

You plugged me into the life you *wanted, making me play house in a family I never asked for.*

The words rattle in my mind, a long-forgotten memory of the blowout fight Kim and I had, and even though I push it away quickly, it leaves an all-too-familiar sour taste in my mouth. I sigh, trying to remember what we were talking about, and the sound of Emma shouting, *"Uno!"* from the living room brings me back. My eyes shift there, catching Hallie laughing as Madden grumbles something, taking a card from the pile of cards in the center before giving her a mischievous look.

"Yeah, well, maybe that means Madden will see it too, one day," I say, giving him a knowing look. His face goes confused for a moment, and he opens his mouth to say something, but he's cut off before he can.

"You should know by now that Jesse's blind, Pete," Mom says, putting a hand to my dad's shoulder and giving me a soft look. "He'll get it one day."

Dad tries to hide an amused smile, and Mom gives me a warm look that is almost *sympathetic*, leaving me completely confused.

"What—" I start, but Mom shakes her head, reaching into her pocket and pulling out a keyring with two gold house keys on it. There's a Holly Ridge Elementary keychain dangling alongside them from some fundraiser Wren helped to host last year.

"Go show Hallie her new place. It shouldn't be dusty, since I was storing gifts in there this year," she says with a tip of her chin toward the den where Emma, Hallie, and Madden are playing.

I grab the keys, eager to get away from my parents' suddenly assessing eyes, before moving toward the living room.

"You lose, Uncle Madd!" Emma calls as she throws down her last card.

"Because you cheated!"

"Are you accusing an eleven-year-old of cheating?" Hallie asks, her voice suspiciously teasing. Her hair is pushed behind her shoulders and tucked behind an ear, highlighting a row of mismatched stud earrings dotted along them.

"No, I'm accusing a twenty-seven-year-old of helping an eleven-year-old cheat." Madden turns to look at me, a stoic look on his face. "Hey, big brother, did you know you're raising a cheater? And letting her spend time with an even bigger cheater?" Madden asks, turning in my direction and knocking me out of my creep mode.

"Just because you suck at Uno does not mean I'm a cheater, Madden," Hallie says with a smirk that is far too guilty to be innocent.

"You were the dealer! That means you cheated!" Madden says, throwing his hands in the air. I'd think he was being dramatic, but then Hallie shifts, revealing a small stack of five or six cards tucked discreetly under her ass, and I have to bite back a laugh.

"You know, if I weren't best friends with your baby sister, I would undoubtedly think you're a spoiled youngest child," Hallie says with a tone akin to a disappointed parent before turning to Emma and winking. Emma giggles, never able to keep a secret to save her life, and Madden narrows his gaze at my daughter.

"He still is," I say, helping to create a diversion. "The youngest son might as well be the baby of the family. Wren has much more responsibility than he does."

"You're so right," Hallie says. "He truly is a big, fat, spoiled mama's boy."

"What the fuck! Why are you two ganging up on me? You two don't even like each other!" Emma reaches over and pats her uncle's shoulder.

"It's okay to admit you're just terrible at Uno, Uncle Madd."

That does Hallie in, and she bursts out laughing. Madden's face turns red with irritation, and it really is entertaining. Madden has always been a sore loser: there's a tiny scar on my chin where he threw a controller at me when he was nine, and I was ten and beat him at Mario Kart. He was grounded for about a month after that, but it didn't ease his hatred of losing.

"You're so cute when you throw a temper tantrum, Madd," Hallie says when her laughter dies down. He flips her off to his side, out of Emma's line of sight, and she blows him a kiss, making Emma laugh out loud. "Don't you agree, Jesse?" Her face is one of pure innocence, even though I know she's doing everything she can to piss Madden off and is obviously succeeding.

"That's my brother, Hallie. That's weird," Madden says.

Hallie turns to him, exasperated. "He can be objective. I'd ask Wren, but she's across the world. Though she would absolutely agree, you look cute throwing a fit because you didn't get your way."

"Wren's opinion wouldn't count. She always takes your side," Madden whines, and Hallie preens. They've always had this back-and-forth bantering relationship, the tension always so high, and I'm always wondering when—if—they're just going to give in to it right then and there and admit they're wild for one another.

"Because it's the right side." She turns to me again. "What do you think, Jess? Isn't Madden just *adorable* when he throws a fit like a toddler?"

"Yeah, the cutest, whatever." She grins, the happy look directed at Madden instead of me as she lifts her hand and leans forward, patting his cheek. It twists something in my chest, and I decide I need to get out of her.

And take Hallie with me.

Mature? No. Rational? Fuck no. But I'm doing it anyway.

"Want to see the house now?" That's why I came here, after all, to show her the house. My sudden need to get out of the house has nothing to do with my lack of desire to watch Hallie and my younger brother flirt the way they always do.

"Yeah, that would be great," Hallie says, gathering her cards and putting them into a pile before handing them to Madden.

"Can I come?" Emma asks.

Hallie looks to me, not wanting to answer before I do, and I shrug and nod. "Yeah, that's fine. Say goodbye to your grandparents and get your boots and jacket on. We'll head home after."

Emma nods, then all three of them stand before Emma hugs her uncle and runs excitedly out of the den toward my parents.

"Later, Madd," Hallie says as my brother moves to pull her into a hug, and I look away, suddenly uncomfortable.

"Later, Hallie. Let me know if you need pictures for the account this week. I know you like to get shots of everything covered in snow. I can take you out on the four-wheeler if needed."

"All right, I'll let you know. Though now that I'll be living here," she starts, excitement clear in her voice despite her previous hesitation, "I can just go wandering on my own."

"Better get better shoes before you do," I mumble under my breath without meaning to.

She turns to me with a wide smile, then rolls her eyes before turning away in the direction Emma went. Before she's through the door, she looks over her shoulder.

"Come on, show me to my new home."

TKBREAK

I walk in silence to Madden's old place, which is basically a two-minute walk from my house, something I'm not totally sure how I should feel about. The girls chatter incessantly the whole walk. Emma is going on about how exciting it will be to have *a girl* nearby, and I'm staying silent. When we approach the small home, I take a wider step to unlock the door first, then turn on the light. Dad keeps the heat on all winter to avoid the pipes freezing, but it's still freezing in here, so I find the thermostat and crank it up before looking around as the girls enter.

As Mom promised, it's relatively clean, though it has a bit of that unlived-in house smell; that's really the only issue. It's not a huge place, intended just for one or two people to live in, but everywhere Hallie goes to inspect, her eyes light up, talking to Emma about decorations or design ideas. It seems she isn't even formally moved in, and she's already making plans with my daughter, promising to take her to one of those big-box home decor stores sometime so Emma can give her input on everything from lamps to throw blankets.

When they enter the kitchen, Hallie talks excitedly about going antique shopping for an old table to fit the small dining area and about finding gingham curtains for the big window over the kitchen sink. I have no idea what the fuck *gingham* is, but Emma seems to, and gasps, "*Oh my god, yes. Totally!*" There's a single large bedroom with sliding glass doors that lead to a small patio facing the woods, where Hallie and Emma plan to get a little table, chairs, flower pots, and fairy lights to make an *oasis*.

The only moment of seeming disappointment is when she pokes her head into the small bathroom.

"There's no tub?" she says, raising an eyebrow. I never really noticed this place had no tub, but suddenly, my mind is racing toward visions of Hallie, her hair in a mess on top of her head, sunk into a vat of bubbles, water steaming around her.

I clear my throat and shrug before answering. "Mom and Dad built this for Madden. Believe it or not, he's not really a tub kind of guy."

She scrunches up her nose, and I watch as the constellation of freckles across it shifts and changes.

"We have a tub," Emma says while I'm distracted, and Hallie and I both turn to look at her.

"Lucky you," Hallie says deadpan.

"You could come use it whenever you want," I say without meaning to, and when her head snaps to me, the burn of a blush forms on my cheeks, and I stutter out an answer. "Because it's closer than my parents. Or you could go there. Either way. Uh, you know. Wherever you want. I just mean...there are options if it's a deal breaker." A small smile plays on Hallie's lips, typical since she loves to see people uncomfortable, especially me.

"We also have a hot tub," Emma says, a calculating look written across her face.

"A hot tub?" Hallie asks before I can step in, raising a speculative eyebrow at me. "You have a hot tub? Where?"

I shrug, suddenly nervous. "Out back. It was a marketplace find that I was surprised actually worked. It's nothing special, just a nice place to relax once in a while."

"You *use* a hot tub? To relax?"

My blush deepens, and her smile widens, but before she can continue her teasing or I can try and redeem myself, Emma speaks.

"You can totally relax in our hot tub whenever you want."

Hallie turns to my daughter and grins, winking as she steps out of the small bathroom and toward the living room and back out the front door. It's nearly pitch black outside, though I'm happy to see the front light works when I flip it on. Mentally, I think to look in the storage barn tomorrow and grab some of the solar walkway lights to add around her walkway and parking area.

To keep her safe, of course. Because technically, she'll be a tenant of my parents, which means her getting hurt would be their problem.

That's the only reason I care.

I lock the door behind us, not that it's really needed around here, then turn to Hallie, who's looking at the little home with unmasked glee.

"All right. Well, I guess...I guess I'll take it."

"We'll be neighbors!" Emma squeals with excitement, hopping up and down.

Hallie looks in the distance, where the lights for our place are visible, not too far off, then looks back at my daughter. "We will, won't we?"

"Not to rush you, but you really should start moving in soon and get it done with before the storm on Tuesday. You don't have to bring everything tomorrow, but you might as well bring the basics."

She nods, that excitement turning more serious. "I should head home, then. Start packing." I nod, and then the three of us move down the gravel driveway toward my house and her car. As we walk, she turns to me. "I know you've got a lot on your plate tomorrow, getting ready for the storm, but do you think it would be okay if Emma tagged along with me? I could leave her with your mom, but—"

"If Emma doesn't get to help, she'll be disappointed," I finish.

"Yes, I will!" Emma agrees.

"I'll pack up my car tonight and head this way tomorrow morning. You can help me get those unloaded, and then we'll head back to my place to do another trip?" she asks.

Emma nods, but I shake my head.

"Dad texted the family group chat to ask when you want him and Madden there to help you bring things over. Emma will come with them, and with Dad's truck and a trailer, you four should be able to get it all in one load, unless you have a ton of stuff."

Her face pales, though her cheeks stay pink with the cold, and she shakes her head. "Oh, no, I don't need—"

My steps slow as we approach her car until all three of us stop.

"Hallie, if you think telling my mom no is hard, you know by now that telling my dad no is going to be like hitting a brick wall."

Hallie sighs, then, dramatic as ever, looking to the night sky with a shake of her head. "You Kings are so damn stubborn."

"Yeah, well, you should be used to it by now. Come on, I'll walk you to your car." I turn to Emma before Hallie can argue and toss her the house keys. "You go inside and get ready for a shower." She opens her mouth to argue, but as I'm learning is her way, Hallie chimes in.

"You've gotta wash the makeup off your face. Put your hair in a bun and keep it out of the water, and it'll stay dry." Emma looks to Hallie for another minute, and I expect an argument, but instead, she nods, then waves.

"Later, Hallie. See you tomorrow!" And then she's off without an argument, unlocking and opening the door before slamming it shut behind her.

"I don't know how you do that," I say with a shake of my head, clear awe in the words.

"It's not magic: I just know how she thinks. I get her. Hell, I've *been* her," she says, stepping toward her car as she digs distractedly in her bag for her keys. I'm about to ask her what she means by that, but before I can, her foot hits a patch of ice, and the shoes with no grip slip, her entire body jolting as she starts to fall. Instantly, I'm there, grabbing her and pulling her up and stopping her from falling on her ass. My hands are on her shoulders, and her green eyes are wide with panic before it slowly recedes. Once she's steady, I glance down at those stupid fucking shoes before glaring at her.

"You need better fucking shoes." She's so close, her head tipped up, her breath caressing over my chin and down my neck, causing a chill I can't seem to fight off to roll down my spine. "If you're going to be on the farm a lot, especially in winter, those aren't going to cut it."

"I'll be fine."

"You almost fell on your ass."

"Well, thank goodness I had a big, strong, handsome man to catch me, huh?"

I stand there, frozen in place with her words, like a kid who just had the popular girl compliment him, and she uses my stillness to get away. She dips under my arm to get away and nearly slips again, but I reach out in time, settling my hands on her waist and pulling her up and toward me. Her hands move to my chest to steady herself, and her eyes are wide, but it doesn't look like panic this time. Instead, it's something I can't quite identify.

"See? What have I told you about those goddamn shoes?" My voice is low and gravelly to my own ears, and even though I try to make it sound annoyed, I don't know if I succeed.

"Just because I work on a farm does not mean I have to look ugly, Jesse." Her words are breathy, nerves and irritation intertwined.

You could never look ugly, I don't say, thankfully.

"They're inappropriate if you're going to be living here. Get new fucking shoes."

Fire flares in her eyes before she narrows them at me, her fingers digging a bit into my chest, something I feel even beneath my jacket.

"You don't get to deem what I'm wearing inappropriate; I am not yours."

Without coming to any kind of understanding of what I'm doing, my body moving without the permission of my mind, I step closer, and Hallie takes one step back, her back bumping against the car. Her eyes widen as I move, and even though some rational part of my brain knows I should stop, should step away, should run to my house, I don't.

I can't.

Instead, I speak once I have her pinned to her car with my body. "Trust me, Hallie, I am incredibly aware you are not mine." A moment passes before the tiniest smirk plays on her lips, almost like it's calculated, a show, some facade she's putting on, but I can't put my finger on why.

"Thank God for that," she says.

"What's that supposed to mean?" She tilts her head a bit, a look I've seen her use in Colt's bar a dozen times when someone hits on her that she's not interested in, almost like she pities him.

"You couldn't handle a woman like me, Jesse."

My cock twitches with the challenge, both in her words and on her face.

"Oh, I could handle you, Hallie Young." Her tongue darts out, wetting her lips, and a panting breath leaves them, coasting along my own lips

It wouldn't take much to bend down and kiss her.

To prove to her I could handle her, that I could *more* than handle her.

"Dad!" my daughter calls from the front door, and I step back as if she'd burned me. "Dad! The hot water isn't working!"

I sigh and nod, taking a step toward the house.

"Give me a sec, I'll be right there," I call, and the door slams shut again without another word. When I turn back to Hallie, whatever moment we almost had is clearly over, her door open as she slides in and starts the car. Still, she looks over her shoulder, something so similar to regret on her face.

"Too bad we'll never find out."

And then she's slamming the door and driving away, leaving me to watch her leave, fully confused.

Later that night, after I get Emma to bed, for the first time in a year, I allow myself to remember that night almost a year ago—the last time she left me feeling confused as she walked away from me.

NINE

JESSE

For Christmas last year, instead of gifts, our parents gave a weekend ski trip in Killington, Vermont, to Madden, Wren, Hallie, and me. They'd planned and pre-purchased the entire thing so none of us could argue and booked three rooms (the girls shared a suite, but they were smart enough to realize that Madden and I might actually kill each other if we roomed together, since they tried it when we were kids for about two years before building an addition on the house, probably sensing the impending bloodshed) and lift tickets for a day. Wren had a long weekend from school and planned to watch Emma for three nights. We left on a Thursday and returned on Sunday afternoon just in time for family dinner.

It was a great weekend spent on the mountain and relaxing with my siblings and Hallie. We spent Thursday, Friday, and Saturday on the mountain before getting dinner and heading to bed tired as could be, but on Saturday night, after a long day on the slopes and then a casual dinner, we all sat in the lodge for our last night, laughing, drinking, and relaxing. It was the most at ease I'd felt in my lifetime. The trip as a whole made me realize that since Emma had come into my life, I hadn't had much time to myself.

Around nine, Wren let out a loud yawn, saying she was tapping out since she rarely got the opportunity to go to bed early, and then it was Madden, Hallie, and me. An hour after that, Madden started flirting with another guest and left Hallie and me sitting around the fire. Both of her hands were wrapped around a warm mug of hot toddy as she sat in an armchair, and I was on the couch catty-corner to her.

"You gonna head up?" I asked since both Madden and Wren were gone, and I knew it had been a long day for her. We'd spent many nights over the years chatting together, usually in situations just like this at her brother's bar, with Madden chasing some woman and Wren running off to do some favor for someone, so it wasn't like it was odd, but I didn't want her to feel forced to sit with me. But then a soft smile spread on her lips, and she shrugged. A cozy look was on her face, a little bit tired from a long day, a little bit recharged after a weekend with people she loved to spend time with, and a little bit buzzed since that was her third cup of the evening.

"I'm not really tired," she said, and the words hung between us as if she was waiting for me to say something—to add something—to extend the night a little longer. It was apparent she wasn't ready to call it a night yet, and honestly, I wasn't either. The next day, we were checking out and driving back home, but I didn't want this feeling of relaxation to end. I wanted living in this small bubble, free from the pressure and stress of my everyday life, to last just a little bit longer.

It was the first time since Emma's mother had left that I'd let myself have a weekend away without the stress of wondering about her, both because I knew my parents were watching her and because I finally felt like she was old enough to leave for a bit.

"Neither am I. Let's hang here for a bit longer," I said, and the widest, brightest grin lit her face. We spent the next two hours talking, laughing, and just enjoying each other's company. Eventually, she moved to sit on the couch beside me, just a few inches apart, and like it had happened countless times before, I felt a pull toward her. Countless times, I've hung around longer than needed or intended, just wanting to stay and talk more, to hear her thoughts and opinions on everyday subjects, or to listen to her talk about some show she was watching or describe a book she was reading.

I just liked hearing her talk.

At some point, she said something that made me laugh out loud, my head tipping back as the sound rolled out of me, and it felt so foreign. Afterward, I looked around the room to see if anyone was staring since it must have been extremely loud or out of place, only to realize everyone in the lodge was still lost in their own conversations.

It wasn't that it was loud or excessive; it's just that I hadn't laughed like that in such a long time that it felt strange to do it. When I turned back to her, she was giving me a soft, knowing smile. "I don't think I've ever seen you look like that."

I know what she meant, but I still asked. "What do you mean?"

She lifted a shoulder, eyes shifting down to her drink before answering. "I don't know. You just...you looked so free for a second. I don't know the last time I've seen you look like that."

A moment passed as I absorbed her words, waiting for her to lift her head and look at me. When she did, her green eyes met mine, and something shifted. My hand reached out on its own, grabbing her hand and squeezing it once.

"Yeah," I said, lifting my beer to take another sip, holding her gaze. A blush spread across her cheeks, and she changed the subject but kept her hand in mine. We sat like that for a while until almost midnight, when only a few others lingered in the lodge, the fire burning in the fireplace louder than the conversations of the few remaining guests. It was then that she tipped her head toward the large windows.

"It's snowing," she said, and I followed her gaze to where thick, heavy snowflakes were falling gently, illuminated by one of the exterior lights. She stood, grabbing her coat off the couch and shrugging it on, and I followed suit, not sure what she was doing, but in that moment, I think I'd follow her to the ends of the earth if it kept that light, warm feeling stirring in my chest.

When she got to the door, she turned back to look over her shoulder at me, her hands moving behind her neck to tuck her hair out of her jacket. "Want to come check it out?"

The lodge we were staying in was a huge log cabin surrounded by trees that even I could admit would look magical in the snow, so I nodded, opening the door and guiding her outside. We started walking in silence along the side of the lodge, not a soul in sight. I placed my hand on her lower back, and she moved closer to me, my heart pounding as possibilities and maybes raced through my mind. It had been a long time since I felt, or more accurately, *let* myself feel attraction to a woman, so caught up in trying to be the best dad I could for Emma, and it felt absolutely wild that this was the time it decided to return.

This was *Hallie*, after all.

Hallie, who had been around for so long, I couldn't clearly remember when she became a fixture in my family—just that she always seemed to be there.

Hallie, best friend of my sister, second daughter of my parents, who works for my family's business. The one who gets all of our family secrets, who laughs at our inside jokes, who has always fit in, and who loves Emma just as much as anyone else in my tight-knit family does.

Hallie, whom I had found myself spending more and more time with over the previous year, making excuses to see or bump into her, had become a fixture in my mind.

I was lost in these thoughts, both exhilarating and confusing, when she hit a patch of the sidewalk where the snow was fresh and lost her footing. The hand on her lower back came in handy as I shifted quickly; my boot caught in the snow with no problem, unlike her soft-bottomed ones, which offered no grip, and I caught her. Her body was pinned to mine, her hands gripping my shoulders tightly before loosening, my arm wrapped around her waist. Her feet found purchase, but I didn't let go, instead pulling her even closer to me without even thinking.

"Those shoes are trash for the snow," I whispered, because I've told both her and my sister that those types of shoes aren't really winter boots and are definitely not suitable for a tree farm in winter.

A small smile tipped on her lips. "Can't exactly complain right now," she whispered.

I looked down at her, her chin tilted up to look at me, our breaths mingling between us, causing clouds in the cold I can't even feel right now, not with the way my pulse is pounding, with the way my body is heated.

Slowly, painfully slowly, I dip my head down, giving her a lifetime to push me away, to say no, to say anything, but she doesn't. Instead, the hands on my neck tighten, pulling me in closer until my lips are on hers. Then we're kissing, her soft lips pressed to mine in a tentative touch. It's almost chaste, almost sweet—the perfect, idyllic first kiss—until she sighs into it, her body going lax, her lips parting just a bit, and her tongue slipping out to glide along the seam of mine. I groan into it, taking control, one hand moving to the back of her head to angle her the way I want her, to deepen the kiss, to slide my tongue into her mouth and tantalize her. She tastes like honey, whiskey, and fucking *Hallie*, and it was perfect. Everything I never knew I needed—the perfect sweet contrast to me—and when her hands tighten, fingers twining in my hair and pulling, I know we're on the same page.

I groaned, my hips moving involuntarily into hers, and she sighed into it, pulling me closer. Never in my life had I felt more like I belonged somewhere, as I fit with another person, and through my lust-driven haze, I remember wondering if maybe this is what—or rather who—I had been searching for all along. Eight years of resigning myself to waiting until Emma was out of the house before looking for a partner, and all along, the perfect one was there, waiting for me to open my damn eyes.

I moved us, stepping back into the snow-covered grass until she was pressed to the side of the building, and my hands went down to her ass, gripping and groaning as I got my hands on the ass that had been tormenting me for much longer than I could admit. Without another word, she shifted, jumping so I could lift her, legs wrapping around my hips until they were cradled between hers, and my already hardening cock ground into her center. A moan left her lips as my lips moved from hers, nipping at her chin, then up to those earrings in her ears that have constantly tormented me. I pulled an earlobe into my mouth, teeth scraping at the skin there, and her hand moved to my hair, digging into the back of it and pulling me closer as a low moan escaped her lips. I smiled, thinking about how, somehow, it was like I already knew what she liked, my mind spending the past year daydreaming of all the ways I could touch and taste her.

I was eager to see if my thoughts were all correct, if all of the places I'd dreamed about tasting and touching and nipping would elicit similar reactions.

"My room," I groan, pulling her closer, my head in her neck, breathing her in.

"What?" she mewled, her hips shifting to get more friction. I chuckled at her distraction, and she sighed.

"My room. You're sharing with Wren, and I have a room to myself. Come to my room."

It was the wrong thing to say.

Her entire body went still, frozen in place before her hands

And that's when it happened: her small hand settled on my chest and pressed there, pushing me away. I look down at her, confused, then see deep regret on her face, her eyes shining, before I quickly step back and set her down, giving her the space she was silently asking for.

Tears shone in her eyes when she spoke. "We can't. I can't do this," she whispered, then pulled away and ran off.

Slowly, I made my way to my room, trying to think of where I went wrong and settling on doing far too much, far too fast. I should have just kissed her, told her I couldn't stop thinking about her, and asked to go on a date when we got home—dinner or coffee or a movie or literally anything other than pressing her to the side of the wall and grinding my cock into her, making her think I just wanted a quick romp in bed.

Because I was starting to think I wanted a fuck of a lot more than just that with her, and that I'd wanted it for some time.

The next morning, I delayed as much as I could as I packed up my things, buying time and letting the nerves win as I thought through all the things I might encounter when I saw her at breakfast. Would she avoid me? Call me out? Pull me aside and explain? Kiss me?

No matter what, I needed to find her, to talk to her, to tell her I knew it was too much, too quick, but that I could move slowly, as slow as she needed.

For Hallie, I would move like fucking molasses if it meant that in the end, she would be mine.

Eventually, Wren texted me asking when I'd be coming down to the lobby to get breakfast together. I realized I'd put things off as long as I could and made my way downstairs, eyes scanning the entire way, on the lookout for Hallie's red hair and for my chance to talk to her. As I stepped into the lobby where we were meeting, I spotted her, my chest tightening and lightening in equal measure, before sinking to the ground with a new option of what would happen this morning that I hadn't accounted for.

Because when I found her, she was clinging to Madden, his hand on her waist, tucking her into his side, and suddenly, I understood.

It wasn't that she was scared or that I moved too fast.

It was then that she realized she was with the wrong brother.

It was further confirmed when I walked over to where the three of them stood, waiting for me, Wren and Madden giving me wide smiles and Hallie refusing to meet my eye, uttering the smallest "good morning" to me before stepping away to check if our breakfast table was ready.

After that night, she did everything in her power to avoid me. In the weeks after, I realized the night before had been a mistake. Not because I kissed her, but because in that moment, I lost Hallie—a friend, someone I enjoyed talking to, someone I looked forward to spending time with at family dinners and random gatherings where we'd sit in the corner and poke fun at Wren and Madden. Eventually, over the next few months, with her constant avoidance, that disappointment turned into frustration, a frustration that surfaced when she walked into my house the day after Christmas as if nothing had happened.

The worst part is that no matter how much I want to be mad, angry, hurt, or disappointed, it makes sense. It was always supposed to be Madden.

They're perfect for each other. Both of them are funny, fun-loving, and chaotic, and I will never be those things. I left home just long enough to go to school, then returned to work on my family farm, a place I'll probably never leave, and I've never once felt like I wanted anything else. If, for some reason, Hallie chose me, she would be tied to this place, part of a family she never asked for. She deserves freedom, travel, and adventure, and I learned long ago that I could never give a woman those things.

TEN

Moving into the house on the King property reminds me of how much I love this family.

On Monday morning, Madden, Mr. King, and Emma arrive at my door bright and early. I'd been up late, packing boxes after talking to my brother, Colton, about my plans and getting his full blessing. I'm pretty sure he was also getting a little tired of our closeness. Even though I love my brother more than anything, he's the one person in my family who has always been there and never made me feel like a burden. I shouldn't need to be on high alert whenever I hear a woman's laughter through the walls, ready to put on noise-canceling headphones or go to Nat or Wren's if I even *sense* I might hear something I wouldn't be able to bleach from my brain.

I left the bar with a trunk full of folded cardboard boxes, and when he got home later that night, he helped me pack my belongings and break down the few pieces of furniture I was taking with me. The place was fully furnished when I moved in, except for a bed I brought myself. Even though he offered to let me take everything, I'm kind of excited to leave it all behind and start fresh.

The following morning, it takes hardly an hour for Mr. King,

Madden, and Colt to load all my belongings into the truck and trailer. Then I drive Emma back to the farm, with Colt following behind to do his big brother duty of inspecting my place since the bar is closed on Mondays. Over the next six hours, the three men helped unload and set up my furniture, and Mrs. King came to help unpack my things. Around noon, she, Emma, and I headed to the main house to make a quick lunch, which we ate amid various boxes, laughing and joking the entire time.

It was the perfect afternoon, and I reminded myself that, even though they might not be my blood, other than Colton, they were my family.

After my mom left, there was a time when all I dreamed of and wished for was this: a close-knit family, picture-perfect in every way, with a mom and dad who loved each other more than anything and doted on their children like they were the most precious things in the world. Over time, I realized my dad and brother *were* perfect, and we were making the best of the hand we'd been dealt, but I still would have done anything to have what Wren had. As I sat there, looking around my new home, I realized that even though it didn't look the way I imagined, I've found it, in my own way.

And in the same way that, as a kid, I would have done anything to get it, I will do anything I can not to jeopardize losing it.

BREAK

Around three, Jesse is done with his chores around the farm and comes over to help unpack a bit. Mrs. King bosses him and Madden around as they put my bed together and lug my mattress inside, while Mr. King and Colt hook up the washer and dryer, troubleshooting a bit when they can't get the washer to fill correctly. Mrs. King has already headed back to the house to get started on dinner, promising to come tomorrow with pantry essentials and a few housewarming things I told her I didn't need, but I know are coming my way regardless.

"Any other boxes?" Madden asks as he and Jesse leave my room. I shrug, washing the few dishes I brought and setting them on the counter for Emma to dry.

"I think there are a few in my car that we haven't gotten," I say, since I know the night before I had put a few boxes into my car to avoid having to do *everything* in the morning. "They go in my room or the bathroom, though they should be labeled."

Madden nods, and he and Jesse head outside. They begin to bring in the boxes of random items, like extra toilet paper, my shower essentials, and clothes, but when I look over my shoulder and see a smallish pink box on top of the larger brown one Jesse is carrying, I panic.

Quickly, I turn off the water and set the plate down in the sink as he moves out of sight and into my room. Grabbing a dish towel, I dry my hands quickly before moving to my room, watching as Jesse looks around to set the boxes down. The brown one at the bottom says "summer clothes," but I pay it no mind and reach for the pink box on top.

"Give me that."

"What?" he asks. I reach for the box on top, but he shifts away.

"Give it to me!" I shout, panicking now. He turns his back to me, then sets the heavy load down before grabbing the pink box and turning back to me.

"Why—"

In some recess of my mind, I realize if I had just ignored it, he probably would have stacked up the boxes along the wall like I see he did with the others, but the voice in my mind is not rational right now. She's fourteen, the girl who made the very first one of the papers that lie in that box, and is panicking that he'll take the top off the pink-wrapped shoe box to reveal them all. Each paper in that box feels like a hidden secret he can never find out about.

I reach for it, grabbing to snatch it from his hands, and then, like a horror movie, the box falls, the top falling off as it does, and a lifetime of goals and hopes and dreams falls out, fluttering to the ground. There's one for every year, and then a few more for the times I felt lost and wanted to create a vision board for the next season, the second half of the year.

I drop to my knees to collect them, my pulse racing as I do, as I try to pile them all as carefully and quickly as possible.

"What are these?" Jesse asks. "I thought it was going to be, like, vibrators or something."

I don't even have it in me to laugh at that, at the idea that Jesse thought I had a box of vibrators just lying around in my car. Not when he lifts one, not when his eyes scan the paper, cut-up magazine words and photos, and doodles, and I realize it's possibly the worst one.

In Jesse's hands is the very first vision board Wren and I made, back when we used to daydream about my marrying her brother so we could be real sisters, so I could be tied to her for real, and so I could really be a *King*.

I'd found the perfect image to add, and it felt like a sign. Wren and I giggled as I cut it out and glued it to the bottom left corner. It shows a redheaded woman in a wedding dress standing beside a dark-haired man with shorter hair, who looks more like Jesse used to than he does now. I could explain that away, really, but unfortunately, the most damning part isn't the photo but the cut-out letters spelling out the dream: *Mrs. Hallie King*.

I wish the world would swallow me up.

"Is this..." he says, his voice low and confused.

"They're my vision boards from when I was a kid. Give them to me," I demand, trying to act like he doesn't see my embarrassing childhood crush. God, could this get any worse? I spot another one from the following year and realize that one says *Mrs. Jesse King*. I grab it, slide it to the bottom of the stack, praying to all that is good in the world that he didn't see it. But when I look at him again, his eyes are still scanning the one in his hands.

I comb my mind, trying to think of something, anything.

"Need anything else?" Colt asks, stepping into my room.

Instantly, Jesse drops the paper and stands, and I scramble to stack them neatly, placing them back into the box as quickly and as delicately as I can. Even if, in this moment, they feel like an embarrassing secret, they're still precious to me: these far-off dreams, memories of who I once was and what I've wanted, and how that changed over the years. Snapshots of who I was each year that I don't want to lose.

"Uh, I think that's it," I say, standing and looking around the room. I can handle unpacking the boxes myself, and honestly, some of it will just go into storage until I get more furniture to put things away. I also very much don't want my brother or either of the King boys to be going through my things.

It's not like there *aren't* a vibrator or two hiding in those boxes. They're just, you know. *Hidden.*

"Okay, well, then I'm gonna head out if you don't mind. I've gotta check Wren and Adam's places on my way home, make sure there's no mail outside, and salt their walkways before the storm comes." He looks from me to Jesse to the room around us. "You sure you don't need help unpacking?"

I shake my head and give him a wide smile. "No, no. I'm good. Really. Thank you. You didn't have to do this."

My brother rolled his eyes and shook his head before stepping to me and pulling me into his arms. "You always say that, and I always tell you—"

"It's your job as my big brother, yeah, yeah, yeah," I murmur into his chest, letting myself soak in this moment with the one person who was always and will always be there. "Go, check Adam and Wren's house, then go abroad in the quiet of a house without me."

His grin widens then. "Oh, it's going to be blissful."

I roll my eyes as Madden enters our small huddle.

"Hey, Colt, do you mind driving me to my place? My dad picked me up this morning, so I don't have my car here," Madden says, and Colt nods before we all say our goodbyes and watch them drive off.

"I'm hungry," Emma says as soon as Colt's taillights are out of view. I let out a little laugh and hook my arm around her shoulder, pulling her into my side.

"You're always hungry, Emma," I say, tugging her along into my place since it's absolutely freezing outside.

"Well, what are we making for dinner tonight?" she asks, and I turn to her with wide eyes.

"Em, I love you and all of your enthusiasm, but unfortunately, I'm old, and today took it out of me. I can't move in and then also make dinner. Today will be a PB&J night for me," I say with a laugh. Her nose scrunches up, clearly not pleased with that option, and I laugh.

"I'll order delivery from Prima," Jesse says from behind us. "We'll have to eat it at my place, though, because I'm also old, which means eating pizza on the floor isn't in the cards for me."

Emma again rolls her eyes, and I laugh, shaking my head.

"You really don't have to feed me. I brought the essentials over—"

'You've been feeding me every night this week," he says, eyes locked on me. I open my mouth to argue that his mother fed him last night, but he shakes his head. "And babysitting. Please. Let me feed you tonight."

His voice is sincere and on his face, and even though he just helped me all afternoon and even though I just snapped at him ten minutes ago, I sigh and grudgingly give in. A small smile tips his lips before I even speak.

"All right, all right," I grumble.

Emma lets out a hoot of excitement as we all put on our jackets, and I lock up my new place. Jesse tells me it's not really necessary, something I know, but it will take me a while to kick the habit. Then we start making our way down the gravel drive toward Emma and Jesse's place.

We have pizza, eating it on the couch while watching some movie Emma picked out, and then half of the sequel. It's long past dark when Jesse tells Emma it's time to pause the movie and get ready for bed. Since it's only seven forty-five, he tells her that if she does it quick, she can watch a bit more before her bedtime at eight thirty. It seems like a reasonable offer, but she clearly disagrees, and that's when I finally see the full brunt of the attitude.

"But I need to watch the end!"

"You've seen it at least ten times, Emma," Jesse says, exasperation in the words.

"No, I haven't."

"Emma," he says, voice steady but his face clearly showing he's losing patience.

Emma stomps her foot, and I have to look away to avoid laughing, knowing in some part of my mind that laughing right now would be the absolute worst thing.

"I want to watch the rest of the movie with Hallie!" she whines, her voice losing some of the edge and exhaustion filling it. I realize then that she was probably up early to head to my place with her grandfather, then spent the entire day unpacking, moving boxes, and helping me clean. Now it's past her usual bedtime, and she's probably exhausted.

"Em, honey, we can watch it tomorrow. You're tired from a long day, you should—"

"No, I'm not! I'm not a baby who needs to go to sleep! Stop telling me what to do!" she says, and my eyes widen since while I've seen her talk back to Jesse, it's never been directed at me.

It seems that was also the last straw, because after that, the couch beside me shifts.

"Okay, that's it," Jesse says, standing. "Brush your teeth, get your pajamas on, and get in bed."

Her body stills, and her eyes go wide as she turns to her dad. "What?"

"You heard me. Brush your teeth, get into your pajamas, then get into bed. I'm done."

"It's barely after seven!" she says, even though it's past seven thirty.

"The time doesn't really matter, not when you're being rude.

You've eaten dinner, so I'm okay with you going to bed early. Now, brush your teeth and get your pajamas on, or there will be no TV or screens at all for the rest of your

"You can't do that!" she shouts, eyes welling with frustrated tears.

"My house, my rules."

"You're the worst!" she shouts, then turns on her heel toward her room, slamming her door behind her as she does. We sit in silence while she changes, hearing her slam things along the way before she steps into the bathroom and brushes her teeth, mumbling to herself as she goes. Finally, she returns to her room, slamming her door once more.

After a moment passes, Jesse sighs. "I'm gonna go talk to her," he says, standing up and looking down the hall toward her room.

"Maybe I should—" I start, and he looks at me with utter exhaustion in his eyes, exhaustion that definitely wasn't there ten minutes ago, exhaustion that is born from the weight of having to raise Emma on his own and being completely and totally unsure of what to do. I know the look, because I saw it on my dad's face so many times when I was a kid.

"Stay. Please."

It's a simple request, but I couldn't disagree if I wanted to. Instead, I nod, and then he turns, heading toward his daughter's room, opening the door, and flicking the light on.

I sit there on the couch for ten minutes, scrolling my phone while Jesse and Emma murmur to one another, a few sniffles and tears and words making their way down the hall to me. Eventually, Emma, in a pair of pink-striped pajamas, shuffles down the hall toward me, Jesse leaning against the wall near her doorway.

"Hey, Hallie, I'm sorry I was rude," she says when she reaches me, her eyes pink from crying, but she seems to be level-headed now. "I was upset, and I took it out on you, and that's not cool."

"All good, girl. I get it. But next time, maybe try to talk about it instead?" She nods, sniffling once. I give her a soft smile, my throat suddenly tight as I open my arms for her, and she gives me a big hug. Eventually, it ends, and she stands, wiping her hand under her eyes.

"Okay, now it's time to head to bed, okay?" Jesse says from the hall, in soft but firm words. Emma looks to her dad, opening her mouth to argue, but he gives her a look I can't see but can feel instead. I roll my lips together and try not to laugh at the battle of wills, knowing it won't help anything. Emma loses when she sighs, nods, and turns to me.

"Night, Hallie. See you tomorrow?" There's hope and nerves in her words, and it sends warmth through me.

"Yeah, Em. I'll see you tomorrow."

She nods and then heads back to her room, with Jesse following her inside. He spends another minute or so talking to her before stepping out, the door softly snicking shut behind him. He pads down the hall, looking like he's aged ten years. Finally, he flops down next to me on the couch, eyes closed. Silence fills the space for a moment before I break it.

"You're a good dad, Jesse." He grunts a sound—half laugh, half argument—but doesn't open his eyes or speak. "I'm serious. My dad was a good dad and handled being a single dad as well as someone who never thought they'd be in that situation could, but I can tell you right now, if I snapped at him, he wouldn't spend twenty minutes quietly talking to me in my room before bed. He would send me to bed and hope that we could move past it in the morning."

I continue to stare at him, my eyes tracing over his face and the minor differences, signs that time has passed since the last time I let myself do this. There are a few light strains at his temples, just a few, and the lines beside his eyes are more prominent. His mustache sits above fine lines I know are from laughing, though I don't know if I see that very often. That thought brings me back to that night, when his laugh nearly startled me, and I'm glad when his eyes open, his words distracting me from going down a path I can't wander.

"I know. I know I'm a decent dad, trust me. I'm not that deluded or in need of a confidence boost. I just think it's harder than I thought. I know how to handle a baby and a toddler, and an elementary school kid. But this is different. This is her turning into a woman. This is her trying to navigate hormones and attitudes and, God forbid, one of these days, boys. I don't know how to do that. I'm ill-equipped, and I haven't made a good enough effort to try and bridge that gap."

"Your mom and Wren—" I try, but he shakes his head.

"I'm so grateful for both of them—really. I wouldn't have made it this far without them, but they also see Emma as a baby. As a little kid. And I think that it gets to her, and I've been ignoring that. But honestly, she's been better the past few days with you around."

I shrug, not wanting to make him feel any worse than he already does.

"I've been like Emma in a way, so I think I understand her in a way your mom and Wren can't really relate to. But also, I think eleven is just a very uncomfortable time, so no matter what, there are going to be ups and downs."

"I think you came in at the perfect time. I'm grateful you're here."

His words have such sincerity that they settle in my chest, a warmth that stays with me even as I walk in the night air to my new place.

ELEVEN

JESSE

I woke up early the next morning, and even though I should be exhausted, especially knowing the long day ahead, I'm not. When I roll out of bed, I notice there's already almost an inch of snow on the grass, but it isn't quite sticking to the driveway yet, and I send Hallie a text.

> Head to my place when you're ready—the snow's only going to get heavier. If it gets too thick, I can clear the way to my place with the UTV

I'm not sure when she wakes up, but in case she's an early riser, I move through my morning routine a bit quicker, brushing my teeth and getting dressed before heading to the kitchen to make coffee.

"Jesse?" Hallie's voice calls quietly after the door clicks open and shut.

"Kitchen," I reply in the same hushed tone from the kitchen, reaching for a mug and filling it.

"Morning," she says, and when I look over my shoulder, I give her a soft smile that she returns.

"Morning. Want some coffee?" I tip my head toward the pot, and she nods fervently.

"Yes, please. I didn't have any at the house. After the storm, I'm going to have to do a major restock at the store."

I nod, having figured as much, then set a pale green mug on the counter before heading to the fridge. I hesitate for a moment, staring at the blue bottle, feeling silly, before I shake it away, grab it, and set it in front of Hallie.

"Yesterday, when I went to the store, I got that creamer you like. I wasn't sure if you were able to grab it when you moved."

She stares at it for a long moment before looking to me with confusion written on her face. "You got me my creamer?"

A blush burns on my cheeks before I turn away from her, reaching into the cabinet over the coffee maker for a thermal travel mug, wondering if this was possibly the weirdest, most creepy thing to do. I didn't think much of it yesterday, just grabbing the bottle and tossing it in my cart, but maybe I should have thought a little more about it beforehand.

"I was already at the store when I saw it, and you've been here most mornings anyway. Seemed to be the least I could do."

"How did you know what kind of creamer I like?"

I shrug, trying to seem as casual and unaffected as possible. "It's always in Mom's fridge, and you're the only one who drinks it when you're there." I move back to the fridge, intentionally keeping my back to Hallie, grab the half-and-half, then pour some into my mug before returning to the coffee maker.

"Are you watching me?" she asks, teasing in her words as I screw the top on my mug.

Finally, I turn back to face her, leaning against the counter with one arm crossed on my chest, the other lifting my mug to my lips. "We're friends, right? Friends do that."

She opens her mouth to speak, but before she can say anything, a familiar voice calls her name—my saving grace in the form of a sleepy eleven-year-old.

"Morning, Hallie!" Emma says, and Hallie turns to her, pulling her into her side. The sight of them settles somewhere in my chest, keeping me warm the entire day.

Throughout the day, I get numerous updates from Hallie and Emma on their progress as they unpack Hallie's place, then go back to ours and make cookies. The snow continues to fall, with it stopping long enough around dinner time to plow most of the town before it starts back up. By the time I make it back to the farm, it's coming down again, and I text Hallie to put Emma to bed at her normal time, since I won't be home until late. I offer to send my mom over to stay with Emma, but Hallie refuses, so when I get home long after nine, she's sitting on my couch, the lights all dimmed, and watching some movie.

Exhausted, I remove my jacket and boots before shuffling toward where she is.

I'll have to go out again tomorrow once the snow finishes for good, but the town streets are mostly cleared, with the heavy layer of salt turning the currently falling snow mostly to slush that I'll clean up early tomorrow.

"Hey," Hallie says, sitting up from the couch with a soft smile, her voice low. "You're home."

I give her a grunt of a response before collapsing onto the couch in an exhausted heap. "Yeah, sorry, that took longer than expected."

"No worries, Emma and I watched a movie and talked. She went to bed super easy. There's dinner on the stove, if you want it. I taught Emma how to make chili, since you had all of the essentials in the pantry and freezer."

Relief fills me at the idea that I won't have to figure out a meal, so without another word, I nod, then turn toward the kitchen.

"I'll, uh, get out of your hair. Let you relax," Hallie says as she stands. I look over my shoulder at her and see her all casual and sweet, her hair over one shoulder, a too-large Three Kings Tree Farm sweatshirt hanging on her body, and a pair of leggings beneath it. I know when she leaves, she'll be slipping on those shoes that are somehow even less suited for the weather than usual.

Knowing a new fall of snow began right as I came home, I speak without thinking. "You in a rush to get to your place? The snow started again; it should be coming down for the next bit. If you give it an hour, you'll avoid the worst of it." She stares at me for a moment, and I add, "Plus, I've been alone, blowing for most of the day. I could use the company."

Hallie rolls her eyes but nods, and I move to where there's a pot on the stove and spoon some of the delicious-smelling food into a bowl before sprinkling on a hefty layer of cheese.

I grab my bowl and some water and bring them into the living room, where a movie I kind of remember her and Wren watching plays in the background as I sit before the coffee table and dig in. When I look up, she's standing at the entryway, arms crossed on her chest, and watching me with a hesitant look, so I pat the couch next to me. As if that's all she was looking for, she moves through my living room and sits beside me.

"Tell me about your day," I say, taking a bite of food.

"My day?" she asks, raising an eyebrow.

"Emma's day, I mean," I clarify, realizing it sounds weird to ask about Hallie's day. "She helped you get settled into your place?"

"Yeah, she was a big help with unpacking. I've still got a few things to do, but I was getting bored, so I imagined she was too."

I sit quietly as she continues to explain the day and my daughter's antics, and I smile as I listen, refilling my bowl once and returning with a beer for me and a hard cider I know she drinks and may have stocked up on for her. When she seems to be done with her recounting, and I'm beyond full, I sit back with a deep sigh. My body melts into the soft fabric, face to the ceiling, before I speak without really thinking.

"Maybe this is what I need."

"A hot meal?" she asks with a laugh.

"A woman to come home to." I'm not sure what makes me say it, though I assume it must be the consuming exhaustion that fills me. My eyes drift shut, and I block out the fact that it's probably weird to say that to my little sister's best friend.

"You know, I don't think I've ever seen you date someone," she says, and when I open an eye, I see she isn't looking at me aghast but more inquisitively.

I shrug. "I don't."

A loud laugh leaves her. "Kinda hard to find a woman to make you a hot meal to come to if you don't date," she says in a teasing tone, poking me in the side. I sit up, reaching over to grab and then throw a toss pillow at her, and she lets out a laugh that fills the small space. When her giggles fade out, and she doesn't fill in the silence, I explain myself.

"I'm too busy. I don't have free time for myself, much less another person." She tips her head, reading me in a way I find uncomfortable, before shaking her head.

"No, that's not it."

I let out a laugh. "I'm sorry?"

She shrugs. "That's not the reason. You might tell yourself that, and you definitely tell everyone else that, to get them off your ass, but that's not it."

"What...are you an expert in human psychology or something?"

She shakes her head and grins.

"No, I'd just been your sister's best friend for almost my entire life, which means I can read *her* like a book. Unfortunately for you, you and your sister not only look alike, but you act alike. You both have very, very obvious tells." She reaches across the space between us and smooths over a line between my eyebrows, the light touch spreading fire where it goes. "This one, for one. And you refuse to look at someone when you're lying to them."

"You pay a lot of attention to my sister, apparently."

"I take note of the people I care a lot about. Now tell me the real reason."

She shrugs, then reaches out and takes another deep sip of her drink. Something about her silence, her lack of pushing, has me confessing things I haven't told my family for fear they won't understand or that they'll find ways to work around it when I'm not looking.

I can barely keep Emma happy enough so that the guilt doesn't eat me alive, and that's supposed to be something I'm inherently good at. I can't, in good conscience, keep another person happy, even if I'm supposed to. Silence comes from the other side of the couch, and when I turn my head, I see her staring at me, confused.

"You know that's not your job, right?" Hallie says quietly, finally breaking her silence. "It's not your job to keep people happy. It's not your responsibility."

"In a relationship, it is," I counter, and she shrugs. Silence looms between us, and I think she's moving past it, but then realizes she was just trying to find the right words to reframe her thoughts.

"You're right, but you're also wrong. In a relationship, there's a balance. It's part of your job, but also the other person's job. If there's no communication to say *hey, I'm unhappy about this,* or *hey, I need more or else of this,* you can't really know. You can do your best, read between the lines, but when you add in being young parents, trying to keep a whole human alive, no one can expect you just to know, you know?"

In that moment, I wonder if maybe she knows more about Kim and why she left than she lets on, or maybe if it's just Hallie's way— her innate ability to read me and know me, for better or worse.

But the truth is, I've never told anyone the full details of Emma's mom leaving. My family knows I came home after a day on the farm to Emma crying in her crib and Kim telling me her things were loaded in the car and she was leaving. But they don't know the rest.

No one knows she left because I wasn't there for her, that I was too caught up in trying to create some idealistic family for Emma, to create what I had growing up for my daughter, to realize she was slowly dying inside, and it was all my fault.

"You plugged me into the life you wanted, making me play house

in a family I never asked for. You never asked me what I wanted. You stole my dreams and expected me just to live yours," she shouted at me when I asked her what was going on and where she was going.

And she was right: the truth of the matter is, from the moment I found out she was pregnant, I pushed Kim into a corner until she couldn't do it anymore and left for good.

That day, I begged her to stay, to talk to me, to give me a month or two of trying a new system where she'd have more time to herself, more time to chase whatever dreams she felt she'd given up. I begged her to try therapy or a new schedule or *anything* other than just giving up, and I watched her taillights drive off not long after.

As I held a crying Emma, I was also trying to keep it together, not because I missed Kim—who had been a one-night stand turned into more than either of us bargained for—but because I felt so lost and terrified. That's when I vowed I'd never put either of us in this situation again.

The closest I'd gotten since the day Kim left was the night in Vermont. The first time in eight years I'd felt willing to throw the promises I'd made to myself away, to give something more a try.

And look at how that turned out.

But I won't be telling Hallie any of that, so instead I shrug and explain what I can. "There are a lot of things I can't control, especially in the situation Emma and I are in, where there's a second parent whom I genuinely have no control over. But I can control who I bring into her life, so that's what I do. I can date when she's out of my house and figure out what the rest of my life will look like then, but she's my number one responsibility. I won't bring in a revolving door of women, exposing her to relationships she may or may not get attached to, but I don't know if they will actually last. She has enough instability in her life."

Silence lands between us after I speak, and even though I stand by my decisions, for some reason, her opinion matters to me. I've told my parents and my sister, and even Madden, about this choice, and none of them understand. All of them tell me I should date, should have "me" time. My mom has even told me it would be good for Emma, but I've always stood firm.

I wait for the disappointment to wash over me when Hallie reacts similarly.

But, as always seems to be her way, she surprises me.

"No one's going to tell you this, but I think you're doing the right thing."

I look at her with utter confusion, since she's right: no one has *ever* told me that.

"I am?" I ask, and she smiles wide before I shake my head, running a hand through my hair. "I mean, I know I am, but you think I am?"

She nods. "My dad had a few girlfriends when Colt and I were kids, and I hated all of them—the way they changed our family dynamic and our ways, even if it was just in small ways—but somehow, I hated them even more when they left. It was a lose-lose situation for me. I don't know if there is a right answer, but I get it. I get what you're going for."

It's another piece of evidence I don't need to confirm just how much I like Hallie Young, even if she never will be mine. I sit back, letting her words sink in, spreading warmth to every part of me before I decide to change the subject, to shift the spotlight.

"What about you?"

"Me?"

I shouldn't ask, but I can't think of a better, more appropriate time to finally quell my intrigue, to appease this crush I seem to have on her.

"Yeah. Why don't you have a man?" She looks at me like she's trying to decide where to start, how to answer, or maybe even whether she should answer. But eventually, I get too impatient and speak again. "Is it because of Madden?" Silence hangs between us, this time different, this time weighed down with my anticipation of her answer. When I look at her face, I expect to see nerves or embarrassment or even shyness written across her face, but I don't. Instead, I see genuine confusion.

"Madden?" she asks, her voice rising with the single word.

"Well, yeah. You two are always very...close. I always thought you would...you know."

A beat passes, and her mouth opens and closes a few times, her head tipping to the side and hair falling with it, draping over her shoulder as her brows furrow together. It's like she's trying to decode me and can't quite do it.

"Are you trying to say you think I have a thing for Madden?"

"Well..." I hesitate, reading her face and seeing a spark of amusement there. "Not anymore?"

A beat passes before it happens: Hallie's head tips back, her hair tumbles down, her face cracks in the hugest smile that I realize now she'd been holding in, and a full-chested laugh fills the room. It goes on for a moment before the laughter slows, before her head lifts and she wipes a finger below her eyes, before waving her hands at them, fanning herself.

"Oh, god. That was good."

"Are you telling me you don't have a thing for Madden?"

"Hell no. I would rather chew a tire than date Madden. Have you ever seen us in a room together? I'm kinder to my *own* brother than I am to him. He drives me up a wall." Another, smaller fit of laughs leaves her before she settles down, shaking her head. "Madden. That was good, Jesse."

"Honestly, I don't see why that's so funny. You spend a lot of time with him. You flirt with him all the time. You two are always going back and forth—"

She shakes her head. "That's not flirting, Jesse. I do all of those things with Colton, too."

A moment passes before I think about how she acts with her brother, laughing and prodding, and I realize she's...not wrong.

This reframes everything I thought I understood.

"I thought that's what happened that night," I say without

meaning to. Suddenly, the room feels too warm, too stuffy, and Hallie too close as she looks at me with a mix of confusion and understanding. "In Vermont."

My breathing stills in my lungs with my words and the way they spilled off my tongue. We've never talked about that night, about the kiss, about her leaving, and honestly, I had planned to keep it that way. But now I'm too tired and comfortable to stop, and honestly, I want to know what happened. It's been eating at me ever since.

"I…" she says, then stops, her face suddenly stark and unmoving. "Jesse."

"I figured that was why. That you realized that you'd kissed the wrong brother. You both were always, and you always seemed to have a thing for him, so the next day, when you avoided me and you were like glue on his side, I assumed that was why."

She blinks once, twice, before a small smirk tips at the edge of her lips. "Well, for one, there was a girl he was avoiding who he had flirted with the night before, so I was trying to help him play defense."

My head snaps back with confusion as I try to piece this new information into what I already know, and, surprisingly, it does fit. I remember Madden flirting with a woman the night before for a bit and then saying something about trying to avoid her because she was far too intense for his taste, but the kiss with Hallie really threw me for a loop, and I completely forgot about it.

"And I was kind of avoiding you," she adds.

My head snaps up at that, and I look at her. "What? Why?"

"Well, you see, the night before, I had gotten drunk and jumped the bones of my best friend's hot older brother and then freaked out and ran away. That's kind of…embarrassing?"

I don't bother to tell her that I was the one who jumped her, more eager to focus on the important parts.

"So you didn't avoid me because you regretted it?"

Again, her face shifts and changes. "I mean…"

Even with her words, a weight has lifted off my shoulders that I hadn't realized had been settled there for nearly a year, and with it, I'm feeling more like joking, letting humor fill my words next as I mime a stake going into my heart.

"Oof, you really know how to make a guy feel better. Was the kiss really that bad?" My comic relief did what it was intended to, and Hallie smiles, pressing gently on my shoulder before shaking her head.

"Now you're fishing for compliments. You know it was good."

"But...?"

"But you're Wren's brother. That's a line I can't cross." My brow furrows, but she continues. "Wren is one of the most important people in my life. Honestly, your entire family is. I would never put that at risk by hooking up with you, even if that kiss was very, *very* good. It would never go anywhere, and even if we just hooked up for fun, it would give your sister ideas of grand white weddings and red-headed nieces and nephews. The reality would break her heart." She says it so offhandedly, like it's a funny joke she's telling, but there's a hint of seriousness to it that is unmistakable, a seriousness I can't seem to touch.

I want to ask her why she would assume it would just be a hookup, but didn't I just tell her that I don't date? That I won't date at all until Emma's out of school? Now wouldn't be the time to tell her that, for a moment, I had contemplated throwing that rule out the window for her. Something tells me she wouldn't be very receptive to that.

Still, I almost do.

I almost open my mouth to tell her that I would take the leap if she were the one doing it with me, but before I can, she lets out a fake yawn, then stands.

"Well, I should get headed home. You'll be out early tomorrow, right?" She grabs the drink she barely sipped at and carries it to the kitchen, dumping it in the sink. "Would five be an okay time to get here?"

I blink at her, following behind her and trying to follow her train of thought.

"Oh, uh, yeah." I take the now-empty bottle from her and place it on the counter to take outside tomorrow. "I'll walk you home," I say as she walks toward the mudroom, but her hair slides along her back as she shakes her head.

"No need." I open my mouth to argue, but she stops me before I can. "I don't want to hear about your mom yelling at you—she would be okay with my walking the hundred yards home alone if it meant not leaving your sleeping child alone during a snowstorm." When she turns to grab her jacket and slide it on, I realize there's a stubbornness on her face, and there's no way I could talk her out of it, so I sigh and acquiesce.

"Fine. But text me when you get home. If not, I'm headed over there to check on you." She nods, then reaches for the doorknob as she slips on her shoes. I should argue with her about it then, but before I can, she's speaking, distracting me.

"And, Jesse?" she says when she turns the doorknob. "If I were to go for a King, it would absolutely be you."

And then, before I can even think of something to say to that, she's opening the door and offering me a quick good night! Then the door shuts. I stand there for a long minute, wondering what the hell that means, only snapping back to reality when my phone dings with a text.

HALLIE

Home! No need to send the cavalry. Night, Jesse.

I clean up quickly, packing up the leftovers and putting the dishes in the dishwasher before getting ready for bed and setting my alarm for the crack of dawn. But even though I'm exhausted, I lie in bed mentally replaying our conversation and, most importantly, those last few words until I fall asleep.

TWELVE

When I show up at Jess's house on Wednesday, I'm all smiles and excitement, chattering on about plans and crafts, then shooing him out the door before he can ask me any questions. Emma and I plan an Emma and Dad night of relaxation with homemade pizzas, a movie, and s'mores, so when Jesse comes in the door looking exhausted, I tell him about tonight's plans, he accepts, and gives me a soft look, and I dip out quickly before he can say another word.

My goal was to give him an easy night since he has to be exhausted after the last two days, but also one he could feel good about when hanging out with his daughter.

It has absolutely *nothing* to do with the intense embarrassment that I feel knowing that last night, I spilled my guts to him about what happened in Vermont, set clear, friendly boundaries, and then completely demolished them with my final words to him.

If I were to go for a King, it would absolutely be you.

Why would I *say* that?

Sure, it was true, but it could have very much stayed an inside thought.

I tell myself it's because he was so damn vulnerable the night before, and I wanted to give him the same. I tell myself that his opening up about his feelings about dating—or more accurately, *not* dating—made me feel brave, knowing neither of us would ever actually go for it. I tell myself it's because I feel bad that he spent the last year thinking I turned him down for his brother.

Okay, maybe my rushing out the door had *something* to do with my embarrassment, but at least this time, my plan isn't to ignore Jesse. I think I've learned that does neither of us any good, and with my living so close and helping with Emma, I know it's impossible. It's simply that I want to put enough space between that night and the next real conversation we have, so there's no way for him to ask about it, no way for the tension to grow between us.

Because for the smallest moment, when I explained to Jesse that I hadn't avoided him because I was actually into his brother, I saw it there: hope. Possibility. The idea that maybe, *maybe* we could try... something. I needed to squash it, and I think I did, until that stupid, stupid moment as I was leaving.

I'm an idiot.

Unfortunately, because I admitted that the last time I made a fool of myself and avoided him, Jesse has gotten much wiser to my antics, and he proves that to me on Thursday night, when Emma insists I stay for dinner, and Jesse agrees. That morning, I had arrived at eight, after Emma was awake and ready for the day, with a giant bag of craft supplies to make decorations for her room, again efficiently avoiding talking to Jesse.

Mentally, I plan to eat and then leave right after, but Jesse thwarts my plan of evasion halfway through dinner.

"You gonna ignore me for ten months again?" he asks after I head to the kitchen to get a drink. I didn't hear him follow me in, but he's standing there, leaning on the pantry doors when I close the fridge door, and I nearly jump out of my skin.

"Jesse!" I gasp. "You scared the shit out of me!" His smile goes wider, thoroughly entertained by me, and he suddenly looks younger, so much more carefree.

"Good. Now, are you going to ignore me again?"

"Why would I ignore you?" I ask, deciding playing dumb is the best plan as I crack open a can of soda.

"I don't know, but you seem to be doing a pretty good job of it."

I scrunch my nose up and open my mouth to lie, but decide it's not what I want to be doing. Not with Jesse, not when he's always seemed to be able to follow my train of thought, so long as I *explain* it to him.

"It's not that I *want* to ignore you," I start.

"But?" I roll my eyes.

"*But* it seems to be my standard reaction when I do something stupid."

"Stupid?" I glare because we both know what I'm talking about, and that grin spreads wider on his lips. "Oh, you mean when you told me you would pick me over Madden?" My face goes somehow even more deadpan. "Hal," he starts, and I ignore the way the single word sends butterflies to my belly. "I have spent my entire life with people telling me Madden is the better brother." I try not to make a face, but I think I fail when his eyes light up before he continues to explain. "He's friendlier, flirty, and dresses like he actually cares about how people perceive him."

"I've always been way more into brooding," I say with a shrug, trying to play this off as fun and silly, but it's Jesse I'm talking to, so he takes it up a notch.

"As far back as when you were fourteen, Mrs. Hallie King?" That blush deepened, and I guess now I can assume he realizes why I didn't want him to see those vision boards. "Thought those were about Madden, too, in case you were wondering."

I roll my eyes, trying to play it off. "As if."

"Hmm. Well, I think it's just fine for friends to be attracted to one another, yeah? Doesn't have to mean anything, much less be something to avoid me over."

"It doesn't?"

He shakes his head, then turns away, headed back toward the

dining room, and for a moment, I think I'm home free. But then his feet falter, and he looks over his shoulder.

"But just so you know, I'd pick you, too, Hallie. Every time."

Then he walks into the dining room, talking to Emma like he didn't just blow me away.

I don't really know what to do with that, so instead, I do nothing. I play the same role I've played for as long as I can remember, of being into Jesse and never, ever doing anything about it.

BreakTK

The next morning, I don't drag my feet when I finish all of my morning tasks and realize it's barely even seven. It's the last day I'll be watching Emma before she goes back to school on Monday, and also the day Wren comes home. Instead of sitting around and waiting until eight to make my way to their house, I'm out the door by 7:10.

I'm already thinking about the coffee I'm going to have once I get there (I don't know how he does it, but even though I have a fancy machine and the same creamer, Jesse makes better coffee in his shitty pot Mrs. King got him for Christmas years and years ago), but when I hear a consistent grumbling and a *thunk, thunk, thunk* sound, my curiosity is piqued, and I decide to follow it.

And then that curiosity turns to something else altogether when I carefully walk the path around the house to the backyard and see Jesse in the corner, a black and red flannel pulled tight across his back, muscles moving with each shift of his body as he lifts an axe over his head and brings it down, chopping wood.

Oh. My. God.

It's possibly the hottest thing I've ever seen, and I don't feel guilty about thinking that. I can't have Jesse King, but I sure as fuck can have this memory for long, lonely nights with my vibrator, right? That's not against the rules, is it?

Plus, I *have* to just stand here and watch. What would happen if I spoke and scared him, and he chopped a toe off or something? That would weigh on my conscience for an eternity.

Instead of interrupting, like the creep I am, I watch Jesse lift thick hunks of heavy wood onto the stump, then step back, lifting the axe high and swinging it down to split the wood effortlessly. After the third or fourth time (or fifth, or sixth, who knows—I'm very distracted, and counting isn't really a priority), though, I start to take note of the words.

Fucking bitch.

Hate her.

Terrible fucking person.

It seems this isn't just Jesse tackling the chore of chopping wood, but possibly him getting out some long-held aggression. Suddenly, I feel less inclined to drool over him and far more concerned.

When he's reaching for another log, I speak.

"Uh, something you want to tell me?" I ask. Jesse's head whips in my direction, and all joking leaves my chest.

He looks *terrible*.

Angry, hurt, and so beyond frustrated. It's intense emotions I've never seen on his face before, and I almost take a step back.

"Tell you?"

"I just...you keep saying you hate some kind of woman and—"

"Not you," he says quickly with a shake of his head.

"Phew, I thought we were about to be back at square one," I say with a laugh, though it's mostly for show because the truth is, I'm concerned. "Want to talk about it?" The humor is out of my words now, gentleness and sincerity taking their place, and I watch as he lets out a breath of air that seems like it comes from the depths of his soul before he sets the axe down, leaning on it before looking to me.

"It's Kim."

"Kim?"

"She was supposed to come tomorrow and spend some time with Emma. She'd been promising it for two weeks, since Emma didn't see her for Christmas."

Discomfort churns in my stomach at the words, even though I don't know exactly where it's going. Old, too-familiar wounds ache, and I hesitate with my following words.

"And...?"

"She texted me sometime late last night to tell me she got into a car accident and she can't come."

My eyes go wide. That is *not* where I thought this was going, especially not with the way he was grumbling just moments before.

"Oh, my god, Jesse—"

"She doesn't know Madden keeps tabs on her on her social media. He saw her stories, and she's currently in Aspen with some new boyfriend doing ski shots."

I blink once, twice, before fire burns through me, leaving understanding in its wake: she told Jesse she'd been in an accident as an excuse for why she can't be with Emma tomorrow.

"Oh my god," I whisper, frustration and self-righteous anger brewing. "That fucking bitch."

He shrugs as if to say, *"See what I mean?"*

"Does she know?" Emma mentioned her mother had gifted her a cellphone for Christmas, which, personally, wouldn't be my first choice for an eleven-year-old, but what do I know, and that she had been occasionally texting her mom with it. She asked for my number, but I told her I needed to run it past her dad first, and I haven't gotten around to it yet.

Another deeply exhausted sound leaves Jesse's lips before he runs a hand down his face. He's wearing a Three Kings beanie this morning instead of his normal baseball hat, a forest green color that brings out the small bits of green in his eyes. "No. Like always, I get to be the one to break the news to her." There's a reluctant acceptance in his words that tears at me.

"Does this happen often?"

He nods. "It used to be worse when she was four or five, before I stopped telling her when Kim was coming. Around then, I realized that more often than not, something would come up, and she'd have to cancel plans to see Emma. Reasonably, each time a visit was canceled last minute, Emma would lose it. That's when I stopped telling her about the visits. If she comes, then it's a fun surprise. If she doesn't, it's no big deal."

It's more evidence of what I already know: Jesse is a great dad. A lot of parents would use the constant disappointments to their advantage, letting it turn their kids against the other parent, but not Jesse. He lets Emma constantly think the best of Kim and makes the few visits she actually manages to have feel like a magical surprise.

"But now she has a phone," I say in understanding, and Jesse nods, misery written on his face.

"Now she has a phone, and she's been texting Emma for a week about their day together—all these plans to go out for lunch and to get their hair done and to go shopping." She's mentioned it to me once or twice, but I never really thought twice about it. "Now I get to be the bearer of bad news *and* deal with the emotional turmoil that will follow."

I can see it happening, too—how disappointed she will be, and the closest one, the one bringing her the bad news, will be the one who gets the brunt of it. Poor Jesse. For a moment, I wonder just how often this happens, Kim bailing, but thinking about that won't help us, so I decide to move forward.

"Okay, well..." I take a breath and start to pace, my mind moving a mile a minute. "What were your plans for tomorrow?" When I look at Jesse, he's staring at me skeptically, but shakes his head.

"Nothing. I didn't make any plans just in case."

I nod, pulling out my phone and opening up my group chat. "Well, Wren comes home today, and while I'm sure she'll be shot tomorrow, I'm sure she'd love to see Emma."

"I don't want to—" he starts, but I ignore him, beginning to type.

"And I bet if I call Nat, she can fit her in for an appointment."

"Appointment?"

"Brunch with the girls, then her hair, maybe? Do something fun for back to school." I turn to him then with a hopeful look on my face. Nat's a hairstylist, and I'm confident I can convince her to fit us in tomorrow. "How do you feel about tinsel?"

"On a tree?" he asks, and it's the perfect amount of comic relief to have me laughing and shaking my head, beating back the anger for just a moment.

"No, no. Extensions. In your daughter's hair."

He blinks at me before shaking his head. "I'm not following, Hal." I take a deep breath and try to organize my thoughts before presenting my plan to him.

"The only way to avoid a disaster is to give her something else that's bigger and better. Tomorrow, I'll come bright and early, and we'll go to Wren's for brunch. She'll probably be awake super early because she's an early riser, plus jet lag. After brunch, the three of us will go to see Nat at the salon. Emma's been talking to me about getting a tinsel extension but was afraid to ask you."

"Is it dye?"

I shake my head. "Basically, Nat will tie little shiny things into her hair. They'll fall out in a month or so, but it's fun and cool."

A beat passes before he nods. "I'm okay with that, so long as it's not permanent."

I smile and then continue sharing my plan. "After getting her hair done, I'll take her shopping, get her a new outfit, and then you'll take her to dinner."

"Me?"

"Yes. You guys are going out on a date. You go to the florist, get her flowers, and make a big deal out of it. We'll make the day really special for her."

A soft look crosses his face. "You're making up for her mom not being here," he says, but somehow, it's not him stating the obvious. There's almost awe in the words, confusion mixed with the gratitude I feel.

I nod, pushing back the lump that has suddenly formed in my throat. "We're all going to make up for it. So what do you think?"

"I think she's going to love it."

I give him one last grin, and he returns it before we work together to move the wood he chopped, then walk into his house with an arm over my shoulder to tell Emma about the change in plans.

THIRTEEN

The next morning, I head over to Jesse's house bright and early, and Emma's bouncing off the walls with excitement before we head out to Wren's place for brunch. Wren fills us in on her whirlwind of a trip, and we laugh and eat far too much before going to the salon where Nat works.

Last night, after I left Jesse's, I called her to fill her in on everything about Kim bailing and wanting to give Emma a magical day, so I shouldn't be surprised when I realized Nat pulled out all the stops for her, but somehow I still am. At some point between last night and this morning, she found an Emma-sized robe and a pair of slippers. She even managed to squeeze in a manicure, pedicure, and facial with some of her coworkers after getting her hair done, deeming the day Emma's luxurious makeover day. Wren and I pull chairs over to her station, and the four of us chat as if we hadn't seen each other in months instead of just over a week.

"We have to schedule our vision board night," I say, the magazines reminding me of the stack I'd been saving in my house for that reason.

"Oh my god, can I come? I want to make one too! Hallie and I found mine after Christmas, and we did a bunch of things on it, and it was so fun!" Nat smiles at me in the mirror, and Wren nods.

"Oh, totally! We'll make a girls' night of it," she says, and Emma's face lights up.

"What do you want to add this year?" I ask, and Emma goes off on a tangent about all of the things she's going to add to her board, and even more heartwarming, how I'm going to help her achieve them, just like I helped last year. Nat smiles at me, and I shift back to the magazine, not liking the assessing look of it. Emma asks Wren what she's going to add to her board, and a blush crosses her cheeks as she says she's planning for more travel with Adam, including a trip to LA since he has to go there anyway to talk to his new agent over spring break.

"I want to be more intentional about how I help out around town, so I'm trying to plan a big fundraiser to see if we can manage to get enough money together to hire a community event coordinator. Adam offered to donate it," she says with a disapproving grimace, and Nat laughs out loud. "But I think it should be done the old-fashioned way by fundraising. I'm thinking of some kind of strawberry festival or something in May, a big event."

I give her a speculative look. "I don't know how that would *remove* things from your pile, Wren."

She shrugs. "I have a meeting next week with Mayor Calloway to talk about options and if we can make it work. I don't want to do everything myself anymore, but community events are important to me." The reality is that Adam will force her to prioritize herself, but Wren will never stop being Wren. We just have to hope she does it smarter, and honestly, hiring someone to manage the big picture makes a lot of sense to me.

Before I can say anything else, the spotlight moves to Nat, who tells us her goals are to build her clientele book, get certified in facials, and continue moving toward buying a house.

"What about you, Hallie?" Wren asks after a bit, and I startle when all three sets of eyes turn in my direction expectantly.

"Me?"

"What are you going to put on your vision board?" Emma asks, a wide, genuine smile on her lips, but nerves take over me as I try and flit through my mind, thinking of how to answer. Instead of things I *want* to do, all that comes to mind are the things I *didn't* do this year and the discomfort that came with realizing that earlier this week.

"I...I don't know," I say, and for the first time in a long time, I mean that.

"You don't know?" Nat asks, raising an eyebrow.

I lift a shoulder nonchalantly, then drop my eyes to the magazine in my lap. "I just...I'm happy with how things are, you know? I wanted to get out of Colt's house, and I did that. I guess I want to decorate it and make it mine."

"What about work?" Wren asks.

"I have enough clients, so I don't get bored, but not too many that I don't have free time." I flip the magazine page, then stop on a picture of a cat. "Maybe I should add a pet to my board." Silence has me looking up, and when I do, Wren gives me a look I know, from years of experience, means I am not going to like what she adds next.

"I think you should add dating to yours."

I choke on air. *"Dating?"*

"Yes. Dating. Your goal has always been to have your own family, but I can't remember the last time you went on a *date*. Or gotten..." Her eyes shift to Emma before moving back to me. *"You know."*

"I can't even think of the last time you were kissed," Nat says, and I roll my eyes at their dramatics.

"I..." I start, trying to defend myself, then freeze when I realize the last time I was kissed was in February, not that I can tell anyone *here* that. Panic consumes me as I try to figure out how to respond.

"See! You can't even remember!" Wren says, taking my hesitation the wrong way and throwing her hands up. "You need to go on some dates. Find your person. Add *that* to your vision board."

I glare in my best friend's direction, though somehow, I'm grateful for the diversion.

"Why do I have to add dating to my board? How come you aren't on Nat's ass about dating?"

"Because Nat actually dates."

I turn to Nat and glare at her because we all know her version of *dating* isn't about finding her person, but about pure entertainment. She gives me a smug, knowing smile, and I flip her off behind Emma's back before returning my attention to Wren.

"Wren, as much as I love that you've found your person and you want that happiness for everyone else in your life, I don't need a relationship. I don't even *want* one."

"Well, too bad," she says, lifting her phone, and suddenly I sense danger. My entire body stills, and I close my magazine, turning to her fully.

"Too bad?"

"Too bad. I'm going to start setting you up with people."

My stomach drops to the floor. "Wren, no. I really don't want—"

"I already have the perfect option. His name is Kevin. He works at the school, and I already—"

"Wren, no. Please tell me you didn't." Nat lets out a laugh, not bothering to hide her amusement, and Emma sits there with a grin, even though I'm not sure she's one hundred percent sure what is going on. She's just happy to be one of the girls right now. "Please tell me you did not already tell a stranger that I would be interested in going out with him without running it by me."

"Just for coffee!" she says in a near plea.

"Wren—"

"I know, I know. You don't want to date, blah blah blah. But he's really nice, and he seemed interested. Would a coffee date be that bad?" My phone dings in my pocket, and with utter dread, I slide it out. When I look at the screen of my phone, there's a new text from Wren, a line of numbers, and the name *Kevin* beside it. "You just have to text him your availability and set something up."

"Wren," I say, giving her wide eyes.

"Just give it a chance! What could it hurt?"

"Well, for one, he could be a serial killer."

"You said that about Adam, too," Wren reminds me, and I shrug.

"Still no definitive proof he *isn't* a serial killer."

Wren glares at me, thoroughly unimpressed by my humor. "He's a *kindergarten* teacher, Hallie."

"I don't think there are rules about where serial killers work," I counter under my breath.

"Who is it?" Emma asks, curious as ever, and Wren turns to her.

"Mr. Klien."

"Oh, he's cute," she says, nodding approvingly, and Nat lets out a loud laugh at that, clearly entertained by this. I would be, too, if I weren't the one in the spotlight.

"Emma! He's an adult!"

"That doesn't mean he isn't cute, though, for an adult," she says with a shrug, and I just blink at her, jaw dropped.

"You're a traitor," I say, and she lifts one shoulder, completely unfazed.

"Or maybe she also wants you to be happy," Wren says.

"I am happy!"

That's when Wren gives me a look, one missing the playful humor from moments before. It moves through me uncomfortably, and the breath stops in my chest, that single look saying so many things while saying absolutely nothing at all. Her mouth opens, and I brace for her words, which, from years of experience, I know will be both heartfelt and cut me to the bone, but then her phone dings with a new message, distracting her. When she looks at the screen, her face goes soft. *Adam.* The source of her own lovestruck state and the reason she wants the same for me.

She sighs and stands. "We'll have to continue this battle another time," she says, and relief moves through me. I know she won't completely let go of the idea, but at least it will give me time to come up with better excuses. "I need to get home before Adam comes by and drags me out of here. I promised him I'd be home by one so I can rest before school starts on Monday."

I can't help but smile, knowing now that he will, in fact, do that. Adam Porter has quite the affinity for throwing Wren over his shoulder and marching off. He values her well-being above all else, which is the number one reason I love him for her.

When she gives us a dreamy look, thinking about her man, I almost contemplate giving the number in my phone a shot. Because, despite my not dating, I want that. I want to fall in love and stay in love. I want to find someone whom I know to my soul will stay with me forever. Who will love me for the rest of my life and won't run off when things get tough. I want someone who will look at me with stars in his eyes, the way Adam looks at Wren, who will stand up for me when I'm being too hard on myself.

I stand with Wren, hugging her, and when she pulls back, that determined look is on her face.

"Give Kevin some thought. He's really nice, and I just want you happy," she says, and I sigh, knowing if she uses this tactic—the soft, sweet one—I'll end up on a shitty blind date sooner rather than later.

"I know. I'll think about it," I say. The grin she gives me tells me she probably knows that is my fate as well, though she's kind enough not to rub it in my face. Instead, she gives Nat and then Emma a hug goodbye before she heads out the door.

Twenty minutes later, Nat finishes up Emma's hair. We both ooh and ahh over it, taking a few pictures to send to Mrs. King and Wren before sending her over to one of Nat's co-workers for a manicure and pedicure. I sit in a chair toward the entrance, flipping through a magazine, but when Nat comes my way with a meddling look on her face, my back straightens. Unlike Wren, who takes things at face value and would rather die than make someone confess their deepest, darkest thoughts, Nat is a viper when she senses something.

And right now, the way she's looking at me is like she's about to strike.

"All good?"

"Yup, Emma just picked out her color," she says, then sits beside me. Silence fills the space for a moment, and I think I might be home free until... "So you're getting close with Jesse King, huh?"

My head shifts to glare at her.

"Don't," I say. She grins as if she already knows she won. Just then, as if the universe were working against me, my phone beeps with a new message. Quickly, I grab it and see it's him confirming that he got a reservation at the steakhouse in town at five thirty tonight.

"He's been texting you all day," she says.

"I'm watching his kid," I explain simply.

"Having his kid in your care requires a series of mirror selfies in tight-fitting button-downs?" she asks, tipping her chin to my phone, the message screen still open. When I look down, I see Jesse's sent me a few different outfit options for his dinner with Emma, and my heart pangs. He's so sweet, wanting to make sure he looks good for her. He also looks unbearably hot in dress-up clothes, and despite my desire to look closer and possibly drool a bit, I play it off with a roll of my eyes.

"He's taking Emma out on a fancy date and wants my opinion on what would look best."

Nat gives me a disbelieving look. "He has a sister and a mom he could ask."

I shrug. "I'm basically a sister to him, too."

With that, Nat lets out a loud laugh, one that has a few eyes in the salon turning toward us.

"Nat, what the hell?" I ask in a hushed, chiding tone. Her laughter dies down, and she wipes a tear from her eyes, catching her breath.

"Sorry, the idea of Jesse King thinking of you as a sister was just too much." She tips her head to the side a bit, assessing me. "Hallie, that man has been in love with you for years."

"Bullshit," I say, shaking my head. In an effort to distract myself, I scroll to a photo of Jesse in a blue button-down and heart it before texting him that that's the right option.

"You're not stupid, you know I'm right."

I shake my head, then open up a solitaire, adamant about not looking at her.

"And you've always had a thing for him."

"I had a crush on him when we were kids, Nat. That's it. And I was a *kid*. I also thought I was going to marry Harry Styles." I thought that would get a laugh, but it falls flat; her eyes are still assessing me.

"So there's nothing there? Nothing at all?" she asks, and I shake my head.

"Nope," I say, popping the p. A beat passes, and she sits back, and a small part of me eases, thinking she's done.

Rookie mistake.

"So you'd be okay if I went for it?" she asks, and my head snaps up to look at her, falling right into her trap.

Shit.

The grin spreading over her red-painted lips is absolutely devious. I fell for it—hook, line, and sinker.

"Yeah, that isn't the reaction of someone who has absolutely no feelings for someone." I roll my eyes and sigh, and she points at me, eyes wide and excited. "I knew it! Something happened." I don't deny it, eyes staying down, not wanting to give her another way to read me. "Oh my god, tell me right now." I don't speak. "Did you guys fuck? Was it so good? Oh my god, please tell me everything. I—"

Without meaning to, in a hushed tone, I spill, not wanting her to continue down this path.

"We kissed, okay? It was a year ago in Vermont. It was late, and we both had drank a little bit too much, and—"

"I'm sorry, what?" Nat says, eyes wide. "A *year* ago?!"

I groan, realizing there's no going back now, and I'll need to tell her the whole story, so I do, telling her everything about that weekend in Vermont and then everything since.

To my surprise, it's a relief to get it off my chest. It's been held so close to me all this time, something I've played over and over but never wanted to talk to my closest friends about. If I did, Wren would either get that look in her eyes and start planning a wedding and birthday party for future nieces and nephews who don't exist and never will, or she'll be hurt and a little skeptical of me.

I've seen it before, a dozen times over: someone gets close to Wren, and Wren gets excited to have a new friend to fawn over and take care of, but in two or three months, it becomes increasingly clear it was an excuse to talk to her brothers. And every time, it breaks her heart a little. Sweet Wren, who couldn't use someone if she really, really tried, will never understand someone becoming friends with someone just to date their brother.

So all this time, I kept it my own little secret, but sharing it with Nat now feels as if a giant weight has been lifted. Her face goes from excitement to confusion to frustration to intrigue as I tell her my story, mimicking all of the emotions I've felt, but she doesn't speak until the very end.

"And now?" she asks after I finish my story.

"And now?" I ask, confused.

"Yeah. You've spent nearly every day together for two weeks. You're living right next door to him. His daughter adores you. There's clearly something between you both that you're ignoring."

"No, there isn't. It was one kiss, and neither of us wants to date," I say with a shake of my head. She looks at me skeptically, but I move past it. "We're just friends."

"Friends," she says, deadpan.

"Why are you saying it like that?" I ask, irritation brewing.

"Oh, no reason at all." She sits back, arms crossed on her chest. "How is he going to feel about Wren trying to set you up?"

My forehead creases. "Why would he have feelings about that?"

"Oh, so you're in denial, got it. Cool," she says with a little nod.

"You're so dramatic. I'm not in denial, Nat. I'm the opposite, actually. I'm being very much a realist."

She looks at me, something too close to sadness on her face for my own comfort, before she sighs and shakes her head.

"I just...I hope you know what you're doing," she says, low.

"I do," I promise, but it felt hollow. And as my phone buzzes in my hand with a *thanks, I don't know what I'd do without you* text, and a little girl turns to look over her shoulder and smiles at me from across the salon, I know it's because it was a lie.

FOURTEEN

JESSE

A week after my date with Emma, life has somehow settled into a sense of normalcy. Every day after school, Hallie meets her when she gets off the bus at the farm's entrance, and they chat as they walk up to the house, where they make sure Emma gets her homework done and then make dinner together. Most nights, I'm able to convince her to stay and eat with us, and a few times after I've gotten Emma to bed, she's stayed to hang out, watch a movie, or chat about everything and nothing.

It's like I have my friend back, and even though the road to get here was bumpy as fuck, I'm glad we made it here.

On Saturday, Emma has a sleepover at a friend's house, so I drop her off around noon and then head back home, feeling unsure of what to do with myself for the next twenty-four hours. I rarely have a weekend without Emma, and knowing I have the entire house to myself suddenly feels daunting. I didn't tell my family that Emma would be gone, desperate for some quiet time and knowing if they knew, it would be filled with well-meaning visits. I'm still trying to think of what to do and how to spend my time when I step out of my truck and see it: footprints in the snow.

Familiar footprints with a star design that I fucking *know* were not meant to be walking in the light dusting of snow we got overnight, much less in the deeper snow on farmland that might be hiding anything from holes to ice. Looking around, I note that they go straight into the woods, and my mind starts reeling, moving to dangerous territory. Thoughts of Hallie having slipped or gotten her foot stuck somewhere deep in the woods, where she has no cell service to call for help, flood me.

Without thinking, I follow the footprints out into the woods on a mission.

Thankfully, it only takes me about five minutes to find her, and even though she didn't go far, I'm still frustrated by the time I make it to her. "Hallie!" I call when I see her crouched in the snow, seemingly unmoving

Maybe my nerves weren't so unfounded. Maybe she's hurt, maybe she fell, maybe—

A bird flies off, and a low curse comes from her direction as I continue storming toward her and she stands.

"Jesus, Jesse, could you be louder?" she asks, standing, her phone in hand, and glaring at me as I close the distance between us. Well, at least she's not injured, I suppose.

"What are you doing out here?"

"I *was* taking a picture of a cardinal in the snow, but then you scared it off like the giant ogre you are."

"Ogre?" I ask with a laugh. She continues to glare at me, though its burn isn't as effective with the way her full lips are tipping at the edges.

"Yeah...you're like, fifteen feet tall and built like a lumberjack. An ogre. A hot ogre, but an ogre."

I shake my head as I slow my steps before her. "I think an ogre is inherently ugly."

"I'm sorry. Next time I compare you to a mythical creature, I'll try to think of something more accurate."

I let out a laugh, then look around.

"You're out here in the freezing cold to take pictures?" I ask. Despite her inappropriate footwear, she's dressed warm, with a hat, gloves, and a thick jacket, so it seems she came out intentionally rather than being lost and needing a rescue.

"Yes. Half of my job is posting pictures to the farms' accounts. And I like to take pictures. When it's all snowy like this, it's extra pretty."

I remember Madden saying he'd take her out on the UTV if she wanted to last week, and I nod, then speak without thinking.

"All right. Well, come on. I'll take you out," I say, and she gives me a skeptical look.

"Excuse me?"

"I'll take you around the property on the UTV. You do that with Madden sometimes, right?" She lifts an eyebrow, head tipping to the side. Her long red hair is in a braid, sliding along her jacket, with small locks sticking out around her face, framing it.

"Don't you have work today?"

"It's Saturday. I don't really work much on the weekend, since I try to spend time with Emma, but she's out for a sleepover, so I have nothing else to do."

"That's kind of depressing," she says, and I lift a shoulder and tip my head for her to follow me toward the house. When she follows, I respond.

"That's me, depressing and boring."

"I don't buy that," she says under her breath, but I don't say anything because I don't know *what* to say. Instead, we walk in silence for a few minutes as we make our way back to my house. During that time, Hallie's phone buzzes a few times, and when I come back outside with the keys, her head is hunched over her phone, an annoyed look on her face. As I approach, her phone dings with another incoming text, and she makes an annoyed grumble this time.

"Who's texting you?" I ask with a laugh, and her head lifts to glare at me.

"Your sister."

"Is she okay? Does she need something?"

Hallie shakes her head and groans. "Nothing, other than for me to say yes to a blind date she's trying to set me up on."

Without my mind's permission, my heart skips a beat, and I try not to show it on my face, instead opening the pack of hand warmers I grabbed from inside and shaking the small packet before offering it to her.

"A blind date?" I ask as casually as I can manage. She finishes her message, accepts the sachet, then rolls her eyes and slides her phone back into her pocket.

"It seems now that your sister is in a happy, committed relation-ship, she's decided I need to be too."

"You two have always done things together," I say, turning the key in the ignition and sitting behind the steering wheel. She walks to the vehicle, sits beside me before I start driving.

"Yeah, well, that's not something I'm looking for, and the sooner she realizes it, the better."

Unsure of what to say to that and concerned that if I do say some-thing, it will absolutely be the wrong thing *to* say, I start to drive, moving into the woods and toward the field where the trees are.

"Where do you want to go?"

"I don't care, wherever," she says, and I hesitate, then look over at her skeptically. Her gaze is locked on trees in the distance, and she seems lost in her thoughts.

"Are you okay?"

"Yeah, why?" she asks, but her tone further proves her anything but dull and emotionless, so completely far from *my* Hallie. Gently, I attempt to explain that, trying to keep levity in my words.

"It's just, you're Hallie. You always care. You always have opin-ions on what to do and where." A moment passes, and I wait for a sassy remark, which doesn't come. The unease builds in my chest. "Is it my sister that's bothering you? I can talk to her, tell her to lay off, or have my mom—"

"No, no...it's not Wren. I'm used to her meddling in one way or another by now. It's different. It's...it's just been a weird day." Her words are weighted down with emotions that are clearly weighing on her.

"Do you..." I hesitate, not wanting to push too hard on our new, tenuous friendship. "Do you want to talk?" There's a long pause, and I continue to drive slowly along the property as she seems to contemplate how to answer before a reluctant sigh leaves her lips and she speaks.

"It's silly, really. I saw that—" she starts, then her words fade off before her hand reaches for my leg and squeezes, hard. "Oh my god," she whispers, then starts slapping me. "Stop."

"What?" I ask, shifting toward her as I take my foot off the gas.

"Stop! Stop the vehicle, Jesse!"

"Hallie—" I start to say, but do as she asks, panic moving through me. Before I even come to a complete stop, she's moving off the UTV and off into the distance, before her steps slow and I see it stepping out from behind a tree, maybe ten yards from Hallie.

A deer, maybe six months old, is chewing on a low-hanging tree branch.

"Goddammit," I murmur as I approach her, then reach down for a pinecone. When Hallie looks over her shoulder, she glares at me, seeing my intention before I even make a move.

"Don't you fucking dare," she threatens under her breath. "Do not scare that deer off, or I will spend the next two years teaching your daughter to be an absolute tyrant." That makes me stop, and I look at her in a mix of hilarity and shock.

"Did you just threaten to indoctrinate my daughter to be a terror?"

"Scare off that deer, and it won't be a threat," she says, then turns away from me again, taking slow steps in the deer's direction.

"It's chewing a tree branch, Hal. Don't know if you're aware, but my family kind of sells those."

"It's winter! She's hungry!" Hallie argues over her shoulder, then takes another step. The deer's head lifts, and Hallie stills.

"That's not how that works," I grumble, but drop the pinecone all the same. Hallie takes another tentative step toward the deer, her phone lifted to take photos.

"Where's your mom?" she whispers, her voice so low it barely carries over to me as she takes another step closer.

"Hallie," I murmur in warning, but there's no way I'm going to stop her from doing what she wants. She's Hallie, after all. So instead, I pull out my phone and, even though I know they won't be as good as hers, I take a few photos of the two of them together. She murmurs a few more soft words to the deer a few feet away from her, and they look at each other as if they're genuinely having a conversation I can't hear or understand. After a moment, Hallie sniffs, then wipes her cheek, and I realize that she's actually crying. Something in my chest tightens as I watch the exchange, as she continues to speak to the deer softly.

After a minute or two, there's a crack of a branch in the distance, and the deer's head lifts, ears perking before she runs off. Hallie stays there, squatting in the snow for another minute before I slowly take a few steps toward her, and she stands.

"That was crazy, right?" she asks, with a smile on her lips. Her eyes are a bit glassy, and I can make out where the tear fell before, but I ignore it, knowing somehow that's what she would want.

"Yeah. You don't normally see a deer that young without her mom, much less this time of year." Hallie looks off to where the deer went, a look I can't decipher on her face, before a chill runs through her, and I realize she's absolutely freezing.

"Hallie, we've gotta get you inside," I say, trying to keep my voice soft. Like the deer, I don't want to scare her off, not now.

"I'm fine," she says, then steps to move around me and back toward the UTV. Her shoes slip, her hands flying up in panic, and instinctively, as I've done so many times before, I catch her, pulling her into my chest. From here, I see her clearly—the whites of her eyes are a bit pink, her eyes are a little swollen—and I wonder if she'd been crying earlier, long before I found her.

"Those fucking shoes," I murmur instead, and she gives me a half smile.

"They're wet, so they aren't even warm right now," she admits. "I haven't been able to feel my toes for a bit."

"Your lips are blue."

I expect her to tell a joke about looking at her lips, of which I'll have to laugh off, even though we both know I am. In the past week, all I've been able to do is look at her, and often, I find my mind drifting to that kiss a year ago. Now that I know the truth of what happened, now that I know she's just as into me as I am into her, and there are just extenuating circumstances making it impossible, I can't seem to think of anything *but* kissing her.

And right now, with her so close, our breaths mingling in the cold air between us, it would take nothing at all to dip my head, to press my lips to hers. Would she meet me halfway?

My heart thunders in my chest as I grapple with the decision, deciding if I should just say *fuck it* or step away, but I can't seem to force myself to do either. We might stand like that for an eternity, but when her teeth chatter just a bit, I'm knocked out of the moment and into the reality where she needs me to take care of her.

"You need to warm up," I say softly, loosening my grip on her and stepping away.

"Yeah, probably," she murmurs. My mind is racing as she shivers again as we move back to the UTV, and she slides in beside me. Without thinking, I say something so incredibly foolish.

"Do you have a swimsuit?" The cold must be getting to me because I can't quite figure out why I would say that.

"I...right now? On me?"

I shake my head and roll my eyes. "No. At your place."

Her brows come together, and she shivers again, a reminder as to *why* I said it. It has nothing to do with the potential of seeing her in a bikini and everything to do with the fact that she's near hypothermic.

"Well...yeah?"

"We'll go to your place. Grab it, and you can warm up in the hot tub." She opens her mouth to argue, but I shake my head. "It's the easiest way to warm you up, Hallie. I won't even bother you if you don't want."

I don't expect what she says next.

In a million years and with a million guesses, I never would have seen her next words coming.

"And if I do want?" she asks. My heart skips a beat, and I hold my breath. Her tongue comes out, licking her lips, licking her bottom lip absent-mindedly as she watches my own lips. I watch every millisecond, cataloging it for future use, for long lonely nights. Then, she clarifies. "For you to bother me. What if I want that?"

My mouth is dry, and my voice is raspy when I give my response. "Then I'll be happy to bother you."

Her pupils flare with my words, and beneath my thick denim jeans, my cock twitches.

This is so fucked up. This is such a bad fucking idea.

But I can't stop it.

"Okay," she says, then nods. "Then let's go get my bathing suit."

FIFTEEN

JESSE

I hold onto my uneasy feeling for ten more minutes, but when I'm sitting on the edge of Hallie's bed at her insistence, while she digs through her drawers for a bathing suit and a *cozy outfit* to put on after, I crack, unable to hold it in anymore.

"So are you going to tell me why you were standing out in the freezing cold by yourself?" I ask, breaking the silence. I tried, but even watching her side profile, the blank look on her face as she digs through the drawers, I know this isn't the normal, happy-go-lucky Hallie.

It isn't the one who is all sunshine and rainbows, the one who laughs and jokes nonstop. It's a different version, a sad one, and even though she'd probably be more than happy with me pretending I don't notice, I can't.

Her hands stop their movements, and her head turns to me. When her eyes meet mine, my chest twists at the pain there. It's so startlingly familiar, it takes the breath out of my lungs. I've seen that look before—not on Hallie's face, but on Emma's. She looks away quickly, standing up with a pair of sweatpants in her hands that she tosses into the small pile on her bed before taking a few steps to the window, staring off into the snow-covered trees behind her house.

"I needed a distraction." I think she's going to stop there, so I'm shocked when her low voice fills the room again. "I did something stupid, got on social media, and started searching for her. I'm a glutton for punishment, I suppose." Despite my confusion, I stay quiet, realizing she needs to get this out more than I need to understand what she's telling me. "My stepsister got married last weekend." The pain in her words has me standing on instinct, taking the three steps to her, and reaching out for her hand. My fingers wrap around hers, twining them together before squeezing, and she returns the move before continuing to talk.

"My mom was at the wedding, and there were pictures of her helping her put on the veil. A small moment, but the look on her face...she was so proud. So happy. If you didn't know any better, you might think that she was *her* mom." She looks out at the woods, eyes distant when she whispers her following words. "She's *my mom*, though." A tear falls, traveling over the apple of her cheek and dropping onto the dark green sweatshirt she's wearing, making a darker spot that spreads slowly. "You know, two years ago, I stopped being the one to initiate a conversation, just to see what would happen. I haven't heard from her since."

My chest tightens with the sadness in her words.

"Hallie—" I start, but she keeps talking.

"My whole life, I always wanted to see the best in her. I made excuses for years about why she left." She shakes her head, a huff of air leaving her lips that is supposed to be a laugh but lacks any hint of humor. "Sometimes, it was my dad's fault. Or Colt's fault. Or the town's fault, even though she is the one who forced Dad to move here, away from his own family. Sometimes, I told myself it was my fault, because at the time, I was being such a dick. I was ten, you know? A lot of feelings, a lot of emotions. A lot of hormones."

She turns and smiles at me, knowing I'm living that currently.

"I held the divorce against my dad most of all, because on the weekends I'd see her, which were few and far between, she'd tell me the breakup was his fault in no uncertain terms. I loved her, and my dad never spoke poorly about my mom, so I believed her. At the time, his not talking felt like a guilty conscience, like he knew it was his fault, so he just kept quiet." My thumb brushes over hers, a silent encouragement to continue. "But I realize now, it was him trying to protect me. He didn't want me to feel all of...this toward her."

She looks up at me with humor on her face.

"Two years ago, Nat made some off-handed remark about my mom leaving my family for another man, and I wanted to argue. But then I realized I couldn't. It was like she took off the rose-colored glasses I viewed my childhood through, and I could finally see it for what it was. My mom let my dad keep the house and have full custody, and she made it sound like it was a sacrifice she made *for us.* She wanted Colt and me to stay in the school system, so she *let* my dad have the house and, in turn, us." I can see how, as a kid, that could be spun as a positive, but as an adult, the reality of that would hit hard and painful.

It seems that reality struck Hallie two years ago.

She sniffs, tears falling quickly now, dripping into her sweatshirt, dark puddles forming. Her hand lifts, smearing the tracks across her cheeks before she continues. "But really, she just...gave up on us. Let Dad keep what she decided she didn't want anymore, and then she started over with her cute little new family an hour away from us. He has two kids: a daughter who is a year younger than me and a son who is a year older, and they all live together. She went to her dance recitals and his football games and then made excuses when she missed mine. I just...I don't get it." More tears, and her voice cracks when she speaks. "What did they have that I didn't? What made her want to be there, with them, but not here, with me?"

Her voice breaks me in two, pain lancing through me as I suddenly understand her just a bit more, her fear and her baggage laid out before me in a way I somehow know she doesn't do often, if ever. "Hallie—" Her head snaps to me, and her eyes are glassy, her jaw set.

"Please," she whispers, her voice strained. "Please do not pity me. I would not be able to handle it, Jesse. Everyone talks to me with soft words and apologies when I talk about this, and I can't take that pity from you. You're the only one who's never looked at me like I'm the girl whose own mother doesn't love her, and if I see it on your face, it's going to break me, Jesse. Please don't."

Her voice is raw, unshed tears burning there, and a million things go through my mind. Thoughts, apologies, and consolations, but none of them are right. And despite the situations being so incredibly different, I get it. The looks I got when Kim left and the looks I still get when people find out I'm raising my daughter on my own sometimes are enough to make me want to hide away.

Instead of speaking, I move, pulling her into me, pressing her chest to mine, and wrapping my arms around her and holding her tight.

I don't say I'm sorry.

I don't tell her that she deserved better.

I don't tell her that her mother is a colossal fucking bitch and an even bigger moron, losing out on the most beautiful, kind woman in the world.

Instead, I just hold her.

For a moment, her body is still, but I lift a hand, grazing it down her back. With the simple move, her body melts into mine. Silent tears come, her body shaking with them, but I don't speak. I just hold her, her face in my neck, as she lets it out. Somehow, I know it's what she needs.

And somehow, in the depths of my consciousness, I know *I* am what she needs.

My mind falters on that thought for long, long moments, tumbling over it like a rough stone I'm trying to polish, to understand. I sit with it for long enough that I don't realize when her breaths even out or when her tears dry, not until she pulls away. I fight the urge to tighten my arms, to keep her close as she shifts back to look at me. Her eyes are red, but she seems better, less weighed down by her emotions. I keep one arm around her as a hand lifts, pushing a loose lock of hair behind her ear.

"You good?" I ask softly. She lets out a laugh, a real one, thankfully, and a smile spreads across her lips.

"Yeah. I think I just needed that."

I nod, understanding, but now unsure of what to do next. She fills in the silence for me, licking her lips before speaking.

"Are you going to be weird with me now?" she asks with a grimace.

"Weird?"

"I had this same breakdown once with Wren, and she brought me baked goods every day for a month. I think she was doing wellness check-ins to make sure I didn't need a grippy sock vacation."

I let out a laugh and shake my head. "No, no, I won't be weird. And I won't bring you baked goods. You wouldn't want them anyway."

"I've heard your baking really sucks." A beat of silence takes over before she sniffs and steps back. Suddenly, my arms feel utterly empty. "You know what I need right now?" The fake levity is back in her words, but I let her have it.

"What?" There's a moment of hesitation, her eyes drifting down to my lips, then back up in a way that sends my entire body on alert. But then she's moving, stepping away and to the pile of clothes on her bed, stuffing them into a bag, and then moving toward the kitchen. I follow her, intrigued, as she opens her fridge and pulls out a six-pack of hard ciders.

"I need to get drunk in a hot tub."

I let out a loud, relieved laugh and nod.

"You know what? I think I can make that happen."

SIXTEEN

JESSE

This was a terrible fucking idea.

Maybe my worst idea ever.

Because moments before, Hallie stepped into my bedroom dressed in her bathing suit, a small string thing with little bows resting on her full hips, an open cider in her hand, and a nervous smile on her lips. I almost popped a fucking boner, like a teenager who just saw the hot babysitter in her bathing suit. I ushered her through the sliding glass doors in my room that led to the hot tub, telling her I'd get my own beers and meet her out there.

But now, I'm panicking, pacing my room, and my eyes keep drifting to the doors. The backlight gleams like a beacon, trying to beckon me on and encourage me to give in to my temptations.

Get it together, King, I tell myself, taking deep breaths to try and settle my heart. *She just opened up to you. She has had a very rough day. Don't be a fucking creep.*

With that final reminder, I head into the kitchen, opening the fridge and grabbing three beers for myself. I'm cracking one open before shucking my shirt off and tossing it onto the kitchen island.

Then I down half of the beer for courage like some unhinged frat boy.

With one last breath, I make my way back to my room, refusing to pause as I slide open the glass door. The vision sends my pulse racing and my cock hardening.

Hallie is in my hot tub, her hair a bunched mess on top of her head, one arm resting along the side of the hot tub. Her head is tipped back to the darkening sky as if she's asleep, her chest rising and falling slowly and gently with each breath.

She looks fucking magnificent, the ties of a bathing suit around her neck taunting me. All I can think about, despite my best judgment, is tugging the strings, letting it fall, and revealing the curves that have been tormenting me for some time now.

I can't deny that, for the past few years, Hallie Young has been someone difficult to ignore, a gorgeous woman I was always able to categorize as *never could be mine.* I managed to because it was always supposed to be Hallie and Madden. One day, they would come to their senses, and my brother would stop fucking around and give her a fresh start, a family, and a white picket fence.

Except she laughed at that idea.

She told me she would never choose Madden.

And more importantly, her final words have been ricocheting through my mind ever since: *"If I were to go for a King, it would absolutely be you."*

Her eyes track me as I move across the patio, setting the extra beers into the snow and a fresh one on the side of the hot tub. She shifts, setting her elbow on the edge of the hot tub, her eyes locked on me as her fingers play with the string of her bathing suit top. It's a nervous move, a mindless fidget I don't think she realizes she does when she's overthinking things, though usually it's with the tiny curl of hair at the back of her head that never makes it into a ponytail.

She watches as I move up the small set of stairs and then climb into the hot tub, settling in with a sigh across from her. At least I still have enough of a rational mind to sit opposite her, I suppose. Without breaking eye contact, I reach over and grab my drink, taking a long pull before setting it back down.

That's when she lets out a laugh, a slight shake of her head. "I didn't think you'd actually do it." I keep my eyes locked on hers, then raise an eyebrow. "Come in here with me."

"Want me to leave?" A beat passes, and she holds my gaze before speaking, challenge in the words.

"No. I could use a little company." Her tongue darts out, wetting her lips, and *that* goes right to my cock, stiffening it. Thank God for the bubbles of the jets, I suppose.

We sit in silence for a few minutes, Hallie off in some other land, and me stuck on not watching her tits or trying to see through the water at her body before she sinks into the water with a groan.

"Okay, we need to lighten this shit up," she says with a laugh.

"What?"

"It's so awkward, Jesse. I can't sit here in silence with you in a glorified bathtub."

"This was your idea," I remind her. She looks me over, eyes lingering on my lips before she takes a sip of her drink and smiles at me.

"I'm aware. But now I'm bored. Let's play a game." She sits up, and my cock does too.

So fucking stupid. That's me. So fucking stupid, sitting in a hot tub with my baby sister's best friend, my daughter's pseudo babysitter, with my cock hard as a rock.

But do I leave?

Hell no.

Instead, I encourage her.

"What's that game you played with Wren on her twenty-first?" I ask about the one time I saw my little sister drunk.

"Never Have I Ever?" she answers, and I nod, remembering the night.

It was the first night I remember actually *seeing* Hallie, after all. It's burned into my memories. We took Wren down to The Mill, before Colt bought it, for her twenty-first birthday. Madden and I were supposed to be DDs, but he ended up getting smashed as badly as the girls that night. Hallie decided they'd play a drinking game, which was very clearly framed to get Wren hammered quickly, with Hallie, Nat, and Madden saying things they knew Wren had, in fact, done. I'd sat back and watched with entertainment before driving everyone back home.

"You want to play Never Have I Ever with me? I know too much about you."

"Excuse me?" I ask, confused.

"If you play Never Have I Ever, you'll be hammered in no time."

Stupid and stubborn. That's me, apparently.

"Try me," I say with a smile. "I've got a full six-pack in the fridge." She crosses her arms on her chest, which, to my utter delight and dismay, presses her tits together, raising them a bit. I'm so distracted by the move, I almost miss the fact that she started the game already.

"Never have I ever played hooky from school," she says, a playful tilt to her lips, probably remembering the time I did just that and got grounded for a week. I glare but roll my eyes and take a sip of my beer, happy to do it to get more of that courage into my veins.

"My turn?" She nods, and I narrow my eyes at her. "Never have I ever gotten high." She lifts an eyebrow and doesn't take a drink.

"Really?" I ask in shock, and she beams before she shrugs. "Not even with Madden?"

"Hell no. That's the kind of thing you do for the first time with someone responsible. Not Madden."

I let out a laugh, and some of the tension leaves my shoulders. We go back and forth like that for a few rounds, in which she tells me she once won $200 on a lottery ticket, and I tell her I've never borrowed anyone's toothbrush before.

This goes on for a while longer, each of us taking a handful of drinks and laughing. I hop out into the freezing cold and grab another drink for both of us. When I step back in, I hiss, my feet tingling with pins and needles as they sink into the hot water, and move to my side of the hot tub once more.

"Can you move closer so I don't feel like I'm shouting?" she asks. I hesitate, not sitting, but staring at her. "I won't bite, promise." After a moment of hesitation, I realize that common sense has long fled, and I nod, moving so we're on the same side of the hot tub. From this angle, I can see through the water and to the ties that sit perfectly on her hips. My fingers itch to tug on them, to loosen them and get a better glimpse of the faded tan lines, but then I remind myself to focus. Despite the attraction, I'm having fun here.

In fact, it's the most fun I've had, the most carefree I've felt in a long time.

Probably since last February.

"Okay, whose turn is it next?" I ask once I settle in, the silence stretching between us uncomfortably. She shakes her head a tiny bit, as if she'd been lost in her head, then shifts, crossing one leg over the other. As she does, her feet graze along the back of my calf, stopping at the back of my knee, and a red flush that has nothing to do with the cold or the warm weather blooms over her cheeks.

"Sorry! I—" she says.

I roll my eyes, and it's probably the now two beers in my system, but I reach under the water, gripping her ankle and tugging her along the seat of the hot tub until she's at my side, legs draped over mine. This close, the golden flecks in her grass-green eyes are startling as she looks up at me, her full pink lips parted. Quiet breaths pass between us as we sit like that for a moment before I speak.

"Your turn," I say eventually, my voice gravelly, and she licks her lips, her eyes a bit hazy before she speaks.

"Never have I ever regretted a haircut," she murmurs, and I let out a low laugh.

"Unfair," I say, knowing she's talking about the time when I was twenty, and Maddon convinced me to shave my head over winter break. At the time, my hair was longer than it is now, and we didn't just buzz it, but we took one of Wren's close-shave razors and made me *bald*. It looked absolutely horrific, and I've never had short hair since.

She reaches up, brushing hair across my forehead, her fingernails scraping at my scalp as she pushes the unruly locks back. I hold my breath through the entire move.

"Never do that again, yeah?" she asks, fingers still in my hair as she takes another sip of her drink. I don't know if it's just to drink or because of the question, but I'm finding I don't even care anymore. "Your hair looks so much better this way."

I stare at her, unsure of how to respond, unsure of what else I could do other than stare at her, trying to talk myself into not leaning in and pressing my lips to hers, into not giving in to the desire pumping through my veins. I'm not drunk, not by a long shot, but I take a sip of my beer and blame my next moves on it.

My hand moves under the water, my head buzzing with my quickened pulse, until it lands on her knee. My thumb moves in rhythmic swipes, her eyes looking through the water to watch the movement.

"Your turn," she breathes.

"Never have I ever worn inappropriate footwear while out in the woods," I say with a tip of my lips, and she rolls her eyes.

She laughs, shaking her head. "You always did play it safe," she whispers.

She holds my eyes as her lithe pink fingertips wrap around the neck of her drink, lifting the dark brown bottle to her lips, then tipping it back and taking a healthy gulp. A drip clings to her lip, and I reach up, swiping at her skin with my thumb and grabbing the liquid before bringing it to my mouth.

"What would not playing it safe look like?" I ask. She's under the same spell as I am, pupils dilated as she moves to her knees beside me, then shifts over me, moving to straddle my lap. Her ass settles on my knees, leaving a gap at least a foot wide between us, and I resist the urge to settle my hands on her hips.

"Never have I ever wanted to see what Jesse King would do if I kissed him." The use of my name is a shot fired and a challenge in and of itself, and she takes a long swallow of her drink. Her breathing has gone heavy, breasts rising and falling with each one, and my hands slide to her hips, resting above the lush swell of her ass. A squeak of a sound leaves her, not quite a moan, but close enough to have my cock throbbing in response.

Her hands move to my shoulders, and she leans in, her head dipping down, her lips just an inch from mine before stopping.

"Can't say I ever thought about kissing myself," I murmur.

"What about me? You ever think about kissing me?" she asks.

"All the fucking time," I say.

That's when I lose the battle.

My chin tips up, closing the gap, and I press my lips to hers, a soft caress that she instantly deepens. One hand on my shoulder shifts to my jaw, lips parting so my tongue can enter. She tastes like hard apple cider, and the vanilla ChapStick she uses, and my fingers dig into her hips. She groans, hips moving, sliding down my thighs until our chests are pressed to each other. I groan as her hot center presses against my cock, and her own little gasp is like music to my fucking ears when she grinds into me. One hand leaves her hip, sliding up to cup her full breast in my hand, the nipple peeking beneath the thin fabric. My lips move, kissing along her neck, and she tips her head to give me better access. My eyes catch on the white ties of her suit.

"Never have I ever wanted to see Hallie Young topless," I whisper in challenge. Instantly, she reaches behind her neck and finds one of the thin white strands. A gentle tug leaves the cups of her bathing suit above the water, and with the boost from sitting in my lap, they drop to show me one dusty pink nipple. I groan at the look of it, but she reaches behind her back, repeating the process until her top is floating away in the hot tub, leaving her topless.

I don't play games; instead, I cup a bare breast in one hand and roll a nipple with the other, a gasp leaving her lips. My hips lift, and she shifts back and forth, gently rocking against me in a shallow mockery of what we'll be doing by the end of the night.

"Never have I ever wanted to hear Hallie moan my name," I say, then dip my head, my chin touching the water as I wrap my lips around her hard nipple, sucking deep before she does just that, her breathy voice a sound I categorize to use for all future fantasies until the day I die.

"Jesse," she moans, and my teeth scratch along her skin, pulling another gasp from her. Her fingers move into my hair, holding me to her as I shift sides, laving her other breast the same way. My hand moves to her knee, sliding up to her thigh with a mind of its own, but then her hand tugs, pulling my head back and forcing me to look at her.

"Are we doing this?" she asks, breathy and panting.

"I sure as fuck hope so," I say, gripping her thigh tightly. It's soft, and I want to see what it looks like, my fingers denting this soft, delicate part of her.

She nods in agreement, as if to herself, before continuing. "If we do, I need to know it means nothing," she whispers. I don't hesitate when I nod, knowing this is where this would go. We both don't want to date, so it's the perfect solution.

This can be nothing but an itch to scratch. Getting it out of my system, then going back to keeping my head down, making sure I make it through raising Emma without completely fucking her up.

That's what my dazed mind tells me, at least. Common sense and logical thinking are a long-forgotten art at this point.

"I don't date, and I'm not looking for a relationship," I confirm.

"Perfect. The word *relationship* makes me sneeze."

I let out a soft laugh at the confirmation of what I already knew. We stay like that for a moment before her hand leaves my hair, trailing down my face, her palm moving to my chin, her soft thumb grazing over my mustache before she licks her lips.

My hand moves up again, my thumb tracing along the line of her bikini bottoms, then over, sliding across her center and pressing where her clit is. She lets out a sharp hiss of mixed pain and pleasure, but when her hips rock toward my hand, I smile. I make a fist, then slide my knuckles up and down the smooth fabric.

"Jesse," she murmurs, a warning in her tone, but I ignore her, continuing to play as I dip my head, pressing a kiss to her neck, then up, kissing the spot beneath her ears. She has small hoops in her ears today, and I pull them into my mouth. She moans, low and needy, when I do, and I grin into it. My hand keeps moving, grinding over her, her hips shifting to get more before her hand slides beneath the water, tugging at the ties at her hips. My breathing hitches, and I move my lips to hers, kissing her deeply. She shifts, keeping at the strings until her bottoms are off, and I have a fully naked Hallie in my lap.

Tentatively, hands shaking as I've never touched a woman before, my hand moves, my thumb sliding along her center, and we both groan as I touch her. I glide up to her clit, circling, and she moans loud, my name following in a breathy sound. My cock throbs painfully, but I won't rush this, no fucking way.

I've been waiting far too long.

After circling her clit, I slide down, the very tip of my thumb dipping into her center, and she tightens, trying to get me to stay, but I move back, sliding to circle her clit before repeating the process. This time, I go a bit deeper, her pussy stretching along my first knuckle before sliding out, and she mewls in protest. I chuckle against her lips, pressing to mine, but no longer able to focus on kissing.

"Jesse," she moans.

"Patience, Hal," I say, circling her clit and then brushing over it, this time making her hips buck.

"I need you."

The sound is enough to give her anything she wants, and I groan a low "fuck" before shifting my hand, widening my legs to, in turn, widen hers and give me room to play. Then I position two fingers at her entrance and press in.

"Wait, wait," she says, and my entire body stills.

SEVENTEEN

"Wait, wait," I say, common sense breaking in for the smallest moment as the tips of two thick fingers pause at my entrance. Jesse's head snaps back, eyes wide, panic on his face, and if I weren't so thoroughly turned on, I'd laugh.

"Do you want to stop?"

"Absolutely not," I say, my words coming in halted breaths. He smiles and starts to slide his fingers further into me. The stretch is absolutely fucking blissful, enough to melt my mind completely, but I know I need to think rationally for just a moment. I wrap my hand around his wrist, my fingers not making it all the way around but stopping his movements either way. He pauses, but his fingers stay half buried inside of me, and I lick my lips, mentally trying to catch my bearings. "We need rules.

"Rules?"

I nod, breathing heavy. "Yes, rules. One night." A finger bends, and I force myself to hold on to the thread of sanity that's becoming harder and harder to grasp. His cock twitches against my thigh, and I want to wrap my hand around it so badly, to feel him, but this is important. "One night. Just to scratch the itch, sate my curiosity." I accidentally shift, and his fingers slide in deeper.

"Get it out of our systems," he says, and I groan in relief that he's on the same page.

"And then we go back to normal," I say. His head drops, pressing a kiss to my neck. If he moves to my ear and tugs my earring again, I'll be a fucking goner. "You don't want a relationship, right?" I ask.

"No," he says.

"And you promise this won't come to bite me in the ass?"

"I mean, I might bite you in that ass but—"

I let out a laugh without meaning to, slapping his arm and giggling. I *giggle*.

I'm naked in a hot tub about to have a one-night stand with Jesse fucking King, and I'm giggling.

Twenty-year-old Hallie would absolutely be *losing her mind* if she could see us now.

Eighteen-year-old Hallie—who thought Jesse King was the hottest person known to mankind—would be squealing.

Sixteen-year-old Hallie—who wrote *Hallie King* in the margins of her journals—would be having a full-on meltdown, but I never plan to tell *that* version of me about this. *That* version would read into things far too much.

And this is just for one night.

A night with Jesse King.

A single night of pleasure and fulfilling this need that haunts me every time he's close enough to touch.

What could go wrong?

Common sense would probably tell me a million different things if it could, but I don't actually buy a single one of them. Every leak is perfectly patched up. He doesn't want to date until Emma is out of the house. I don't want to date *him* because when things go wrong, because things *always* go wrong, I'd be the one left with nothing.

We're on the same page.

"One night," I say, letting go of his wrist and moving that hand to rest on his chest.

"Then I'd better get started now, huh?" he says, and then, without any warning, he fully seats his fingers into me. I groan, but it's swallowed when a greedy hand moves to the back of my head, pulling my face to his and devouring me in a deep kiss as he pulls out and slides back in. My hips move, riding his fingers as pleasure ignites, flooding my veins and taking over every aspect of my consciousness. All I can think about is Jesse, his fingers, feeling good, and getting *more*.

I try to reach between us, to grip him through his swim shorts that perfectly cupped his cock when he was getting in, but he breaks the kiss, shaking his head.

"Hallie, if you put your hands on me, it's going to be a short fucking night." I smile then, continuing to move, reaching for him, and then gripping and stroking him over his shorts. His fingers twitch inside of me, and I lift my hips, then drop them, in essence fucking myself, and hands down, this is the hottest sexual experience of my life.

"Hallie, you gotta stop," he groans, head dropping to my neck. His hot breath there eggs me on, the idea of getting to him fanning the flames in my belly.

"No," I say simply, gripping him harder, then moving to slide beneath his shorts. I just about have my hand around him, almost finally able to feel his smooth, hot skin beneath mine, when he grumbles to himself.

"Why do I feel like you're never going to do as you're told?"

"Not in my DNA, baby," I murmur, then groan when I hit paydirt, wrapping my fingers around him. He's thick and hot, and the idea of him filling me—the way I already know he'll stretch me with the perfect edge of pain—has my pussy tightening around his fingers. He twitches in my hand, and I manage to stroke him once before his hand leaves me completely, wrapping around my wrist, tugging it away, and out of his shorts. I pout pitifully as his hands move to my waist.

"Tell me if you get too cold." I open my mouth the respond, but then I'm gasping as he's lifting me out of the water, setting my ass on the edge of the hot tub against the house, and positioning me so I'm spread wide before him. "Oh fuck." The air is cold, but my body is on fire, especially when I see the heated look that crosses his face as he takes in my naked body.

"Jesus Christ, Hallie. Look at you." He leans forward, pressing a kiss to one thigh and then the other, his mustache scraping along delicate skin and sending a shiver through me that has nothing to do with the cold air around us. In fact, I can barely feel the cold, not with the way my skin is on fire right now.

Especially not when his head dips, tongue flattening as he licks me from entrance to clit before tipping his head back to look up at me. I'm staring down at him, his grin wide, mustache dotted with water, and his thumb grazes along my center.

"Better than I fucking imagined," he says, and I barely have time to think about the fact that he *imagined* this because his head is dipping again, his face moving to devour me.

"Oh, fuck," I groan as his tongue flicks at my clit, putting a hand on the edge of the hot tub so I don't fall, my head tipping back. My free hand travels up to my breast, and the warmth of my hand over the quickly cooking water makes me moan again. He makes a satisfied noise, and when I look down, his hair is pushed back, his mouth is on my pussy, thick fingers are on my inner thighs, denting my skin and holding me open, and his eyes, hazy and needy and filled with fire, are locked on mine. When his finger pinches and rolls my nipple, he groans into me, the vibrations taking me higher and higher.

But I need more.

"Jesse," I murmur. "Fuck me. Please. Just fuck me." His eyes spark, and for a moment, I lose his mouth.

"Make it quick." Three fingers slide into me, fucking me hard and fast and pulling a guttural sound from deep in my chest. "Make it quick, and then I'm bringing you inside and fucking you hoarse."

I tighten around him, and he smirks.

"Is that a promise?" I ask, lifting an eyebrow.

"You said one night, Hallie, so I'm taking the whole fucking night." The most devious smirk graces his handsome face before it dips, and all of the breath leaves my lungs, his lips circling my clit and sucking hard.

As he does, his fingers continue to move, fucking me like he's on a mission, pushing on my G-spot like he's known my body for years. It's building and quick, and my hand leaves my breast, fingers threading into his hair and pushing his face closer, getting him right where I need him. "Right there, Jesse. Fuck."

Another deep groan leaves him, his eyes drifting shut. It's not his mouth or his fingers that do it, but it's him so clearly enjoying this that sends me over the edge, the orgasm washing over me, waves and waves of the most intense pleasure I've ever felt crashing through me until I'm shaking. He continues licking me and fingering me until it's passed before he pulls back. A self-satisfied smirk is written on his face, and he stands, reaching out to cup my face in his hands, then pulling me to him for a searing, white-hot kiss. The taste of me is on his lips, on his tongue as it slides along mine, and I groan into it, the need that was just sated flaring back up in an instant.

When he pulls back, he gives me yet another knowing smirk before stepping out of the hot tub. I watch, shifting toward the edge myself as he drops his wet swim shorts to the ground, leaving him just as naked as me. His hard cock bobs, and I tighten my legs. I barely notice him grabbing a towel before he's wrapping me in it and then lifting me, his hand on my ass, my legs wrapped around him. His lips move to mine in an instant as he walks both of us toward the house, sliding the glass door open, stepping into the warmth, and then sliding it shut again.

My hips move and rock against him, his dick right beneath me. I need him. I need more. I need it *now*. My lips shift down his neck, biting and sucking, and when I hit where his neck meets his shoulder, he groans, stopping his steps toward his room and pressing me to the wall.

"I could fuck you right here," he groans, thrusting so his cock slides between the folds of my pussy, teasing and taunting but never giving me what we both need.

"Do it," I groan, shifting my hips to get something, anything. Suddenly, I'm so empty and filled with need. He chuckles, then pulls back, stepping away from the wall and taking us toward his room once more.

"Need a condom," he says, and embarrassment floods me. Of course, we'd need a condom, even if neither of us, from my understanding, has been intimate with anyone in some time, no matter that I'm on the pill. I'm sure one accidental pregnancy is enough to last him a lifetime.

"I'm sorry, I—" I start, then he tosses me onto his bed, climbing over me, planting kisses as he does, and knocking any thoughts out of my mind. One on my ankle, another on my calf, and another on my inner thigh. He plants a longer, hotter one right on my clit, then moves up to my belly, to the underside of one breast, to the nipple of the other, before finally reaching my lips.

"Shh," he murmurs there. "All good, Hallie. In another world, another life, I'd love nothing more than to slide into you bare. But neither of us needs that kind of stress."

Then, before I can say another word of apology, he reaches over to the bedside table, opens a drawer, and grabs a condom. When he returns, kneeling between my spread legs, I take it from his hand, inspecting it before tearing and unwrapping it. My eyes are locked on his hard cock as I slide the condom out, and my free hand wraps around him, jacking once, twice. His hips thrust forward into me, and I can't help but smile. My hand continues to move on him, in awe, before he groans loudly.

"Get that on me, Hallie. I need to be in you."

That's all I need to hear. My hands move quickly, rolling the condom down his thickness before he's moving again and settling between my thighs, forearms planted in the bed on either side of me. My hand is between us, gripping him and notching the head inside of me before moving to cup his face.

His head dips to kiss me as he slowly, torturously slowly, stretches and fills me. We're a mess of teeth and tongues and pants as he slides into me, but when he bottoms out, he pauses, head falling to my neck and breathing heavily there.

"Fuck, Hallie," he groans, his chest against mine and his voice vibrating through me. My throat is suddenly tight as I nod.

"I know." It's all I can say, and when he lifts his head, for a moment, I worry about what he might see there. Suddenly, it feels like he can see past every wall, past every whisper of *just this once,* and *I don't need anyone,* to the soft place I've kept to myself for seventeen years.

But then he blinks, and his face is nothing but heat and need as he slides out and then slams into me. My head falls back, and I moan his name.

"The most fucking perfect sound I've ever heard," he groans, eyes locked on me, and he pulls back and thrusts again. "My name on your lips when you're full of my cock."

In another world, I'd have a million different witty comments. Instead, I just nod, lips parted as he fucks me, hard and fast, the orgasm in me building faster than ever in my life. His head dips, kissing me for a moment, and my legs lift to wrap around his hips and get him in deeper. Each slam into me makes a satisfying noise that fills the room, his balls slapping against me and adding to it, his grunts and groans blending with my mewls and moans and creating the most erotic soundtrack.

"Jesse," I pant after a few minutes with panic in my chest as the most all-consuming pleasure builds in my stomach, something so big I've never experienced it before.

"So fucking good. So fucking tight. So. Fucking," he says, then stops, groaning. "Need you to get there." I nod quickly, my pussy tightening. "Your cunt's too fucking good. Need you to come with me."

I nod again, and then when his thrusts speed up, each one hitting deep, hitting me right where I need it—each one building that ball tighter and tighter—until on the third or fourth thrust, I fall apart, screaming his name. He slams into me one last time, then groans into my neck, my name sounding like a prayer as his cock twitches inside of me.

For the smallest, most insane moment, I think that I'd really like to know what it felt like for him to fill me with his cum. I blink that one away, shaking my head as he pulls out.

"Holy shit," I murmur, panting as he rolls off me, lying on the bed beside me.

"Yeah."

"Holy. *Shit*," I repeat, because what else do you say when your childhood crush fucks you into another century?

"Yeah," he says again, this time with a chuckle. He turns to the side, planting a hard kiss on my cheek before rolling out of bed. I shift to my side and watch his tight ass as he goes. I didn't get a chance to really look at him naked before, but now I take my fill.

"Where are you going?" He turns to face me, his cock still semi-hard, a hot-as-fuck happy trail moving down his chest, leading straight to his cock. His arms are muscled, his shoulders broad, and suddenly, I want him all over.

He smiles at me with the most devious grin on his lips. "Gotta go throw this out, then get refreshments."

"Refreshments?" I ask with a laugh.

"I've got one night with you, Hal. I'm using it to my full advantage."

And then he turns to walk off. When he's out of sight, I reach over for the pillow and let out a girly squeal into it.

EIGHTEEN

Hallie

I wake against a hard chest and, for a moment, panic.

But that panic eases when a familiar pine smell fills my senses and when a rough hand scrapes along my back, gliding up and down.

"You up?" a familiar voice rumbles, and I lift my head, looking at him through squinted eyes.

Everything aches in the most delicious way, and memories from the night before flood my mind.

Jesse finding me in the woods when I went out looking for the deer.

Having a full-on breakdown in Jesse's arms.

The hot tub.

Never Have I Ever.

Everything after that.

With the memory, a chill runs through me.

Nope, I tell myself. *No way, Hallie. That was yesterday. It stays in* yesterday. *We are not mentally recounting that right now, not when* we're still in bed with the man.

In fact, right now, my only goal should be to ensure that this impulsive decision doesn't impact the rest of my life or the relationships with the people I care about, including Jesse. And with the way he's looking at me, a wall pulled down over his face so I can't read him in the slightest, my stomach churns.

"Yeah," I say, even though that's obvious. His lips tip at the edges, and it sends the smallest wave of relief through me.

"Are you...good?" he asks, and I let out a small laugh.

"Yeah." I lift a hand to wave between us as I shift away, putting a much-needed gap between us. "Are...we good?"

"I don't know, you tell me," he says, and my stomach churns as panic floods me. "Are we going to avoid each other for a year again?" The panic subsides, leaving relief in its wake.

"If we can joke about it, that's a good thing, right?" I sit up, pulling the sheets up to cover my chest and giving him my signature snarky look. "Do you promise you won't get weird?"

He's let out a loud laugh, shaking his head, and it hits me: we can do this. One night, one *unforgettable* night, and we're back to normal.

"Promise. Want breakfast?" he asks, rolling out of bed and moving to a dresser in the corner. I try not to watch his ass, but I can't stop myself. That's allowed, though, right? I would have absolutely watched his ass as he walked away before we fucked, *especially* if it was a naked ass. In fact, it would be weird *not* to do it afterward. He opens a drawer and grabs out a pair of sweats before bending to put them on.

"Hal?" he asks over his shoulder, smiling at me. I shake my head, trying to focus.

"Sorry, you've got a good ass." No point in playing coy, I suppose. He laughs again, and I don't know the last time I heard him this *light*.

"You too. Now, do you want breakfast? Or are you going to sneak out and make it weird by trying not to make it weird?" He knows me too well, and with that realization, the vise in my chest has loosened entirely.

That's why this isn't going to be an issue: we both know each other so well that it can't go bad.

Right?

Right.

"You got bacon?" He rolls his eyes, then throws a sweatshirt at me. It's going to be far too big, but I also know it's going to be worn and warm. I hope he doesn't like it too much, though, because I am never returning it. A souvenir, so to speak.

I throw the sweatshirt on and stand, noting that it's so big it covers my ass, and then spot the bag with my leggings in it on the floor. Grabbing them, I slip into his bathroom. After I use the toilet, I slip my leggings on, and when I spot his toothbrush, I grab it, coat it with minty toothpaste, and brush away. Now he can't use that for Never Have I Ever, I suppose.

"You're a shit cook from what Emma tells me," I say as I walk into the kitchen, a bowl with batter before him and bacon already sizzling in a pan. He smiles at me over his shoulder.

"I am, but bacon and pancakes? That's the only thing I've mastered."

"Good to know," I say, even though I'll never have a use for that info again. I help set the table and clean up a bit as he goes, throwing out eggshells and starting coffee for us, and in ten minutes, we're sitting at his kitchen table, a stack of admittedly delicious pancakes before each of us.

"What do you have on the agenda for today?" I ask after I've eaten two full plates, far too full for another. Still, I dip a piece of bacon in the puddle of maple syrup on my plate and pop it into my mouth. He shrugs across the way from me, leaning back with his arms behind his head. Again, I tell myself it's totally okay to admire his arms like this. It's what I would have done anyway.

"Nothing, really. Gotta get Emma around noon, then family dinner. The norm. You?"

I nod. "Same. I've gotta batch some content for the week's social media channels. The pictures of the deer should go over well." He glares at me, and I smile. "I'm thinking of seeking her out once a week and trying to make them the mascot of the farm."

"You're not going anywhere with those boots." I roll my eyes, then stand and move toward the sink to rinse my plate and put it into the dishwasher. He stands as well, his own plate in hand, but he sets it aside before grabbing mine.

"Who's going to stop me?"

"I think I proved I will," he says, and suddenly, the friendly air that I've been forcing to hang between us feels decidedly *less* so. "You know—" he starts, and I hold my breath, unsure of what he's going to say next and equally uncertain of what I *want* him to say next, but then my phone dings once, twice, three times, with incoming texts. I glare at the device on the table like the traitor it is, then reach for it and let out a groan.

"What is it?" he asks.

"Your sister," I mumble, seeing that while it sounded like three new messages, it's closer to six, since the first three hit my DND. He lifts an eyebrow before I continue. "She is trying to convince me to text that guy she wants to set me up with." I regret saying it for a moment as the words hang between us before he speaks. His face shows no change, though, no hint of irritation or dismay or hurt.

"Are you going to?" he asks, and I sigh.

"I don't know. I mean, does anyone really say no to Wren?" He laughs and shakes his head, knowing that even though Wren is sweet as pie and will do anything for anyone, when she gets an idea in her mind, she's unlikely to drop it, especially if she thinks it will benefit someone she loves.

"What do you think?" I ask, eyes still assessing him carefully.

"Me?"

"Yeah. Do you think I should text him?"

It's a stupid question, especially today, especially this morning. Still, I think a part of me does it intentionally, pushing the boundary to see just how he reacts and how honest he is about it being just *one night*.

"Do you want to go on a date with him?"

"I don't know him, so I'm not sure." A moment passes before he shrugs, grabs his plate, and stands.

"I mean, if you don't care either way and it would get Wren off your ass, it probably couldn't hurt," he says, back to me as he scrapes the remnants of a pancake into the trash.

I force myself not to feel that flash of disappointment and fail miserably.

It's what I wanted. It's what I asked for, actually.

I should be happy he's acting normal now that this is out of our system. And I *am* happy. Right?

I'm lost in my own pondering as his own phone dings with a new message.

"Shit," he says with a sigh. My head lifts. "I thought Emma was getting picked up at twelve, but it's eleven." My eyes move to the clock over the oven to see it's ten.

"Oh, I'll help you clean up a bit and then head out." He shakes his head to argue, but I refuse. "I'll get this, but can you just, uh, get my swimsuit?" A blush burns over my face as I remember that it's probably still floating in the hot tub. He lets out a laugh.

"It's in the dryer. Sometime last night, I grabbed it." I try to pinpoint when he could have done that, but that requires me to think about rounds and breaks, and my mind *cannot* go there right now. I nod. "Leave this. I'll grab it. Just get your things together, and I'll walk you home," he says.

"You don't have to," I say with a shake of my head, but he just glares at me. Knowing better, I don't bother to argue, instead getting my things together and letting Jesse walk me to my house.

"Thank you," I say when he stops at my door, the words spilling out even though I tried to keep them in. His head tips as he turns to me, his face a mask of intrigued confusion.

"For what?"

"For...yesterday."

He lifts a brow. "I don't know, Hal, I feel like I should be thanking you."

I laugh, happy for the moment of levity, and shake my head. "I meant before all of that. I was having a shitty day, and you made a shitty day much better." His face softens, and he steps closer, pushing a piece of hair behind my ear. He hesitates for a moment, then seems to win the battle in his head as he pulls me in for a hug.

"Anytime, Hallie. I mean it."

I take in a deep breath as my face settles into his chest, his familiar leather and pine smell enveloping me and relaxing me for a moment before his body goes still.

"Hallie," he whispers.

"Mmm?" I ask into his chest. He shifts slowly, pulling back, and when I look up at him, his eyes are focused somewhere behind me and wide.

"Turn around."

"Huh?"

"Hallie, turn around. Slowly."

I do as he commands, his hands staying on my waist, and when my back is to him, I notice the deer from yesterday ten feet away.

"Oh my god," I whisper, then gasp when she meets my eye and comes even closer. Jesse's fingers dig into my hips, and I whisper over my shoulder at him. "Go inside and get celery."

"What?"

"Go in my fridge and get celery, Jesse. For the deer."

"I'm not leaving you alone with a wild deer, Hallie," he says, and with his words, the deer snorts as if annoyed by his belief she'd be anything but kind to me.

"He's just protective," I tell her, then turn to Jesse. "It's Jane Doe. She's very trustworthy." He pauses, looking at me like I've completely lost it, but I give him a fierce glare and then speak through gritted teeth. "Go. Get. The. Celery."

"When did you name her?"

"This morning." He looks at me for a long moment, then closes his eyes and shakes his head. "Go get the celery!" I say again. With a resigned sigh, he turns to my house and disappears, and I take another tentative step toward the deer. Soon she's just two feet from me, and I'm moving to bend to her level.

Yesterday, I saw Jane Doe in the woods, which is why I was out there taking pictures, not that I told Jesse that. Bumping into her again felt magical, but now I wonder if she found me on purpose. Yesterday, I felt so miserable after seeing those pictures of my mom and stepsister; I thought I'd imagined the deer. But when we found her again, it felt like it was meant to be, some sign from the world that it would be okay, that navigating this world without a mom wouldn't be the end of me.

Just like her.

Her head lifts as Jesse's boots crunch behind me, and then there are green celery stalks in his hands before me. I take them and then reach out, offering the leafy side to Jane. She steps closer, sniffs once, then gently takes it from my hand, crunching through the vegetable happily.

"Oh my god," I whisper in awe.

"I haven't believed this," Jesse murmurs. "Only you would bond with an orphaned deer as soon as you move in here." All the same, he has his phone out, taking pictures as if he knew I'd want him to.

"We're the same," I murmur, emotion in the words, then offer the second celery stalk to her. "I wish I had more in my fridge, but when I go to the store, I'll get you more, okay?" I ask, then reach out and pet her nose. She blinks at me, then stands for a few more moments as I talk to her in hushed tones before turning and walking away. When she's completely gone, I stand with a sigh.

"That was amazing," I say, turning to Jesse excitedly. "Did you see it?"

He's smiling and shaking his head.

"Yeah, I saw it, Hallie. But your lips are going blue again. You've got to get inside." His eyes dip down to my lips, and again, memories flash through my mind. The way blue lips and that very deer led me to his hot tub. His eyes were hooded, and he was doing that same move before dipping to kiss me. The way I felt in his arms, free and light and like I had not a single want or desire in the world, so long as I was there.

My phone beeps in my pocket, a reminder that brings me back to reality.

A reality where Jesse and I can and will never be anything more than one night.

"You've gotta get Emma," I say. Now it's his turn to nod. We stand there awkwardly for a moment before I step closer and give him another hug. "Thanks again, Jesse. I'll see you at dinner tonight?" He nods, and then, before I can make a fool of myself, I turn around and head into my house, closing the door behind me. I lean against it, closing my eyes and taking a deep breath, sliding my phone out of my pocket to read Wren's most recent inquiry to see if I've texted the kindergarten teacher or not.

Fuck it.

What better way to prove to myself I'm not going to be hung up on Jesse than to say yes to this? Quickly, I tap out a text, introducing myself and asking if he wants to get coffee sometime next week, and get a reply almost instantly. I clue Wren in, and she sends me back a text with far too many exclamation points and emojis, and I smile, though I can't quite find it in me to be nearly as excited as her.

NINETEEN

JESSE

That night, family dinner is normal.

Hallie smiles at me.

She jokes with Madden.

She giggles with Wren.

She passes the butter.

She acts like I didn't make good on my promise the night before and fuck her hoarse.

"I've rented a bunch of rooms up at the lodge in Killington next month for my birthday, and I'd love you all to come. Wren told me you went last year and had a blast, and, well, I know I'm kind of new here, but Jesse and Madden, I know we talked about going snowboarding, so I figured we could make a weekend of it," Adam says when we're sitting in the den after dinner, and when I turn to Hallie, she gives me a small, knowing smile, not a hint of the usual shyness on her face that's usually there when that trip is mentioned.

"Oh, fuck yeah," Madden says, pumping a fist. "I'm in. But I'm not rooming with Jesse."

"I've already told him that is the sure-fire way to have a miserable trip," Wren says.

"Everyone gets their own room. Hallie, I already talked to Colton, and he's coming."

"So is Nat!" Wren says with a wide, excited look, and I realize now she's probably been planning this for a week at least. It's another check in Adam's *pros* column, because somehow, the man is willing to spend *his* birthday getting his girlfriend's favorite people all together and footing the bill.

"We already agreed to watch Emma, so you're free to go, Jesse," Mom says. I shrug, eyes locked on Hallie.

"I'm in," she says, looking at Wren.

"Me too," I say, continuing to watch her.

It's as if not only last night didn't happen, but like *none* of it happened, as if one night truly did get me out of her system.

I fucking hate it.

By the time Hallie, Emma, and I walk home, I feel like I may have imagined it all. We drop Hallie off first, and she smiles, hugging Emma and then me before telling me she'll get Emma off the bus like she did every day last week.

It's all totally fucking normal.

All I can do is think about her. What she sounded like, what she felt like. What she fucking *tasted* like.

I'm going insane. Absolutely fucking insane.

That night, I tell myself it's because she's the first woman I've fucked in a long time.

I tell myself it's because I can still hear her moaning my name if I close my eyes.

I tell myself it's because there are still scratches on my back from her nails.

I tell myself a lot of things that night, trying to convince myself I'm okay with *just one night.*

But when I fall asleep in the sheets that smell like her, I still don't believe it.

Monday, I find myself finishing my work quicker than usual, heading home around four instead of my usual five o'clock. I tell myself it's because it's after the holidays and I have less to do. Still, I know there's a list a mile long of things that need doing around the farm, things that need checking, and a dozen things I should be doing to continue preparing for the rough winter that's predicted to come over the next two months.

But it's much easier to say that than to admit I want to get home to see Hallie and watch her interact with my kid.

And if I *did* say that, it would have nothing to do with Hallie. It's just that I rarely get to see Emma interact with people who aren't her direct family. Watching Emma and Hallie gives me hope that I'm actually raising a good kid, like Hallie said, instead of a chaotic gremlin who

When I step into the mudroom, I kick the seat of the small bench, undo the laces on my boots, then kick them off and remove my jacket. I toss my hat in a bin along with my gloves and follow the sound of giggles and laughter into the kitchen.

"Hey, girls," I say, and both sets of eyes pop up to me, surprised smiles over their faces.

And with it, all of the stress of the day fades away because right now, this is all that matters.

After dinner, I walk Hallie home while Emma finishes up some homework she forgot about. We're silent on the way there, and I mentally take note of a few places I need to salt better. If she insists on wearing those shitty shoes, then I need to make sure it's safe for her.

"Tomorrow work?" I ask when we get to the door. A blush pinkens her cheeks in a way I don't understand. At least, not until she speaks.

"It should be. I have that, uh, coffee date at one." My body stills. "But it should be done by two, and I'll have plenty of time to get back here and get Emma off the bus."

"Oh, well, uh," I start, running a hand through my hair, suddenly unsure of...everything. "If you can't get her off the bus, it's really no big deal—"

"No, I can. As I said, it's just coffee. And it's probably going to suck."

I lift a shoulder, somewhat appeased.

"Who knows, it might be good," I say quickly, and she hesitates, looking over my face and shrugging a shoulder of her own.

"Maybe. Either way, I should be able to get her off the bus."

I nod, because what else can I do?

"Okay. Sounds good. Just, uh...let me know if something comes up. Mom can get her, or I can, no problem."

She nods, then opens her door, gives me a wave and a *thank you* for walking her home, before disappearing inside.

When the door closes behind her, it feels like it's being slammed in my face.

I tell myself it's fine.

I tell myself it's just one date.

I remind myself that I practically insisted she go on it.

And most of all, I tell myself it doesn't matter, because it could never work between us.

But when I drive past her house at one fifteen the next day and see her car isn't out front, my stomach drops to my feet, and I still don't believe it.

On Tuesday, my mind races all day, wondering how her date went. I fight the urge a dozen times not to text her or even drop in at her place to ask, not wanting to give in to the voice in my head. I tell myself I won't, but the first chance I get, I ask her about the date.

"How'd that date go?" I ask as I load dishes into the dishwasher while Emma gets ready for a shower. Once more, Emma insisted Hallie stay for dinner, and once more, I didn't argue.

"Oh," she starts, a blush burning her cheeks, and my chest tightens. "It, uh, it was pretty good, actually. I was surprised. We have a lot in common."

"That's good," I say, suddenly very interested in organizing the dinner dishes in the machine, separating forks and spoons into their own segments. It'll make unloading easier, of course.

"Yeah, I think we're going to meet up at The Mill on Friday and get some drinks with Adam and Wren."

I force my hands to continue their task, with no hesitation that she might notice.

Inside, I'm fighting back an internal crisis as I realize the woman I can't stop thinking about is going on a second date with some asshole who definitely doesn't deserve her.

Outside, I'm just Jesse King, organizing silverware. Nothing to see here.

Like the saving grace she is, before I have to say anything else, Emma comes into the kitchen to ask if she can have dessert, and Hallie takes that as her cue to leave.

"I'll walk you home," I say, and she shakes her head.

"No, no, it's all good. I've got it."

"My mom—" I start, attempting the argument that's worked in the past, but knowing it's probably no use.

"Like I said the last time you tried that, your mom would understand not leaving an eleven-year-old in a house alone to walk me one hundred yards. I'll be fine." The knife twists at the idea of not being able to steal those extra minutes, but what can I do? Arguing would look suspicious, and something tells me if I push too hard—if Hallie gets even the tiniest whiff that I might not be okay after our weekend together—this entire thing might implode.

So I nod.

"At least text me when you get inside." She gives me a mock salute, and despite the dread in my heart, I smile before she wishes Emma and me goodnight and heads out. Minutes later, I get a text from her.

H: Made it home safe and sound.

J: I'm glad. Thanks for humoring me.

H: Always.

That night, I tell myself one successful date doesn't mean anything.

I tell myself that it was just coffee.

I tell myself that she isn't making dinner for him and his kid.

But the tiny, cruel voice in my head whispers, *yet*.

On Thursday, a storm hits Holly Ridge, and Emma has the day off, and Hallie shows up bright and early to watch her. I barely have time to talk to her before I have to head out, but I get plenty of texts throughout the day from both Emma and Hallie about their shenanigans. I eat a quick lunch and dinner out on the road and don't make it home until after eight.

"Surprise!" Emma shouts excitedly when I walk in the door. "Come on! We have to show you!" She grabs my hand and tugs me past a smiling Hallie into the dining room, decorated for a birthday. I'm very confused. My birthday is in July, and Emma's is next month.

"I..." I stare, looking around, and then see a chocolate cake on the table. Or, half of a chocolate cake.

"Happy half-birthday!" Emma shouts.

"A half birthday?" I ask, raising an eyebrow.

"It's your half-birthday today," Hallie answers low. I stare at her for a moment, trying to pin the date and do math, and I realize she's right: it *is* my half-birthday. "Half birthdays are very important to celebrate."

It's so incredibly *Hallie* to celebrate half-birthdays.

"How did you know it was my half-birthday?"

"I know everyone's half birthday. I usually just grab a cookie or something from the bakery and hand-deliver it, but Emma wanted to celebrate and try her hand at baking. She made it all herself. I just helped with getting it in and out of the oven."

I look to my daughter, who smiles at me with so much pride it hurts my heart. "Really?"

She nods excitedly.

"But," Hallie says, giving my daughter a bit of a side-eye. She rolls her eyes, and I want to tell her to drop the attitude, but it seems Hallie has some balance of her own on what she calls out and doesn't. "But like I said, when he texted that he would be late, there's a chance your dad wants you to go to bed." Emma opens her mouth, but Hallie keeps talking. "And like we talked about and *like you agreed to thirty minutes ago*, if that's the case, we will save it for tomorrow night."

There's a mini staredown between Hallie and Emma before my daughter turns to me, her face sweet as the cake sitting on the dining room table, as she smiles up at me.

"Daddy, can we please eat cake tonight?"

I hold it in for all of ten seconds as I stare at Emma, whose eyes are comically wide, her hands slapped beneath her chin like a caricature of someone who is well-behaved. I let out a loud laugh soon, though, shaking my head and scrubbing a hand over her hair.

"Dad!" Emma whines as I walk away, moving to the kitchen to open a drawer where the lighter is, then turning to the girls with it in the air.

"Do we need candles for a half-birthday cake?" There's a squeal of excitement and a *yes!* from the dining room, and I can't help but laugh. I might be bone tired, but somehow a slice of cake with my two favorite girls feels like exactly what I need right now.

"What were you guys watching?" I ask an hour later as I sink into the couch beside Hallie after getting Emma to bed. A movie is paused, with a familiar set of actors I can't quite place on the screen, but it looks much older than anything Emma enjoys watching.

Hallie laughs, then shakes her head. "I found out today your daughter has never seen the classics."

I lift an eyebrow at her. "The classics?"

"Mary-Kate and Ashley movies."

I blink at her, then let out a laugh. "I don't know if those are considered classics."

"Excuse me, they absolutely are. Wren and I watched them a million times. Hell, one year we made an entire vision board based on them," she says with an amused laugh. "We made this whole plan, basically *Around the World in 80 Days*, but with Mary-Kate and Ashley."

I wonder momentarily if it's in that pink box with the rest of her vision boards.

"You know, I remember Wren loving them, but I don't think I ever watched one."

She looks at me, her jaw dropping and her eyes wide. "You've never seen *one*?"

"Hallie, in what universe would I have watched a Mary-Kate and Ashley movie?"

"You have a little sister. You have a *daughter*!"

"My sister is five years younger than me, and I hate to tell you, Hal, but kids these days aren't sitting around watching Mary-Kate and Ashley movies."

"Maybe it would solve a lot of the youths' issues if they did."

"Did you just say *the youths*?"

She rolls her eyes at me, then reaches for the remote.

"Okay, which one do you want to watch first? We're going to start your education now. Honestly, it should be a required watch for girl dads." She expects me to argue, raising an eyebrow at me, anticipating the impending challenge, but I just sit back and smile. No way am I missing out on an opportunity to sit with her for two hours.

"Whichever you suggest."

Ninety minutes later, after watching blond twins evading mobsters in Australia, the credits are rolling, and a yawn escapes Hallie's lips. She sighs, sitting up from her slouched position on the couch, and turns to me, biting her lip. "I should get home."

"You could stay here," I murmur without thinking, but don't take it back. Her eyes scan my face, looking for jokes or maybe waiting for me to take it back, but I don't.

Each day, I become more and more deluded in my thoughts of Hallie. More and more lost in the idea of her, of having her, I almost can't remember why I decided I couldn't in the first place.

After a moment, she stands up, gives me a soft, tired smile that makes me want to kiss her, and shakes her head, yawning again.

"No, I shouldn't. My house isn't too far."

For the first time, I regret her living so close, if only because if she didn't, I might be able to convince her to stay tonight, to sleep in my bed. Even if I took the couch, I'd get the perk of my sheets smelling like her again, the scent having faded two days ago.

Knowing there's no use in arguing, I stand and follow her to the mudroom, where she slips on her shoes, and I'm grateful I spent a few extra minutes slating and plowing the path to her place. We stand in the mudroom, and after she slips her jacket on, she tugs a dark green Three Kings beanie over her head, and suddenly, an unignorable thought slams through me: I want to kiss her.

So fucking badly.

I take a step closer without thinking, closing the gap between us until it's barely a foot. My eyes move from hers to her full, pink lips, and they part, a tiny breath leaving. When my eyes move back to hers, I see it there: that wall is down, one I didn't realize she had erected sometime between Saturday night and Sunday afternoon.

Need.

Want.

Disappointment.

That's when I realize I'm not the only one struggling. Hallie is facing the same problem I am; she's just far better at burying it than I seem to be.

She wants me to kiss her as much as I want to kiss her.

With that knowledge, I almost do it.

I almost lean in, nearly pull her into me. My hand reaches out with a mind of its own to grab her hip and pull her into me, but then she shifts, looking away, tugging her full bottom lip into her mouth and biting down on it.

"Oh, uh, remember, I won't be here for dinner tomorrow," she says, and the moment is broken.

"What?" I ask, confused. The only thing keeping me going these days is knowing I'll get her at night and get to steal these precious moments with her.

"I'm going to The Mill," she whispers, apology in the words, and I know why instantly. She's going back out with that fucking guy.

"Oh, yeah, of course. No problem," I lie. "I can also get her off the bus if you'd like."

She shakes her head. "No need, just wanted to remind you. I probably won't be making dinner, since I won't have time to help her finish."

I shake my head, waving a hand as if it's really no big deal, then tuck my hands into the pockets of my jeans to avoid doing something incredibly fucking stupid.

"All good," is all I can say, and she stares for a moment before nodding.

"Okay, well...night, Jesse," she says, stepping back and heading out the door.

I wait by my phone for her to text me, staring at it like a madman. When it dings minutes later, I jump and read the message.

> Made it home! Night, Jesse. I had fun tonight.

I smile at the message before getting ready for bed. The sheets no longer smell like her when I lie in bed staring at the ceiling, long past when I should be asleep.

I tell myself I won't do it.

I tell myself I'll let her live her life and stick to the plan.

But the next morning, I still find myself texting Madden and asking if he wants to get drinks that night.

TWENTY

Two drinks, I tell myself. *Two drinks, and then you can head out.*

The fact that I feel an all-consuming dread as I park behind the bar my brother owns to get drinks with my best friend, her boyfriend, and my date can absolutely not be a good sign, but I push myself to smile as I step out of my car. Kevin is standing beside his car and gives me a small wave as he makes his way toward me, and I fight back a sigh.

It's not that he's not nice: he is. Incredibly. Sweet and kind and everything I should want. Wren did well, setting us up, and I wasn't lying when I told Jesse we had a lot in common.

The problem is, he doesn't make my heart flip when he looks at me, and I don't feel butterflies when he gives me a small, polite hug or tells me I look beautiful. When I slip on ice in the parking lot, he asks me if I'm okay.

"Oh, yeah, I'm good. I really shouldn't be wearing these shoes, not with the storm that just came through," I say as we walk around to the front, gesturing to my Uggs.

He tips his head at them. "They look warm," he says.

I give him a nod. "Yeah, but they have no grip. I'm toast on ice."

He shrugs as if that doesn't matter. "Sometimes you just want to be cozy."

I nod and then politely smile as he opens the door, but all I can think about is the grumpy face Jesse would have made if he saw me slip yet again in these.

"You know what I was watching last night?" I ask twenty minutes later, turning to Wren. We're sitting at a four-top table, Kevin next to me, Adam beside Wren with his arm over her shoulder. "*Our Lips Are Sealed.*" Since settling in, the night has been fine, and a fraction of my desire to head home instead of spending the night out has died down, and I'm enjoying myself for the most part.

"The Mary-Kate and Ashley movie?" she asks with a laugh, and I nod. "Oh my god, I haven't seen those in years. We loved them."

"I know. I found out Emma's never seen any of them."

"My sister liked those," Kevin says, and when I look to him, his nose is scrunched up. "They were so bad." I tilt my head a bit and force a smile, shrugging.

"That was kind of the best part. It added to it. Plus, they were a sign of the times, you know?"

"I suppose. There are just so many great movies out there—I can't imagine intentionally watching them as an adult."

I let out a laugh, trying to lighten the mood. "Would this be the wrong time to tell you that I rewatch them regularly? They're kind of a comfort watch for me," I admit.

He shakes his head and lets out a little huff of a laugh. "No, it just means we'll just have to watch some of the classics, broaden your horizons a bit."

I blink and then nod, unsure of what to say. I'm sure he means well, but it grates against my nerves in a way that can't be a great sign. Wren gives me a strange look, and I put on a friendly smile, shrugging it off, but all I can think about is Jesse staying up all night, even though he was dead tired from working all day, to watch it with me.

Thankfully, Wren takes over the conversation, talking about the kids in her class, and I'm grateful for the distraction as I look around.

At the bar, I catch Colt's eye, and he gives me a skeptical look, but I just give him a polite smile and a shrug.

"I'm gonna go grab another drink," I say, a bit too loud. "Anyone else?" Everyone shakes their heads no, and I'm relieved when Kevin doesn't follow as I walk over to the bar where my brother is standing.

"What's going on over there? You look like you need me to rush over with an emergency to save you," Colt says with a laugh when I walk over to him, and I let out a laugh, shaking my head, the tension leaving my shoulders.

"No, no. It's all good. It's kind of a blind date, someone Wren works with. Can I get a Coke, please?" I ask, deciding that one cider would be enough.

"What is a kind of blind date?" Colt asks, reaching for a glass and filling it with ice.

"We got coffee together earlier this week, and he seemed normal."

"But now?"

"Now..." I shrug. "I don't know. We don't have much in common." He tops the drink with dark soda, then adds a straw and slides it to me.

"Well, at least Wren is with you to make it less weird."

I nod, agreeing, but before he can say anything else, the door opens, a bell jingling up above it. All of the heads in the bar shift to the entrance as always happens, and the air halts in my lungs as Jesse and Madden walk into the bar.

"Well, looks like tonight got a bit more interesting," Colton murmurs, and I turn to him with a furrowed brow, but he grins at me and gets a wave over to a customer as I watch the King brothers walk straight to my table with a mix of relief and overwhelming dread.

Jesse ignores me for the first twenty minutes he's here, grabbing a beer for himself and Madden. We shift to one of the large tables so we can all sit together, Madden sitting on one side and Kevin on the other side of me, while Jesse sits directly across from me.

"So how long have you two been going out?" Madden asks, sitting back. He looks at me with a smirk that I can't quite decode, and honestly, with the dumpster fire that is becoming this night, I don't want to.

"Oh, this is our second date," Kevin says, then loops an arm around my chair, smiling at me. I return it, but it feels forced, and I hope no one else picks up on it. Eyes burn on me, but I don't let myself look across from me to where the glare is coming from. I lift my cider and take a sip, but find it's empty. Sullenly, I take a sip of my soda and wish I'd gotten a second drink instead.

"Want a sip of mine?" Kevin asks, tipping his beer in my direction. I open my mouth to decline, but I'm cut off.

"She doesn't like beer," Jesse says, the first real sentence he's said since he sat down.

Wren snaps her head to me, a questioning look on her face, but I ignore it, smiling again at Kevin.

"No, thank you," I say, trying to be as polite as possible, then tipping my soda in his direction. "I'm good."

Finally, I direct my gaze to Jesse, giving him a dark glare.

He doesn't even flinch.

The conversation continues painfully with Madden and Wren tugging it along. We ordered some food—a bunch of random appetizers, since that's all The Mill offers—and even though I don't order it, Colt sends out a big pile of fries for me. When they arrive, Kevin grabs the ketchup and moves to start squirting it all over the top of the fries, and I flinch.

Before he can, though, Jesse reaches across the table, grabbing the ketchup from his hands and setting it to the side. Then, as I've done so many times before, he slides half of the pile of fries to a separate plate and adds a small pile of ketchup to the side before handing the plate to me without a word.

I sit in silence, incredibly annoyed and uncomfortable, but also inconveniently touched, the feelings warring in my chest as the table sits in awkward silence.

"Hallie doesn't like the ketchup to touch anything," Wren explains with a kind smile.

"Oh, shit, sorry," Kevin starts, but I shake my head before he can continue.

"No need to be sorry. They've all known me almost my whole life, so they know my silly quirks." I look to Jesse, all kindness leaving my face. "There's no way you could know that after just two dates." Jesse holds my eyes for a beat longer than necessary before looking away and grabbing an onion ring and eating it.

Ten minutes later, we're all chatting, and for a moment I think I can survive the night. Kevin tells some stupid joke that I don't want to laugh at, but when he looks at me with a wide grin, like he's proud of it, I let out a little laugh.

"That was the fakest laugh I've ever heard," Jesse says with his eyes burning on me.

"Dude," Adam says low, a hint of entertained humor in the word.

"Jesse," I say low, but he ignores me.

"It was. She hates jokes like that." Jesse's speaking to Kevin, but he doesn't even look at him. His eyes are locked on me.

"Jesse, stop it," I say through gritted teeth.

"I'm not wrong," he says. "You hate jokes like that. It was a fake laugh." He stares me down as he takes a sip of his drink. It's barely half drunk, and I can't help but wonder why the fuck he's even here. It's clearly not to enjoy himself or have a drink with a friend.

I want to scream at him.

I want to make a scene. I want to ask him what the fuck is wrong with him and why he's ruining this for me. He *knew* I'd be here, and there is absolutely zero chance he randomly and impulsively found a sitter for Emma and decided to come to The Mill *tonight*.

I said yes to the original date in an effort to move on quickly and efficiently from my one night with Jesse, but that's proving increasingly impossible. Even more impossible now with the glaring reminder of who I can't have while I'm out with the one I'll allow myself to have.

"Sometimes it just takes the right person to tell the joke," I say through a brittle smile.

"Bullshit," he says quickly.

"Come on, Jesse, you're being an ass," Madden says.

"Jesse—" Wren starts.

"What? If someone's going to date her, he should at least know the basics." Turning to Adam, Jesse asks, "Don't you think?"

Adam lifts his hands in surrender. "I am playing Switzerland here, I'm the newcomer," he says.

"That's smart, honey," Wren says, patting his hand.

"What color are her eyes?" Jesse asks, eyes locked on my date, and Kevin stutters beside me.

"They're, uh," he starts, pausing, clearly unsure. I turn to him, and there's an embarrassed blush on his cheeks.

"They're green. Grass green in the winter, but they get closer to evergreen in the summer. Sometimes they're emerald if she wears red or purple," Jesse states.

The breath stops in my lungs, and the entire table goes absolutely silent. I assume the chaos of the bar continues to swirl around us, unaware of how my entire world is shifting on its axis, but my focus is laser sharp, looking straight at Jesse, who suddenly looks both crushed and furious.

"But what do I know, right? Fuck it. I shouldn't be here. Have a great date, Kev. I wish you both the fucking best." Then he stands, leaving his half-drunk beer on the table and walking out the door.

BREAKTK

Wren gives Kevin her profuse apologies for her brother, who, to his credit, doesn't also storm out. Instead, he finishes his drink before making his excuses, saying he has an early morning the next day and needs to get home. I wish him a good night, and he gives me the world's most awkward hug before heading out the door.

But when it's over, and Wren tries to get my attention, giving me wary glances across the table, I know she probably wants to drag me to the bathroom and ask what happened and if I'm okay, but I ignore her. Instead, I act as if everything is totally and completely normal as Madden, Wren, and Adam all try to pretend that wasn't the weirdest exchange. Thank God for good friends who know when you need to sit in your delusion.

When I finish my drink, I stand and let out the world's fakest yawn ever. "I think I'm going to head out. I'm super tired. Madden, do you need a ride?"

He looks at me assessingly, checking his watch that shows it's barely even nine, then shakes his head. "No, I'm okay, but let me walk you—"

I give him a firm shake of my head. "No need."

He assesses me, reading me the way only a friend can, before he nods his acceptance with a defeated sigh.

"Text me when you get home," he says, but I don't answer, my mind long past what happened at the bar and turning into anger.

Quickly, I bid everyone goodbye and wave to my brother, who gives me a similarly confused look, before I nearly run to my car. I drive home with my mind in a daze. I don't go to my place, though. I drive straight to Jesse's, slamming my fist on the door as soon as I'm there.

Then I decide he doesn't deserve the decency of my knocking, so I fling the door open, letting myself in and storming inside. He's on his way to me, his hair an absolute mess, irritation on his face, and dark circles under his eyes as we meet in the living room, where I push his chest as soon as I'm within touching distance, fighting the urge to slap him instead.

"What the fuck, Hallie?" he says, stumbling back, and his indignance stokes the flames of my anger.

"What the fuck? *You're* asking *me*, what the fuck?"

"You just stormed into my house and pushed me? Yeah, I think I'm allowed to ask what the fuck."

"What in the *fuck* was that, Jesse?"

"What was what?"

I step back, taking in a deep breath through my nose with my jaw so tight, my teeth grind.

"Don't play stupid. What was that at The Mill? Interrogating Kevin like that?"

He rolls his eyes at me like I'm being dramatic. "That was me protecting you."

I shake my head, jaw dropping as I let out a scoff of a laugh. "*Protecting me?* From what? A man not knowing my favorite drink on the second date? I didn't realize that was a threat to my well-being."

He shakes his head. "I was just trying to show you he doesn't know anything about you! You shouldn't be wasting your time with him."

"We've been on *two dates, Jesse!* And even then, *who cares?*" My voice is taking on a frantic edge, and his face is taking on a similar one. Somehow, I know this tentative friendship we've formed is about to implode.

"He's not good enough for you."

"What do you know about good enough for me? He's fine," I say, and he shakes his head mournfully.

"You don't deserve *fine,* Hallie. You deserve perfect. You deserve spectacular. You deserve a man who knows you hate when ketchup touches your food. You deserve a man who knows you would rather die than drink a beer and that you never wear the proper footwear because you'd rather be comfortable than safe. And I don't expect him to know all of that on the first or the second date, but at the very least, he should know your eyes are fucking green."

Something warm blooms in my chest, and I fight it back. Unfortunately for my sanity, he's not done.

"I know your favorite color is robin's egg blue and that you keep celery on hand even though you don't eat it because you made friends with a deer. I know you take too much fucking creamer in your coffee and that you have a freckle on your hip that I really can't stop thinking about. I know what it sounds like when you're laughing because you feel like you're supposed to, and what it sounds like when you're laughing because you really thought a joke was funny."

His voice lowers, and my throat aches as he takes a small step closer.

"Jesse," I say, my voice frail even to my own ears.

"He doesn't know those things, but I do. I do, and it kills me to know you'll give him a shot, but not me. Because what I know most of all is that you are meant to be mine."

All of the fire I stormed in here with is gone, leaving smoldering embers in its wake.

He closes the gap between us, and my breathing halts, my heart beating so hard in my chest I'm shocked it's not audible. He shifts his arm, sliding it along my lower back and pulling me into him, and against my better judgment, I let him.

"I can't do it, Hallie," he murmurs so low, but I hear him all the same.

"Do what?"

"Watch you fall in love with someone else, watch you let him in and give him a chance. I can't do it." From the look on his face, it's a startling confession even to him, but he gives it to me nonetheless. "Not when I want that to be me."

Everything in me comes crashing down.

Reality merges with girlish dreams and shatters into new understanding as panic fills me. "Jesse—"

"I know you said it was temporary, and I got it. I still do. I was all for it, but you and I both know that night wasn't just sex. It wasn't just getting out of our systems, Hallie. It was more. It was us. It worked so well because we were always supposed to be that, and it terrifies you."

My jaw slackens, and my breath comes in short, panicked breaths as I stare into his hazel eyes. I can't help but recognize that he knows my eyes the same way I know his gold and green flecks, the tiny freckle beside his left eye, and the scar on his chin.

"You're out of your mind," I whisper.

"Fuck it. Then I'm out of my mind. That doesn't change how I feel about you." And then his head is dipping, his lips are on mine, and the world melts away.

It's just as perfect as the first time in Vermont. It's as healing as it was on Saturday and filled with need and desire and *adoration* as it was that night. Its lips and tongues and teeth, and my hands move up to cup his face, to hold him closer, to stop him from retreating. I have no idea what will happen next, but in this moment, I need this. I need him.

We continue like this, his body pressed to mine, a hand in my hair holding me where he wants me, my hands on his jaw grounding me before he finally pulls back and looks down at me, pleading and need on his face.

"Please," he murmurs against my lips. "Give this a shot, Hallie. You belong here. With me. With Emma. I know you see that."

For a moment, I almost give in. I almost say *fuck it*, throw all my worries and concerns away, and do as he asks—as he *pleads*. Maybe I could be brave, maybe I could try this, maybe I could give in to what I've always wanted for more than just a night.

"Let's see if we can make it work," he adds, and the voice in my head whispers to me. *See? Even he doesn't think it could really work. Don't be stupid. You'll do something stupid, and he'll leave you the first chance he gets, and then what will you have?*

I'm fighting with myself, battling to try and convince myself it would be worth it, worth the risk, worth the heartache, when my phone dings with a new text in my pocket, followed by another, and then my phone rings with a call, and reality sets in.

It's probably Madden checking to see if I got home or Wren calling to see if I'm okay.

Good people.

My friends.

The family I've forged for myself. And with those tiny mechanical sounds, reality comes in.

"I can't," I say, dropping my hands and stepping back. Resignation washes over his face, shoulders dropping with my words.

"Can't or won't?" Jesse asks softly, though he doesn't stop me from moving away.

I shrug, my eyes stinging.

"Does it really matter?" I ask, my voice cracking as I take a step back. I need to go back to my place. I need to get out of here, out of this familiar place that feels too much like home for my sanity.

Again, he doesn't stop me.

Instead, the look of confusion, hurt, and, strangely enough, determination crossing his face is the last thing I see before I turn and run out the door, get into my car, and drive the short way home.

I unlock the door with shaky hands, then lock it behind me and text Madden that I made it inside, adding some stupid GIF in hopes that he'll think I'm fine. Next, I quickly call Wren to tell her I'm okay, knowing if she doesn't hear my voice, she'll panic, and the last thing I need is her showing up at my front door.

I hold it together.

I assure everyone I love that I'm okay.

And then I lie in my bed and cry until I fall asleep.

BREAKtk

I bow out of family dinner on Sunday, citing a stomach ache, and no one questions it. Monday, I'll deal with reality, but this weekend, I just want to wallow.

But when Monday comes, and I step out my front door for the first time since Friday night, there's a box with a light blue bow on top. I look around, confused, before bending to lift the box and heading back inside to carefully inspect it. When I lifted the lid, though, a rock settled in my chest.

A pair of boots.

A note written on a slip of paper, like he tore it off the bottom of some paper Emma brought home from school. *Stop being stubborn.*

The boots fit perfectly, in case you were wondering.

I tried not to think about it too long, what he meant by *'stop being stubborn'*.

The simple explanation was that he wanted me to stop being stubborn and wear boots acceptable for living on a farm in the middle of winter, so I wouldn't slip on ice and fall on my ass and get hurt.

But another part of me thought he meant it differently: stop being stubborn and give us a chance.

Can't or won't—the answer is the same. Jesse and I can never happen.

TWENTY-ONE

JESSE

On Monday, I texted Hallie asking if she could get Emma off the bus, but I didn't get a response. Instead, an hour later, I got one from my mom, telling me she's on Emma duty that day.

The same happens on Tuesday. I got into an argument with Emma that day about cleaning up after herself, which ended with her slamming her door and not coming out for an hour. After, she apologizes to me tearfully, and we sit on the couch to watch a movie together.

I'm a glutton for punishment, saying *"fine"* when she picks *In a New York Minute.*

I don't see Hallie on Wednesday or Thursday. On Friday, I got a text from my sister saying she's picking Emma up from school to spend the afternoon together. For a moment, I think maybe Hallie is meeting them there, but when I drive past her place on the UTV and see her car in the same place it had been all week, I assume that's not the case.

I fucked up.

I got angry, and then I pushed too hard, too fast, when I needed to go slow, to ease her into the idea of giving this a chance between us.

Despite what she wants me to believe, I don't think she's as opposed to the idea of us being together as she wants me to believe she is; she's just absolutely terrified for some reason. In fact, on Friday, there was a moment where she almost said yes, almost took the plunge, and then thought better of it. I've gone over it a dozen times, trying to understand, but haven't been able to figure out where I went wrong. And without that knowledge, I can't figure out what to do next.

I get home late, spending more time out on the farm this week than I have in a while, trying to keep myself distracted, so when I make it home, Wren already has Emma in bed.

"How was she?" I ask quietly, assuming Emma is probably still reading in her bed, and my sister shrugs.

"A little moody."

"It's been a pattern this week," I say with a deep sigh, running a hand over my face.

"Hallie said she was fine when she was watching her." I shrug as if I didn't notice it, though I did. And I've noticed the stark difference now that Hallie isn't here again and how she seems to have reverted to her earlier attitude. She might be feeding off of my own shitty mood, but either way, without Hallie around, the house is far less peaceful.

"Maybe she was being extra good for her. I have no idea."

"Or maybe she just really likes her, and they get along," Wren says, and I shrug as if that never crossed my mind. "Maybe she's acting out because she misses her."

"Yeah, well, Hallie's been busy." My sister looks at me skeptically, head tipping to the side as she leans her ass on the table, crossing her arms on her chest. I try not to pay attention to her, knowing that look is her assessing one, the one she gives parents and students alike when she thinks they're not being entirely truthful.

"Is there something going on with you two?" she asks, tipping her head to the side.

"No. Why?" I quickly respond. Probably too quickly, if I'm being honest.

"Uh, because that was weird as could be at The Mill?"

"I acted the same way I would if you brought Adam home and I could tell he was a fuckwad."

Wren's nose scrunches up, annoyance taking over her face before she sighs and confesses.

"Don't tell her because she's really mad at you and wouldn't want to hear it, but Adam said the same thing."

I nod. "That's because Adam's a good guy with a brain in his head." Relief washes over me as she seems to accept my statement, standing and shaking her head.

"You three are miserable."

I shrug and don't speak, not even as she stares at me, waiting for me to crack. Unfortunately, while Wren is good at guilting people into talking, she was taught by our mother, whom I have also learned to shield myself from.

Eventually, she sighs and stands. "Anyway, I should get home."

I nod with relief, then walk my sister out and head back inside, checking the fridge for dinner and grabbing a leftover container from the freezer. I don't let myself think too hard about the fact that it's a meal Hallie and Emma made together, or that Hallie had the foresight to make individual portions with the leftovers and freeze them for later.

I eat standing, straight out of the microwaved container, as I move through the house, cleaning up a bit and tidying up things before heading to my room for the night. As I'm wiping the counter, the light on Emma's phone flashes from where it's charging on the kitchen counter with a new text from *Mommy*. When I catch the first few words, I groan, then open the text, the dread sinking deeper as I scroll to the top of the most recent conversation with her mom.

> Hey, baby! I want to throw you a birthday
> party this year with a bunch of your friends!
> I'm going to rent a bunch of hotel rooms.
> How many friends do you think you'd like?
> What about a theme?

I groan, wishing I had seen this earlier so I could fucking *delete* it, but Emma already responded with a dozen exclamation points and three GIFs of dancing cats, then told her ten friends would be good. They've gone back and forth a few times with dates, with both the weekend before and after her late March birthday in the running.

If it were anyone else, I'd think it was just a kind gesture, but with Kim, I always mentally prepare for things to fall through. I think sometimes she genuinely has good intentions, but when kids are involved, you can't just run on good intentions, especially not when the chances of her actually following through with this party are slim to none. This is exactly what I feared when I realized Kim and Emma would have a direct line to one another, without me as a buffer to filter out the chaos and protect her from disappointment.

Mentally, I plan to call Kim sometime this week to see just how real these plans are and to try to come up with a way around it—how to plan a party for Emma without stepping on toes. I sigh, marking the message as unread for Emma to see in the morning and closing out of the screen, and I'm about to shut it down when I spot another name on the message screen: Hallie.

Hallie's been ignoring me for the past week since our blowup, but thankfully, she hasn't been ignoring Emma, who has been texting her nightly.

I hesitate for only a moment before opening the conversation thread. It's not something I usually do. Emma has never done anything to make me feel like she doesn't deserve privacy or trust, but seeing Hallie's name is like a beacon I can't resist.

I find myself smiling at the incredibly wholesome conversations about hair and makeup, and music. Emma sent her a couple of pictures this past week, and Hallie sent her one of the deer she must have taken.

Can we have a girls' day again?

Absolutely. We'll set something up with Wren.

Can you have dinner at my house again soon?

That answer took a bit longer to come, and when it did, it was less promising.

We'll see. Did you do your homework yet?

As I scan over their conversation, it's clear Hallie's been keeping tabs on Emma's life, asking about tests and girl drama that I skim over, not wanting to learn anything my daughter hasn't told me about, but with each conversation, my heart warms in my chest and the realization hits yet again, though this time it settles even deeper.

Hallie is perfect for me.

She's not just perfect for me, but perfect for *us,* for this tiny family Emma and I have.

I want Emma to have this—to have Hallie, a woman who, unlike anyone else in her life, understands what she's going through and the complicated relationship with her mother and could probably hold her hand through it all.

Despite what she wants to believe, Hallie belongs here.

TWENTY-TWO

I haven't seen Jesse for two weeks.

In my defense, I don't *usually* see Jesse that often, but now that I'm living on the King farm, it seems a bit more inevitable. Unless, of course, you're avoiding him.

Which I am.

I feel bad, knowing from Wren that Emma's been acting out a bit more over the past two weeks, but it's what I need to be doing right now to protect my sanity and my heart.

But two weeks and a day after the night at The Mill, my phone rings as I'm folding laundry, and when I see Emma's smiling face on the screen, my brow furrows. She texts me occasionally but never calls me. Quickly, I tap the screen and cradle the phone between my ear and shoulder as I answer.

"Hey, girl, what's up?"

"Hallie?" she says, and pain lances through me at the realization of how much I miss her.

"Yeah, babe?"

"It's Emma."

I let out a small laugh. "Got that. You need something?" There's a moment of silence that sits uneasy with me, and I drop the shirt in my hands, giving the conversation all of my attention.

"I...I need help." Her voice is shaky, and she sniffs like she's been crying for a bit, and panic takes over, my mind going through a million and seven different outcomes while I try to remain calm.

"Okay. Where are you? Are you safe?" That's when she starts to cry, delicate sniffles and tiny whimpers that tug at strands in my heart. "Emma, are you okay? Are you safe? Are you hurt?" She sniffs again, but relief floods me when she finally responds.

"I'm, I'm okay. I'm at home. I just don't know what to do." Her voice breaks, a squeak coming through the line. My brow furrows as I check the clock. It's eleven on a Saturday—Jesse should also be home. Why is she— "I could ask Dad, but he's a boy. We learned about it in school, but they said it would happen in a few years, and none of my friends have gotten it." Understanding slams into me, grief riding its tail. "And it hurts, and I don't know what I should do, and I don't have anything and, and, and—"

I can sense her spiraling, and I take in a deep breath and nod, even though she can't see it, before sitting on the edge of my bed. My pulse is pounding with nerves, but I try to calm myself.

She needs that from me.

Emma just got her period, and she's upset.

Emma, who lives with her dad and rarely talks to her mother, just got her period for the first time.

And for some reason I don't quite understand, she called me.

I don't ask any other questions.

Instead, I stand, nodding again as if she can see, and start making a list in my mind.

"I'll be there in five minutes, okay?"

"Thanks, Hallie," she whispers, and the relief and gratitude are clear in those words.

"Any time. Hang tight, I'm on my way."

I don't even knock when I get to Jesse's front door, and I'm relieved when the door opens easily, though that feeling is gone in a moment when Jesse's booming voice reaches my ears. I move toward the sound quickly.

"Emma, open the goddamn door," he says, looking at his feet as he stands at Emma's door, hands on his hips.

"Go away!" Emma calls through the door, her voice full of frustration and tears. It breaks something in me, and in a few steps, I have a hand on Jesse's shoulder, tugging him to face me. He jolts with shock as he looks down at me, forehead furrowing.

"What are you—"

"You gotta go," I say, putting a hand to his back and pushing him away from her door, but he doesn't move, the giant lug.

"What the—?"

"I said, you have to go." I tip my head toward the front door, and he looks at me in utter frustration and exasperation, but I don't have the time or energy to deal with him and his ego.

"This isn't the time for your games. Hal, seriously."

"I know, which is why you have to go."

"Hallie—"

I sigh, grabbing his wrist and tugging him away from the door, where a scared eleven-year-old girl is most definitely listening to this conversation, and dragging him toward the kitchen.

"Hallie, what—"

"Jesse, you're a great dad. The best, really, but you are not what she needs right now." He opens his mouth to argue, but I break the news to him. "She called me." That silences him, and I take a deep breath before spitting the news out. "She got her period," I say low, and in a moment it's all written over his face in heartbreaking detail.

Confusion, followed by understanding.

Understanding morphing into hurt.

Hurt moving into pain.

Pain turning into acceptance.

His eyes shimmer with tears right before he closes them and whispers a low, quiet, "*Fuck.*"

A single word saying so much.

Fuck, my baby is growing up.

Fuck, she didn't tell me, or maybe *fuck*, she didn't feel comfortable enough to tell me.

Fuck, I'm ill-equipped to handle things.

Without thinking, I reach up, resting a hand on his cheek, and his eyes open again, hazel eyes I've seen so many times over my entire life, but somehow, in this moment, they look brand new. Open, unshielded. Terrified and trusting and confused.

My Jesse.

In another world, this would be my Jesse.

"I've got it," I whisper.

"She called you," is all he says, and I nod.

"She called me, and I've got her. She's scared and going through a lot right now. Go. Go to Madden's, work, hang with your dad, go to The Mill, go distract yourself. Honestly, I don't care what you do, so long as you're not here. Nat's on standby to bring me anything I need. I've got it."

"Nat? Not Wren?"

I smile at him, letting my thumb move over his high cheekbone as I watch him wistfully, his light scruff scratching at my thumb.

"I love Wren to pieces, but if she wanted Wren, she'd call Wren. If she's up for it, we can have a girls' day with Aunt Wren tomorrow, but right now, I'm not bringing anyone she hasn't explicitly invited here, and if I call Wren, she'll be well-meaning, but she'll want to stay." A look of understanding passes over his face, followed quickly by appreciation.

His arm moves, pulling me into him, and I let him, mostly because of the soul-deep sigh that escapes his chest when he does—a shaky sound that tells me this impacts him more than he knows what to do with. When he pulls back, he looks down at me, and I look up at him, taking in his handsome face and forcing myself to remember that there's a little girl in the other room scared out of her mind because of the changes she's experiencing.

"I've got this," I whisper, patting his cheek. He stares for another moment before another sigh leaves his lips, though this one is different, pained, but in a disappointed way.

"I want to kiss you right now," he whispers, and even though I want to argue with him, even though I should argue with him, I don't.

Partially because, while I managed to find the willpower to walk away that night after a long, emotional day and avoid him for the past two weeks, now that he's here before me, staring down at me with his guard absolutely obliterated, I can't exactly say I don't want him to kiss me.

Instead, I stay on the topic at hand.

"I've got this," I say, a small smile on my lips, before I tip my chin toward the front door. "Go."

He stares another moment before nodding, and I drop my hands, expecting him to step back, but he doesn't. Instead, he bends, dipping to press a soft kiss to the top of my head. He holds it for a moment before he whispers, "Thank you," there. Then he lets me go and turns, grabbing his phone, keys, and jacket before making his way out the door.

I stand there in shock for a moment before I remember what's important right now, then turn on my heel, moving back toward Emma's door and knocking gently.

"Hey, Emma? It's me, Hallie," I say against the door, my hand on the stiff handle. "Can you unlock the door for me?" I hear a sniffle and feel a click under the cool doorknob before I turn it, and she's moving away to sit on the floor beside her bed. Her eyes are red from crying, her long hair pulled into a bun on the top of her head, and she's still in her pajamas, despite it being lunchtime.

"Is my dad still here?" I shake my head.

"I had him leave. I figured you'd want to be alone for a bit." She nods, and I move to sit on the floor next to her. I'm not sure what to do here. I never had to help a girl through her first period, but Mrs. King helped me through mine, so I pull from that.

I remember sniffling in a school bathroom stall, and Wren finding me there, asking what was wrong. When I told her, she nodded, then called her mom, who picked both of us up for the day. My mom had left barely six months earlier, and my dad and brother were so ill-equipped to help, but it didn't matter. I had Mrs. King. Wren wouldn't get her period for another two years, but when she did, Mrs. King pulled both of us out of school, and we repeated the process with Wren.

"How do you feel?"

She looks at me, those big eyes watering again.

"Terrible."

I let out a light chuckle, then put my arms out to her. "Come here, babe."

Instantly, she does, moving to my side and letting me hold her, and she feels so much younger than she actually is right now.

"I was so excited because everyone says it's this big moment, but this sucks."

"Yeah, well, welcome to the next thirty years, at least." Her head snaps back to look at me with horror, and I bite back a laugh, cutting through the heaviness of the moment. "But don't worry. I'm here to help."

The afternoon went as well as one could expect, with a few tears, a lot of junk food, and some female bonding. I've made sure to send Jesse a text about once an hour to keep him in the loop and reassure him that she's safe, without sharing too much information. Hours later, Emma and I are sitting on the couch in pajamas, watching another Mary-Kate and Ashley movie she requested, when I finally get the nerve to ask her.

"Hey, Emma?" I ask.

"Yeah?" She's happier now as we sit on the couch, in full veg-out mode. For dinner, we had a Chinese food takeout extravaganza, ordering way too much, though I know the leftovers won't go to waste. I've seen how much Jesse can eat, and if he doesn't want it, I can probably tell Madden there's leftover up for grabs at his brother's place, and it will be gone in an hour.

Nat, being the best, even brought a tiny cake with *Welcome to Womanhood!* written on the top that made Emma laugh. With her permission, I texted Wren an hour ago to update her, and we made plans to have another girls' day tomorrow at Wren's place.

"Why'd you call me?" I ask finally. There's a pause, and her face loses some color, so I quickly add, "Not that I'm complaining, of course. I'm honored. I'm just wondering. Your aunt would drop everything to be here, and your grandma was just as close." Her eyes are locked on the bowl of candy before her, her fingers move through wrapped packages as if looking for something, but clearly she's buying time before she finally speaks.

"You don't treat me like a baby, for one," she says, and I can tell she's giving me the easy answer first. "Aunt Wren is the best, obviously. But she's Aunt Wren. She babies *everyone.*" I let out a little laugh in agreement. "And Grandma, she's great, but I'm her baby's baby."

I nod, understanding in part, but not in total.

Until she says her following words.

"You get it. You're...you're like me." An arrow pierces my heart with her words.

"Like you?" I ask, but I already know before she says her next words.

"You get what it's like, not having a mom."

The breath leaves my lungs.

"Well, honey, you know," I start, unsure of what to say because every variation of words that could leave my lips feels...wrong. The truth is, Emma and I are much more alike than I'd like, not because she's not the most amazing, gorgeous, cool girl I've ever met, and it's an honor to be like her, because she is, but because I don't want that for her.

Both of our moms left, though I was lucky enough, if you want to call it that, to have the illusion of a perfect family for my first ten years.

In contrast, Emma's mom was in the picture for just a few years that Emma probably doesn't even remember before she told Jesse that she didn't want to be a full-time mom, instead wanting to follow her dream of being a model or singer or actress—honestly, I can't really remember, mostly because I don't care—and leaving Jesse full custody of their daughter. And just like my mom in the first few years after she left, Kim occasionally makes plans to see Emma, but, more often than not, backs out at the last minute with some elaborate excuse as to why she can't come.

"You didn't have a mom to help you through this, either. You get it." She says it with cheer instead of the sadness I feel settling in my chest, and I force myself to mirror it.

She doesn't have to know what I'm thinking or how it clearly isn't weighing on her in the same way.

"Well, I'm honored you called me, Emma. And any other time you need something, I'm your girl." She gives me her soft Emma smile, then nods.

"Yeah. I know."

Emma then turns back to the movie and starts chomping on chips, but all I can think about is just how right it feels to be back here.

TWENTY-THREE

JESSE

"Everything okay?" my dad asks when I walk into his office, brows furrowed, the lines deep from years of my siblings and I putting him through the wringer. I rarely show up unannounced on a Saturday, much less go right to his office rather than go bug my mom for food or a babysitting favor, so he knows something is off.

I sigh, running a hand over my hair as I try to sort through a million and seven thoughts, all of them conflicting and new and uncomfortable.

Emma locking herself in her room.

Emma calling Hallie.

Emma getting her period, which, in the grand scheme, I know was to be expected, but it still feels like it came out of nowhere, this moment where my kid is no longer my little girl.

And, of course, Hallie.

My girl called Hallie.

My girl called *Hallie.*

I think if I were someone else, I could get jealous of that, of her turning to someone else during a moment of vulnerability, especially since Emma has always been *mine*. But Emma called Hallie, and it made sense, in a way.

She's as attached to the woman as I'm realizing I am.

"Emma got her period," I say low before thinking that I should keep that to myself. It's Emma's story to share, or not if she chooses, but when a look crosses my dad's face, a mix of understanding and solidarity, I remember that he's been here and had to watch his own little girl grow up.

"Who's with her? Wren?"

I shake my head, then sit in the chair across from him, sinking in.

"She called Hallie."

I expect him to be confused. To ask a question. Something. *Anything*, because when I realized my daughter called Hallie this afternoon, I was all of those things.

But as it seems to be my dad's way, he confuses me.

"Makes sense." I shouldn't be surprised. My dad's always been able to see what I couldn't long before I could. Silence spans between us before he speaks again. "How's it going with her?"

"Emma?"

"No, Hallie."

I tip my head to the side. "I don't—"

"Oh, come on, Jess. You two have been inseparable for the last few weeks. So, how's it going with her?"

I sit forward, putting my elbows on my knees, head in my hands, and groaning aloud before I speak. "It's going terrible. She hasn't talked to me in two weeks." My dad chuckles, and when I look up, he's thoroughly entertained by my current misery.

"Does this have anything to do with you having a throwdown at The Mill?" I sit up then, glaring. Before I can ask, he continues. "Your brother's a bigger gossip than any of the old women in town."

I roll my eyes, shake my head, and rest my head on the back of the chair.

"We got close when Wren was in Paris," I say.

"Figured that. Your mom thought her moving in might help things along."

"Help things along?" I ask, confused.

"Oh, your mom's been waiting years for this, for one of you boys to make Hallie a King." My jaw tightens at the memory that I thought she wanted Madden, but he corrects me quickly. "It became clear to me it would be you when she was twenty, or maybe twenty-two, but your mom is convinced she knew when Hallie was fifteen."

"I was twenty when Hal was fifteen," I say, in disbelief, but my dad just lifts a shoulder.

"I don't question your mom's ways, kid. You'll learn that one day. You hit a point, your wife says something, and you say, *Sounds good, dear*."

With his words, my mind doesn't go to some far-off wife I might have one day, but to Hallie, and the idea of telling her *sounds good, dear*. She'd probably roll her eyes and smack me upside my head, thinking I was being sarcastic with her.

I smile at the image, and Dad laughs.

"See, she wasn't wrong."

I try to figure out what to say, moving between wanting to keep everything to myself and wanting to have someone to talk to about this finally. I settle somewhere in the middle.

"Yeah, well, we had a moment," I say, and try to move past it quickly. "And we thought we could keep it casual."

"Never works," my dad says with a laugh.

"I thought I could handle it, but then Wren started trying to set her up on dates." Dad's head nods, knowing where this was going. "I kind of crashed their date, as you know. After, she stormed over to my house and yelled at me, which I deserved, even if I'd do it again." It's a strange feeling, knowing I was an ass but not being sorry about it. "Then I kind of confessed I didn't want to be just friends." I groan, remembering that night, how I pushed her too far, too fast. "She hasn't talked to me in two weeks. Today was the first time she came to see Emma."

My dad stares at me for long moments, reading me, taking me in before speaking.

"So, what's the problem? Go get her. Make her yours. The two of you were meant to be together. Hell, the only thing that makes that clearer is the connection she and Emma clearly have." At the very least, it's good to know other people see it—that I'm not deluding myself in ideals and what I want.

"She doesn't want a relationship," I explain, and Dad lets out a laugh.

"I'm sure she tells herself that."

"What do you mean?"

He sighs, the kind I heard a ton as a kid when he thought I was being too stubborn or irritating or frustrating, before he looks at me sternly.

"Hallie went through a lot as a kid—her mom leaving, her dad leaving the second he got a chance. She clung to this family as if it were a lifeline. You gotta hold that woman with kid gloves, Jess. Give her time. Don't rush her, don't scare her. Just be there, giving her what she needs a little at a time. Make her feel safe, make her feel loved. That's all she wants."

I sit with his words, seeing the truth in them, and trying to understand what that means for me. Before I can ask anything else, though, we're interrupted by my mom calling for lunch, somehow knowing I was here. We don't talk about Hallie again, even though I spent the rest of the day at my parents' house. The entire time, my dad's words move around me, swirling with ideas, thoughts, and realizations.

One way or another, I have to make Hallie feel safe enough to give us a shot.

I don't return to my house until I get the *all clear* from Hallie that Emma had gone to bed, happy and healthy, and even then, I stay at my parents' place for another thirty minutes. I'm nervous as all get-out when I walk home, my new plan formulating in my mind: be firm, don't let her run, but don't rush her. Let her take the reins, but make sure she's listening to her heart, not her fear.

Easy enough.

BREAK

When I walk through the door of my home, my heart moves into my chest, seeing Hallie curled up on my couch. I have to slide my hands into my pockets to remind myself of my mission, of moving slow and giving her space, because when I see her, I just want to hold her.

"How is she?" I ask softly.

She sits up and gives me a soft look. "She's good. Asleep. She ate a lot of junk, but I figured today was kind of a pass. There's more left-over Chinese in the fridge than either of you can probably eat, but she seemed okay by the end of the night. I got her everything she needs, and...yeah." I stare at her, her eyes that pretty grass color, the freckles across her nose barely visible in the dim room.

"Thank you," I whisper. A beat passes, her eyes meeting mine, a patient and kind smile tipping up the edges, and without meaning to, I move closer, a step, then two.

"Anything for her," she whispers. "You know that."

I nod, and then she bites her lip, looking over my shoulder toward the door.

"I should probably go—" she says, starting to get up, but I step closer to her, putting a hand to her waist and pulling her to me. She doesn't push me away, though. Instead, she rests her head on my chest, a soft sigh leaving her lips as if she can't resist giving herself this one small moment of peace.

I know the feeling.

"Stay," I say, and her head tips up to look at me. The shield is gone, the same as it was that Friday night, and it's all there: fear and trepidation and need and desire and, buried beneath all of it, love.

She's so fucking mine, and she doesn't even know it. Or she does and doesn't know what to do with it.

"Jesse—"

"I just found out my only child is no longer a little kid. Please. Stay with me for a bit." She hesitates for a bit, looking over my face, and she must see something there that makes her sigh, then agrees, stepping back and sitting on the other side of the couch from where I settle.

"Thank you. For coming today. I know..." I take in a deep breath, trying to find the right words, but I just go with my gut, throwing elegance to the side. "I know I fucked up that night. I got jealous, I got mean, I let my emotions win. We..." I shake my head, not wanting to say that night was a mistake, not wanting to give her that line to move forward with, not if I'm going to take my dad's advice and move with kid gloves, but still move *with* her. "Thank you for being there for her even when you have all the right in the world to be mad at me."

A soul-deep sigh leaves her chest, and she shakes her head after a moment. "I'm not mad at you, Jesse."

I raise an eyebrow at her.

"You're sitting on the other side of the couch from me." She sighs, rolling her eyes, and I have to tell my heart to calm down as it flutters with hope as she shifts, closing the gap between us until it's barely a foot.

"Better?"

"You have no idea," I say.

She smiles, then shakes her head before continuing, something I have to interpret as a good thing.

"I'm not mad at you. I'm...confused. I feel lost."

"Why?" I expect her to brush past it, but as seems to be her way, she surprises me, giving me more, and I'm filled with relief that she's *talking*.

"Because...when this started, I knew what I was getting into. I knew what to expect. One night, and then I'd move on with my life. One fun night and then back to normal." We were delusional to think that was feasible, to believe we could ever go back to *the way things were*. That was assuming there wasn't an *us* before, but we were something long before that night. We just hadn't added the physical complication yet. "We had a deal. We had a plan. We had rules."

"Rules were meant to be broken," I say.

"Not rules like that."

"Why not?" She doesn't answer, and I reach out for her hand, holding it in mine across the small gap between us. The touch grounds me, and I continue. "Why can't we break those rules, Hallie? What makes them different?"

She hesitates, opening her mouth, then closing it, so close to confessing the truth before she chooses a different route.

"Because you don't even date! The rules were in place because you don't date. I can't get tangled up in fairy tales when you don't even want someone right now."

"You're right. I don't want to date you," I say, and disappointment flashes on her face before it's buried once again under indignation.

"See! Exactly, that's why we—"

"I don't want to date you, Hallie, because I want to start forever with you. I think we're well past dating and getting-to-know-yous, don't you?"

Her face drops, confusion taking over.

"What are you...?" There's a hesitation as her eyes scan my face, and what she sees there—the sincerity and the fact that I'm dead fucking serious—has her eyes widening. "No. No. We can't."

"We can, Hallie I—"

"*I* can't. And you can't throw around ideals and promise me forever, because forever doesn't exist. It's all a myth, and I know...I *know* if I believed in a forever with you and it fell apart, I could never come back from that," she says, tears brimming.

"Hallie," I start, shifting closer and squeezing her hand. "I know you're worried about Wren, but I promise, she'd be thrilled, she—" She stands then, shaking her head, and I see what I didn't before: the utter panic written across her face as she lifts her hands in the air.

"No, you don't get it. You don't *get* it, Jesse. You're amazing, and that night was the best of my life. I haven't been able to stop thinking about it, trust me." A prideful smile tips at my lips, and despite her emotional turmoil, she rolls her eyes. "But I can't let a single moment of good make me lose everything."

"How would you and I, trying to make a go of things, ruin everything?" I'm using the soft voice I use with Emma when I'm trying to reel her in and speak rationally and calmly and with kindness. Kid gloves that, in any other situation, Hallie would absolutely hate, but she's so lost, she doesn't. Instead, she stops her pacing and looks at me with wide, apologetic eyes that cut me to my core.

"Because if something goes badly, I lose it all." Her voice cracks, and I open my mouth to speak, but she continues before I can, almost frantically. "That's how it works, Jesse! Every time someone gets the opportunity to leave me, they do. It's happened with friends and boyfriends. It happened with my mom and my dad. The only people I have left are Colton and your family." Pain, sharp and hot, slices through me, bringing understanding on its heels, but she keeps going, resolution on her face as she shakes her head.

"You have all of this, and you always will. That's a guarantee. Your family will always be there and love you no matter what. You could fuck it up to hell and back, and they'd still be there. In a way, I have them too—your family as mine—but I don't have the same guarantee. One bad move and it's gone. If we tried and it failed, you'd get them."

Suddenly, it clicks into place with a heartwrenching understanding. This is the missing piece, what my dad either wouldn't share or couldn't fully grasp, laid out before me: how deep Hallie's hurt and fear go.

She continues, oblivious to my revelation.

"They would be nice about it, of course, and pretend it was fine. I'd still be invited to family dinner, and I'd be involved, but I couldn't put them through that awkwardness of trying to appease both of us. It wouldn't be fair. I'd stay away, then fade away, and then it would be gone. I'd rather have Wren and your family and Emma and you from a safe distance than try this, fuck it up, and lose it all. That might be a risk you're willing to take, but I'm not."

It's the most honest reaction I've seen from carefully constructed Hallie, the one who puts up her tough, fun-loving, easy-going front. A front she's erected as a defense mechanism, a safety net to keep people in her life for fear they'll run from the mess of emotions she harbors beneath.

I've never seen her more beautiful.

But with the look and her confession comes a sharp understanding.

It's not just Hallie being stubborn or worried.

This is Hallie, absolutely *terrified.*

It's not about giving Wren hope that Hallie doesn't want to get her hung up on.

It's not about my not dating.

It's not even about messing with Emma's head, I don't think.

It's about losing the safe space that my family has given her over the years.

I was wrong all those weeks ago in thinking she couldn't be or wouldn't want to be tied down with a premade family. The truth is that Hallie plays flighty and fun and no-strings attached because she's terrified of hoping for stability. For family. For love.

She's never had anyone in her life show her unconditional love, other than her brother and my family. Love has always come with those conditions, starting with her mother's leaving. Coming to the realization and understanding that I would do anything to stop her from feeling that panic, but knowing I can't fix it—at least, not right away—is nearly suffocating.

Forcing her hand will only push her further away, so instead, I'm going to play reverse psychology on my sweet girl.

"Okay," I say, and she stops pacing, her brow furrowing. I force myself not to smile.

"Okay?"

"Okay. I get where you're coming from. Now sit so we can finish our movie."

"I don't know if it's—"

"Jeeze, Hal," I say, reaching up, wrapping my fingers around her wrist, and tugging until she's stumbling to the couch, sitting next to me. As much as I want to pull her into my lap and hold her there until I get my fill, I sit her next to me, then turn to face her. I don't resist the urge to reach up, though, to tuck a strand of hair behind her ear, to reveal the row of glittering earrings and her pretty green eyes I could drown in.

"I get it now. I get where you're coming from." I don't tell her that I don't really care where she's coming from, that I'm going to continue to push for what I know we both want, what we both need, but I'm going to do it with care. "Stop avoiding me, Hallie," I whisper, and to my own ears, it sounds like a plea.

It is one, really.

"I wasn't—"

"I was an ass. I'll give you that. I was way out of line, but I'm trying to battle with all of this. You, me. Things I don't think either of us is ready to look closely at yet." She opens her mouth to argue, but I keep going. "I should have kept my mouth shut, and I'm sorry for that. I was an ass."

"This is complicated," she conceded, and it feels like a confession.

"The best things always are," I murmur, and I believe that to my core. It's the wrong thing, though, something I know when her face goes hard again.

"Jesse—"

Shaking my head, I shift so we're not so close, so the temptation of kissing her isn't as obvious, so we're sitting next to one another, facing the TV.

"Another day. Today was a long one." She looks at my profile, and I watch the two tween girls on the screen, pretending like I'm not fully in tune with her every move, every gesture. Finally, she sighs, then turns back to the movie, and something in me eases.

"And I'll give you all the time you need, but only if you stop avoiding me like the plague. My sister is starting to get suspicious."

It's a low blow, but it does what it needs to, so she nods, taking in a deep breath.

"Okay," she murmurs, and her head drops to my shoulder.

It's not much—nothing, really, in the grand scheme of what I'm realizing I want with her—but it's enough.

I convince her to stay for another hour before she yawns, and despite myself, I sigh and tell her she should get home. In a perfect world, I'd say *fuck it* and convince her to sleep in my bed or with me on the couch, but that's not for today.

Today is for baby steps.

So instead, I walk her to the door. When we're at the mudroom, she bends, pulling on and then tying up familiar shoes, the ones I left on her front step last Sunday.

"They fit," I say once she stands, and even in the dim lighting, I catch a blush moving over her cheeks.

"I've worn them every day. Haven't fallen once, to my disappointment." Warmth overtook me at the idea that even when we weren't talking, even when she was so mad and confused, she put those shoes on, and that I was able to keep her safe. "I kind of wanted you to be wrong so I can wear my comfy ones."

I step closer, grabbing her chin between my thumb and pointer finger.

"When you're with me, you can wear the comfy ones. I'll always catch you," I whisper, and I hope she knows I mean more than if she slips on life when her face goes soft. She shifts closer, moving on instinct, I think, a hand going to my cheek, her thumb brushing over my mustache.

"Jesse," she murmurs, and I smile.

"I'm not going to kiss you tonight, Hallie." Confidence moves through me, warm and thick, when a flash of disappointment crosses her face, but my decision is made ironclad when it's quickly covered by relief. "You're not ready for that, so I'll wait."

"You'll wait?"

I shrug.

"The thing about forever is that it'll be there tomorrow," I whisper. When her face goes soft, I know I said the right thing, but I still second-guess my decision not to kiss her; the desire to do so is strong.

But I hold steady, and instead, I pull her into me, holding her there tight in my arms until her body relaxes, until her shoulders soften, and she melts into me. Her arms wrap around my back, and her breathing slows. We might stand there for one minute, we might stand there for ten, but I don't care. I'd stand here all night if I knew she didn't need the sleep.

Regrettably, I step back, then help her slide on her jacket. Reaching over to the bin of winter gear, I grab one of my worn Three Kings beanies and slide it over her head. "You didn't wear a hat over."

"I was kind of in a rush to get her."

That now familiar warmth settles in my chest, and I lean down and press my lips to her forehead.

"Well, you can have mine."

Because *she* is mine.

And as I watch her walk off and then wait for the confirmation text that she made it home safe, I conclude that she came into Wren's life all those years ago so she could be mine one day.

No, not mine—*ours*. Emma's and mine and Wren's and Mom's and Dad's and, fuck, even Madden's.

Because Hallie was born to be a King.

TWENTY-FOUR

JESSE

Hallie's at my place early the next morning to pick up Emma, but she doesn't do more than give me a small smile and a wave before driving off with my girl. Nerves churn in my stomach the entire morning as I try to play it cool despite having no idea where we stand. But when she texts me a selfie of her and Wren, that tension eases.

She's not ignoring me. She's not avoiding me. She's just overwhelmed and unsure.

I can work with this.

She pulls up at four to drop off Emma, but when she hesitates when Emma asks if she's coming inside, I remember my mission. Play it slow. Play it safe. Give her space, but not too much.

"We'll see her in an hour at the family dinner, Em. Let her have some space." Emma glares at me but nods, and when she does, Hallie gives me a relieved look.

"Yeah, I desperately need to wash my hair, Em. It's getting gross." She motions to her head, where her hair is in two French braids.

"Looks good to me," I say, eyes on Hallie. A blush spreads across her cheeks, and I smirk just a bit. But she doesn't look away. She holds my gaze, eyes lighting up with challenge.

God, I'm so gone for this woman.

I tap the top of the car instead of begging her to stay, insisting she showers at my place, preferably with me, and turn to my daughter. "Let's go, Em. Get your things, and let Hallie get ready." Emma nods, slides out of the car, and I wave to Hallie as she drives off.

At family dinner, her hair is freshly washed and down—isn't that strange?—but the fact that she's in a pair of jeans and a sweater rather than a Three Kings sweatshirt and leggings and wearing makeup is. Almost as if she wanted to look good for some reason.

"Hair looks good, Hal," I murmur when she walks into my parents' place. Again, that blush, and this time, it's accompanied by a soft, shy smile.

After my talk with my dad and my admitted tantrum at The Mill, I'm a bit nervous about dinner. I assume everyone understands at this point that there is *something* between Hallie and me, and I don't need them poking and prodding and scaring off Hallie. Thankfully, my entire family also seems to understand the assignment of taking things slow and letting Hallie steer this ship, and doesn't say a single word of teasing or question.

It's further proof that her fears are unfounded. She's so worried about losing them, but I don't think she realizes there is no world where my family would simply let her go. I'm pretty sure they'd get rid of me before they got rid of Hallie at this point; she's such an integral part of this family.

After dinner, Hallie, Emma, and I walk back together, and when we reach my house, I turn to my daughter. "I'm gonna go walk Hallie to her place. Go get your pajamas on, and you can get some screen time."

Emma's eyes light up, and she nods.

"Thanks, Dad!" she says, heading inside at warp speed.

I smile at her predictability and turn to Hallie. "Come on."

"You don't have to—" she starts, and I shake my head. She rolls her eyes but doesn't argue.

As we're walking, I think about how I want to be holding her hand, about how I want to give her a goodnight kiss, and about how I want to drag her inside and do a lot more than kiss.

But I don't. Instead, when we get to her door, we both stop, facing each other. Silence spans between us, and I lift a hand, letting the very tips of my fingers move along her earrings. I like these, Hal. Really pretty." Then the backs of my fingers move down, coasting over the side of her neck, and her breath hitches. I can't help but let the tiniest, teasing smirk play on my lips before I step back. "Are they new?"

"I got them today with Emma and Wren at the mall."

I nod. I wonder if she knows I'm thinking about the sounds she makes when I tug her earrings between my teeth. When her cheeks go pinker, something I know has nothing to do with the cold, I get my answer.

"I like them a lot." We stand there for another moment before I give in. "Anyway. See you tomorrow?" I ask. There's a single moment of hesitation before she nods.

"Yeah. I'll get Emma off the bus. Any dinner requests?"

God, she's so mine.

"Whatever you guys want. I'll make a grocery run in the morning —let me know if you need anything." She nods, then I pull her in for a hug. Her body doesn't tighten as it did yesterday. She takes in a deep breath and just melts as soon as she's in my arms. I hold her for as long as I can without pushing it too far before stepping back, dipping to press my lips to her cheek.

"Night, Hallie. Sweet dreams."

And then I head back home, feeling like the day was a success.

The next night, I managed to convince her to stay for dinner with the help of Emma's pleading. After we're finished eating, I clean up while she helps Emma pick out an outfit for school the next day, but when she steps out and tells me she's going to head home, I nod.

Confusion and surprise cross her face—she's clearly expecting me to argue, which only tells me she doesn't realize my game yet.

"I'll walk you home," I say, calling out to tell Emma what I'm doing, and pleased with the fact that Hallie doesn't argue at all anymore, instead just moving to the mudroom to get her shoes and jacket on.

"Hallie," I murmur when we're halfway to her place, tipping my chin to the woods to see the deer again.

"Jane Doe! How are you?" Hallie says as if she's an old friend. When the deer approaches with zero trepidation, bumping her snout into Hallie's hand, I can't help but shake my head. Only Hallie would make friends with a motherless doe.

Since that day in the woods, I've wondered if Hallie and her deer share some kind of kinship, and the more I think about it and see them together, the more I realize the answer is absolutely yes.

Hallie murmurs and chats with the animal for about a minute before Jane hears something, breathes out a noise that is alarmingly close to a goodbye, and walks off.

"Does that happen often?" I ask once the deer is out of sight and once Hallie moves back to me.

"She comes to my place for snacks. I got her a salt block. We're friends," she says as we start to walk. I let out a small laugh and shake my head, but my chest freezes when our hands bump. With the move, she looks up at me, gives me a tiny, hesitant tilt of her lips, then twines her fingers with mine.

I walk as slowly as I can, wanting to devour the moment, and when we get to her door, I do the same as the night before: a long hug, a kiss to her cheek, and wishing her goodnight.

On Tuesday, Emma convinces Hallie to stay for a movie, and Hallie puts up even less of an argument than she has in the past. It's getting easier to convince her to spend time here, and I wonder if I'm already weakening her walls just a bit, or if she's falling back into comfortable habits.

One movie turns into two, and there's an hour or so left before I send Emma to bed. Once the house is quiet and Emma is in her room, I sit back down on the couch and pat the seat next to me. Hallie eyes it skeptically.

"I should go," she says.

I lift an eyebrow at her. "You're going to make me finish this movie alone?"

"You don't have to—"

"How else am I going to know how their Italian internship goes?" She stares at me like she's not buying it before rolling her eyes and sitting again, but unlike when Emma was here, when she sat on the complete opposite side, my daughter between us, Hallie sits a mere foot from me on the couch. I smile to myself.

Ten minutes later, I move, closing the gap between us, looping an arm around her shoulder, and pulling her into my side.

Ten minutes after that, she shifts, resting her head in my lap, and I run my fingers through her hair, watching her eyes flutter shut as a pleased sigh leaves her lips.

If this were all I got from her for a lifetime, I could be okay with it, but when she speaks after a bit, I know we're easing our way toward more.

"When you said you'd wait..." she starts, then hesitates, unsure of how to continue, but I don't speak or pressure her. My fingers keep moving slowly, waiting for her to finish, and eventually she does. "When you said you'd wait, what did you mean?" I respond with no hesitation.

"I meant that I know in my heart of hearts that you're exactly what I need. What Emma needs. What *we* need. And I know we're what you need. But I'm not in a rush to make that happen, so I'll wait, Hallie."

She doesn't speak again, but she doesn't have to. When I walk her to the door that night, she stands before me, head tipped back, almost like she's waiting for a moment, waiting for me to make a move.

To kiss her, I realize.

I don't.

Instead, I hug her and press a soft kiss to her cheek.

The flash of disappointment that crosses her face feels like the biggest win yet.

This goes on for two more nights before she gets brave. On Friday, when I walk her home, she turns to glare at me, hand on her hips.

"Are you ever going to kiss me?"

I lift an eyebrow at her. "Are you saying you're ready for me to kiss you?"

A blush burns bright on her cheeks. She hesitates, but not for long.

"I mean, a goodnight kiss would be nice."

"You've got the reins, Hallie. You call the shots. If you want a goodnight kiss, ask for one."

She doesn't.

I shouldn't be surprised.

Instead, she moves to her tiptoes and takes one hand on either side of my face and pulls my face to hers. My arms tighten around her, my heart racing as she presses her lips to mine and holds them there for a beat. It's fucking perfect, her soft hands on my cheeks, her lips sliding against mine, her body pressed to me.

I want more, but I don't take it.

When she pulls back, her cheeks are flushed, her pupils are dilated, and her breathing is heavy as if we had made out for an hour, despite it being a chaste kiss. I know the feeling, because I'm breathing similarly.

Kissing Hallie is intoxicating.

She stares at me for a moment, hands still on my face, before she nods, as if she found that acceptable. I bite back a laugh but don't fight off the smile.

"Good night, Jesse," she says.

"Night, Hal."

She bites her lip, then surprises me with another soft, closed-lipped kiss before stepping away and through her door.

On Saturday, I get a text before Emma's up, and the grin that spreads across my face might just light up the entire room.

> Do you have my creamer?

> Yeah, why?

> I'm out. Can I come for coffee?

I'm not sure if she's actually out of her creamer, but in this moment, I do not care. Hallie is initiating contact, coming to my house outside her regular after-school hours on a Saturday, a day when I wasn't sure I'd actually see her.

> Only if you stay for breakfast.

The dots appear and disappear a few times before she replies.

> Do you have bacon?

I don't reply; instead, I send her a picture of the bacon and pancake ingredients.

She's at my door in five minutes, her face fresh and clean without any makeup, her hair in a knot on top of her head. She's in the boots I bought her and a pair of leggings, and when she takes off her jacket, I notice the sweatshirt is the one she stole from me after our night together.

It could be a coincidence, but that's not Hallie's style.

Everything Hallie does has an intention.

"Morning, Hallie," I say with a grin. Her smile returns hesitantly as she walks toward me. She steps close enough so I can smell her toothpaste before hesitating, her tongue coming out to wet her lips.

"Where do we stand on good morning kisses?" she asks low.

I grin.

"Big fan," I whisper, then put a hand to her waist and pull her into me. I kiss her hard, but not deep. No parting of lips, no nipping of teeth. Just her lips on mine, her body pressed tight. Her hands on my neck hold me tight, and when I pull back, she pulls me in again for another, then another. A series of five kisses, as if she can't stop, as if she's trying to sate that need brewing without pushing herself too far. Eventually, she pulls back, and I rest my forehead against hers.

"Morning, Jesse," she whispers.

"Let's get you some coffee, baby," I murmur, and she grins wide.

That night, she stays at my place after Emma goes to sleep, this time watching some comedy that I barely know what is happening in because at some point, we lie down on the couch, her head on my bicep, her back to my front. All I can focus on is her soft, easy breaths, the occasional laugh, and the way it felt to have my entire world happy and safe and under one roof.

When the movie ends, she rolls, turning to face me, lifts a hand to cup my cheek, leans in for a soft, gentle kiss, then pulls away. We lay like that for a while, my hand wrapped around her waist to keep her close, our eyes locked.

"I want to make out with you," she whispers.

"Then do it."

"I don't know if I'm ready for that."

The words sound like a confession of sorts, and I lift a shoulder.

"Then don't. I'm happy just lying here with you."

Again, time passes, and she stares at me, trying to read past the walls that have long since been obliterated, before she speaks.

"You mean that, don't you? Taking things slow, waiting me out?"

"Hallie, if this is all I ever get from you—long nights on the couch and sweet kisses and hearing you laugh—I'd be happy."

Her nose scrunches up. "I wouldn't," she says, and I laugh.

"Good to know. When you're ready for more, let me know. Or take it. I don't care."

Again, she stares, and again, I hold her gaze. Eventually, she nods, believing what she's seeing and what I'm saying, then rests her head on my chest and lies there quietly.

That night, Hallie falls asleep on the couch with me, and even though it's uncomfortable and I have to shake her awake at five to get her out of the house before Emma wakes up, since I know that's what she would want, it's the best night of sleep I've had in weeks.

TWENTY-FIVE

The week after Emma gets her period is everything I didn't know I needed, but I think somehow, Jesse knew. He seems always to know what I need, and if I let myself believe it, I think he's known what I need for some time.

And up until now, that was sweet kisses and nothing more. But by Tuesday, the soft, chaste presses of our lips aren't doing it for me. I think about it the entire night as we watch some movie I can't even pay attention to, Jesse's warm back against mine, his arm looped around me, holding me tight.

I want more.

I need more.

And when I turn in his arms when the movie is over and lie face to face,

"Hey, Jesse?"

"Mmm," he says low, reaching up and pushing some of my hair back over my shoulder in a delicate brush.

Gentle. So, so gentle. He's always so gentle with me, and this past week has shown me that he's not only gentle with his actions but also with his intentions. Gentle so as not to scare me, gentle so as not to push me too far, too fast.

And suddenly, I realize I want more.

"I want you to kiss me," I whisper. He looks at me a bit confused, but then I clarify. "Really kiss me." I lick my lips, and his eyes follow the movement before a low curse escapes his lips, the sound of it resonating right between my legs.

And then his lips are on mine, but not in the safe, sweet way I've become used to. It's heated; his hand is resting in my hair behind my head, using his grip there to position my head where he wants it. His lips move over mine, his tongue wasting no time as it slides along the seam of my lips, requesting entry. I open quickly, and when his tongue touches mine, we both sigh.

Fuck, I missed this. Missed *him*. The taste of him, the way he sounds, the way he feels against me. Every touch sends fire through my veins, and it builds and builds until all that exists in my universe when his lips are on mine is him and me. There are no complications, no fears, no daughter, no family—nothing but Jesse and me.

We kiss like that for long minutes, my heart racing and need building. His hand moves to my hip, gripping tight as if he needs it to keep him tethered to reality, to remember whatever plan or mission he's laid out for himself.

I suddenly want him desperately *un*tethered.

"Jesse," I breathe, needing more. "I need...more."

He groans, his fingers tightening on my hip, and I tighten with anticipation. But instead of getting his hand or literally anything to ease the ache between my legs, I get a soft, sweet kiss, remiss of any fire that was there moments ago.

And then I get cold air as he sits up. I'm appeased just a bit when he reaches down, lifting me from where I'm lying and pulling me to his side, his head going into my neck and breathing me in, but I'm still left reeling by the sudden and abrupt change.

"That's enough for tonight," he says against my skin, leaving goose bumps in its wake, before pulling away like it pains him and turning to the television.

"What?"

"That's enough for tonight."

I shift away to look at him, but his face is locked to the screen as if it's the most interesting thing he's ever seen.

"We don't have to stop," I say, reaching up to cup his cheek and turning his head to look at me. He gives me a soft look, then bends and gives me a sweet, chaste kiss.

"Yes, we do."

I scrunch my nose in irritation, and he laughs, leaning in to kiss the tip of it.

"We're going slow, Hallie."

And it's sweet. So fucking sweet that I can't find it in me to argue, so I smile at him, then snuggle into his side and watch the rest of the movie.

The next night, I find it far less sweet.

Again, we kiss, lying on his couch, making out like teenagers. After long minutes of it, I'm desperate to find some kind of friction to ease the throbbing between my legs. I lift a leg to hook it around his hip, but his palm meets my knee and stops me before I get even the slightest brush of the bulge I felt between us, where I want it.

"Please," I whisper, trying to shift around to get what I want, but his head shakes.

"No, Hallie girl. Not tonight."

"Why not?" I pout.

I *pout*. I'm twenty-seven, lying on Jesse King's couch, making out with him, and I'm pouting because he won't do anything. Hell, I'd take *dry humping* right now.

"Because you're not ready," he murmurs, brushing his fingers along my jaw reverently.

"But I want to do...*something*," I whine.

"And we will. Trust me. When you're ready."

I feel like stomping a foot like a petulant child.

"So you're not going to do anything with me until I'm ready to, what? Tell the world I have the hots for you?"

"If that's the word you want to use, sure."

I scrunch my nose up, and he laughs, then shifts, rolling so I'm on my back, and he's hovering over me. I would say something like, "*Now this is what I'm talking about*," but the look on his face is far too serious for me even to begin to believe he's about to let me ride his thigh, much less anything else.

"I messed up once already with you by moving too fast. I'm not going to risk scaring you off again, Hallie. Try all you want, but I'm not moving any further with you until you feel secure in what we have.'

Again, I want to argue.

But again, his face is so sincere, and his words are so fucking *perfect* that I can't. So instead. I sigh.

"Fine," I grumble. He laughs, shaking his head and giving me a soft kiss. "But I'm not going to make it easy on you."

"You never do. And I wouldn't want it any other way.

On Valentine's Day, even though it's a Saturday, I get to Jesse's place at my normal time for coffee before Emma is even awake. Still, unlike normal, instead of giving me a soft kiss, he drags me into his room, pressing his lips to mine, and makes out with me for a full five minutes before he pulls away, resting his forehead on mine.

"Happy Valentine's Day, Hallie," he says, and I can't help but grin.

"Happy Valentine's Day, Jesse." He steps away then, moving to his bedside table and grabbing a small box before handing it to me. It's light, one of those pre-wrapped boxes, but it's the same: a gift.

A Valentine's Day gift from Jesse Peter King to me, it seems.

"Jesse..." I say, hesitating.

"It's nothing crazy, trust me. Just something I saw and thought you needed."

"It's—"

"Let me have this, Hallie," he murmurs, pressing his lips to mine and pushing the small box into my hands. When I look at him, his face is soft, and I can see it means something to him that I'm accepting this, so I sigh and nod, then open the small box.

Inside are a pair of dainty hoop earrings, silver and gold twisted together in hoops just bigger than huggie earrings. They're simple and beautiful and so very *me*. Because, as he shows me every single day, this man knows me more than anyone ever has in my life.

"I know you switch your earrings often, and you don't stick to just gold or silver, so I thought these would be a good addition—something you could rotate in."

I stare at them, touching the delicate metal gently and wondering why on earth he would think I would be *rotating* these into my earring sets.

These are going to be worn every fucking day of my life.

When I look back up at him, he is looking at me with anticipation, nerves clear. I let him out of his misery. "They're gorgeous, Jesse. Perfect."

"Yeah?"

"Yeah," I say with a laugh, setting the box aside and taking out the small gold hoops from my first hole. I have four on each side, and I've never missed the way Jesse always looks at them, touches them, or, like that one night, tugs them between his teeth. A shiver runs through me before his hand reaches up, replacing mine.

"Can I?"

I nod, then he delicately and tenderly removes the other earring before sliding in the new hoops, clasping them, and reverently rubbing his fingers over the new set. It sends a wave of adoration mixed with need, and even though I know I'll be touching and staring at them all day, I don't need to look at them in the mirror. Not when Jesse is already looking at them like they're the most perfect thing he's ever seen.

"Gorgeous," he says, and then he leans forward and presses his lips to mine in a hot, sweet kiss. Minutes later, I'm gasping, and I know we're running out of time, since Emma will be up soon, and regrettably, I step away.

"Well, this makes my news for you even more awkward."

He lifts his eyebrow at me.

"Are you breaking up with me on Valentine's Day, Hallie?"

"We have to be together to break up." His eyes narrow, thoroughly unentertained by me, and I bite back a smirk. "No, I'm not breaking up with you. But I don't have a gift for you."

"I told you—"

I interrupt him and finish giving him the news.

"But I did plan a daddy-daughter date night tonight with Emma yesterday." He tilts his head, clearly not seeing that coming. "At home. But it means we're kicking you out today. And when you come back, you'll spend the night with Emma." I read him, but he's a blank slate as he stands with his eyes locked on mine. Long moments stretch between us, as does my patience before I finally crack. "Are you...okay with that?" I ask nervously.

"Okay with what?"

"Your day with Emma. I mean, it's Valentine's Day. You got me these." My fingers reach up to touch my new earrings reverently. "And in turn, I set up a whole date for you with someone else." I let out a laugh, and he shakes his head, confusion and awe on his face.

"There are only two people I would want to spend this day with. This year, Emma gets it. This is a gift, Hallie, even if you don't see it. I don't think I have much longer that she'll be willing to have a daddy-daughter date on Valentine's Day."

I understand what he's saying, but I still want to clarify.

"I just...this isn't..." I bite my lip and wait for him to fill in for me, but he doesn't, the infuriating man. "I want you to know this isn't me avoiding you. Or...us."

His eyes light up, and he pulls me in closer.

"That's the real gift, Hallie." I tip my head, not understanding, but before I can ask, he fills in for me. "I think that's the first time you've agreed there's an us," he whispers, breath ghosting over my lips. "That's the best gift I could have gotten today."

I open my mouth to say something, and even though I don't know what I was going to say, I know it's not a denial.

We're long past that.

But my words are cut short when there's a noise down the hall. Emma's door opens, then her feet are padding down the hall to the bathroom, and I step away, quietly following him to the kitchen for coffee.

And we both do so with smiles on our faces.

Unfortunately, it's not just Valentine's Day I don't spend with Jesse, but most of Sunday, the next day. I drop by in the morning for coffee, but soon after, I'm headed to Wren's to decorate. I tried to get her to skip or postpone our annual get-together, since this year she actually had someone to spend the holiday with, but Wren's guilt that we'll feel left out now that she has a man in her life runs deep, and there was no dissuading my stubborn best friend.

Still, Jesse and I text back and forth all day, but when I get to his parents' house, Emma whispers to me that her dad's in a bad mood, something I pick up on quickly. When I first got there, he tugged me into a corner for a quick (sweet, not hot, *ugh*) kiss, so I'm pretty sure he's not mad at me. He also seems to find every opportunity to casually touch me or talk to me, almost like he's grounding himself with my presence. But after dinner, we're all in the den when Jesse gets a call and abruptly stands, heading outside.

I wait a few minutes, but when he doesn't return, I quietly go to find him. I make it outside just in time to see him grab a small planter that holds marigolds in the summer and toss it, hitting a tree. The terracotta shatters impressively.

"Pretty good aim," I say with a raised eyebrow. He turns to me, then sighs. "Everything okay out here?" He glares at me, and I bite back a smile. "Your mom really liked that planter, you know?"

"I'll get her a new one."

I nod, then sit on the edge of the patio table with my arms crossed on my chest, watching as Jesse paces back and forth.

"You gonna tell me why you're murdering perfectly innocent planters?"

"Kim canceled."

My heart drops at the disappointment that's about to hit Emma, but I resolve to fix it.

"Okay, so I'll do another girls' day. No big—"

"She canceled her fucking birthday party." The small bit of hope I'd fostered dies out, and anger floods my veins. He sees it on my face and nods before explaining. "She texted me this morning with some big tale, I don't know. I didn't even bother to read it, but she said she wasn't going to be able to be there for the party. Stupid of me to hope she wouldn't be a fucking cunt."

He sounds so angry, and the worst part is knowing it's not only at Kim, who is the only person who deserves his wrath right now, but at himself for falling for it. "Kim gave her invites and everything to give to her friends. Said she was renting her hotel rooms for a big sleepover, making a big thing out of it. I didn't think to double-check..."

My stomach sinks at his words, remembering Emma telling me she has a big birthday sleepover next weekend. I never got around to asking Jesse about it or how I could help, but now I'm thinking I should have.

"Right after she texted me, I called up the hotel in town she said she had booked rooms in, and I was waiting for them to give me info on what was already planned. They called to tell me that not only did

Kim never book the rooms she told Emma she was reserving, but the hotel is fully booked now, so *I* can't do it."

I step closer, unsure of what to do or how to help. The only thing I'm sure of is that I want to touch him, so I do that, closing the gap and placing a hand on his chest. He looks down at me with forlorn eyes and shakes his head.

"I should have fucking known. I should have *known* not to trust it. But she can be so convincing when she wants to be." He lets out a sad laugh. "I really thought that this *one time* she'd be there for her."

The hopelessness in his voice pulls me into him. When I do, he crushes me to him, burying his face in my neck. My mind is reeling as I try to piece things together and formulate a plan, caught between wanting to track down Kim and get into a fistfight with her.

"I'm so fucking tired of this, Hal," he says into my neck. His voice cracks, and it pulls at something in me as I rub his back, biting back my own emotions. He needs a safe place to vent to, and I'm determined to be that for him.

"I know, babe."

"It's so unfair to her. She deserves...fuck. She deserves better. It's my fault."

I shake my head, putting my hands to his cheeks, forcing his head off my shoulder to look up at me.

"No. No, Jesse. It's not. It's hers. She's a fucking bitch, a waste of space who doesn't deserve to be in the same stratosphere as Emma, but that isn't anyone's fault but hers."

He pulls back, eyes pained as he takes in a deep breath. The anger is gone from his face, leaving disappointment and sadness.

"How am I going to break it to her?"

Now it's my turn to step in when he needs me, just like he did for me the day he found me in the woods.

"I'll handle that. Do we have the info for the girls who are supposed to be coming?"

Jesse nods. "I got the RSVPs since I knew they wouldn't want to agree to a sleepover with a relative stranger. I'd planned to spend the

night in the same hotel. The only reservation they *did* have on file,"
he grumbles. I ignore the irritation and instead nod.

"Okay. I've got it. Sometime tonight or tomorrow, call them all
and tell them the party will be at your parents' house," I start.

"Hallie—"

"Wren and I have done this a dozen times. Trust me when I say,
we've got this. We will make this the best sleepover any of them has
ever had. Just get me the date and time, and we've got the rest."

He stares at me for a moment.

"You'd do that for me?"

I shrug and let a small smile tilt my lips, a moment of sunshine in
this shitty hurricane.

"I'd do it for Emma." He glares at me, and I laugh, shifting and
moving to my tiptoes to press my lips to his. "And I'd do it for you, but
mostly because I need you in a better mood. I'm gonna get you to
crack tonight, I think."

We both know that's not true, that he won't crack until I'm ready,
but I like this game between us a bit too much.

"Oh yeah?"

"Mm-hmm."

"Well, I feel my mood perking up already." My head tips back
with a laugh that has a few birds scattering. "All right, let's get you
inside before you freeze. I'll clean up my mess later."

Even though he drops my hand as soon as we walk into the living
room, I feel more like a team with Jesse than ever before as I pull
Wren aside and we start to plan.

And even though I fail at my task of making him crack, I have fun
trying.

TWENTY-SIX

The day of Emma's party, Jesse's parents take her to breakfast while I bring everything to the Kings' house and into the furnished basement to set up with the help of Jesse. Wren will be here in about an hour to help once she's done making the birthday cake.

"Hallie," Jesse says, his voice a low warning that, despite being in his parents' house, settles in my stomach with warmth. He sets the helium tank I bought for balloons next to the three giant boxes and a dozen or so bags filled with decorations and party things that he helped me carry in.

"Yes?" I say, as I dig through bags and start unloading them to set up.

"Did you leave anything at the store?" I look over my shoulder and grin.

"A bit, but not much." His eyes narrow. "You only turn twelve once, Jesse. Go big or go home." He fights a smirk, wanting to pretend he's annoyed by me, shaking his head and taking off his hat, flipping it around, and taking in the room.

"I'll pay you back," he says, and I don't even bother to look at him, continuing to take out the seven boxes of air mattresses and adorable bedding I got to go with our decorating theme.

"Sure, you will," I say.

"I mean it, Hallie."

"I'm sure you do."

I move on, sorting through the bag where the goody bags are: a tote bag with each girl's name on it, filled with various fun things I know will totally blow them away.

"The way you're saying that makes me feel like you aren't going to take the money when I give it to you."

I stand and pat his cheek. "Now you're catching on." I attempt to step back, but his warm, rough hand wraps around my wrist and stops me.

"This shit wasn't cheap, Hal." I lift a shoulder but don't reply, and his eyes narrow on me. "Let me pay you back." When I don't respond, irritation flashes on his face. "Hallie," he says, his other arm wrapping my waist to hold me in place.

"I have too much money," I say in defense. He gives me a disbelieving look, and I shrug. "Talk to your mom about it. Colt already got a new tenant, so he won't take my rent, and neither will your mom. I have to spend it somewhere."

"Bank accounts exist, Hallie. Saving accounts exist."

"So do shopping sprees and birthday parties."

He sighs but drops my wrist, using the hand to tuck hair behind my ear. The back of one finger grazes the earrings he got me, his eyes lighting up when he sees them, the way they always do.

"She's my kid, Hallie. My responsibility."

For a brief moment, I think about brushing it off, about playing it safe. But lately, I'm not feeling like playing it safe is actually the right choice anymore or even what I want.

"The goal is for her to be mine, too, right?" I ask low, and his breath stops. It might be wrong to use this against him, so I can help pay for Emma's party, but I don't feel bad about it. Especially not when it feels like the truth. In fact, if I'm being honest, it very much feels like Emma is *already* mine.

"You're a pain, you know that?" he murmurs, then leans down to give me a soft kiss before resting his forehead on mine. "Does that mean you're ready to admit you fit here with us perfectly?"

My pulse pounds, and I tell myself it's the proximity, his voice, his touch, but I know it's what he's saying, how he's saying it—the confidence in his words.

I part my lips, second-guessing and old worries flooding me, but Jesse just smiles and presses his lips to mine again.

"I'll wait."

Before I can respond, a familiar voice calls out from upstairs, and he steps away.

"Hello?" Wren moves down the stairs, coming into sight just as Jesse turns to start unpacking the helium tank. "Hey party people!" In her arms is another giant box, and behind her, Adam has another with two bags over his shoulder.

Jesse looks at me with a glare, and I just laugh before we all get to work.

"Can you believe Kim messaged me?" Wren asks hours later, her fork moving through the frosting on a piece of leftover cake.

The party is well underway, with every inch of the basement decorated and individual sleep stations with blow-up mattresses and canopies for each girl. With the help of Nat, who came around five, we created a spa night for the girls with facials, mani-pedis, and clip-in colored extensions. When I headed upstairs an hour ago, the girls were settling in for a movie on the projector screen Mr. King set up.

My entire body stills as I turn to her.

"Kim, as in Emma's bitch of a mom?" Nat asks, and Wren nods, her brown curls bouncing with each movement.

"No fucking way," I whisper in utter disbelief.

"Yes! I posted a story last night about the banner I made, and she replied, telling me to give Emma a big hug and a kiss and saying she's so bummed she can't make it. As if she isn't the entire reason we're scrambling to do this as it is."

My eyes travel across the room to the living room, where Madden, Jesse, and Adam are chatting, but I don't miss the fact that when I catch him, his eyes are already on me. He winks at me, tipping his beer in my direction, and I roll my eyes.

"I didn't even know she followed you," Nat says.

"I didn't either, but I think sometime last month she must have. I don't really pay attention, so I'm not sure."

"I hate her," I say under my breath.

"You and me both," Wren says. Then she gets a text and stands, waving her phone. "Oh my god, it's time!"

I stand and squeal, the excitement building in my chest and washing out the irritation. The guys laugh but stand, and we all move downstairs. When there, Wren and Adam move to the computer attached to the projector while I stand in front of the screen, facing the girls. Jesse stands near the stairs with his phone out, fixed on Emma.

"Okay, so we have one last surprise for the night, a gift from your Aunt Wren," I say with a broad smile, knowing this is going to lock in this being the most epic birthday party ever.

We are *never* going to beat this party, that's for sure, though I'll have fun trying.

"So Adam managed to pull some strings and called up a friend," Wren starts, moving to stand beside me. A grin takes over her face as Emma gasps, her eyes going as wide as plates. The girls around her look at each other, confused, but Wren continues. "And when he told her—"

"NO WAY," Emma calls out before she can continue, and Wren laughs.

"When he told her that we had a birthday girl in the house, she wanted to call up and say hi."

"*No way!* No way, no way, no way!" Emma says, standing now. Her friends continue to look lost, though they're smiling now. But when the projector screen flashes to a video of Willa Stone backstage at her concert, they all start screaming.

"Hey, Emma! Happy birthday!" the pop star says with a wave as the chaos continues. Willa laughs, and after a moment, they quiet down so Emma can chat for a few minutes with her idol. A lump forms in my throat as I watch from the back of the room, and when I shift my gaze to Jesse, he's suspiciously glassy-eyed as well as he takes in his daughter's genuine and utter delight.

It was a Hail Mary, Wren asking Adam to see if there was any chance we could get a single signed album for Emma's birthday. But as soon as he called and asked for a favor, something we later learned he had *never* done before, since he loathes feeling used or making othersthinkl used, Willa jumped at the opportunity to help. Not only did she line up a quick video call with the girls, but she also set up a front-row livestream of her concert, including a shout-out to Emma halfway through, which will be projected for the girls. In the goody bags are relatively useless, but still very fun, VIP lanyards, signed albums, and tour sweatshirts that Willa's team overnighted.

Once again, we are *never* going to beat this one.

Once the call ends, the girls are all squealing and giggling as Wren hands out the goody bags and Adam makes sure the live stream works, since the concert starts in five minutes. Emma moves through the room, coming straight to me with a dazed look on her face.

"I can't believe this," she says.

"Are you happy?" I ask. She nods, then surprises me by coming closer and wrapping me up in a big, tight hug.

"Thanks, Hallie," she says, whispering the words into my chest. I return it, my hand brushing over her hair, and when she looks up at me, tears glisten in her eyes, tears I know are mirrored in my own. "Thank you. This is the best birthday ever."

"Anytime, girlfriend. Love you."

"Love you, too." I take in a shaky breath and then pull her in tight again, and when I look over her shoulder at her dad, he has his phone up, capturing the whole moment.

That night, I sleep in the guest room at the King's house so I can get up early to set up breakfast. Usually, Wren and I would stay in her bedroom, the only kids' bedroom that the Kings haven't touched since she moved out, but she conned Adam into staying there with her, so I'm in the guest room alone.

The guest room that used to be Jesse's room, and the irony is not lost on me.

I'm texting the man in question while lying in bed, too amped up from the successful night of surprises and, admittedly, way too much sugar, when there's a near-silent knock at the door before it creaks open and Jesse's head pokes in, a broad grin on his lips.

"Hey," I say as he closes the door behind him and presses the lock. He's in a T-shirt and sweats and tosses his sweatshirt to the floor before padding across the room. "What are you doing here?"

"Going to bed."

"No, you are not," I say, but he ignores me and climbs into bed behind me. "Jesse!" His arm warms around me, pulling my back to his chest and pulling the blankets up around us.

"Shh. It's bedtime."

I bite back a smile, trying to sound firm. "Jesse, this is so stupid. Someone will find us!"

"The door is locked, and I have an alarm set. It'll be fine." He tightens his hold on me and presses a kiss to my neck. My fight starts to melt; his proximity is too nice, his warmth too calming.

"Jesse—"

When he cuts me off, the teasing is gone from his words, his voice a bit gravelly.

"I just need to hold you, Hal. You saved the day and loved on my girl, and I don't know what to do with this feeling."

A beat passes before I speak, and I snuggle in a bit deeper into his hold. "I'm not helping you with your horniness under your parents' roof. Not even if you're going to finally fuck me."

He huffs out a laugh, his mustache scraping against my neck, and shakes his head.

"Jesus, Hallie. Can't you let me be serious for one minute? I meant gratitude. I'm so fucking grateful for you, and it's overwhelming me."

His words and their sincerity stop any further jokes or protests in their tracks.

"We're lucky, Emma and I. We have a lot of people in our corner, and we always have. My parents, my sister, and my brother...they've always been there from the moment Kim told me she wasn't in this for the long haul, and long before that. I've spent years struggling with guilt and stress and the repercussions of Kim's flightiness. I've had to comfort my girl, hold her while she cried, or listen as she raged. But I've never had anyone to do it with me until lately."

My breathing stops, my ears ringing as he continues to set my world on its axis.

"Lately all I can think is that we're lucky to have you, Hal," he whispers. And for the first time, I know he doesn't mean his family, his sister, or the Kings as a whole.

He means him and Emma. Their little unit. The one he's slowly trying to invite me into without scaring me off. I let my head fall onto his shoulder, take a deep breath, and nod, giving him what I can in the moment.

"Me too, Jesse." And when his hands tightened on my wrist, when his shoulders released some of the tension he's been holding, I know he knows all of the things I left unsaid.

"You know, I never had a girl in this bedroom," he says after a while, and I laugh a bit.

"Really?" I ask because that does genuinely shock me. He shakes his head, his lips grazing over my pulse, and despite myself, it starts to speed.

"Are you kidding me? And face the potential wrath of my mom finding her in here with me?"

"Oh, but now you're fine with it?" I ask with faux irritation.

"For one, I'm thirty-two, so the worst she can do is tell me she's disappointed in me."

"Still a killing blow," I say with a laugh, because everyone knows that Mrs. King's disappointment is worse than her wrath, and his own reverberates through me.

"And two, if she found me in here, she would absolutely blame me, not you. She'd think I corrupted you."

"If only," I murmur. He laughs again and presses his lips to my neck.

"Another time," he murmurs. "When things are more settled, if you really want, I'll fuck you in my childhood bedroom."

"Promises, promises," I say with a sigh that morphs into a yawn. He laughs one last time, presses his lips to the back of my head, and settles us further into the blankets.

"Go to sleep, Hallie."

And even though I should argue, even though I should kick him out, I don't. Instead, I fall asleep in Jesse's arms, waking up only when the alarm he set for far too early goes off so he can sneak out.

TWENTY-SEVEN

The week before we go to Killington for Adam's birthday, we continue our routine. Every day, Emma and I hang out after school and make dinner. When Jesse gets home, Emma insists I stay to try it, something he agrees is necessary, with a smug grin as if he realizes, as I do, that his daughter is trying to push us together in her own way.

Each night, he convinces me to watch a movie on the couch together, one we barely watch because not long into it, we inevitably end up horizontal, making out. Every night, I try my best to get him to crack in his efforts to refrain from going any further than heated kisses.

Each night, he stops me before things get too good, telling me in soft words and gentle touches he's not moving too fast, not until I'm ready. Then we spend the rest of the night holding each other and talking about everything and absolutely nothing at all.

I want to be annoyed by his method, but the truth is, each night, my fear of this failing lessens, and my need for him grows, so maybe he really does know what he's doing.

But right now, that acceptance is nowhere to be found, not when I'm panting and needy as his lips move over mine.

I want more. *Need* more. I feel like a horny teenager, making out while their mom is in the other room, except I'm ten years out of high school and Jesse has a whole-ass kid. But every time I try for something more, Jesse stops me.

Like right now, when his lips trail to my ear and pull the hoops between them, nipping at me there and sending heat straight to my core.

"Please," I whisper, shifting to slip my hand between us, to touch him or maybe myself, I don't know, and really, I don't care, but his fingers loop around my wrist, and his head shakes.

"No, baby. Not tonight." He looks at me softly, not annoyed, but with all of the patience in the world as his hand moves, his thumb running over my bottom lip. "We have all the time in the world for more. I'm not rushing things until you're ready to admit there's something between us."

I roll my eyes. The idea still shoots nervous energy through me, but it's less sharp lately, overshadowed by my need for him and, admittedly, though I'm not ready to say it, my recent desire to show everyone what he means to me.

That development came as a surprise at Emma's birthday party, when I found myself gravitating toward Jesse and, more than once, found myself having to stop from touching or kissing him. It's only gotten worse.

"What's between us right now is your hard-on," I say, soft and seductive, trying to shift my hips to graze his.

"You know what I mean," he says, not rising to the bait, unfortunately, and I groan in defeat once again.

"Every night you make out with me," I say, sitting up, and Jesse follows. His hair is a tousled mess from my hands, and I'm sure mine looks just as wild.

"Are you unhappy with that?" he asks, and the words sound genuine, but his face is smiling as if he already knows the answer.

"No? Yes? Maybe?" I ask, and he lifts an entertained eyebrow at me. Clearly, he loves my suffering. "Yes."

"You're unhappy with that?"

"I'm unhappy that that's all you'll do with me." He grins then, eyes crinkling at the sides, and my glare intensifies. "Stop looking so pleased with that!"

"I can't. I'm incredibly pleased that you're getting all riled up."

"Is this your plan then? Making out like teenagers until I get bored?" His face goes serious, his head shakes, and he reaches out to grab my hand.

"Hallie, I don't want either of us to think that sex is blurring our common sense and use that to doubt what we have. We're building a foundation for forever, Hallie."

His words settle in my chest, but after the last week, after the last month, they don't sound as scary as they did when this first started.

I don't tell him that, though, not wanting him to realize his method is actually working.

"You're infuriating," I grumble, and he laughs but reaches over, pulling me into his lap. My legs drape over him, and he pushes my hair back from my face before cupping my face.

"We'll have the rest of our lives to fuck, Hallie."

"We don't even have to fuck!" I say, shifting so my center rests against his still hard cock. "We can do other things."

"Hallie," he says in warning, but he feels so good between my legs that I decide I don't care about his protests. Not right now. Not when I can take what I need and still follow his rules.

"Fine," I grumble, mostly to myself. "I can take care of myself."

"Hallie." His voice is a warning, but I'm liking the idea brewing in my mind more and more by the moment. I just need to take things into my own hands, to take a hit I need. He's pushing me in the direction he wants, so why can't I push him in the direction I want, too?

I shift, grinding myself gently against his hardness beneath me in his sweats, and a heavy breath leaves my lips. I'm in thin black yoga pants and a pair of silky underwear that I definitely didn't put on just in case he finally decided to move further, and I'm grateful for the way they sit against me now. My hands move to his shoulders, pressing to lift myself and readjust, and a mewl leaves my lips as the thick length of him settles right where I need him. I move my hands up to his jaw, cupping them and leaning in to kiss him, to continue with what we started. He accepts the kiss eagerly, and when I realize he's not stopping me, I have to fight back a squeal of delight.

Instead, his tongue twines with mine, stoking the fire that never went out, and slowly, my hips start to rock on him.

"What are you doing?" he asks, breaking the kiss, his hands moving to my hips, though he doesn't stop me. He just rests them there, fingers tightening just as I shift my hips again, the head of his cock brushing over my oversensitive clit. My breath hitches before I answer, hips rocking again.

"Taking care of myself," I whisper back, leaning in to kiss his again, deeper. The hand on my hip grips me tighter, the other moving up my back and tangling in my hair at the back of my head as he groans into my mouth. I can't help but grin triumphantly into the kiss, but when I tip my hips back with my next line, the grin turns into a soft moan.

"Fuck, Hallie," Jesse groans into my mouth. "Fuck." The second one sounds more pained, more needy, and it sends me higher.

"I'm more than—" My breath hitches as pleasure shoots through me unexpectedly. I am already so close after a week of foreplay. "More than happy to fuck. You're the one who refuses."

"No, no. This is fucking perfect. I'm not complaining in the least. This is the most beautiful torture."

He's not going to stop me.

Need and heat crash through me with the realization, and my hips start to move faster, taking what I need without abandon. I tip my head back, moaning low, and his head drops forward to press kisses to my throat, my chest, whatever exposed skin he can reach.

"Fuck, you're beautiful," he groans into my neck. "Moaning and using me. Fuck Hallie." My hips rock with more speed, my breath coming in short pants, the pleasure building between my legs.

"You could take over," I manage to breathe, watching the look of pained pleasure on his face through hooded lips.

"And miss the show? Fuck no."

His hand leaves my hip for a split second, shifting to hover over my breasts before thinking better of it and moving back to my hip. He grips me there harder than before, as if he has to remind himself of the boundaries he set. I really thought he would cave, that this would tip the scales in my favor, and he would fuck me, but it seems Jesse King has the restraint of a much stronger man.

"Fuck," he groans, his hips lifting as I move, chasing my pleasure. My hands slide to cup my breasts, the thin bra I'm wearing barely offering any resistance as I roll my nipples. His eyes watch, enraptured, jaw loose, breathing heavy, and the look alone sends me higher.

"I'm gonna come," I whisper, staring down at him with hooded eyes. His eyes shift to lock on mine, burning with unsated need. A hand moves up, gripping the back of my head and pulling me close until my forehead is pressed to his, never breaking eye contact with me.

"So am I," he admits, then presses his lips to mine.

I don't know if it's the confession that he's as lost as I am, that he's so far gone and so needy that he's like a fucking teenager, about to come in his pants, or if it's the kiss, the need and desire and something I won't quite name but know lingers there all the same, pouring from his lips to mine, but I come, lights flaring behind my eyes.

A deep, pleasure-filled groan leaves his lips, and his hands move to my hips, holding me down onto him, pulling me tighter, as I shatter, rocking my hips as wave after wave of pleasure crashes down over me. Eventually, it wanes, and my body goes slack. Jesse's head falls to my shoulder, and I try to catch my breath as I come back to reality.

I just dry-humped Jesse King until I came, and I think I may have made him come in his pants.

More importantly, it was hands down the hottest sexual experience of my goddamn life.

"Like high school, huh?" I say with a laugh, and he lets out one of his own. "If I knew that was an option, I would have been doing that every night."

He shakes his head. "That can't happen again, Hallie."

I pull back as my face falls, panic filling me. "Was it—"

"It was fucking phenomenal, and after you agree you're mine, and after you agree to take a chance on this, on us, I'll let you do that every fucking night if it's what you want. You want to make me blow in my sweats like I'm fifteen? Have at it, so long as you make those pretty noises again."

I just came harder than I ever have, and yet, my pussy tightens. He senses it, like he has some kind of sixth sense of Hallie's pussy, and a wicked, boyish grin spreads on his lips.

"But until you're ready to move forward with this. To be an us, to tell Wren and Madden and my parents, and eventually, my daughter, then no. We're not doing this. We're not muddying the waters."

I try to move, to get away, but his arm is on my back, holding me close to him. It forces me to face my thoughts and fears head-on. I don't know if it's the calm brought on by the killer orgasm or his closeness or something different altogether, but for some reason, I drop my head into his neck and whisper to him.

"I'm not ready for that," I confess, then add, "yet."

His hand comes to my jaw, cupping it and lifting my face so he can press his on mine. "I can wait, Hallie." He kisses me again, and with the gentle press, the lingering panic recedes, leaving warmth and tenderness in its wake. "Now, I'm gonna go clean this up, if you don't mind."

I smile, grateful for the break in heaviness.

"What, you don't want to sit in it?"

He lets out a bark of laughter, lifting me with ease and tossing me onto the couch. I sit as he stands and stare at the damp spot in his sweats with a strange pride. But when I look at the clock and see it's nearly eleven, I sigh.

"I should actually head out," I say with regret, and a moment passes before he pulls me up and into him, holding me tight.

"Spend the night," he whispers against my lips.

"Jesse—" I start because that's precisely the opposite of *taking things slow*.

"I'll set an alarm." I tip my head, and his face goes so sincere, so soft before he speaks. "We can stay on the couch if you want. I just want to fucking hold you, Hallie."

It's a similar plea to the one from the night after Emma's party.

"Promise you'll wake me up before she wakes up?" He nods fervently, like a little kid promising to clean up his room in exchange for ice cream. I let out a small laugh and shake my head. "I don't want to sleep on the couch." I stood, and disappointment crossed his face. "Let's go to bed, Jesse."

And then I take his hand and lead him to his room.

Hallie

On Friday, Wren takes a half day at work, and we pile into two cars to head up to Vermont, Madden and Adam both driving. I was confused that Jesse chose not to drive, but it made more sense when he sat in the back with me, Madden, and Nat in the front, since Nat gets car sick in the back. The entire drive, he finds excuses to brush against me.

We get to the lodge by four, and after settling into the hotel room Adam so graciously paid for, Wren begs me and Nat to come over to their room to get dressed and do our makeup for dinner and a night at the bar at the lodge. It's fun and silly, the three of us laughing and giggling as we get dressed. Nat leaves to answer a call from the salon, and a bit later, Adam returns to the room.

"You look gorgeous," he says, pulling Wren into his arms after taking in her tight burgundy dress. He presses his lips to hers, and a blush burns on my best friend's cheeks as she pushes on his chest.

"Adam!" she says with a giggle. "You're going to mess my makeup up!"

"I'm okay with that," he murmurs, and her eyes go wide.

"Hallie is here!" she says under her breath, and I laugh, taking a hint and standing.

"Okay, on that note, I'm going to head down to the lobby."

"We'll meet you down there in ten," Wren says, biting her lip.

"Make it forty," Adam says.

"Adam!" she says, slapping at his chest. "Everyone is here for you!"

"It's my birthday trip, Birdie. I'm sure everyone will understand me wanting to spend some time alone with my girlfriend."

"It's still rude!"

I shake my head and laugh at their antics.

"It's all good, Wren, enjoy your time together. I'll make sure no one bugs you two for an hour."

"You're my favorite, Hallie. Remember that."

"Yeah, yeah, yeah," I say with a wave, then walk out, the heavy door slamming behind me.

I head down the hall, shaking my head, and then stop when my brother steps out of his room. I'm still not sure how Adam convinced Colt to leave the bar in his assistant manager's hands for the weekend, but I'm grateful. I don't know when I last saw my brother enjoy himself outside of work. He smiles wide, waiting for me to catch up before throwing an arm over my shoulder.

"Hey there, Hal. Where are you headed?"

"Downstairs. I was getting ready with Wren, but they started getting all touchy-feely and, well, you know."

Colt nods with a knowing look. "Well, that means I can get a drink with my favorite sister before dinner, I guess."

I look up at him with a smile, warmth in my chest since I have missed spending time with my brother, and then we head to the lobby bar together.

I should have known it was coming, but I'm on a vacation high, or maybe it's the elevation, but barely five minutes after settling into a corner bar table, he strikes.

"Hear you've been spending a lot of time with Emma and Jesse," he says, and I force my body to remain loose, not to get too tight, since if anyone can read me, it's Colton.

"Yeah, I watched her while Wren was out in Paris."

He nods, taking a sip of his beer and keeping his eyes on me.

"Word on the street is you're there a lot."

I lift a questioning eyebrow. "Word on what street?"

He grins. "Madden,"

My jaw tightens, and I shake my head with an irritated sigh. "Madden has a big fucking mouth," I say, taking a long sip of my drink. Bad move, since Colton takes the opportunity to land his next hit.

"Are you finally going to admit you're in love with your best friend's brother?"

"What—" I start, but his face is so sincere, so kind and nonjudgmental, I hesitate in my argument, in my denial.

At some point, I'm going to have to make a choice, and I'm realizing that choice, made rapidly, is never going to be letting Jesse go. Eventually, everything will be out in the world if I'm going to confess this to anyone before we tell everyone, Colton's the safest of them all.

"I think love is a bit of an exaggeration," I murmur, though these days, I don't actually know if that's it.

A moment of surprise crosses my brother's face as if he thought he'd have to work harder for a confession, but he bounces back quickly, crossing his arms on his chest and sitting back.

"So you're together?" he asks, taking me in.

"We're not...I don't know. I've been trying to do a friends-with-benefits thing with him, but he isn't into it. He wants all or nothing."

Colton let out a short huff of a laugh. "He's Jesse King. That doesn't surprise me in the least. So, you're the one looking for just friends?"

I brush off the disbelief in his words.

"I...I don't know. I like him a lot, of course. But it's...complicated."

"I feel like you two getting together would be the least complicated relationship that Holly Ridge has ever seen. You're already a King by extension."

"That's the problem," I say with a shake of my head and a sigh. My brother looks at me with a raised eyebrow but says nothing else. "Wren is my best friend, more a sister than a friend. Her parents are more like parents to me than our own. I work for them and work right with Madden. Fuck, I live on their property."

"Okay..." he says as if he doesn't understand, but I can tell from his face he does. He's just waiting for me to say it out loud, as is his way. A bartender through and through, the man is half therapist, always waiting for you to process all of your thoughts before he adds any of his own. "So, are you afraid that Wren and the rest of them are going to be mad?"

"No," I say with a choked laugh and shake of my head. "Are you kidding me? Wren would dance with joy. When we were kids, we made plans for me to marry one of them so I could be her real sister."

"Good choice with Jesse. You'd eat Madden alive," he says with a laugh, and I return it, then nod in agreement, and wonder how on earth Jesse never saw that.

"Exactly," I take in a deep breath. "But if I tell her there's something with Jesse and me, and we start dating, she'll be thrilled. She'll more than likely start planning our wedding, and Mrs. King will be right with her, happy at least one of her boys is settling down." Colt nods, knowing this to be true. He was in the same grade as Madden, and he's always been friends with both of the boys and thus knows all about Mrs. King's woes. "But what happens when it ends? What happens when we break up or decide it just doesn't work the way we thought, and it ends?"

He tips his head, assessing.

"Interesting that you said *when* and not *if,*" he says after a moment, and I roll my eyes.

"You know what I meant."

"Do I?" I glare at him, giving him a taste of his own medicine before he adds, "I just think it's interesting that your instinct isn't to think that things will work out and everyone will be happily ever after, you know?"

"It's not like I had the best example of a happy, loving relationship," I say under my breath, my finger playing with the condensation on the side of the glass.

"Mr. and Mrs. King?" he asks, with a pointed look.

"They're a freak relationship, meant to happen."

He shrugs. "Adam and Wren are pretty perfect."

"They started dating three months ago. And, besides, Wren is a fairy princess who gives everything to everyone. She deserves the most amazing happiness."

"And you don't?" The question comes so quickly, like he'd been waiting to ask it, and it makes my defenses go even higher.

"What is this, therapy?" He looks at me, unyielding, and I try to explain, to get him to understand where I'm coming from. "I have to be rational, Colton. It might not end, but what happens if it does? What happens if it ends and ruins everything? I'd lose them all." His face goes soft, and he leans in, reaching across the table to grab my hand and squeeze it.

"I think you have to decide if you want to live your life or keep yourself safe, Hallie. It's clear you've been doing the latter for most of your adult life, but have you been happy?" I think about the vision boards in my room, all of them ambitious and exciting, yet incomplete. While some of those items aren't crossed off because they were entirely unattainable, others are simply because I was too scared to try.

"The truth is, you'll never know if something is going to last forever. If you look for the potential bad, you'll always find it. Sometimes you just gotta jump and believe in the *promise* of forever." My heart races with his words. "The promise, the hope of it—isn't that what love is all about? What *is life* all about? Knowing you won't be promised forever, knowing it could destroy you, and trusting in reaching for it anyway?"

Suddenly, it's like a new door has opened, a new choice that I didn't realize was there. It's not just saying yes and worrying for the rest of my life or saying no and regretting it. There's saying yes and trusting in my choice. Saying yes, and trusting that when I slip, Jesse will catch me before I fall.

And when I ask myself that—when I ask myself if I can trust that Jesse will catch me—the answer is clear.

It always has been.

I'm mulling over his words and my new realization, about to speak when a familiar voice calls. I turn and see everyone coming out our way—all three Kings, plus Nat and Adam—walking our way, and I smile.

Break TK

My brother, just as bad as Wren, plays matchmaker that night when he manipulates the table seating so I sit next to Jesse, not that I'm complaining.

The only thing I *am* complaining about is the constant teasing.

Jesse's arm lies casually along the back of my chair, which is normal for him, but occasionally, there are the most gentle touches of his skin on mine.

My bare shoulder in my off-the-shoulder sweater dress.

The back of my neck.

Somehow, he does it so smoothly that when I glance around the table, no one has noticed. Each time I look at him, his head shifts to mine, and he smiles.

Smiles.

He knows exactly what he's doing to me, and I can't find it in me to hate it.

Halfway through dinner, I set my hand on his leg beneath the table, and for a moment, his entire body tenses, pulling a smirk to my lips. I'm talking to Nat when I feel his gaze burning on me, and even though Nat gives me the most sly, skeptical look, I ignore it.

Ten minutes later, his fingers gently move over my earlobe, the backs of them brushing over my earrings, sending a shiver through me, and I wonder how the hell I'm going to survive this trip.

When dinner ended, we all decided to head to the hotel bar and hang out. On the way over, I stop in the lobby bathroom, tell everyone to head over, and I'll meet them there.

Leaving the bathroom, I step out into the dark hallway, and in a moment, there's a hand around my wrist, and I'm being tugged, moving until I'm in a hidden alcove, my back to a wall, a body over mine. I open my mouth to scream, but then a familiar woodsy scent, pine and leather and whatever body wash Jesse uses, fills my senses.

I relax but slap at his chest. "What the fuck, Jesse?"

"Exactly what I was thinking." His hand is warm on my waist, and suddenly, my pulse is racing, but not because of the panic of being potentially kidnapped. It's from something altogether different.

"Are you trying to drive me crazy, Hallie?" he asks, dropping his head and pressing a kiss to the pulse in my throat.

"How am I driving you crazy?" I ask, my voice sounding breathy.

"Existing for one." Despite my irritation, I can't help but let out a small laugh as he kisses up my neck, then to my jaw, before pressing another kiss on the side of my lips.

"You're out of your mind."

"For you."

"You're the one who refuses even to touch me," I ask, lifting an eyebrow.

"What do you call this?" His hand tightens on my hip, his hips pressing into mine. I shift my hip against him, and heat rockets through him. Just like last time we were in Vermont, the need between us strains tight. It seems once Jesse gets away from his responsibilities, he untethers a bit, his restraint slackening as he becomes more carefree, if only for a weekend. I wonder for a moment if I can use that to my advantage.

"Not touching me. You're *teasing* me, which you've been doing for a while. I'm tired of it," I pout. Something flashes in his eyes, and before I can say anything else, his words fill the small space between us.

"Fuck it."

Confusion settles over me, but it's fleeting when his mouth drops, moving to press his lips to mine. Then he's kissing me, hard and deep, nothing like our late nights on the couch. It's not slow, hot kisses, but needy, consuming ones: ones that say so much, a promise for what I might get sooner rather than later. My hands move to behind his neck, my fingers moving into his hair to hold him to me, to get more. As he kisses me, he shifts, his thigh moving between my legs, and a hand moves to my hips, tilting them so I grind against him. I gasp at the sensation, at the way it sends heat spiraling in my belly, curling in on itself.

"Jesse," I whisper.

"You're mine, Hallie. The sooner you admit that, the sooner we'll both be a fuck of a lot more satisfied." His hand moves me again, grinding me, muddying my mind as I try to grasp a response, to even begin to process his words.

I open my mouth to argue, to tell him he's wrong, to say to him that I can't take that risk, but my brother's words move through my mind in place of my usual common sense, soothing over my typical panic.

What if he's right?

What if it's not nearly as much of a risk as I think it is? If things ended messy, the Kings wouldn't just toss me aside. That's not their style, and if it were, I wouldn't have them on such a pedestal, right?

And in a dark hallway in the hotel where things started a year ago, I give in. "What if you're mine?" I murmur.

He grins wide, his smile lighting up the area. Somehow, as he always seems to, he knows exactly what I really meant with my words.

I expect him to take the olive branch. To toss me over his shoulder and bring me to his room or, at the very least, kiss me.

Instead, he steps back then, leaving me feeling cold, needy, and frustrated.

"Then you've gotta claim me, baby."

Jesse walks off, leaving me in thought and stewing for a moment before, dazed and turned on, I make my way to where everyone is. Despite the buzzing bar, as if he senses me, Jesse's head swivels, and the most handsome grin spreads on his lips. I roll my eyes, but approach our group to get on with the night. Right now, it's about hanging out with our friends and family.

What's a few more hours stoking the heat burning in my belly going to hurt? We have all night to enjoy each other.

Hell, I'm starting to believe we'll have the rest of our lives.

BREAK tk

We're sitting without drinks at a bar table an hour later, when Madden turns to his brother, determination evident on his face.

"Come on, Jess. Let's go scouring."

Jesse's brows furrow as he stares at his brother dumbly. "Scouring?"

"For ladies! You don't have a kid tonight, and you don't have to rush home tomorrow to get back to her. It's the perfect time to find someone to get that pent-up sexual tension out of your system."

There's a moment of hesitation before Jesse scans the table where we all sit, settling on me.

"Come on, Jesse! I need a wingman," Madden says.

"He really does," Nat says. "Madden's shit at picking women."

The table laughs, and Colton stands.

"Come on, let's go help him out, Jesse." Then my brother gives me a knowing, challenging look before guiding the King brothers toward the bar.

"Looks like the guys found their marks," Wren says with a smile ten minutes later.

I've been diligently ignoring them, not wanting to be too obvious and have to endure questions, not with a long weekend ahead of us. I also, despite everything, trust Jesse. He might tease and fuck with me, and he might be willing to help Madden out, but that's it.

"She's cute," Wren says, but there's something in her tone, something I can't quite pinpoint. Until I look at her face, that is. "Don't you think so, Hallie?"

That's when I see it. Wren, my sweet best friend who is always worried about everyone and always concerned with making everyone feel loved and included, is *teasing me*.

Adam's grin is just as wide as Wren's, and when I turn to Nat, she has a *"told you so"* look, and I realize that all my weeks of trying to be sneaky and stealthy may have been for nothing.

Or, more likely, I am not nearly as sneaky as I thought.

I don't respond. Instead, I watch as one of the women they're standing with reaches out and touches Jesse's bicep. He steps away, giving her a polite nod, but the suddenly very possessive part of me doesn't care.

"Fuck it," I say under my breath, then slide off my stool and head in their direction, my shoes clicking against tile as I do. I think I hear Wren, Adam, and Nat laughing behind me, but I can't focus on that. Suddenly, I have tunnel vision. All I can see is Jesse standing with another woman, one who is very clearly into him. It's polite laughter, and Colt and Madden are with him, but *I do not care.*

It's time to claim him.

"Excuse me," I say, pushing my brother aside. The grin on Jesse's face is megawatt-level when he sees me.

"Hallie," he says, all casual and coy as if he has *no* idea what he's doing.

"Shut up," I say, taking the final step to him until our chests are touching, placing my hands on his shoulders, moving to my tiptoes, and pressing my lips to his in front of everyone.

TWENTY-NINE

There isn't a moment of hesitation as my lips touch Jesse's, no surprise or confusion, just his arm wrapping around my waist, pulling me flush to him as we meld together.

It's not a sweet kiss—it's a claiming. Lips and teeth and tongue, and then he's moving, shifting me, lifting me. My legs move to wrap his hips, and he's laughing as he kisses me, smiling into it as he starts to move us, leading us out of the bar.

Somewhere in the back of my consciousness, I hear cheering, and I know it's from our friends. Continuing to kiss Jesse, I flip them off, and a chorus of laughter follows us out of the bar.

We're headed to the elevators as my lips move down his neck, deciding he probably needs to be able to see as he moves us through the lobby with a purpose. It might be faster if he puts me down, but neither of us wants that; neither of us wants any kind of distance.

I just want his skin on mine in any way I can get it.

When we step onto the elevator, Jesse hits the button for his floor. Before the doors even close, he presses my back to the wall, grinding his already hard cock into me, and I moan.

"You're mine," I murmur as his hand lifts my head from his neck so he can kiss me.

"And you're mine." His tongue tastes me, and my chest feels lighter than I think it ever has in my life. "No going back, Hallie," he says when he pulls back, and I shake my head.

"No going back."

He smiles, head dropping to my neck and kissing me there. The elevator is criminally slow, but I can't deny it to myself. "That was the hottest thing you've ever done."

"Hotter than when I dry-humped you on the couch and made you come in your sweats?"

His laughter fills the small space, and I love that—love this—how when we're so on fire, we can still joke and laugh. In fact, I feel like I'm floating with happiness.

"A million times hotter."

"Hotter than when you ate me out on the edge of the hot tub?"

"Definitely."

"Hotter than when I got on my knees and sucked you off in your bedroom?" I ask, and he hesitates for a moment, making me laugh again.

"Hotter, Hallie. You claiming me in front of everyone? Nothing will ever top that."

"I have forever to try, though," I say the words without meaning to, but I know once they leave my lips, when his entire face lights up, they were the right thing to say. His hand glides down over my hips and under the skirt of my dress.

"What the fuck are these?" he asks, pinching at my thick tights, pulling them away, and realizing they're not actually sheer and thin.

"They're lined tights. They're very warm," I inform him as his lips move down my neck, nipping and kissing and sending my need higher and higher as the elevator climbs.

"They're criminal, Hallie."

"What? Why? If I weren't wearing them, the entire bar would

have seen my ass," I say with a breathy laugh that cuts short as his hand finds its way beneath the waistband and cups my pussy.

"Because if you weren't wearing them, I'd be on my knees eating your cunt right now."

And you know what? He makes a great point.

His finger presses my clit over my underwear, and I suck in a sharp breath. "Jesse," I murmur, about to tell him to take them off, destroy them, ruin them—I don't care so long as it gets his mouth on me—but then the elevator dings, opening on our floor, and Jesse is moving us out the doors, his hands gripping my ass as I suck on his neck. I give an apologetic look to the elderly couple, who look alarmed as we pass them, then laugh when the woman gives me a wink and thumbs-up. When we turn the corner, that laugh turns to a gasp as one of his hands slides down, fingers grazing over my entrance, and for the second time, I vow never to wear these fucking tights again. Always easy access only.

Finally, we reach a door, and Jesse fumbles in his pocket as I press kisses to his neck before he finally gets the key out, scanning it and opening the door. It slams behind us, and then my back is pressed to it, Jesse's body pinning mine in place. His lips crash down on mine with need and ferocity as my hands move to either side of his face and pull me to him. Our teeth clash, lips smashing together, tongues tasting one another.

I've never felt more needed, more desired, in my entire life. But over the past month, I've realized that's how Jesse always makes me feel—like there's nowhere he would rather be and no one he would rather be with than me.

When he grinds into me, his cock already hard and moving over my swollen clit with perfect precision, I groan.

"Please tell me you're not going to cut me off again," I beg, desperate for him.

He lets out a laugh and shakes his head. "Oh, Hallie baby, we're not leaving this hotel room until you're good and sore."

A chill runs through me as he sets me on my feet, then tugs my dress off as I kick off my boots. His fingers tuck under the waistband of my tights and pull them and my underwear down, moving to his knees as he does. I step out of them with his help, and then I'm naked before him. He shifts until he's face-to-face with my pussy, and the man *groans*. He groans loudly, and I tighten at the sound. A finger trails up my inner thigh, and I slowly step to widen my legs and give him room, a smirk forming on his lips, though he doesn't look up my body at me. Instead, his eyes stay locked on my center.

"I've fucking dreamed about this cunt, Hallie."

"You could have seen it in person weeks ago," I say, words shaky as that finger slides over the crease where my leg meets my hip.

"No, no. This is so much better. Now it's mine." He leans forward and places a soft, almost chaste kiss on my clit, and I sigh.

"Jesse," I murmur, fingers moving to his hair, but he doesn't move. Instead, his other hand moves up, thumbs parting me, and then he groans again when my cunt is revealed to him.

"So fucking pretty."

His head drops, lips circling my clit and sucking deep. My head falls back, knocking on the door, but I can't focus on anything but the way he feels on me, the way his fingers bruise my thighs, and the way his tongue flicks over my clit. My eyes snap open to look at him, and when I do, he's standing, tugging his sweater off in one smooth move, tossing it aside without a care.

"I want to eat that all fucking night, Hallie. I really do. But right now, what I really need is to be inside of you." I nod, eyes wide.

"Yes," I say, and he laughs as I step closer, his hands hesitating on the button of his jeans. I reach up, brushing his hair back and looking in his eyes. Even now, even in this moment of need and desire, I need him to know it's not just one night, like last time.

"We've got time for the extras. This first time, I just want you."

It's written clearly on his face, the understanding of what I'm saying crashing over him—joy and acceptance and gratitude I don't deserve.

In that moment, I knew for sure he would wait an eternity if I asked it of him. He'd wait for me for as long as needed, and that means more to me than he'll ever know.

Thankfully, he doesn't have to wait, and he knows that now. He bends, grabbing my hips and lifting me again. His lips are on mine as he takes long strides to his bed, then tosses me onto it, just like that first time. I find a giggle leaving my lips, and I hope it's always like this with us—fun, hot, and filled with need but also friendship.

God, I love this man.

The thought crashes through me, a realization that isn't necessarily new or groundbreaking, but still, I sit with it as he starts to undo the button on his jeans. I find that it's not scary at all, just warm, comfortable, and safe.

Just like the man before me.

"What are you thinking?" he asks, pushing his jeans and boxers down. His cock bobs free, and my lips part, my pussy tightening with sudden need, and I say the first thing that comes to mind.

It's not a prolific confession of love.

"Please, for the love of God, tell me you brought a condom."

He lets out a deep laugh that fills the room, reaching for his pants, forgotten on the ground. His pecs flex, and I lick my lips, taking in his naked upper half as he rifles through his pocket, grabbing his wallet and pulling out a condom, then tossing it on the bed. I sigh with relief before he tosses the wallet on the ground and takes two long, prowling steps toward the bed, climbing on. His movements are graceful and precise, and just like last time, he dips his head to my ankle, pressing a kiss there, then to my calf.

Despite the need, desire, and feat, suddenly my throat gets tight.

Jesse has never hidden anything from me, not when it comes to how he feels. He may have played things down to avoid scaring me off, but he has always deeply cared for me. That night, he was showing me the same things he's showing me now—pressing a kiss to my thigh and then my hip. He loves me, every bit, every inch, even the flawed, scared part of me.

"Wait, wait," I say, trying to keep my head on straight when he reaches my belly. He raises his eyebrow at me and smiles.

"Is this your kink?" he asks, and I roll my eyes, shaking my head before moving to my knees and then grabbing his wrist and pulling him toward me.

"No. I just. I want..." I take a deep breath, trying to muster the courage before I close my eyes. We're on our knees before each other on the bed, and I reach up to cup his jaw, my thumb moving on his mustache I am so obsessed with. "I love you, Jesse King," I whisper into the room. It's too soon—far, far, too soon—but also, it's so late. Because I've loved Jesse for years, my feelings have evolved, but I can't deny that over the past few months it's become glaringly apparent.

I am head over heels in love with Jesse King.

He takes in a deep breath, and his face goes blank for a moment, and panic fills me. Maybe it was too soon. Maybe it was the wrong time. Maybe...

"Fuck, I wanted to take this slow," he says. I stare at him, confused. "But now I've gotta fuck you."

"That was kind of the goal," I say with a laugh, but then the breath is gone from my lungs as he takes the condom from my hands and pushes me to my back. I watch with rapt attention as he rolls the condom on, and he smirks at me when a small squeak of arousal leaves my lips. Then he shifts down my body and starts where he ended, kissing between my breasts, then one nipple and the other— my collarbone, my shoulder, kissing me as he goes. For a single lucid moment, I wonder if this is *his* kink.

I can't say I wouldn't be into that.

When he makes it to my face, he holds himself above me and presses a long, sweet kiss to my lips.

"I don't know when I fell in love with you. I think it happened slowly, over time. You took a little bit of my heart here and there until one day I woke up and realized I didn't have it anymore. But I know the moment I realized I was crazy for you, and there was no going back."

"The Mill?" I ask, filling in. Part of me fell in love with him when I was a teenager, back when I would have done anything for him to just smile at me, but I fell hard the day he found me in the woods. It became unavoidable—and unignorable—when he told me he'd wait, and I came to terms with it that night when he held me in his childhood bed.

"No, no. God, I was already far gone by then." He lines his cock up with my entrance, and I hold my breath, but he doesn't push in; instead, he settles over me, keeping my eyes. "I fell in love with you a year ago, here in Vermont, that first time I caught you. That night, I realized I would do anything to ensure you never fell without my being there to catch you. I've been waiting for you to fall ever since."

The lump forms in my throat again, and it hits me just how long we've been building to this moment.

"You're really ready for this?" he whispers, reading my mind as always, but in that moment, I remember why we're actually here.

I narrow my eyes, my pussy tightening around the tip of him, and glare at him.

"Jesse, I swear to God, if you don't fuck me tonight, I'm going to—"

I don't know how I was going to finish that threat, but it doesn't matter, because before I can say another word, he's sliding in, filling and stretching me, and I'm gasping, back arching, and taking him even deeper. There's no real foreplay, because we've had weeks and weeks of it. I'm wet, and he's so hard and thick, and when he settles in deep, I have to catch my breath. He rests his head against mine, eyes hazy and filled with a need I know is reflected on my own face.

"I fucking love you, Hallie Young," he whispers, pulling out before sliding in again.

"You're mine," I say through heated breaths, and his head drops to my shoulder, groaning deep as he retreats and then thrusts back into me.

My hips rise to meet him, my breath catching as he fills me. Common sense leaves me as he fucks me, as my legs wrap around his hips, trying to get more, trying to get everything. My hands move to his jaw, and I pepper kisses everywhere I can, any inch of him I can reach. One of his hands cups my breasts, rolling the nipple, and I tighten around him.

It's too much.

It's not enough.

It's everything I never knew I needed and everything I always wanted.

But most of all, it's Jesse and me.

"Jesse," I whisper, a frantic edge to my words as the pleasure builds in my belly, spiraling in on itself.

"I know. God, I know." His words are a groan as his hips snap into mine, the tether he has on his restraint loosening.

"Jesse," I repeat as it builds. The orgasm is going to wash over me soon, but I focus, trying to keep it at bay because some part of me wants to hold on to this for as long as I can, drag it out, and cherish it.

"It's okay, Hallie. I've got you."

"I—" I start, and his head pulls back to look at me, pupils blown as his hips continue to rock into me, his pelvis bumping into my clit with each move, tipping me closer and closer to the edge.

"We have forever, Hallie."

And that's when I fall.

As I come, he slams in deep, and his lips move to mine, smothering my moans, his chest rumbling with a groan of his own as he follows me over, as he comes with me.

Long minutes pass, and he continues to kiss me, the hard edge of him melting into something soft and sweet, before his lips move, trailing over my cheeks, chin, and nose. Finally, he pulls out and off me, disposing of the condom before crawling back into bed beside me.

"Well, I guess we can confirm it was not a fluke," I mumble under my breath, still panting and wrung out. There's a beat of silence, and I tip my head to the side to look at Jesse, only to see his eyes on mine, a broad smile on his lips, before he bursts out laughing. Before I can say anything else, he rolls to his side, hugs his arms around me, and tugs until I'm moving on top of him. "Jesse, I'm sweaty and gross!"

"Don't care," he says, settling my naked body on his, then locking an arm around my lower back to hold me in place before burying his face into my neck.

I sigh, but stop fighting him, not that I really want to. I can't think of anywhere else I'd rather be right now than right here.

THIRTY

The next morning, I wake in an unfamiliar bed, my head on a familiar chest with light streaming into the room, and I have to fight back tears when everything feels so perfectly right.

This is what I've wanted. This is what's been missing. His warm chest beneath my cheek, his thick arm around my back, the even sound of his breathing, not a worry about sneaking out before anyone catches me here. Even though part of me is nervous, worried about what happens next, another, louder part screams that it doesn't matter: it's going to work out.

"Morning," Jesse's gravelly voice says, rumbling against my cheek. I lift my head, and his hand moves, brushing hair back from my face and smiling softly down at me.

"Morning."

A moment passes between us before he speaks again.

"How do you feel?"

I barely had a full drink at the bar last night, and while we fucked —a lot—last night, I know he's not asking how I feel physically. He means with everything that happened the night before.

Instead of answering right away, I think and try to sift through my thoughts and feelings before responding. How do I feel? There's no world where Wren and Madden missed the show I put on the night before, so the cat is kind of out of the bag about that, but when I dig deep, I find, strangely enough, I feel...relieved.

I don't have to hide my feelings anymore, and I don't have to force Jesse to conceal his. Things are out in the open, for the most part, and it feels good. It seems the most challenging part was just taking that jump.

"Good," I murmur with a smile, and when Jesse grins back, his is nearly blinding. It warms my chest to see it and know I did that, knowing that the small feat of my being open about my feelings for him is what put that look there.

"Yeah?"

I nod. "Yeah."

My phone blinks from where it is charging on the bedside table, though I don't remember plugging it in. Jesse must have further proof that he always takes care of me in the smallest ways. "I'm sure your sister has texted and called me eight million times," I groan.

"I texted her last night and told her we'd talk to her in the morning," he murmurs, his fingers moving through my hair, scraping at my scalp as he does.

A pleasant shiver moves through me. "You did?"

He nods. "There was a good shot that if neither of us responded, she'd show up at my room demanding answers last night or first thing this morning, neither of which I was interested in."

That's a great point.

"I can't believe you dragged me out of the bar," I murmur.

"I can't believe you kissed me in front of everyone," he counters, and I smile, mirroring the one on his lips.

"I was tired of playing games."

"Well, I for one am very glad you did."

I nod, agreeing, leaning up to kiss him. As I do, my stomach growls at the words. He laughs, then rolls both of us off the bed and to our feet.

"It's almost eight. I'm sure everyone is waiting for us for breakfast," he says.

"We slept till eight?" Usually, if we're on a ski trip, we're at breakfast by seven to get on the mountain early. I wonder if Jesse included a delayed morning in his text to Wren, too.

"We had a long night," Jesse says with a grin, and I roll my eyes.

"I need to go to my room. I can't wear the same outfit I did yesterday." A blush blooms on Jesse's cheeks before he goes to his bag, digging before lifting something. "Are those my leggings?"

"You left them at my place the night of the hot tub. I washed them, of course. I was hopeful you'd be stuck there one morning."

"Wow, condoms *and* a change of clothes? I really was a sure thing, wasn't I?" I ask with a laugh, snatching the fabric from his hands. He shrugs but grabs one of his sweatshirts and tosses it my way as well. I start to change, then stare at the heels I wore yesterday with an irritated glare. "Unfortunately, we still need to go by my room. I can't wear those."

This time, his smile isn't embarrassed but excited as he digs in his bag. Grabbing a box, he hands it to me.

"What is this?" I ask, though it's clearly a shoebox.

"Shoes." I furrow my brow, then open the box to find a brand new pair of my comfy slipper shoes, but these have a more durable sole. "The best of both worlds. Cozy and grippy."

"Oh my god, where did you get those?" I ask with a laugh, opening the package and then sliding one on. It's a perfect fit.

He shrugs one shoulder as he pulls a sweatshirt over his head.

"I was going to give them to you for Valentine's Day, but you wouldn't have accepted them. We weren't there yet."

I let out a loud laugh. "And now we are?"

"Now you're mine, so you can't argue as much when I spoil you."

I tip my head. "I don't think that's how that works." Still, I slide the other shoe on and stand, smiling at the exquisite coziness. God, this man gets me.

"It definitely is, trust me." He pulls me into him. "You spoil

Emma, I spoil you. The world keeps turning." I'm warm and comfortable, and everything feels perfectly right as I sigh, leaning my head into his chest. His fingers move through my hair, gently brushing it, before tugging a bit so I look at him. "Come on. Let's brush our teeth, then head down. You can even share my toothbrush." I grin, then nod, and we finish getting ready before stepping out of Jesse's hotel room hand in hand.

"Good morning, lovebirds," Wren says, and I shriek with a bit of surprised panic. She stands in front of us, hands on her hips, face unreadable. Adam stands beside her, back against the wall, scrolling on his phone. At this point, the man is entirely immune to her quirks.

"Oh, my god, Wren, you scared the shit out of me!"

"Told you it was creepy," Adam says, but Wren glares at him.

"You used to watch me through my office window. I don't think you have a leg to stand on."

He shrugs as if he knows that, and Wren turns back to me.

"We have to talk," she says, and my stomach drops. Then she turns to Jesse. "Everyone is downstairs for breakfast; we'll be down in five."

Jesse stares at her for a moment before he must conclude that there's no point in arguing. He pulls me into him, giving me a soft kiss and a reassuring look before abandoning me with his sister, who is holding open the door to the hotel room.

With dread, I follow her inside, the door slamming ominously behind us.

"Oh, my god, it smells like sex in here," Wren says, looking like she might gag.

"It does not, you're so dramatic."

"Are you denying you fucked my brother in here?" she asks with a raised eyebrow.

My pulse is pounding, and my throat is tight, but I force the words out before I lose steam.

"Wren, I'm so sorry, I—"

She lifts a hand and closes her eyes as a mother at her wits' end might do, and I stop talking.

"If you apologize for being the one to put that smile on my brother's face for the past two months, I'm actually going to scream." She steps closer to me, and I stand frozen, unsure and nervous. She stares at me for long moments, and I realize she's waiting for me to say something, anything. I'm not sure what to say or where to start, so instead, I tell her the only thing I think actually matters in this moment.

"I love him."

"I'm glad you can finally admit it," she says pointedly, sitting on the edge of the bed. She must have read the look of utter confusion on my face, because she explained further. "Hallie, you've been in love with my brother for years." I stare blankly, and she shakes her head, as if I'm being hardheaded. "You used to write his name in the margins of all your notebooks."

"Yeah, but back then I was a kid."

My best friend shrugs, reaching out to grab my hand, her eyes suddenly going so sincere as I move to sit beside her.

"And then you weren't." It's as simple as that, I guess. And then I wasn't a kid, and it wasn't a cute crush, and we suddenly were...everything. "So, when did it happen?"

"When you were in Paris," I whisper, and she smiles, then gives me an all-knowing look.

"All according to my plan."

I laugh, rolling my eyes and pushing her shoulder. "You're so full of shit. You didn't even know you were *going* to Paris."

She grins and shrugs.

"I mean, maybe not my *plan,* but I could hope." She takes me in, tipping her head in assessment. The thing about Wren is that she can read people better than anyone I've ever met. It's why she's so great as a teacher and so great at helping everyone. "And last year? In Vermont? After, you two got super weird."

I sigh, then explain. "We kissed, and then I ran off because I got scared. I avoided him, and he thought it was because I had a thing for Madden, so he let me have that space."

A look of incredulity crosses her face.

"You and *Madden?* You'd kill each other if you dated."

I laugh, loving that everyone but Jesse could see that.

"Thank you! That's what I said." We sit in silence before I take in a deep breath. "So, you're not mad?"

"That you're with my brother? No way. Just as long as I don't have to hear the details." Wren goes a bit green, and I laugh.

"Nat's going to want them all, you know."

"And I hope you and Nat have a jolly good time yapping about it every moment I am not around," she says deadpan, then pauses. "Did you really think I'd be upset? Is that why this took so long?"

I scrunch my nose and shake my head.

"No, not really. Honestly, kind of the opposite. I thought you'd start planning our wedding." She lifts an eyebrow, then tips her head as if to say it's not *totally* out of the question. "If you start planning mine, I'll start dropping hints to your mom that you'll be getting engaged soon."

She gives me a horrified look, and I let out a loud laugh.

"A truce," she says, standing and putting a hand out. I follow, and when she takes my hand, she pulls me into her, a familiar hold I've felt a million times over my lifetime. "I'm happy for you, Hallie. I know this was a big step for you."

And this is why Wren King is my best friend in the entire universe, more sister than friend: she knows me. I don't even have to tell her I was scared, why I was scared, or why I fought the pull to Jesse for so long. She gets it, accepts it, and appreciates it. When I pull back from the hug, her eyes are as watery as mine, and we let out teary laughs.

"Now, let's get downstairs before our guys come barging in to check on us." Then we walk hand in hand out of the room, and I'm not even a little surprised that Jesse and Adam never actually went downstairs without us, instead waiting near the elevator just in case we needed them.

As a group, we move downstairs and find the rest of our crew in the lobby. Once Colton catches sight of us, he grins wide and starts clapping, and Madden, Nat, Adam, and Wren join in quickly, hooting and hollering and generally causing a scene as my face burns.

"That was hot," Nat says as the ruckus dies down. "Hallie going over there, claiming him? Hot. And then, of course, the kiss."

"I'm still trying to bleach my brain of Jesse's hands on my sister's ass," Colt says with a grimace.

Nat lifts her shoulder. "It still was hot."

"I'm just glad we can all finally admit that the temper tantrum Jesse had at The Mill was because he had the hots for Hallie," Madden says.

"I don't have the—" Jesse starts.

"Excuse me?" I say, turning on my...boyfriend? Lover? Shit, I suppose I should have talked *that* part out. He grins at me, an arm moving around my waist and pulling me into his side.

"Oof, already headed to the doghouse. Come on, Jesse, you just got her. Don't fuck it up this fast," Madden says. Jesse looks down at me with a soft smile.

"I don't have the hots for her. I'm in love with her. There's a big difference," he says, and I think I might melt into a puddle.

"Oh, he's good at this," Wren whispers.

"Told you he would be," Adam says. "I saw the looks he gave her."

I'm sure Wren rolls her eyes, but I don't. I'm too busy moving to my tiptoes and pressing a kiss to Jesse's lips in front of everyone.

And god, it feels good.

THIRTY-ONE

JESSE

When we get home from Killington, everything and absolutely nothing at all changes. Hallie and I are, for the most part, out in the open and actually dating, and most nights, she sleeps in my bed. Sometimes, I fuck her at night with her face in the pillow to muffle her moans, but more often than not, we opt for a midday quickie when Emma's at school. A perk of working for ourselves, I suppose.

The main thing that doesn't change is the fact that we don't tell Emma about our change in relationship status. Both Hallie and I agreed to let things settle a bit longer before telling my daughter, though I mostly agreed so as not to scare Hallie off. Her throwing her fears to the wind and telling all of our friends and, on Monday morning, after Emma went off to school, my parents about us was a big step for her.

This means, for the most part, I keep my hands to myself when my daughter is around, and we still set an early morning alarm for Hallie to head home, change, and shower before coming back over for coffee. I'm sure to outsiders it seems silly, her still having her place and us pretending we're anything but fully committed to each other, but if there's anything I've learned over the past year, it's that when it comes to Hallie, patience is always worth it.

Today, two weeks after that trip, I'm looking forward to an easy Friday night. While the worst of the winter weather has passed with spring coming up quickly, today's slushy rain was somehow colder than any typical winter storm. After a full day out in it, all I want to do is eat the dinner I'm sure Hal and Emma made and spend the night on the couch with Hallie.

It's strange, looking forward to long, boring nights, but I covet them now. I didn't realize how lonely my life had become until Hallie started spending more time at my place. Most of my nights were spent doom-scrolling and watching shit TV alone before I moved to bed, then I'd be up at six, get Emma ready, and start it all over. More often than not, we were scrambling to make a simple meal or heading to the main house for dinner, but these days, I come home to my girls waiting for me, both of them excited to share whatever new culinary masterpiece they've created.

When I walk into my front door and spot Hallie's shoes lined up next to Emma's, the ones I brought her two weeks ago, I smile. But it fades when I hear my younger brother's groan filter into the mudroom. Sliding off my jacket and hanging it up on a hook beside Emma's backpack, I flip my hat around and head to the living room.

"Hey, brother. Do you think I look beautiful?" Madden asks, a pair of yellow clip-on earrings hanging from his ears. Emma is wearing similar ones in pink, plus a necklace, and Hallie has just one purple one on, plus a crown.

"Uh, no," I say. "What are you doing?"

"We're playing Pretty Pretty Princess," Madden explains as if I'm a moron. I bought that game for Emma on her fifth birthday, and she hasn't played in years, but somehow, she convinced her uncle to play.

I glance at Hallie, who is fighting back a full-blown laugh, before I turn to my brother.

"Why are you here?" I ask. "What are you doing here, in my house?"

"Hallie wanted to hang out with me. I am her favorite, after all," he says, and despite knowing it's my bed she's sleeping in every night, a flash of jealousy flares. My brother knows it, a smirk spreading on his lips.

"She's busy babysitting Emma. She doesn't need to be babysitting you, too."

My brother throws up his hands, offended. "Excuse me, she was *my* employee first."

Hallie throws one of the plastic rings at his head. "I work for your parents, Madden. Not you."

"You do marketing, and that's my side of the business, so you work for me."

Hallie reaches for her phone, unlocking it while lifting a challenging eyebrow at Madden. "Want me to call your mom again? I'm sure she could iron out that small confusion real nice."

Hallie gives him a look that both entertains me and, strangely enough, turns me on. Granted, everything she does turns me on these days, but that's neither here nor there.

"Jesus, Hallie, why do you always resort to calling my mom?" Madden whines.

"Because you're a little bitch who always folds once I do."

Emma lets out a laugh, and I narrow my gaze on both of my girls.

"Hallie—" I start, but she turns to Emma with a stern look.

"Remember what I said."

Emma nods before filling in. "I can't curse until I'm eighteen and I'm out of my dad's house, even if it seems stupid and totally misogynistic that the world thinks it's okay for boys to curse but not girls," she says, and Hallie smiles wide before nodding. When she turns to look at me, I can't do anything but grin and shake my head at her.

"Anyway, we're all going to The Mill tonight. Colton threatened to kidnap me since he can't check on me next door anymore, and he whines about it to Adam, who whines about it to Wren, who told me she needed me to come. And when your sister calls, I come."

"What does that have to do with me?" I ask, crossing my arms on my chest, even though I know anywhere Hallie goes, I'll be going.

Hallie stands, looping an arm on my shoulder and leaning her head on me. I fight the urge to pull her in close and press my lips to hers, but just barely.

"You have to come, or else I'm going to be stuck with Madden and Nat arguing all night and Adam and Wren making out and Colton doting on me like I'm five." I look down at her and know that what she's saying is the truth: all of those will, in fact, happen. "Please? I'll do anything," she says, and my mind goes places that she clearly can follow. A grin spreads on her lips, and she winks at me. "Emma's going to have a sleepover with your parents tonight, so you'll have a night of peace if you agree."

I know she doesn't actually mean a night of peace, and the true promise she's dangling before me is what has me nodding.

"Okay, fine," I say, stepping back to get much-needed space. We're in mixed company after all. "Are you okay with that?" I ask Emma.

"Yeah!" she says excitedly, nodding. "Grandma said we could watch movies and bake a cake."

"We covered all the bases, so you can't bail," Madden says.

I look to Hallie for confirmation, and she shrugs.

"It'll be fun."

I kiss my peaceful night goodbye, but I don't think I'll miss it too much.

"All right. The Mill it is."

Three hours later, we're at The Mill when Hallie sidles up next to me while I sit at a table with Adam and Madden. The girls have been off, being social butterflies and dancing, occasionally stopping for a drink or to chat before heading back off. It's fun to watch, especially now knowing she's completely mine.

"You're not drinking," she says, and I shake my head.

"I've gotta get us home one way or another."

She bites her lip, pushing her drink away. "I'll stop—"

I grab it and pull it closer. "Hell no. I want a drunk and wild Hallie on my hands tonight."

There's a moment of hesitation before heat flares bright in her eyes. Then she grabs the drink from my hands and downs it before dancing off back to Wren and Nat.

I find out an hour after that, when Hallie is drunk, and we're not hiding out, that Hallie is handsy.

So very handsy.

Every time she passes me, her fingers graze my arms, and her lips brush my cheek, or my temple, or my lips. When she spends longer at the table, she sits in my lap even though there's an empty chair for her. She holds my hand and leans her head on my shoulder. It makes me both want to stay here indefinitely, enjoying being out in the open like this with her, and take her home to show her *exactly* how much I appreciate it and her.

I choose staying, if only that every time I turn, she's laughing loud, dancing, and chatting, and I get to not only see the version of Hallie I loved from afar for years but also to claim her. It's fucking heaven.

I'm chatting with Madden and Adam at the table when Hallie comes back from dancing on the small, makeshift dance floor. She's panting and reaching for her drink when I pull her into my lap and slide a glass of water before her. "Drink this."

"No fun."

"Neither is a hangover or passing out before I get my fill of you tonight. No Emma means no muffling."

She looks at me with a pout, but drinks the water all the same. Once she's done, she reaches for her drink again, and I laugh, shaking my head and pulling her into my lap before pressing a kiss to her neck. She sighs and melts back into me for a moment, and I could sit like this for the rest of my life, happily.

"Gross," Wren says with a grimace.

"This is what you asked for, Wren," Hallie reminds her.

"I did *not* ask for this."

"*All according to my plan*, were your exact words," Hallie counters, and my sister narrows her eyes at Hallie.

"And then I specifically told you I don't want any of the details."

"This is not me giving you details. This is me literally *sitting on my boyfriend's lap*," Hallie says, and when I look over Wren's shoulder, Adam is watching them and fighting back a laugh. It seems he knows better than to laugh out loud at them.

I decide I should step in and end things before they go sour. My hands tighten on Hallie's hips, and I press a kiss to her neck. The distraction works as planned, and she turns her head to look at me, a soft smile on her lips.

"Let's dance," she says, sliding out of my lap, grabbing my hand, and tugging it. "Come on."

I let out a chuckle and shake my head. From beside me, Madden laughs as well. In his many attempts to get me to go out with him as a wingman, he's seen the fact that I cannot dance proven time and time again.

"Not my thing, Hal, you know that." She scrunches her nose up at me, and I bend a bit, pressing my lips to the tip of it. "Hallie, I can't dance."

"A slow dance. I know you can do that, at least," she whines, her arms locking around my neck.

Suddenly, dancing doesn't seem so bad, not if I get a full three minutes with Hallie pressed against me. As if my weakness has been sensed, "Landslide" by Fleetwood Mac interrupts some new pop song, and I look over my shoulder to my sister, who is smiling wide as if they had planned this. I shake my head, but slide my arm along her waist as I pull her in close.

"You're kind of a tyrant," I murmur against her lips, unable to stop myself from pressing them to hers.

"You love it," she murmurs, and I don't argue, because I do. We sway to the song for a minute or so, and I can't seem to remember why I didn't want to dance. Getting her all to myself for just a few minutes is exactly what I needed.

"I always loved this song," she whispers after a bit.

I listen and let the words of the song move through me, since Hallie rarely says she likes something for no reason, without some more profound meaning. She might play whimsical and silly, but everything she does holds meaning, from half-birthday cakes that whisper that someone means so much she wants to celebrate them twice a year, to finding and relating to a motherless deer in the woods, to keeping all of her vision boards as reminders of who she's been and what she's wanted over the years. This song is no different, and when the lyrics sink in, I realize it's the perfect song for her, about finding love but being afraid to chase it, about life changing around you and not being sure if you can handle it.

As I hold her, swaying with our friends and family around us, I can't help but picture dancing again to this song in a different setting. When she speaks, I realize that despite all of her hesitation, we're always on the same page.

"I want this to be our wedding song," she murmurs into my chest. My heart races with her words and the meaning behind them, at the acceptance in them, at the trust they hold.

"Promise?" I ask, looking down at her. She tips her head back and gives me the softest, sweetest look I've ever seen in my life, and somehow, I fall even harder.

"Forever," she whispers. She's been drinking, but she's not blackout drunk, just loose and carefree, and I know that this is a confession in a moment of openness, a moment when her walls are completely down.

"I love you," I tell her, and then my lips crash down to hers. Her arms move to wrap around my neck, to hold me close and deepen the kiss. We're no longer dancing, just standing and kissing as the song fades off.

"Get a room!" my sister calls from behind me, and I let out a small laugh.

"That's not a bad idea," Hallie says with a lifted eyebrow, and that's all the encouragement I need.

As I did weeks ago in this bar, without a goodbye to anyone, I head for the door.

But unlike last time, I do it with Hallie over my shoulder, our friends and families cheering behind us as we go.

We're barely a block from the bar when she starts.

"I'm so hot, Jesse," she whispers, leaning over and pressing a kiss to my neck.

"We'll be home soon." I put a hand on her knee and squeeze. She reaches down, grabbing and slowly sliding it up her soft thigh until I reach her center.

Her bare center.

"Jesus fuck, Hallie. When did you do this?"

She giggles, the sound going breathy as, unable to stop myself, my finger slides along her center. Her hips shift to try and get more, and she's already soaked.

"When you walked around the truck. You took a while chatting with Madden."

Madd had called out to us when we were almost to the car, waving me down because Hallie's purse was left on the table when I carried her out.

"You took your panties off while I was talking to my brother?" I ask, wanting to sound aghast but unable to as my fingers slide up, circling her clit, and her breath catches.

"Gotta do what you gotta do." Her hand shifts, moving to my crotch, where I'm already growing hard, and strokes me through my jeans. "You don't seem to mind much."

"You're in my truck, no panties on, wet as fuck, and we're

heading home to an empty house. No, I'm not complaining." She lets out a laugh that moves to a moan as I slide one finger inside her, then back out.

"You know, I think you deserve a prize for being so responsible tonight," she murmurs. Before I can question what she means, her hand is moving up to the button of my jeans and deftly undoing it.

"Hallie," I say, a warning with no heat behind it. A warning she ignores, which is no surprise. Instead, she undoes my zipper, then slides her hand beneath my underwear. "Hallie."

This time, it's more of a sigh as she wraps her hand around me, then pulls my cock out as I drive out of town toward the farm. I allow myself to glimpse down for just a moment at her small, soft hand that is wrapped around me, then tugging gently. A bead of precum is already on the tip, and I groan as she dips her head to lick the tip.

Never in my life have I been more grateful I have this shitty old truck with a bench seat instead of a fancier model with a center console than I am right now.

I'm even more grateful as her head dips further, wrapping her lips around the head of my cock and sucking. A strained breath leaves me, and I wage an internal battle. I should tell her to stop, to be responsible, and wait until we get home. But as her head lowers, bobbing over me, lips sliding down, I can't find the words to get her to stop.

"Hallie," I say, my voice low, forcing my hips not to lift and go deeper as my fingers grip the wheel tightly. After a few sucks, she pops off and looks at me.

"Come on, Jesse. Take what you need." Then she reaches up, taking my hand and putting it on her head before sliding down on me, the tip of my cock hitting the back of her throat as we turn onto the King property, thankful that the rest of the drive is so familiar, I could probably drive it with my eyes closed, not that I'll be doing that.

I keep my fingers in her hair, but don't tug, don't push her deeper, don't fuck her face the way she clearly is asking for. Instead, I make it to my house, park out front, then turn the key to kill the engine, a bit of relief.

"Come on. Inside," I demand, and she pulls back and shakes her head.

"I'm not ready," she mewls, then shifts, her knees going to the bench seat, ass tipping up, back arching as she moves to lick the tip of my cock again before sinking her head. When I look over, her skirt is bunched at her waist, and I hit the overhead lights to get a better view of her peach-shaped ass in the air as she sucks me off.

Fucking magnificent.

I slide my fingers into her hair and pull, then press her back down, giving her what she wants. She moans around me as my other hand reaches over, sliding down her back and between her legs to finger her. My head falls back, my eyes drifting shut as I fall into my own personal form of heaven: Hallie's wet pussy on my fingers, her mouth around my cock, her muffled, needy moans filling the space.

I could easily come like this.

But I have bigger plans for tonight, so I pull her head back, her eyes watering and lips puffy as she looks at me, and I groan at the sight, my resolve weakening. My hand reaches up, brushing the spit along her lip before sliding my fingers, wet from her, into her mouth. She laps at them greedily, sucking the same way she did on my cock, and I groan again.

I need to get her inside.

Now.

Sliding my fingers out of her mouth, I tuck my cock back into my pants, though I don't bother with redoing the button or zipper. "Get inside, strip down, and bend over the couch." She looks at me dazed, brows furrowing. "I've been dying to fuck you on that couch, Hallie. No one's home, I'm taking you there first. So go inside, strip down, and wait for me bent over the arm of the couch." Her eyes lit, hearing the *first* way I hoped. We have the house to ourselves tonight. I plan for it to be the first of many.

Hallie licks her lips, grins, and then nods.

"Okay," she says, then shifts, tugging her skirt down a bit and stepping out of the truck before moving quickly to the house.

I move slowly behind her, watching the door slam behind her, and the lights flick on, then laughing when the green fabric of her skirt hits the glass of the front window. By the time I make it inside, Hallie is nowhere to be seen, but there is a trail of clothes leading toward the living room. Quickly, I take off my boots, hang my jacket, and then strip off my shirt.

Reaching into my pocket for my wallet, I grab the condom I slid in there, replacing it after Vermont. Hallie's on the pill, and I am desperate to feel her tighten around me without anything between us, but I don't think tonight is the night to tell her I want to fuck her bare and hope her birth control holds.

Or that if it doesn't, that's a risk I'm willing to take with her.

Baby steps with my Hallie.

So instead, I palm the small packet as I move through my house and slip off my jeans and underwear as I do until I'm in the living room, where I told her to wait for me.

The sight takes my breath away.

Hallie bends over the arm of the couch I've dreamt about fucking her on for weeks, legs splayed, hips rocking as she moans, her fingers working her clit. I stand there for a few moments as she slides her fingers into her, fucking herself with two fingers before moving back to her clit. The sounds she makes are breathy and needy.

"*Fuck*," I groan, standing to watch the show for a moment, wrapping my hand around my cock to stoke it. One day in the far future, I'll come like this—jacking off while Hallie fingers herself bent over the couch, ending it by spilling over her back.

But not tonight. I need to be inside her far too much.

And especially not when she looks over her shoulder at me, moans louder at the sight of me stroking myself, and then gives me wide pleading eyes before speaking. "Please, Jesse."

Another pained moan leaves my lips as I take long strides to her, unwrapping and rolling on the condom in record time. But instead of slamming in deep, I move to my knees behind her. My hands move to her ass, tipping and spreading her, her toes barely on the floor as I lean in and eat her pussy. My tongue dives in deep, and her fingers continue to work her clit. I groan into her as she tightens around me, and my fingers bruise the flesh of her as I grip her tighter as she screams my name, coming hard and fast.

Before she's even finished, I move to standing, grab my cock, and slide into her hard and fast. Her head snaps back, and she cries out, her cunt pulsing around me as she continues to come or maybe comes again.

I don't know, and I don't care.

I'm already so fucking close after hours of torturous foreplay followed by the last ten minutes in my truck.

"This one's going to be quick," I say, sliding out and then slamming back in.

"Yes, yes, yes."

"Such a fucking tease," I groan as her hips back into me, back arching, hands in the cushion of the couch. "Fuck, you're so tight like this. This pussy is so fucking good, Hallie." She tightens around me, and I clench my jaw, then shift her a bit so her clit will rub against the arm of the couch she's bent over.

"Fuck!" she shouts as I pound into her, my hand sliding up her back to her neck, then wrapping her copper strands around my hand. Her head moves back, and I tug, a deep, guttural moan leaving her lips. The sound goes straight to my cock, and I let out a groan.

Sometimes, Hallie likes it soft and sweet.

Sometimes, she needs it rough, and it seems this is one of those nights.

I continue to fuck into her, her hips bucking back into me, tipping and taking me deeper, before I can't hold out any longer. "Get there, Hallie," I grit out, my balls drawing up as the orgasm starts to become imminent.

"Jesse."

"Fucking get there, Hallie."

"Jesse." It's a more frantic sound, filled with need and tinged with panic as she tightens around me.

I tug on her hair again, and she gasps.

"Fucking *get there, Hallie*," I demand, my hand pulling back to come down hard on her ass, the slap echoing in the room.

That's what it does.

Her entire body tightens before she comes, the sound starting with a *J* before melting into a scream, and her entire body shakes with her orgasm.

That's what sends me over the edge, slamming in deep one last time and coming hard and long into her, my body collapsing over hers. My arms on the couch are the only thing stopping me from crushing her as I pepper kisses along her neck.

THIRTY-TWO

JESSE

The sun floods my room the next morning, waking me up instead of a blaring alarm, and the first thing I register is Hallie's naked body glued to mine, her cheek smooshed to my chest, a leg hitched up over mine as she holds me in her sleep.

I'm the luckiest asshole on earth, and the woman before me is undeniable proof of that. I lift my hand and slide my fingers through her hair, pushing it back and away from her face so I can take in her beauty. Her long eyelashes resting against her cheeks, the freckles that got a bit lighter with summer so long ago, her pink lips pouty and full. After our first round, I managed to convince her to wash the makeup off her face, knowing she'd hate waking up with it on, so the flush on her cheeks is all hers.

She's beautiful.

The most beautiful woman on earth and all mine.

Eventually, after another ten minutes or so of lying like this and watching her sleep, she starts to stir, eyes moving beneath her eyelids, her tongue coming out to wet her lips before she blinks, then looks up at me, groggy and sleepy. "Morning," I whisper. It's my favorite part of every day, though there's usually little to no light to see her with when my alarm goes off at the ass crack of dawn so that she can sneak out.

Then she grimaces.

"Why did you let me drink so much last night?" She puts a hand over her face and buries it further into my chest.

I let out a laugh and shake my head, moving and shifting her until she's lying on top of me.

"I think you're very aware that no one can ever tell you what to do, Hallie, much less *let* you do something."

She groans, head falling into my neck and breathing there for a few moments.

"Well, maybe you should start."

"Are you sick?" Worry trickles in because if she's contemplating letting me tell her what to do outside of the bedroom, she must really not feel well, but she shakes her head.

"Just a headache." Well, that's fixable.

"Water, meds, breakfast. You'll be good as new," I say, hands going to her hips and moving us both so I'm sitting on the edge of the bed with her in my lap. On instinct, her legs wrap around my hips, and I stand, walking us to the dresser, where I set her before digging through my drawers for a sweatshirt. She has some clothes here, but I know she would rather steal another of my sweatshirts.

"Pancakes and bacon?" she mumbles as I pull one over her head.

"Only option," I say with a smile, leaning in to press a kiss to her lips before sliding a pair of my boxer briefs up her legs and then helping her off the dresser. "Go use the bathroom, I'll meet you in the kitchen."

She nods, then shuffles off.

I get dressed in a T-shirt and sweatpants quickly before moving to the kitchen. I start the coffee, then pull things out of the fridge. When she shuffles in, I move to her, grab her one last time, and set her on the counter next to where I'll be making breakfast before handing her a glass of water and two pills.

"Coffee?" she asks, and I'm glad to see her eyes have cleared.

Most of her sluggishness seems to have been grogginess, not a terrible hangover.

I press a kiss to her lips, then make her a coffee and bring it over to her.

"I love you," she mutters, then takes a long sip of the drink.

"Love you more," I murmur, then stand between her legs, my hands moving to cup her jaw and press my lips to hers. She sets the coffee to the side before her hands move to the back of my head, playing with the hair there and kissing me softly and slowly when it happens.

The door opens.

Feet hit the floor.

And then a shriek fills the kitchen.

"*Oh my god!*"

Hallie is still in my arms, and I turn quickly to see my daughter, her jacket and boots over a pair of pajamas, her eyes wide as she takes in Hallie and me.

"*Oh. My.GOD!*" she yells again. "Ahh!"

"Emma, honey, what the fuck?" I ask, staring at her. Panic fills me, not only because she just caught me kissing Hallie, who is wearing nothing but my sweater, which thankfully covers more than enough of her, but also because there's no good reason for her to be here this early in the morning after Mom watched her. "Is everything okay? Why are you here?"

She stares at me for a moment, confused, before shaking her head.

"Oh, yeah, I just forgot my charger, so I ran over to grab it to show Grandma a video on my phone, but *oh. MY. GOD.*"

Well, that answers that. My phone on the counter blinks with a new text I can only assume is from Mom, warning me. I'll have to talk to her about that, though, in her defense, Emma dropping in to grab something she forgot has never been an issue before.

"Emma," Hallie starts, voice soft and nervous, but Emma doesn't let her speak any further.

"You two are TOGETHER!" she shouts, then starts jumping up and down, and that's when I realize it's not horror she's experiencing after catching Hallie and me together. It's elation.

Relief floods me, and I reach back to put a hand on Hallie's knee and give it a reassuring squeeze. Her hand covers mine, returning the gesture.

"Uncle Madden SO owes me money!" she shouts, then starts moving, running through the house with her arms up as if on a victory lap.

I don't know what to do about my brother making bets with my daughter, even though it's a sure-fire loss for him, but I decide that's something I can handle another day.

"Hey, hey," I say, stopping her with an arm on her waist when she passes through the kitchen again. When I look at Hallie, she's grinning, clearly not as nervous about this conversation as I thought she might be. I return her smile, then put my hands on my daughter's shoulders, looking at her seriously. "Are you really okay with this?"

"Are you and Hallie dating?" she asks, getting right to the point.

"Yes."

The answer comes from Hallie, all confidence and no hesitation, and the single word settles warm in my chest. Emma was the last barrier between us being *everything*, and she just tore it down in a moment.

Emma turns to her, nods, then returns her gaze to me.

"Are you going to marry her?" Emma asks as if she's Hallie's father instead of my kid. Hallie coughs, but I keep my eyes on my daughter.

"Yes," I say, just as confident as Hallie just spoke. Emma grins.

"Then I am so totally okay with this."

Emma turns to look at Hallie behind me, and I do the same. I expect to see a hint of the panic I'm used to on Hallie's face when I move things too quickly, but surprisingly, I don't. Instead, there's simply happiness, and maybe a little surprise, on Hallie's face.

That's when I know I did it.

I made it past her walls, battled her fears, and while I didn't slay them, they're safely in cages now.

I have Hallie. All of her.

Forever.

THIRTY-THREE

The next six weeks move by in a haze.

Not long after Emma finds out about Jesse and me, Mr. King installs a greenhouse for Mrs. King, and Emma and I help her plant hundreds of flower seedlings over the course of a week. At the end of March, I watch Emma during spring break, while Jesse, Madden, and Mr. King rip up an entire field over three days to make Mrs. King's pick-your-own flower field. Each night, Jesse comes home and grumbles about it, and I smile. Still, when I offhandedly mention that a little garden would be fun for Emma and me at dinner, the guys spend the fourth day building raised beds complete with a fence and trellis to keep Jane Doe out.

Despite the fact that I'm rarely at my house, I keep the feed that I leave for her stocked, as well as adding a second salt block to Jesse's place, and in early April, Emma meets my deer friend for the first time.

"What's her name?" she asks, holding out a piece of celery. Even though Jesse isn't a fan, so we rarely cook with it, I make sure both houses always have a bundle of celery on hand, and when I spotted

Jane while we were out in the garden thinning the carrot seedlings, I was glad I did.

"Jane Doe," I tell her.

"She looks like a Jane," Emma says simply, further proving that we just *get* each other. "How'd you meet her?" Unlike her dad, Emma doesn't question my quirks or show any fear when the deer approaches us; instead, she takes my instructions to get the celery quickly and eagerly offers some to my friend.

"I saw her back in January. Deer this young usually stick with their moms, so when I spotted her alone, I kind of made it my mission to find her." I turn to smile at her. "Your dad was not pleased that I was wandering out in the woods alone."

Emma laughs, then nods as Jane accepts the stalk, pulling it gently from her hands.

"She doesn't have a mom?" I shrug.

"If she does, she's not around."

Emma pauses, not even looking at me as she reaches for another piece of celery.

"She'll be okay. We'll look out for her."

I don't know if Emma meant the, *just like we look out for each other*, that I insert in my mind, but when she looks at me, giving me a soft smile that looks so much like her dad, I hear it all the same.

And more and more, I'm realizing that's the truth.

We have each other, so we'll always be okay.

BREAK TK

By late April, I spend barely any time at my place. When I do, it's alarmingly quiet, and I almost always find an excuse to leave, to go to the main house or to Wren's or Madden's or just wait at Jesse's until he or Emma comes home.

"You know, you should just move in, Hallie," Emma says offhand-edly during dinner one night, and my fork freezes halfway to my mouth.

"What?" Out of the corner of my eye, I can see Jesse is smirking wide, probably because for about a month he's been saying the same thing. I repeatedly tell him I don't think it's fair to force that on Emma, but now I think I'm about to lose the argument.

"You're here, like, all the time now. Why bother with a whole other house? I mean, most of your things are here as it is. Just another place for you to have to clean."

"I've been telling her that, too," Jesse adds, his smirk moving to a full-blown grin at this point, and I glare at him.

"Did your dad put you up for this?" I ask, and when genuine confusion crosses her face, I know the answer.

"No. I just think it's kind of stupid for you to be split between two places. At this point, your house is just overflow storage."

I spear a baby carrot on my fork and try to play it as casually as humanly possible.

"Would you be okay with that? If I moved in?"

"Why wouldn't I?" she asks, her face filled with genuine confusion.

"Well, it's just that it's always been you and your dad here. I would be another person in your space."

Now she looks at me like I'm the one losing it.

"Aren't you going to move in eventually anyway?" I hesitate, then nod, and Emma nods like it's common sense. "Then there's no need to put it off."

I set my fork down and look to Emma, assessing her face and trying to read any hidden feelings she might be hiding. I've learned to read her pretty well over the past few months, but right now, there's nothing but genuineness, and just like that, one last barrier is gone.

"Okay, well...then, I guess I'll move in."

Emma shrugs like it's no big deal to her. "I can help you start packing up the rest of your stuff after school."

I nod, then look to Jesse. He's grinning wide, eyes shining, joy emanating from him, and I know I just made the right decision.

BREAK TK

Over the next few days, Emma helps me box up my things, and the Thursday before Wren's spring festival, knowing we have a busy weekend of helping her out ahead of us, Jesse helps us bring the last of my things to his house.

"What are these?" Emma asks, lifting a familiar pink box. I catch Jesse's eyes across the room, and an entertained look spreads over his face, but I no longer feel the need to hide them away.

Hell, he already knows all of my secrets, after all.

"Those are all of my vision boards since Wren and I started making them."

Emma's eyes go wide with excitement, and she sits on the edge of my bed before removing the lid and taking out the stack of papers. Carefully, she starts to flip through them, each a time capsule of sorts for a year in my life.

"How many of these have you done?" she asks, looking at me.

I shrug, sifting through the pages. Some of them have hand-written lists of the items I wanted to do that year on the back, and I scan them.

"I did that," I say, pointing to the one from last year that said to get three more clients.

"And I guess you've *almost* done that," she says with a laugh, showing me one that says *Mrs. King*.

Just like last time, a deep blush burns on my cheeks.

"I always had a crush on your dad, even when I was totally invisible to him."

"And let's be grateful for that, yeah? When you made that, you were, what? Fourteen? That would have made me nineteen. Pretty happy I didn't notice you then."

I let out a laugh and shake my head, but nod all the same. He lifts some and sifts through them, the same as Emma is doing. I've never shared these with anyone other than Wren and Nat, and whenever someone has tried to dig through them, an acute sense of panic and a need to hide them has washed over me. But now, I don't feel that. Instead, they feel more like an artifact from my childhood, a bit of nostalgia I'm happy to share with these two.

"Learn to surf?" he asks, looking at me with a raised eyebrow.

"Wren and I watched that movie *Blue Crush* and thought it sounded so fun."

"Go to the Bahamas, go to Paris, go to London, go to Rome," Jesse reads on the back of one, and I laugh, grabbing it from his hands and flipping it over. It's one of the very first vision boards I made with Wren, and the front is mostly cut-out photos of movie covers of all of the Mary-Kate and Ashley movies we watched and loved.

"You really wanted to do a lot and go everywhere, didn't you?" he asks, voice soft.

I smile up at him and shrug.

"There was a long time when I didn't feel like I belonged anywhere. If you don't have a place you belong, I think inherently, you want to wander to try and find it, even if you don't realize that's why." He continues to flip through vision boards where travels and career goals, and personal desires are all laid out. All of my hopes and dreams were glued to 8.5 x 11 pieces of cardstock. I reach out my hand, grab his, and his head lifts to look at me. "I found that place, finally."

His eyes warm, and his smile softens as his hand squeezes mine, and we sit like that for long moments before Emma breaks into our bubble.

"I love the ooey gooey, but I'm also starving," she says, and I snap my head to her to see that while I was distracted, she stacked up all of my vision boards and slid them back into the box. The only one left is the one in Jesse's hands. He stares at it one last time before handing it to Emma and standing.

"Well, that sounds like my cue to get these in the truck so I can get my girls fed."

"Prima?" Emma asks, placing the lid on the box and standing. Jesse agrees, then lifts the boxes and heads out the door.

Later that night, when the three of us are sitting on the couch watching *Holiday in the Sun*, which is arguably one of the best of the Mary-Kate and Ashley films, it clicks that for the first time in my life, I feel settled.

I spent so much of my life trying to think of things to fill a void in my soul. New hobbies, picking up odd jobs, and visions of travel and far-off accomplishments, but even when I did manage to cross things off, it didn't fix it, didn't fill that spot inside of me, never made me feel settled.

But here on the couch, watching a nostalgic movie and listening to Jesse and Emma jokingly tear apart its admitted plot holes, I feel whole.

THIRTY-FOUR

The Sunday between Mother's Day and Memorial Day is Wren's strawberry festival. After talking to the town board, they agreed that a community event coordinator would benefit the town, especially since many of their events attract tourists. Even though they told Wren that they could move things around and find money in the budget for the position, Wren went ahead with planning the spring festival anyway, and she's done a fantastic job at actually delegating tasks for it.

"I can't believe you did this," I say to my best friend, looking around at the county festival grounds as we stand in the exclusive area behind the giant stage currently blaring music from a local band. Hundreds of cars are neatly parked in the grassy lot, and from what I've heard, they sold two thousand entry tickets. At the center of the fairgrounds are many food trucks and vendors, mostly businesses from Holly Ridge. On one side is a handful of rides and games, and on the other are some animals from the 4-H club, but the real draw for the day is the giant stage where, an hour ago, Atlas Oaks played a full set as a favor for Adam.

That said, I'm pretty sure the community coordinator's salary will be paid for years to come.

Jesse and Madden just ran off to grab us food, and Emma and I are standing in the VIP section with the band, Wren, Adam, Nat, and Leo, Adam's publicist and the band's manager.

"It's wild, right? I was just going to do it small, but then Adam mentioned a micro-festival vibe could be cool. I didn't want him to feel like I was using him for his connections, but he made the call without my even knowing, and the band was on board before he even suggested it." Wren grins wider. "He even got their event management company and security contacts to donate free services as well, so I didn't even have to do much. Isn't that wild?"

I don't tell her that the reason Adam did all of that was so he could ensure she wouldn't overwork herself with this event. Knowing Adam, he foresaw her burning herself out in her effort and did anything he could to stop it.

"Do you think he could get Willa Stone next year?" Emma asks, nearly skipping as she goes. From her neck dangles a VIP badge that gives her backstage access. Last night, we had dinner at the King house with the band, and after spending most of the night with Stella Greene and Harper Holden, she's told me that next year's vision board will include learning to play the guitar, writing a song, and learning to sew. I mentally added a guitar and sewing machine to my potential Christmas gift list.

"I could probably make that happen," Reed, the bassist for Atlas Oaks, says, putting an arm around Emma's shoulders. A blush burns on her cheeks, and I bite back a laugh.

"No, you could not," Beckett, the drummer of the band, says deadpan. "No one tells Willa what to do." I've learned in our small time with the band that Reed is the goofy, happy-go-lucky one and Beckett is the serious one.

"I wouldn't be *telling her what to do*. We just have to tell her how great this event was, and she'll totally do this for Adam," Reed says.

"Or I could ask her. We're kind of friends," Emma says with a proud smile, and my heart swells at the look. In the past six months, Emma's confidence has absolutely skyrocketed, and it's so fun to see.

"I heard about that," Leo says, tapping his phone screen and sliding it back into his pocket. The man seems to be on that thing constantly. "Heard you were a cool kid and that the town seemed full of good people. It's why when Adam asked about this festival, I knew the band would be interested." I don't know if he means it, if he and the pop star actually talked about Emma, but I could hug the stoic man for putting the excited look on my girl's face

"I hear you're thinking of leaving the city and might be looking at a house here?" Stella Greene, the wife of the lead singer, Riggins, says as she shifts a baby on her hip. A sparkle comes to her eye when Leo nods in his agreement. "You know, there are plenty of houses in Ashford for sale."

Leo shakes his head at her suggestion. "I'm kind of liking this place. Far enough away from the chaos without being too far from airports and transportation. Ashford is in the middle of fucking nowhere. I could never live there."

Riggins hooks an arm around his wife's waist and tugs her into his side.

"Plus, I don't need Leo near us. Ashford is where we go to escape him. If Leo were nearby, he'd be knocking on our door every day with some new idea."

Leo glares at the rockstar, who seems so much more like a regular guy than I expected.

"I'm so sorry, I want to get you guys' work. Maybe if you stopped dropping off the face of the earth, I wouldn't feel the need to show up at your front door."

"We'll go on tour sometime. I just need this guy to be a bit bigger, you know?" Riggins says, leaning to poke his son in the belly, a loud baby laugh filling the air.

"Yeah, yeah," Leo starts, then goes to say something else before they're interrupted by a man in a tight-fitting black T-shirt with

Wilde Security stretched across the front, and Leo's stern manager face returns. "All good, Jaime?"

The man nods, then looks around the group.

"There's a woman at the entrance trying to get access, and she's starting to cause a scene. She doesn't have a pass and isn't on the list, but is insisting she belongs back here."

"Did she give a name?" Wren asks, confused.

Jaime nods. "Name was Kim Dunne. She said she knows you, specifically, Wren."

My entire body goes still, and I turn with wide eyes to my best friend, who is looking at me the same way.

"Kim? Like, my mom?" Emma asks, and panic moves through me, utterly unsure of how to handle this. Jesse and Madden just left to get us some food before the show starts, but I need him here now.

"Text Jesse," I say to Wren, but don't stop to see if she followed my command, since Emma has started to move toward the gates of the VIP section. Jaime jogs after her, and I follow closely behind.

"That's her! That's my baby!" a woman's voice calls out, and my attention moves in her direction, seeing a familiar blond arguing with a couple of security guards. Jaime calls something, and the guards step aside, letting Kim inside the VIP area. She moves quickly to where Emma stops, and I stop right beside her. "Emma! Give your mom a hug!"

Emma stands, confused and awkward, as her mom pulls her into her arms.

That's when I realize everyone we were talking to came with us, not because I saw them, but because when Kim hugs Emma, her eyes never meet her daughter; instead, they widen with excitement at the group behind us.

The hug breaks, and Emma takes a step back, closer to me, something Kim notices but doesn't get a chance to question.

"Kim?" a familiar voice asks, and with it, relief washes through me. A moment later, Jesse, his anger barely masked on his face as Madden moves behind him, comes into sight.

"Hey, Jesse. How's it going? Sorry, I didn't call," Kim says as he joins our growing group.

"What are you doing here?" Jesse says, cutting straight to the chase.

"I thought I'd surprise my baby girl! Surprise!" she says as she puts her hands out to her sides.

I take in the gorgeous blond woman, seeing Emma's features in her face, in the blue of her eyes, and in the way her smile tilts more on one side than the other. Emma has the King family nose and smooth dark hair, making her often look like she could be Wren's kid, but there's no way you couldn't see the resemblance between Kim and Emma.

"How did you know we were here?" Jesse asks, and Kim bites her lips.

"I saw Wren posting about the festival a bunch on social media, and then this morning she posted to her stories a picture of Emma with everyone. I was in New York, and I figured it would be a good day to head over here for a fun surprise."

Wren pales, more likely than not taking the blame for this mess now, but I try to remember the pictures Wren posted this morning. The only one I can think of with Emma in it was Emma with the band, and my stomach sours.

An uncomfortable silence hangs between us, and I don't have to look at Jesse to feel the fury rolling off him in waves, but I do catch eyes with Wren, whose jaw is tight and her eyes are narrowed. There aren't many people whom Wren hates, but Kim is on that very short list.

"Emma, introduce me to everyone," Kim says, but Emma stands there, her own quiet skepticism brewing. It's a perfect storm, and it crashes down all around me with no real way to stop it from happening.

When no one speaks, Kim turns to Adam. "You're Adam Porter, right? I'm Kim. I'm a big fan," she says, batting her eyes at my best friend's boyfriend. Wren gets a confused look on her face, mainly because, while in the industry, Adam might be a notable name, outside it, he's not an extremely noticeable face, which is how he likes it.

"Uh, yeah," Adam says, clearly just as confused.

"God, it's so crazy you're here in Holly Ridge. Nothing ever happens here. It's why I had to get out, you know?" There's more uncomfortable silence before Kim's now stiff smile turns to Leo. "And you're Leo, right? Adam's agent? I thought I recognized you on Wren's socials. I'm a singer myself."

A cold rush moves through me.

You have *got* to be fucking kidding me.

Beside me, Jesse goes still as well.

But it's Emma's cold words that cut through the group like a knife.

"Did you come here to talk to Adam?" Emma asks before I can think of anything to say to avoid this inevitable mess, and with her questions, my heart breaks.

"What?"

"Did you come here to talk to Adam? Because, you know, he's in the music industry and you want to be a singer or whatever, right?" God, the girl is smart. Too freaking smart. "And Willa Stone is his friend."

"I did see that you had a little chat with Willa on your birthday. What a sweet surprise! You know, I have a demo. Maybe next time you talk to her—"

I watch as recognition and understanding filter over Emma's face, the small spark of hope that she held for her mom when she saw her here flickering out as she realizes the truth.

I hate this for her. I hate it so much, and even more, I hate that there was nothing I could do to protect her from it. I remember when she backed out of the party, Jesse said something similar, and now it's my turn. Unfortunately, there are no planters nearby to throw at trees, so instead, I use my words.

When I speak, my words are laced not just with anger and frustration for Emma but, embarrassingly, my own hurt and anger, years and years in the making, and all of it erupts.

"Emma, come here." I put a hand out to her, and something in me eases when she takes it without a moment of hesitation before I tug her to me.

"Excuse me?" Kim asks, a sneer in the words as she steps closer to us.

The need to put something between Kim and Emma racks through me, and I shift my body. "Emma, get behind me. Actually..." I turn my head, my eyes wide and wild, I'm sure, looking for Madden. I spot him, and relief courses through me. "Madden, can you take her? Bring her home?"

"I came all this way to see my daughter. Who do you think—"

I shake my head, the fury nearly unmanageable now.

"You cannot get away with this bullshit anymore," I say, my words firm, and a dozen eyes turn to me, but my gaze is locked on the woman in front of me. "You missed Christmas. You missed her birthday. You missed a dozen other opportunities to see your daughter without a moment of hesitation. You do not get to come in and claim her when you decide she can benefit you. When you decide she has some use to you. There are a dozen people here who love that girl to pieces right now, but you are not one of them."

"I don't know who you think you are, but—" Kim says, her sweet demeanor melting quickly and turning to venom.

"Madden, take Emma. Bring her home. We'll be home soon after you guys," Jesse says, cutting her off. Madden nods, and Jesse steps in my direction, putting an arm around my waist, and Kim's face tips with a cruel smile. She opens her mouth to speak, but Jesse raises a hand, fire in his words. "Shut up until she's gone."

Kim's jaw goes tight, but she stays silent as Madden walks Emma off, which really says everything I need to know.

If it were me, I would be throwing a fit if someone led Emma off without me, without my even saying goodbye to her, and she's not even my daughter. In contrast, Kim just stands there, staring Jesse down like she's ready for a fight.

When Emma's out of earshot, Jesse speaks. "This is fucking low, even for you."

That cruel smile spreads, making her pretty face ugly as she shifts her gaze to Jesse's arm around me.

"I see you're back to playing house," she says, eyes flicking to me and ignoring his accusation. "You finally found some poor, stupid girl to slot into your perfect family, huh?"

Jesse goes still beside me, and I try my best not to look confused.

"Does she keep the house clean for you? Does she make you a hot meal every night and watch the kid while you're off doing God knows what?"

The blood drains from my face with her words, not because they hit too true, but because of the way Jesse's hand tightens on my waist. A dozen tiny conversations make more sense now, and each of them makes me want to hit the woman before me.

"Have you drained all of the life out of her yet? Crushed all of the dreams she had so you could force her to be your perfect little Stepford wife."

"Who the fuck do you think you are?" I ask, that fury coming back tenfold. I've never hated someone with such vehemence as I do this woman. First, she put that sad look on Emma's face, and now she's making Jesse look like he saw a ghost.

Her attention turns to me, that malicious sneer making my stomach churn. Her head tips, faux kindness rolling off her. "You seem sweet, but if I were you, I'd run, or else all those hopes and dreams you have for yourself will disappear before you know it." She gives me a once-over, eyes pausing for a moment on Jesse's hand at my waist. "Just a fair warning," she says with a single, carefree lift of her shoulder.

I open my mouth to speak, but I'm interrupted before I can.

"You said you're a singer?" a voice behind me says. I don't turn to look, but I don't have to as Leo steps forward, eyes locked on Kim.

He's all business, his light brown hair perfectly coiffed and combed back, and a white button-down tucked into slacks despite the casual get-together. Most importantly, the way he looks down his nose at Kim gives the vibe as if he thinks she's no better than the scum beneath his shoe.

"I am," Kim says, ignoring the look. "Kim Dunne. I would love to get a moment of your time. I have a demo—" She moves to dig through her bag, but Leo stops her.

"Don't bother. I am not a fan of people who manipulate and use their children for personal gain," he says. From the look on his face, I can tell he means it to his core, that it's something he's seen before and absolutely loathes. "If I were you, I would find a new hobby."

"Excuse me?"

"My reach is broad. Jesse is a friend of Adam's, and he's Wren's brother. From what I've seen, you are neither a friend to either of them nor a good person. After the scene I just saw and the few details I know, I feel confident in saying that by the end of the week, I will make it known to all of my contacts that you are a talent I will never touch, nor will any of my many, many clients and colleagues."

Her face goes ghostly white, and I have to admit, a bit of a rush runs through me.

She deserves nothing but the absolute worst.

"You didn't even hear my side—"

"I'm very much uninterested in hearing another word from your mouth, much less an entire fabricated tale." Leo speaks with such precision, with such malice in his words, that Kim doesn't know how to respond, her mouth opening and closing a handful of times before she speaks.

"You know what? Fuck all of you. I should have known better than to come back to this shithole of a town. Only fucking has-beens would play here, anyway."

"Is she talking about us?" Reed asks in a stage whisper.

"I think she is," Wes replies.

"That's such a bummer for you guys," Harper, Wes' wife, says, and despite myself—despite the shit that this afternoon has been—I find myself starting to smile, but it melts when Kim's ire turns to me.

"When he drains you dry, feel free to reach out. We can compare war stories," she says to me before turning on her heel and walking off into the crowd.

Without a word, Jaime follows her.

I can't help but hope she's walking out of our lives for good.

THIRTY-FIVE

We drive home in silence, both of us lost in our own thoughts. I check my phone and see Madden texted the group chat that he's with Emma at our house, then a second, private text from Wren telling me not to worry about coming to help with the cleanup. Usually, I'd argue, wanting to help my friend after her long day, but right now, my little family is my priority.

And today, I realized we're just that: a little family. A bit unconventional and surely not the family I ever thought I'd have, but still *my* little family, and one I'll do anything to protect.

Still, with the way Jesse's jaw is set tight, the way he's barely said two words since we got into the car, I worry if I went too far with taking the reins this afternoon, with talking that way to Kim the way I did, and with telling Madden to get Emma out of there. At the time, it felt right, like I was doing what I had to for my girl, but maybe that's not my place yet. Perhaps it will *never* be my place, something that I would understand at the end of the day.

"I'm sorry I snapped at her," I say quietly when we turn onto the Three Kings property. "I should have cooled down, walked away, and let you handle it. My own emotions clouded my judgment, and I didn't—"

"What?" Jesse finally averts his gaze, which has been deadset on the windshield, to look at me, with genuine confusion on his face. The county fairgrounds are about fifteen minutes from the house, and he hasn't looked away once that entire time.

"I'm sorry that I told Madden to take Emma, and I'm sorry I yelled at Kim. It wasn't my place, and—"

"The fuck it wasn't," he says, voice low.

Well, now I'm confused.

I assumed his silence was irritation with me, but if that's not the case...

"Then why are you mad at me?" I stare at his profile and watch his face shift, but I can't decode it.

"I'm not mad at you, Hallie." Silence fills the cab of the truck again before he sighs and reaches for my hand, finding it without even looking. He squeezes it, and some of the panic in my chest fades. "I'm just...thinking."

"Well, the way you're doing it makes me assume you're pissed at me, and it's kind of sending me into a spiral."

He laughs, shaking his head, and more of that panic fades.

We're good.

He's laughing.

"I'm just stuck in my head. Not your fault." I stare at him for a moment, but then we're pulling into the gravel drive beside Madden's truck. After turning off the engine, he turns to me with a smile on his face that feels forced, and whatever unease that had left comes right back into my chest. "Now we have to go in and relieve Madden and talk to Emma."

I nod, a bit appeased, but that knot is still settling in my chest.

Time. Time is all that can help with this.

"Can I talk to her first?" I ask in a whisper. His face softens as if he already knows where this is going, but I continue. "I need to apologize for acting like that in front of her. You thank Madden, say goodbye to him, kick him out, then hang out in the living room."

His hand lifts, cupping my cheek, his thumb brushing over the skin there.

"That works. While you do that, I'm going to call Adam to see if his security guy can confirm Kim is gone."

I nod in agreement.

"Yes, do that. Make sure that witch is as far gone as possible. And then, call your lawyer, do whatever you have to do to make sure she can never just show up like that again, or the next time, I'm not going to use my words." He raises an eyebrow. "I'm going to hit her, Jesse." Despite everything, the edges of his lips tip up. "I'm serious," I tell him, and he nods stoically before leaning in for a gentle kiss. When he pulls back, he opens his door, then slides out before moving to my side of the truck and helping me out.

Hand in hand, we move inside.

"Hey," Madden says, standing from the couch. "How was everything after we left?"

Jesse sighs, his eyes moving down the hall toward Emma's room.

"A shit show."

"I didn't punch her, so there's that," I say, trying to lighten the mood. Madden grins back at me.

"A valiant effort, since I know you're such a scrapper," he says with a sarcastic nod of his head.

I laugh a bit, but then my gaze follows Jesse's down the hall.

"I'm gonna go talk to her," I say with a tip of my head toward Emma's room.

"She went in there soon after we got home and didn't say much."

I nod, then squeeze Jesse's hand, signaling for him to let it go. He stares at me for a long moment before nodding. I think he's going to turn away, to do as I ask, but instead he pulls me closer to him, puts a hand on my waist, pulls me into him, and presses a soft kiss to my lips.

"Take care of our girl, okay?"

I know it's not a slip of the tongue.

I nod, then he nods, pressing his lips to my forehead before stepping away, grabbing his phone and his jacket, and heading out the door. I wonder what his plan is, if he's going to talk to his family, who I'm sure have a million questions we'll have to face later, but right now, all that matters is the lost little girl sniffing in the room.

"Emma, babe?" I call out with a soft knock at the door. "It's me, Hallie."

"You can come in," she calls, and I try to dissect the words to get an idea of what to expect when I open the door, but I can't, so I turn the knob and open the door.

When I walk in, she has a notebook before her, sitting criss-cross applesauce in her bed with headphones on, and she smiles at me as I gently close the door behind me.

For a moment, I'm utterly confused.

I expected to see a completely different person, or at least, an entirely different version of Emma. But she's content. Smiling. Her eyes aren't puffy and red, and there isn't a pile of tissues beside her. There's no anger or hurt on her face as she closes her notebook and sets it on her bedside table before removing her headphones and doing the same with them.

"Hey," I say, stepping to her bed and sitting on the edge of it, a few feet between us. "How are you?"

"I'm good. Just doing some journaling." She started a month ago after reading an article about how Willa Stone journals every single day, and I catch her jotting things down in one of her dozen notebooks often now.

"That's good. Um, about today," I say, biting my lip. I look down at my nails and pick at a cuticle. Nat would yell at me if she were here, I'm sure. "I'm sorry I got a little heated."

"Heated?" she asks, and when I look at her again, her face is confused. Right now, she looks so much like Jesse, it aches.

"Well, I kind of..." Somehow, talking to Emma feels more embarrassing than talking to Jesse about it. "I kind of flipped on your mom."

"I don't think you *flipped* on her." She pauses, her head tipping, and her hair falls to the side, sliding over her shoulder as she reaches out to grab my hand before smiling at me. "You stood up for me."

Warmth settles in my chest as I squeeze her hand back.

"I always will, Em." The words come through a tight throat, and she nods as if she knows that.

"I told you, you get it. You're just like me."

"I wish I weren't, Emma. Trust me. I wish you had your mom and your dad and that everything was peachy keen."

She shrugs like it's no big deal.

"I get it. I guess I also wish my mom wasn't the way she was, but she is, and there's nothing I can do about that." She's twelve and so much wiser than half of the adults I know. "I didn't get the picture-perfect family like Dad, Uncle Madden, and Aunt Wren got, but that's okay. Today, I realized I got something better." My brow furrows, and her grin goes beaming. "I get proof that you'll stand up for me even if you're not sure if you should because you care about me. And that's better than a mom who won't even come to my birthday."

My chest aches, and I wonder if this is how Jesse feels all the time: so, so proud that he's raised such a clever, self-confident, and empathetic daughter, but absolutely crushed that she had to learn those skills so young.

"You really mean that, don't you?"

She sighs and rolls her eyes like I'm a brick wall she is tired of talking to, then shifts closer to me on the bed so she can hold both of my hands. It's like she's suddenly the adult, trying to gentle-parent me.

"Hallie, you've been here for me more in the past six months than I remember her ever being. And that's not even counting all of the times you and Aunt Wren hung out with me or the millions of things that I don't even realize were things you guys did to protect me from being disappointed. You do it because you love me, and I love you too." My pulse pounds with her words, and I swallow, trying to fight back tears. "She hasn't made time to see me in at least nine months, but she finds out I might have some kind of connections, and suddenly she can make a surprise trip to me. Meanwhile, you, Dad, and everyone drop everything at the drop of a hat whenever I need something. I'm young, but I'm getting older. I see what you guys have been doing, and I appreciate it. You protecting me once again today is not something I'm going to hold against you."

"You know, you're really smart for a twelve-year-old," I say with a sniff, a tear falling.

Her eyes water, but she brushes past the emotions as she gives me a cocky grin.

"I'm glad you're finally noticing."

I roll my eyes and take a deep breath before pulling her into me for a tight hug. When I finally release her, I pull back and scan her face once more. There's a bit of hurt beneath her tough exterior, but that's normal. I also see genuine gratitude and love for me on her face.

"So you're good?" I ask, and she nods.

"I'd be even better if you could convince Dad that we should bake some of that cookie dough we put in the freezer last week."

I give her a stern look, but I'm also secretly grateful for the slight comic relief.

"You had a funnel cake with ice cream and split a bag of zeppoles with your uncle, Emma."

"It was a very trying day," she says, suddenly looking worn out and weary, and I can't help but let out a laugh. "I bet I could convince him to let me."

I smile. "You're on."

Then we both leave her room, and when Jesse gives me a questioning look, I give him a subtle thumbs-up. And even though the look of introspection doesn't leave Jesse's face all night, we do have cookies.

The next morning, I wake up with the sun barely creeping into our room, but I do it to an empty bed. Sitting up, I look around the dim room but see no trace of my boyfriend. Rolling out of bed, I blink tiredly as I slip a pair of sweats under the oversized T-shirt I slept in, then quietly pad to the kitchen. Relief floods me when I spot Jesse holding a mug of coffee and staring out the kitchen window.

"Morning," I whisper, knocking him out of his daze. He turns to me, but when I catch sight of him, my stomach sinks to the ground at the blank look on his face.

"Morning," he says, setting his mug down, then moving to the coffee pot on autopilot, grabbing a mug, and pouring me a cup. I watch as he moves to the fridge for my creamer and tops it off. "Want to drink on the patio?"

I lift a shoulder but nod, and he tops off his mug before we move through our room in silence with our coffees. It's cool but not cold in the early morning, but the birds are up and singing as the sun creeps up over the trees, and I can't say it's not a perfect morning.

Except, of course, for the look on Jesse's face.

We sit in silence for a bit before finally, I set my coffee down. "You gonna tell me why I woke up in an empty bed this morning?"

It was the first time I could remember waking up that way since we told Emma about us, and I didn't like it, if I'm being honest. Now, mixed with the look on his face and his introspective silence, nerves are coursing through me.

"I couldn't sleep, and I didn't want you to wake up from my tossing and turning," he says, and I try not to point out that he always wakes up before me, but he never leaves the bed before me.

"Something on your mind?" I ask. A deep sigh leaves his chest, and he looks out over the woods. Silence spans, and I think I'll have to say something more to fill in the gap, but finally, he speaks.

"I did that, you know." I don't speak, unsure of what to say or what he means, but eventually, he continues. "To Kim. I did that. I fit her into my vision of a picture-perfect family when Emma was born and never took her into account."

My heart breaks, realizing that this is what's been weighing on him since yesterday.

"Jesse—" I start, but he keeps speaking.

"I did. I found out she was pregnant, and I made a plan. I barely involved her in those decisions. I decided we'd live near campus until we graduated, then move to my parents' property. She said she wanted to be a singer, but she was getting a marketing degree. I told her we could figure out what she wanted to do once Emma was a bit older, and she agreed. After that, she took on raising Emma, and I took on making the money we needed to survive. We were young, and I was scared, and if I'm being honest with myself, I don't regret it. I did what I had to do to make a stable life for Emma. At the end of the day, I think at some point, it would have ended the same regardless. But my part in it, the way I forced her into that life, that was my fault. Sometimes I think if I didn't, she wouldn't be so adamant to stay away from here, from the town I chained her in. She might visit more and might have more of a relationship with Emma."

"She was an adult, Jesse. Did she tell you that wasn't what she wanted?" He shakes his head. "That was her responsibility. You can't read minds, much less when you're unexpectedly raising a child and trying to keep a roof over everyone's heads. I'm not saying you were perfect, but she is just as much at fault. Your relationship with her does not explain or cancel out literal years of her ignoring Emma and neglecting being her mother." He sits back in his chair but still doesn't look at me.

"What if she's right? What if I'm doing it all over again?"

For a moment, I pause, unsure of what he's saying, but then it clicks: he means with me.

Her nasty words come back to me then, asking if he found another woman to con into raising Emma, and I realize that those are the ones that stuck deep for him.

"With me?"

"I decided I wanted you to be mine, to be ours, and I shoved you into my life. You make dinner, and you clean the house, and you watch Emma—"

I can't help but roll my eyes at him.

"All of those are things I do because I want to, Jesse. In fact, I was doing those things before we were even together." Finally, he looks to me, and his conflicted look nearly takes my breath away. This is *eating* at him.

"I've seen your vision boards. You have dreams. You want to travel, you want to see things, and you want to go places." I remember the look on his face when he and Emma were going through my vision boards, and nervous energy creeps in on a cool breeze, chilling me to the bone.

"What does that have to do with anything?"

"You have dreams outside of this." He gestures around the property, and somehow I know he means him and Emma. "But all of mine have always been here. The farm, growing it, building it. One day, I'll take over, and it'll be mine. I've always wanted that—to have a family and build it at Three Kings, to give my kids the childhood I had. Travel and bucket lists and new hobbies and passions were never in that plan, but they are for you."

I shift then, moving to the edge of my seat and reaching out to grab his hand. He stares at our twined fingers, but when I speak, his eyes go to me.

"My entire life, Jesse, I've had one consistent dream. I've made a dozen vision boards, and they've always had one thing in common." I reach my other hand up to cup his face, brushing my thumb along the edge of his mustache and over his cheek, his hazel eyes soft as he stares at me. "All I've ever wanted was to have a family. To find someone who will love me, who I can chain to me, and make it hard just to leave. I have that here, with you." I smirk then. "Unless you have some kind of exit strategy I don't know about." My joke doesn't land, and he shakes his head.

"I'm less worried about wanting to leave you and more worried about not fulfilling you. I've fit you into the life we already had, Hallie. I don't want you to look back in a year, two, or four and realize it's not what you wanted, that you gave up everything you wanted to stay here."

"That won't happen," I say with complete confidence.

"You can't know that." There's a hint of panic in the words, his eyes wide and pleading for me to understand, and I wonder for a moment if this is what I looked like months ago when I was terrified to take that step with him.

What would he have done in this situation? He took baby steps, doing what he could to ease me into things and reassure me. Made a plan.

I can do that.

I can be that for him, the same way he is for me.

"I do know that, but I know that's not something you can know. We'll figure it out. We can do check-ins weekly, monthly, or whatever we need to make sure you feel secure in this, and that I do too. We can go to therapy, or journal, or make a yearly bucket list, if that helps. But right now, I'm happy. Right now, there's no other place I'd rather be. Right now, we're good. Right?"

He hesitates, and my heart pounds with that hesitation.

"Right," he says finally. Another moment passes, silence filling the space before he lets out a heavy breath and leans down, pressing his lips to mine. Relief washes through me, and when he breaks the kiss, he presses his forehead to mine.

"I want all of your dreams to come true, Hallie. You've changed everything for me, made me realize what my life was missing, but I'm terrified that in five, ten, fifteen years, you're going to look around and realize you're now the one missing things."

"In five, ten, fifteen years, am I going to have you?"

"That's the plan," he says.

"Then I'll have everything I need. If I have you, and I have Emma, and I have this life we're building, I'll have the whole world, Jesse." He stares at me, and my pulse races when I don't see the understanding or acceptance I thought would cross his face. Instead, I continue to see that battle, that doubt on his face.

I open my mouth to speak—to try and continue to reassure him, though I have no idea what I'll say—but before I can, Emma's voice trails through the door, and my head turns toward it.

"Dad? Hallie?"

"Be there in a sec, babe," I call through the door. When I turn back to Jesse, he's already standing, grabbing both of our mugs and moving toward the doors.

"I'll get breakfast going, but I have some errands to run later. Will you two be good today without me?"

My brows furrow in confusion as I stand, following him through the door, sliding it shut behind me.

"It's Sunday," I say.

"I know. I'll be done by dinner, but I spent a lot of time this week helping out Wren and moving you, and I need to catch up." He doesn't catch my eyes as he speaks, and that unease continues to move through me. He's almost at the bedroom door when I reach out, grab his arm, and stop his retreat.

"Are we okay?" I ask, anxiety running through me. His face goes soft, and he wraps his free arm around my waist, pulling me closer to him.

"We're good, Hallie. Sorry, I'm just in my head."

I nod, though it's half-hearted, but when he dips his head, softly pressing his lips to mine, some of the nerves melt away.

Though they manage to creep back in throughout the day when I don't hear from him at all.

THIRTY-SIX

I haven't seen Jesse since he walked out the door at seven this morning, and it's nearly five thirty. Thankfully, my texts have not gone unanswered, though they all received little more than a single-word response or worse, a thumbs-up emoji, which has done nothing at all to ease my anxieties.

H: Hey! Emma's getting antsy. Should we wait for you or head over to your parents' house without you?

Every moment since he left the house has been drenched in nervous energy, though I did my best not to let Emma feel it. I texted Nat and Wren a bit throughout the day, and both checked in to ask how Emma is doing. At midday, Wren called to chat and told me that the fairgrounds are already all cleaned up, thanks to a group of volunteers Adam coordinated without her knowledge. That, at least, gave me a bit of joy, knowing my best friend found the one person who is genuinely the perfect match for her.

When my phone beeps with a new text, I reach for it quickly, and when I read it, my heart drops to the ground.

J: Head over, I'm running late.

Dread curls in my stomach, but when Emma speaks, I force a happy smile to my lips.

"Was that Dad?" I nod.

"Yup! He says he's running late and to head to your grandparents'." She nods, then heads to the kitchen for the cookies we baked today, when I needed to distract myself. The house is also sparkling clean, and I spent extra time on my hair today, blowing it out sleek instead of letting it air-dry.

No matter how many times I tell myself not to worry, it creeps back in, that lost look on Jesse's face haunting me.

What if he's off trying to figure out how to let me down easy? What if all of my worst fears are about to come true? What if he decided he actually doesn't want a relationship and wants to revert to his old plan of not dating until Emma's out of the house?

Where will that leave me?

And more importantly, how the hell will I survive that?

These are the questions that have plagued me all day, mixed in with the voice of that hurt little girl whispering in my ear that maybe I really am just that easy to leave.

But I push all of it aside, putting on my widest, fakest smile as Emma and I walk over to the main house for dinner. I grin as I greet everyone, giving out hugs as if I haven't seen them in days, versus hours. Madden asks me quietly how Emma's doing, and Mr. King gives me more than one sly smile that makes absolutely no sense to me.

But even stranger, no one asks where Jesse is.

Dinner is long over, and Mrs. King and Wren are setting the table for dessert while Madden, Emma, and I play a lackluster round of Clue in the den when the front door opens. A moment later, a very frazzled-looking Jesse stands in the doorway. His hair is tousled as if he's been running his hands through it nonstop, and there's what looks like a folder in his hand as he scans around the room, his eyes finding me quickly.

The brightest, widest grin takes over his face, eyes crinkling with the move, and even though I'm still an anxious, stressed mess, some of his clear joy sifts through me. He takes three long strides to me before he bends, grabbing my hand and tugging me up.

"Jesse?" I ask, but he doesn't say anything, just starts moving with his hand in mine, leading me out of the den. He pauses in the hallway, looking around as if unsure of where to go next. "Jesse." My voice is firmer now, but his hand tightens on mine, and he turns, moving toward the stairs and pulling me up them. When we're at the top, he moves toward what used to be his room and steps in, closing the door behind him.

"Hey," Jesse says, casual as could be, pulling me into him and pressing a hard kiss to my lips. I return it for a moment before I pull back, looking at him with irritation.

"What the hell, Jesse?" I ask, stepping back. "Where have you been?"

"Sorry, I missed dinner. I was running errands all day."

"It was family dinner. What kind of errands could have been so important? What is happening?" I cross my arms on my chest and stare at him, the speech I'd been planning flying from my mind. "Were you trying to get space from me?" I ask, suddenly feeling that vulnerability I've been trying to hide away all day come out.

"What?" he asks, confusion taking over his face. "No. Why would I do that?"

"I don't know. So, could you let me down easy? Set me free to chase my dreams or whatever bullshit you were rambling on about this morning?"

His look of confusion turns to entertainment, and he shakes his head, stepping closer to me and pulling me in with one arm.

"Hallie, I love you. I'm not letting you chase anything without me," he says, then shakes his head, stepping back. "I'm fucking this up." He moves to the desk, slapping what I thought was a folder onto the table. His back blocks my view as he opens it and starts looking for something.

"I talked to my dad, and we agreed I've gotta be home at least every other week this summer, but next year we can probably add it into the budget to have someone here part-time to help him out so we can leave for longer stretches," he says, confusing me further. "So we'll start small this year."

"Start small?"

"Nothing too long or too far," he says confidently, turning back to face me.

"You aren't making any sense. What are you talking about, Jesse?"

He smiles, then gestures toward the desk again. "We're doing it all, Hal."

"I don't—" But then my eyes drop to the desk. It wasn't a folder he was holding at all, but a calendar that's now flipped open to the current month. I recognize it as the one from his kitchen, the one I've admired a dozen times over, not because I particularly enjoy the naturescapes, but because I love seeing his life all in one place. I love seeing Emma's sleepovers and days off from school in hot pink, alongside Jesse's plans in dark blue. Family events and birthdays are in green, and more recently, he has started adding my plans in purple.

"I used the most recent one, since that felt the most doable. And I used Emma's too, though that one was a bit more...reckless."

"The most recent what?" I ask, but he doesn't explain. Instead, he flips to June, where Emma has put hearts and stars in her signature hot pink around the last day of school, then points to the Tuesday after.

"This week, we're heading to Seaside Point. It's not on your vision board, but it was on Emma's. Learning to surf is on yours, though, which is good because Madden's got a buddy down that way who gives lessons." I open my mouth to ask a question or maybe argue that he's lost his mind, but he speaks again. "I know it's not crystal clear like the water in Hawaii, but we're working with what we've got." When I step closer to look at the calendar, the last week of June has *SEASIDE POINT* written there in Jesse's messy scrawl.

"In winter." He moves to the front of the calendar, where there's a calendar for the next year, much smaller, and he points to what I know from experience now is Emma's winter break. "We're doing Salt Lake City, like in that movie." He pushes the calendar aside, and beneath it, there's a recognizable stack of papers. Gently, almost reverently, he sifts through them and finds the vision board in question, pointing to the *Getting There* movie cover. My pulse races as pieces fall into place. "I think I can get Emma ice skating lessons for Christmas. That's on hers."

"Jesse," I whisper as realization begins to crash through me. He must know because he turns to me, a broad, happy, love-drunk grin on his lips, before he pulls me into him.

"We're doing it all. Not right now, but eventually. Over time. Everything on every one of your lists—we're doing it. You're going to have it all, because I'm going to give it to you. A family *and* adventure."

My throat swells with his words.

"This is why you were ignoring me all day?"

He blushes and shrugs. "I had to talk to Wren this morning, then I had to talk to Colt, *then* I had to go a town over to find a travel agent open on a Sunday. Then I had to get Wren and Nat again."

"You talked to Colt?" I ask, confused, and then the rest of his sentence settles in. "You were with Wren and Nat today?" The bitches didn't even say a *word* to me about it, and I talked to them multiple times today. He just grins. "While I was panicking that you were trying to plan how to dump me gently, you were bebopping around with my best friends?"

"I had to make sure it was just right," he says.

"What was just right? This..." I gesture to the table, at the evidence of how much he knows me, how much he cares about me, my eyes welling again. "This is perfect. You didn't need them for this. You didn't even have to *do* this."

He nods, then once more sifts through the boards, pulling out five and lining them up. They're from various years, including the very first one Wren and I ever made.

"There's one last thing I needed to get straight, and I needed their help for it. One thing on your boards that I wanted to make happen as soon as possible."

My brow furrows as I scan the pages and try to figure out what he's talking about. But it doesn't take long to realize, there's only one thing all of them have in common.

"Jesse—" I start, but when I turn back to him, everything stops.

Because Jesse King is on one knee before me, a black box in his hands.

"On all of the boards, you never put your dream ring on it, so I needed backup." He flips open the ring box, and inside is a simple gold ring, one larger diamond with two smaller triangles on either side, and a hand flies to my mouth, a choked sob escaping my lips—his tip up in a soft smile. "I thought I'd wait to do this, give you time to settle. Give us time to ease into things so I don't scare you, but I think you need this as much as I do."

"Jesse," I whisper, watching as he removes the delicate ring and holds it up to me.

"I want you forever. I want to take care of you and keep you safe, to catch you well before you fall. I love you, Hallie. I might not be everything you deserve, but I love you enough to work every day to be what you need. I know your favorite color is blue and that you hate ketchup touching your fries. I know that your eyes are green and that you made friends with a deer because she made you feel seen. I know that you love the Mary-Kate and Ashley movies because they were what you binge-watched when you were sad when your mom left. I know I'll never have to worry about you fitting in with my family because you're already family. I know that you'll do anything to put a smile on my daughter's face. I still know that you have a freckle on your hip that drives me wild." I let out a tear-filled laugh when he winks at me. "But most of all, I know you are meant to be mine, forever."

He reaches out, grabbing my hand, and when I notice his is shaking, the first tear falls.

"Jesse." The word aches as it moves through the tears building in my throat.

"Marry me," he whispers, his own eyes shimmering.

"It's the only thing I've ever wanted," I reply, a confession and an answer all in one, because it's the truth. All I've ever wanted was to be someone's, but most of all, Jesse's. Those fears have melted away, fading to nothing in the bright sunshine of his love.

With my words, he grins wide and slides the ring, a perfect fit, over my finger before leaning down to press a kiss to the three stones that somehow, I already know are symbolic of the three of us becoming one family, a reminder and a tie to them both to carry with me always.

When he stands, he cups my jaw and pulls me in hard and fast for a kiss. My arms move around his neck, and tears fall as I melt into him. In this moment, I know I have it all. Everything I never thought I could have in my arms, and that void in my chest is filled once and for all. He kisses me and kisses me, then peppers more, softer, sweeter kisses over my face. My chin, my cheeks, my forehead, my nose, as if he doesn't want a single part of me not to feel wholly and completely loved. Finally, he pulls back and rests his forehead against mine as I grin up at him.

"We're getting married," I whisper as it sinks in.

He nods, then worries his lips before speaking.

"I'll wait. A month, a year, ten, but I want you walking down an aisle toward me sometime in the future. There's no rush, Hallie. I just needed to give you that ring, to take that step now. But I'm a patient man. I can wait until you're totally ready."

I shake my head against his. "I don't think there's any reason to wait. I don't want to wait to marry you. I don't need time anymore," I say, my eyes watering again.

"Well, good, because Wren's looking at a fall wedding," he says with a smirk. I let out a laugh and shake my head, the tears finally falling freely. "Are you happy?"

"Are you blind?" I ask.

He shakes his head and swipes a thumb over my cheek. "Hallie, baby, you're crying. I think I should probably ask if you're happy when you're crying like this."

"Yes, I'm happy, you big idiot. Though the next time you have some grand gesture, would a couple of texts that are longer than a single word hurt?"

"What?"

"I spent the entire day thinking you were trying to figure out how to let me down easy and break up with me." His face goes soft, and he continues to wipe at my cheeks. The tears haven't stopped, and I don't think they will anytime soon.

"I knew if I texted you, I'd spill everything. I was too excited. I was trying to preserve the surprise." I glare at him, and he laughs, pulling me into him and kissing me again like he can't help it before sighing with regret. "I hate to say this, but we have to head downstairs soon, or else they're all going to barge in on us."

As he finishes his sentence, there's a gentle knock on the door, and Mrs. King's voice sifts in, soft and cautious. "Everything okay in there?"

I beam up at my fiancé.

Another woman might find his family barging in on a private moment annoying, but not me. I've waited my entire life for a noisy, intrusive family, and just like everything else, Jesse just gave that to me.

"Let's go," I say with a whisper, pressing my lips to his one last time before moving for the door.

When we step out of Jesse's childhood room, everyone is standing in the hall, and I laugh, realizing that he really was planning this all day. I even spot Nat and Colt, who were definitely not here for a family dinner an hour ago.

"SISTERS!" Wren shouts, lifting her hands into the air and running toward me, pushing her brother away. We hug, and when we pull back, I look at my best friend for a beat before we both squeal, jumping up and down. Jesse laughs from beside me, and then there's a soft hand on my shoulder as a teary-eyed Mrs. King pulls me away from Wren and into her arms.

"Now you really have to call me Mom," she murmurs into my hair, and I start to cry in earnest. She holds me for a moment before passing me off to Colt, who wraps me up tighter than anyone else.

"Happy for you, Hallie."

I look back at my big brother, the only real family member who has ever mattered, and I have to swallow back even more tears. "I love you, Colt."

His eyes soften a bit before he presses a kiss to the top of my head and steps back. Jesse is wrapped in a back-slapping embrace from Madden, and I smile as my attention turns to Emma, who is standing there patiently, a knowing smirk on her lips.

"You're good with this?" I ask. She looks at me like I'm a moron, all pre-teen attitude.

"Hallie, who do you think I was texting all day? Someone had to check your ring size," she says with an eye roll, and I remember her playing around with my jewelry box in our room while I did my hair, not thinking a thing about it.

"Oh, you're so sneaky," I say with a laugh, then pull her into me for a hug. But when she hugs me tight and looks up at me, the attitude and sass are gone, and a contented look settles over her face. I put a hand to her cheek and blink back more tears.

"I love you, Emma."

Her eyes shine the same way I know mine do, and somewhere to the side of us, I hear sniffling that is definitely Wren and probably Mrs. King.

Or Mom, I suppose.

"I love you," she whispers.

I look over her head to her dad, who is watching us with warm eyes, his own glassy from tears.

"My girls," he mouths.

"Forever," I promise.

EPILOGUE

Hi, friends!!

Thank you so much for coming for Hallie and Jesse's story. It means the world to me, and I hope you enjoyed it as much as I loved writing it. Next is the epilogue, set two years after the engagement. It features pregnancy, something I always like to disclose in case my friends experiencing infertility, miscarriage, or mixed feelings about that topic aren't interested or in a place to read. Please, please take care of yourself first—reading is supposed to be our happy place! Hallie, Jesse, and Emma get their happily ever after, and the next chapter doesn't change that in the least.

Love, Morgan

Hallie

I'm pacing the house, unsure of what to do with myself. Emma's at school, her first week of high school going well so far, and Jesse is out on the farm, continuing to prep for the busy season.

I should be outside, taking pictures of the property, posting to the accounts I manage, getting stuff in the crock pot for dinner, cleaning, or doing any of a hundred different productive things.

Instead, I pace, trying to keep my pulse from skyrocketing. As I pass a gilded frame on the far wall, my steps falter to take it in like I've done a million times before. It's just one of two dozen photos on the gallery wall Emma helped me hang last winter, something Jesse was very unimpressed by when he found out we'd teetered on chairs to hang the high-up ones instead of waiting for him.

It's not even my favorite picture on the wall—that one's the picture taken last June at Emma's middle school graduation, Jesse and me on either side of her in her red graduation gown, pride on both of our faces, and Emma giving the most exaggerated eye roll possible. I don't remember what she was annoyed by—probably that four different people had already asked her to stand for this same photo on six different devices—but it's the perfect snapshot of our little family.

Instead, the photo that stops me is from Jesse's and my wedding, almost two years ago to the day. It's just like that one I saw on my stepsister's social media, the one that sent me into a spiral and, in turn, into Jesse's arms.

Except better, of course.

In the photo, you see the back of a woman in bridal white, though instead of her hair being brown, it's a shining strawberry blond, the hair falling in waves down her—my—back, while a woman in a baby blue mother-of-the-groom dress slides a veil into my hair with tears in her eyes.

The moment I never thought I'd get, given to me freely.

Mrs. King—Mom, as she continues to remind me to call her gently, a name I always dreamed of calling her but can't seem always to remember—has the same photo framed in her craft room, beside a matching one from Wren's wedding last spring.

My girls, she says, the words carrying both lightness and nostalgia. I wonder sometimes if she always knew I'd end up here one day.

The day was beautiful and simple, a small occasion on the Three Kings property with barely forty people in attendance. Wren was my maid of honor, Nat was my bridesmaid, and Emma was my junior bridesmaid. I'd had a full breakdown a month previously to Wren about who would walk me down the aisle, since as much as I love my dad, I thought Mr. King might be more fitting, or even Colt, but I didn't want to hurt anyone's feelings.

Being the genius she is, Wren suggested I walk down the aisle with Emma to Jesse, and instantly, I cried, knowing it was the right decision. It was further confirmed when I saw Jesse's face, the tears shining in his hazel eyes, when we started down the aisle, Emma and I walking hand in hand.

I probably should have warned him ahead of time, but, as he loves to remind me, I love the drama.

I held it together for the most part as we walked down the aisle to an instrumental version of Mumford & Sons' "I Will Wait." When we reached the end, he took Emma's hand first, pressing a kiss to her forehead and whispering something softly to her before tipping his chin for her to stand beside her aunt. He turned back to me then, putting a hand out, a tear falling, and somehow, in that moment, I knew what he was thinking: that in ten or twenty or, more preferably for him, thirty years, she'll be wearing white again as he walks her down that aisle to give her away.

That's what made my own tears start.

Even though it's not part of the ceremony, and even though Madden, who somehow convinced us to let him officiate, groaned aloud, Jesse pulled me into him, pressing his lips to mine, hard and fast. He whispered, *"I love you,"* one last time before we were legally tied together, like a reminder or a reassurance he knew I needed.

I stare at the photo fondly, marveling at how different my life was just a few years ago. I guess if I have one thing to thank my mother for, it's pushing me to the place where I was always meant to be.

The alarm on my phone rings, and I race to the bathroom, checking to see the results before closing my eyes and letting out a shaky breath. Then, without a second thought, I make my way to the front door, where I put on a pair of boots, ugly as all get out, but since I'm headed out to find my husband on the farm, they're my only choice. In a last-minute decision, I grab the thin jacket I wear when I go out to do farm chores with Jesse occasionally. Once outside, I slide out my phone and open up the app for Jesse's location and find he's not far, at the field closest to our house, and make my way there.

I'm not far from him when I spot her, and despite my desire to find Jesse as quickly as possible, my steps slow, a smile spreading on my lips.

She always finds me when I need her most.

Jane moves out from behind a tree and moves closer to me. Behind her, a smaller deer stumbles, white spots covering her back. I don't speak as she comes up to me, then lets me pet her as is our way. Reaching into my pocket, I grab the treats I carry just in case, handing one to her and dropping another for her baby. They both chew happily, and I watch them in silence for a minute before Jane steps closer, her nose bumping at my still flat belly.

"How do you know?" I whisper, my eyes watering. It happens a lot lately, something I thought was because my period was impending. But when Emma's came and went with no sign from mine, I wondered if maybe it had happened. I'd stopped my birth control in May, though we weren't actively trying, instead going with a *when it happens, it happens* mentality for a bit.

The test on my bathroom counter says it happened.

"I guess we did okay for ourselves, all things considered," I murmur to her, my hand smoothing over the top of her head. As if she knows what I'm saying, she looks behind her at her baby, then back to me. Her baby nibbles on some grass, impatiently waiting for her mother to finish. "We'll give them what we didn't have." The words come out in a croak, my throat aching. When Jane nudges my stomach again, I shake my head.

It might be strange, talking to an animal, but I've always thought of Jane as like me—a lost girl, navigating things alone, as well as someone who, by some chance, brought Jesse and me together. "I haven't told him yet," I murmur. "That's why I'm looking for him. Have you seen him?"

Just then, Jane's head lifts, a twig snaps behind me, and I look over my shoulder to find my husband just a few feet behind me. His hair's a bit lighter after a summer in the sun, both from working the farm and a week in the Bahamas over summer break.

"Hey, Jane," he says softly, putting an arm around my waist and pulling my back to his chest. His hand rests on my stomach, and warmth moves through me. "What haven't you told me?"

A wash of nerves hits, but I take in a deep breath, smiling at Jane before turning in Jesse's arms.

"How do you feel about another unplanned pregnancy?" I ask, and his brow furrows.

"What?"

"Okay, so it wasn't necessarily unplanned this time, but I haven't really had time to think of a fun way to announce it to you. I kind of just headed out to find you." He stares at me for a beat before his face clears, hesitant excitement on his face.

"You're pregnant?" he asks.

"I took a test this morning after Emma got on the bus. It was positive." I bite my lip, even though I have no reason to be nervous.

"Really?" he asks, hesitant excitement in the word, and I lift a shoulder before nodding.

He lifts me, that giant grin on his face as he spins me around, and I giggle. Jane and her baby trot off, but I'm barely paying attention as his lips press to mine, hard and deep.

"You're having my baby," he whispers.

With watery eyes, I nod, then giggle as he lifts me again, then makes his way back to our house to remind me just how beautiful our forever is.

Eight months later, Emma's brother, Peter Colton King, is welcomed into our little family.

ACKNOWLEDGMENTS

Thank you so much for reading this story that means the absolute world to me. I love Jesse and Hallie, but know that they wouldn't have made it into the world without some very special people helping me out.

Always, to Alex, my very own Jesse, who showed me it was okay to trust that something good could last. I remember when we first started dating, and I chose 'Mine' to be our song. You made a rebel out of a careless man's careful daughter, since my dad has always seemed so carefree and goofy. Watching my parents' relationship fail, I figured being cautious with my heart was the only way to fight that—to ensure that one day, when I finally settled down, I'd never spend a moment worrying if it would end. But it only took two weeks for you to tell me you loved me and for me to say I was going to marry you. Even though that felt reckless at the time, I knew even then I was right and that you'd be my forever. Thank you for giving me that, for always catching me, and for helping me chase all of my dreams.

Thank you to Ken. You'll never see this, and I'll never tell you about it (if you do, don't tell me, gross, put this book down), but thank you. You didn't expect to be a single dad, but you did it the best you could, and I think we turned out pretty good. Sorry, I made you literally throw me in the pool that one time I wouldn't get out of bed. Thank you for smacking that kid upside the head when he tried to make out with me at the movies while you were sitting literally two rows behind us. Let's both be thankful my taste in boys got much, much better in the coming years.

To Ella, my absolute best friend, even though you're only five. I usually bundle you and your brothers together because playing favorites isn't cool. Honestly, I write a lot of books, and there's only so much I can write each time, but this book feels like you need your own section. I am so honored to be your mom, and that you're my daughter. I work every day to make sure you feel loved, appreciated, and safe, and I hope I'm doing an okay job. Right now, you can only read easy 3-letter words, but if that changes and you pick this book up, never talk to me about it. Thanks.

To Ryan and Owen, sorry that I had to give your sister her own line this time. It's a mom-daughter thing. But thanks for letting me be your mom, for being the coolest kids I know, for pretending you need my help with your writing assignments just to make me feel good. I love you both, and I'm so proud of the little people you've become. And if you've gotten this far, as if the norm, you are so grounded, put this book down.

To Regan, the best PA and best friend a girl could ask for. Thanks for always sitting with me on silent calls while I attempt to write, and for not thinking I'm the worst when I disappear because I'm a stressed girlie. I really and truly could not do this without you, and I hope you realize that by now. Please never leave me and make my abandonment issues even worse. I hope this self-harm book makes up for that time I accidentally used your own trauma in a book. My bad, you know?

Ashleigh, thank you for being the best friend a girl could ask for, and I'm so sorry we occasionally (often, I'm sorry I have bad time management and think I can write way more books in a year than I can) have to work when you want to yap. I can't wait to see your baby goats next year (manifesting this for you)

To Taj, the best agent a girl could ask for. Thank you for always sending me seven follow-up texts when I ignore the first six, and for not firing me when I ignore the seventh as well. I'm SO EXCITED to see what 2026 brings because you made ALL of my 2025 dreams come true and then some.

To Cat, who made the most GORGEOUS cover, and Jess, who brought my characters to life.

To Christine, for always jumping in at the last moment to make edits because I'm just a girl with no actual reference for how time works.

To Becca for helping me realzie that I might actually need to plot things out and helping me come to terms that the answer is almost always *you're overthinking it.*

To Marlee and April, and Kylie, thank you, guys, for being the best alpha readers known to man. I'm sorry I can't respond to a single email or DM (there's a theme here, if you can't tell), but thank you for helping me realize that whatever I'm working on isn't a total dumpster fire, and I'm just worried because, oops, I wrote a slow burn. Also, thanks for always ignoring my typos. Sorry, I accidentally implied that Jesse fucked a horse. (I meant HOARSE!)

Thank you, thank you, thank you to my ARC and content team, who always shout about my stories from the rooftops. This book would be absolutely nothing without each and every one of you, and I am forever grateful. I owe any success it gets to you all, and I will never take that for granted.

And finally, you, my dear reader, for always trusting me. For grabbing my stories off of your startling high TBR pile and falling in love with my characters. I somehow managed to end up with my dream job, and I owe it to you, the people who actually read the stories. I hope you love Jesse and Hallie.

ABOUT THE AUTHOR

Morgan is a born and raised Jersey girl, living there with her two sons and daughter, and mechanic husband. She's addicted to iced espresso, barbeque chips, and Starburst jellybeans. She usually has headphones on, listening to some spicy audiobook or Taylor Swift. There is rarely an in between.

Writing has been her calling for as long as she can remember. There's a framed 'page one' of a book she wrote at seven hanging in her childhood home to prove the point. Her entire life she's crafted stories in her mind, begging to be released but it wasn't until recently she finally gave them the reigns.

I'm so grateful you've agreed to take this journey with me.

Stay up to date via TikTok and Instagram

Stay up to date with future stories, get sneak peeks and bonus chapters by joining the Reader Group on Facebook!

Enter the Morganverse by catching up on your favorite Morgan Elizabeth books!

All books are interconnected standalones, which means you can jump in wherever you'd like, regardless of series or number in that series!

The Springbrook Hills Series

The Distraction

The Protector

The Substitution

The Connection

The Playlist

Season of Revenge Series:

Tis the Season for Revenge

Cruel Summer

The Fall of Bradley Reed

Ick Factor

Big Nick Energy

The Ocean View Series

The Ex Files

Walking Red Flag

Bittersweet

Evergreen Park Series

Passenger Princess

If This Was a Movie

Never Been Worse

Down the Shore Series

Tourist Trap

Mavens Series

Maneater

Holly Ridge Series

The Bright Side of Christmas

The Promise of Forever

The Mastermind Duet

Ivory Tower

Diamon TikTokress

All My Love